Love by Design

Book Two in The Meraki Series

Effie Kammenou

Printed in the United States of America

First Edition:

10 9 8 7 6 5 4 3 2 1

ISBN 13: 978-0-578-83535-8

Library of Congress Cataloging-in-Publication Data Case # 1-10037792531

Kammenou, Effie. Love by Design

Cover Design by Deborah Bradseth of Tugboat Design

Interior formatting by Melissa Williams Design

Author photo by Alexa Speyer

In dedication to my baby grandson, Michael Alexander,
the joy of our family.

Meraki

A small Greek word with a complex definition. In essence, it means to put your soul into something—anything done with great passion, absolute devotion, and undivided attention—a labor of love.

Acknowledgements

To my husband, Raymond, and my daughters, Eleni and Alexa, for your never-ending love, support, and encouragement.

To my sisters, Kathy and Jeanine, who inspire me with their compassion and kindness.

A special acknowledgement to my daughter, Alexa, who inspired this story with her passion for her work in the creative industry.

To Valerie Gildard, my most trusted beta reader—the first set of eyes on my manuscripts. Thank you for your attention to detail.

To Deb/Dee, writer and beta reader. I value and respect your opinions and suggestions.

To Marisa and Chris Raptis, who brainstormed the historical subplot in the storyline for this book with me.

To Aphrodite Papandreou, who supplied me with much-needed facts and shared personal accounts of a tumultuous time period in Greece.

To my editor, Katie-bree Reeves of Fair Crack of the Whip Editing, a master at her craft and a pleasure to work with.

To Deborah Bradseth of Tugboat Design, for this incredible cover and all my other equally beautiful past covers.

To Michelle Argyle of Melissa Williams Design for formatting this book. Thank you for fitting me into your schedule on such short notice.

To all my friends and family, too many to name, who support and inspire me every day—you know who you are. You may have even found traces of yourselves within the pages of my books.

To my parents. To my father, who amazes me every day. I pray I have inherited his longevity and sharpness of mind. And to my mother, no longer with us but never forgotten. If not for her, my first book would have never been written, much less this fifth one. I hope she is smiling down from above.

*"Design creates culture. Culture shapes values.
Values determine the future."* — Robert L. Peters

Chapter 1

Mia

November 2018

Mia was convinced she was born in the wrong era. While her friends listened to pop music and followed DJ Khaled waiting for local concert dates, she preferred the classic sounds of Benny Goodman and Tony Bennett. Classic rock was as contemporary as she got, and the same could be said about how her tastes ran with just about everything.

Mia considered herself a 'Charlotte,' the prim and proper character from the *Sex and the City* series. And although the sitcom represented women living in Manhattan from two decades ago, she shuddered at the thought of comparing herself to any of her contemporaries in the series *Girls*. If they were the representation of her generation with their highly dysfunctional lives and bizarre choices of male companionship, then she had to say a firm, 'No, thank you.' Charlotte was refined, cultured, and at least somewhat discerning with her men. And the clothing! Mia envied her sophisticated designer dresses, tailored to accentuate her slim figure.

In truth, Mia preferred to daydream of a more genteel time. She yearned to live like Audrey Hepburn in *Sabrina* or *Roman Holiday*, back when women dressed fashionably and men knew what it meant to be a gentleman. Give her the classic style of Jacqueline Kennedy in the days of *Camelot*, or the stylish dresses Lucy wore in her sitcom as she played bridge with the ladies. The iconic little, black sheath dress and string of pearls worn in *Breakfast at Tiffany's* was her go-to look for any occasion.

Mia was seated, perched upright at her computer, a support pillow resting at the back of her chair. Some days she could spend as many as eight hours focused on the monitor editing short videos or creating print layouts. Other days were spent running from department to department, directing photo shoots, attending pitch meetings, or hiring set designers for future campaigns.

Leaning back, Mia clasped her hands together and stretched them over her head, loosening out the kinks from sitting in one position for so long. She kicked off her black, spiked-heel pumps, removed her dark-rimmed glasses, worn only to magnify the images on the screen, and rubbed her tired eyes.

Homelife was one of *Aris Publications'* smaller staffed magazines. It was most likely Mia's diverse skills that had first won her the position she now held. It was rare for a graphic designer to have the capability to also take professional-grade photographs and edit the raw footage of a video shoot. But Mia could do all of it, and she hoped these skills would make her not only more marketable but also invaluable to her employers.

"Do you want to grab something to eat before we go to the CCP meeting?" Jenny, one of Mia's co-workers, asked, rolling her chair back so she could peer around the cubicle partition separating their desks.

Mia pressed the home button on her iPhone. The display read six-fifteen.

"Sure," she said. "We'll have to make it quick, though. I don't want to be late for our first meeting." She slipped back into her shoes, opened her desk drawer, and retrieved her bag.

Mia waved goodnight to her other co-workers as she and Jenny walked past long, white tables, partitioned with adjustable slats hosting several computers for employee stations. The walls were painted a soft rose, giving the room a fresh, light atmosphere, and despite a nearing deadline, there was nothing about this space that seemed chaotic. As they made their way to the glass door, etched with the magazine logo, leading to the elevator, Jenny turned to Mia.

"Le District?" Jenny asked.

"I never say no to French food!" Mia agreed eagerly.

Aris Publications was located in Brookfield Place, a shopping center and office building adjacent to the World Trade Center. Anything Mia needed was at her fingertips, from the high-end designer boutiques where she could only afford to window shop, to the more sensibly priced stores, to a couple of high-end food courts offering a variety of unique foods from which she could never tire.

Mia found two vacant high-top seats by a counter situated around the open cook station in Le District. They each ordered a glass of rosé and shared a charcuterie board while their paninis were being prepared.

"The guy was a total drip!" Jenny said, filling her in on her date from the night before.

Mia laughed into her wine glass as Jenny regaled her with her latest online dating disaster. Normally, she would have heard all about it when she'd come home, but Mia had fallen asleep early and didn't hear her roommate come in.

"I mean, I filled out this long, extensive profile with a ton of detailed questions, and they sent me that guy?" Jenny went on. "He droned on for forty-five minutes about the benefits of the statin his company developed over the competing pharmaceutical companies."

"So, no second date?" Mia joked.

"I didn't finish the first one. I went to the ladies' room and asked my sister to call me in ten minutes," Jenny said. "Then, I got the hell out of Dodge on some lame excuse."

"Have you sworn off dating apps now?" Mia asked, spreading some brie on a paper-thin cracker.

"That one, definitely! But I'm on Zoosk now, and they have the best success rate."

With her auburn hair and green eyes, Jenny's face was striking. Her figure was a bit too curvaceous for her own liking, but Mia pointed out to her more than once that women like Marilyn Monroe and Jane Russell flaunted their bodies proudly and that she needed to as well.

"Why don't you give it a try, Mia? What do you have to lose?"

"Precious time," Mia answered. "That's not for me. How did couples meet before all this online stuff? What happened to the old-fashioned way of meeting by chance, or at work, or through a friend?"

Jenny raised an eyebrow. "And how many men have you met that way?"

"Point taken." Sweeping her lustrous, sable hair from her face, Mia sighed.

"You know, for a person living in the most progressive city in America, you sure have some small-town ideals."

"Not small-town," Mia corrected. "I just like things to happen a certain way. I like romance and instant chemistry, not profiles and clinical checklists."

The grill man served up their plates, interrupting their conversation, and Mia thanked him. "We have about fifteen minutes before we have to make a dash for it."

After they finished dinner, Mia and Jenny headed to the bank of elevators. They rode up to the twenty-first floor and looked for the suite where the CCP meeting was to be held.

The Community of Creatives in Publishing held a yearly awards event. In addition, they introduced high school students to the many positions the publishing industry had to offer and helped to place college students with internships.

A portable stage had been erected at the front of the room; behind it a large viewing screen was set up. A podium was placed off-center, and seating had been arranged in rows beyond the stage. Seats were filling up quickly. Mia and Jenny found chairs in the fifth row, seated themselves quietly, and waited for the meeting to begin.

Mia was doodling on her notepad when the chairman of the organization stepped up to the podium. She didn't even notice until he began to speak, looking up when she heard a voice as smooth as velvet, laced with a slight indistinguishable accent, seduce her ears.

And then she saw him. Tall, dark, and handsome was too vague a description for this man. His double-breasted suit looked as though it had been tailored specifically for him, and she was sure it had been. He wore a cuffed shirt with gold and onyx cufflinks, and she'd bet any amount of money his ensemble cost more than she made in three months.

Mia wasn't one for dramatic overtures but she latched onto Jenny's arm. Her nails dug into her friend's skin in an involuntary reaction to the man standing on the stage before her. He was gorgeous.

As if his face wasn't perfect enough with his square jaw and the deep dimple in one cheek, he pulled out a pair of black-framed glasses and slipped them on before beginning his speech.

"Oh-my-God," Mia whispered, trying to contain herself. "Now that's a Clark Kent who doesn't need the Superman costume."

"He is hotter than hell," Jenny agreed. She glanced at Mia with a raised eyebrow. "I've never seen you react this way to anyone—ever."

"That's because I don't recall Adonis coming down from Mount Olympus before."

"You'll just have to find a reason to speak to him when the meeting is over," Jenny suggested.

"Shh, he's about to begin." Mia put a finger to her lips to silence her friend before adding, "Besides, I can't do that. I'd die of embarrassment."

She fell silent as he began his speech.

"Good evening and welcome. For those of you who don't know me, my name is Nicholas Aristedis of *Aris Publications* . . ."

Chapter 2

Mia

May 2019

A string of luxury cars lined the street by the main entrance of the St. Regis Hotel. Gentlemen clad in bespoke apparel exited chauffeured vehicles, escorting elegantly dressed women, their gowns billowing behind them as they were guided into the ballroom for the annual CCP awards.

Mia looked like a goddess dressed in a pale pink, one-shouldered gown accented with delicate rose-gold braiding around the waist, yet she did not arrive in the style fit for a deity. No, she and Jenny, in dresses they could barely afford, called an Uber to transport them to the most elegant event they'd ever attended.

The only saving grace was they had arrived well over an hour before the other guests. Mia had volunteered for the awards committee, and both she and Jenny had several assigned tasks to perform throughout the evening. Mia was to check in each guest as they entered, and Jenny was to hand out a small box of gourmet chocolates, labeled to identify each guest's table seating.

Guest after guest arrived, and Mia greeted each one, many of whom were icons of the industry, professionals she could only dream of emulating one day. She was polite and gracious, efficient in her task until she saw him—Nicholas Aristedis, accompanied by one of the most beautiful women she'd ever laid eyes on.

"Dear? Are you alright?" an elegant, white-haired woman asked. Mia had just confirmed her on the list of guests.

"I'm fine, Mrs. Wasserman," Mia lied. "Just a bit lightheaded for a moment."

But she wasn't fine at all. Being this close to Nicholas made her insides flip. Seeing him with a woman knocked the wind from her lungs.

Throughout the months of CCP meetings, she had never once spoken to him. Instead, committees had been formed, the members in the group being her only contacts. Mia had no delusions that a man like Nicholas would ever notice her, yet nonetheless, there was something about him beyond his devastatingly handsome appearance that drew her in. Mia had scrutinized every inch of this captivating man. But alas, she'd once noticed a gold band on his left ring finger, dashing any unrealistic fantasies she may have coveted. Mia assumed the woman on his arm must be his lovely wife, and she had to admire her beauty. They made a stunning couple.

Mia's heart thundered in her chest when Nicholas stopped in front of her. As the master of ceremony for the event, he wasn't required to sign in. Still, he followed protocol.

"Good evening," Nicholas greeted her politely. "Checking in for Nicholas and Penelope Aristedis."

Suddenly, Mia's mouth was as dry as the desert sand. A quick nod and a fleeting smile were all she could manage. If Mia made eye contact, she'd lose all control and probably faint on the spot. It was confounding that he had this effect on her. He wasn't the only handsome man she'd come in contact with. But he was different, and she didn't know why. Her throat constricted as she grew more nervous in his presence. She couldn't even muster the words to welcome him, as she had for the other guests. Instead, she stood there gaping like a deer caught in the headlights. Mia checked off his name from her list, and as Jenny gave the couple their welcome gift, Nicholas turned to glance at her, expressionless, before continuing down the corridor. There was something about the way his eyes penetrated hers for a brief second that rattled Mia. It wasn't until he was out of her line of sight that she was able to catch her breath.

"He must think I'm the world's biggest moron," Mia whispered to Jenny. "I couldn't manage to utter a single word."

"I'm sure he didn't even notice," Jenny assured her.

"Did you see the way he looked at me?" Mia asked. "He was probably thinking, 'Why the hell did they give such an awkward girl this responsibility?'"

"You're overthinking it. Relax."

"I can't," Mia said. "His grandfather owns the company we work for. What if he tells him I'm incompetent or something?"

"I don't think I've ever met anyone who worries about nothing as much as you do," Jenny said, cuffing her friend's shoulders. "Trust me, you're giving this more thought than he is."

"You're probably right." After all, why would Nicholas give Mia a second thought?

Once the last guest was accounted for, Jenny and Mia found their seats at a table with the rest of the committee members. Nicholas offered a champagne toast, welcoming everyone to the annual event. Courses were served in between the presentation of various awards—heirloom beet salad with pistachio-crusted goat cheese, seared Chilean sea bass complimented with lemon and dill, and individual flourless chocolate cakes dusted with gold leaf sugar powder.

Mia was no stranger to good food. Her family was made up of home cooks and professional chefs. But every morsel was divine, and she savored each bite as the flavors exploded in her mouth.

"You look as though you're having a religious experience," Kyle joked, amused by Mia's enthusiasm. Tall, blond, and nice-looking in his own right, he had not been able to hold her attention at meetings until they broke up into smaller committee groups and he was seren-dipitously assigned to hers.

"Because I am." She closed her eyes in pure indulgence, running her tongue along the last bits of chocolate left on her fork.

"If that's all it takes to get you to dance with me," Kyle laughed, slid-ing his plate toward her, "then I'll gladly give up mine to you."

Mia glanced over at the dance floor where Nicholas chatted easily with Penelope as they gracefully moved across the floor. This was the amiable man Mia recognized from the many meetings she had attended. Not the man who had flashed her a menacing stare. Mia sighed.

When the song changed over from a Cole Porter classic to a more contemporary, yet still soft, melody, a woman tapped Nicholas' wife on the shoulder. Stepping out of his hold, Penelope smiled, offering a double-cheek kiss to the woman before handing her husband over for a dance.

"So, what do you say?" Kyle asked, interrupting her thoughts.

"About what?" Mia asked vaguely, her eyes still fixed on Nicholas. "A dance?"

"Oh." Mia shook the dreamy reverie from her head. "Sure."

Kyle held his hand out to her and led her to the crowded dance floor.

They danced in silence until Kyle nervously cleared his throat. "I've been trying to find a chance to ask you out for a while but you always run out so quickly as soon as the meetings end."

She had sensed Kyle's interest, but it was Jenny who longed for him, not Mia. "I have a busy schedule," she replied. "I'm always running from one commitment to the next."

"Is there a little wiggle room in there for a date?"

Mia inwardly groaned. "Kyle, you're a great guy."

And now he outwardly groaned. "The words no guy wants to hear. The beginning of the letdown."

"I highly doubt you're let down often, if ever."

"Except right now." Kyle continued to hold her in his arms, gently rocking her as they danced.

"I don't leave much time for dating. I'm focusing on my career right now."

"Why do I have the feeling if the right man came along, you'd squeeze him into your schedule?" His question was laced with disappointment.

She looked over at Nicholas, unconsciously running her hand through her glossy, dark hair. Hers was the exact color of his wife's sable tresses yet so different compared to the tall redhead currently holding his attention. Every woman in his sphere had an air of glamor and sophistication. She imagined they were wealthy, well-traveled, and worldly in every sense of the word. Mia was just a girl from Long Island, barely making rent, much less jet-setting around the globe.

"I don't think there's much chance of that." Mia patted Kyle on the shoulder. "Take a look around you. I have a feeling someone fantastic is right around the corner." She gave him a friendly peck on the cheek. "Pay attention," she advised with gentleness in her tone, yet with a firm stare, cryptically signaling her message.

Mia walked back to the table to retrieve her evening bag. "I'm going to the ladies' room," she told Jenny.

"I'll come with you." Jenny draped her arm around her friend. "If Kyle asked me to dance, I wouldn't have been ogling the hot, married guy."

"Was I that obvious?" Mia whispered.

"Only to me."

"Good." She was relieved. "Think of it like when you google your favorite movie star or go to see his movies over and over again. It's not real. I'm admiring an image."

"Except here he is in living color," Jenny reminded her. "Not just on a movie screen or in the pages of a celebrity tell-all."

"But just as unobtainable," Mia sighed. "Married. Rich. And the most beautiful man I've ever seen."

As they exited the bathroom, Jenny checked her phone for the time. "It's later than I thought. We should probably set the swag bags on the gift table."

"Good idea," Mia agreed.

* * *

"Nice job tonight, girls," Diana Blackman complimented.

Although Nicholas Aristedis was influential as the new head of the CCP, Diana had run this prestigious event over the past ten years, and gaining her praise was golden. At forty-nine years old, she had achieved more than most people had in two lifetimes.

"Thank you, Ms. Blackman," Mia replied as she gathered up the remaining programs.

"Goodnight," she said with a nod of her head. But before she stepped out the door, she halted. Turning, she called out to Mia, "Send over a copy of your resume to my office by Tuesday."

Mia's eyes grew wide. "Yes, of course, Ms. Blackman. Goodnight."

The second Diana was out of view, Jenny grabbed Mia's hands and squealed with delight. "Do you think she wants you to come work for her at *Moi*?"

"I don't know." Mia was stunned into silence. "But I need to update my resume. I haven't changed it since I landed the job at *Homelife*."

"From home décor to high fashion!" Jenny exclaimed. "So glamorous!"

"It would be a big opportunity to work for such a high-profile magazine but the work itself is still pretty much the same," Mia mused. "I don't suppose I'll be in on any of the glamor of it all," she continued as they exited the venue.

Still, it was all Mia could think about as she and Jenny returned to their modest walk-up apartment in Lenox Hill. The possibilities—a new position, a promotion, a higher salary; they swirled through her head in a flurry of anticipation. She was barely surviving on what she was earning now, and aside from a new and exciting challenge, the money would be awfully helpful.

Beet and Pistachio-Crusted Goat Cheese Salad

Ingredients

3 large beets

Olive oil

Salt & pepper

4-ounce block of goat cheese

¼ cup honey

4 ounces of crushed, unsalted pistachios

2 – 3 ounces of baby arugula

Dressing

¼ cup olive oil

Juice from 1 lemon

Salt & pepper to taste

A pinch of sugar

A pinch of dried tarragon (optional)

Method

Cut the ends off both sides of the beets. Individually wrap them in aluminum foil, drizzling them with a splash of olive oil and a dash of salt & pepper before sealing the foil. Place the beets in a baking pan and place in the oven for 45 minutes at 400° F. Allow to cool a bit and then peel off the skin. Cut into quarters or sixths, depending on the size of the beet.

Slice the goat cheese into ½ inch thick rounds. Pour the honey into a dish and coat each goat cheese slice in the honey. In another dish, place the crushed pistachios. Coat the goat cheese with the nuts. The honey will adhere the pistachios to the cheese.

Place the arugula evenly on a platter. Add the beets and drizzle the dressing over the beets and greens. You may not need to use all the dressing. Scatter the goat cheese rounds between the beets.

Chapter 3

Mia

It had been well over a week since Mia had submitted her resume to Diana Blackman, and she hadn't heard a single word. Trying to put it from her mind, she concentrated on the layout she'd been assigned to work on. But Jenny's constant inquiries and solicitous stares were distracting.

"Jen!" Mia scolded, "If I had any news at all, don't you think I'd tell you?"

"I guess."

"You're more anxious about this than I am," Mia laughed. "It's possible that I might have been considered for a position I wasn't qualified for. She never said why she wanted my resume. It could have been for a completely different reason than we thought."

"You're taking this awfully well," Jenny said.

"There's nothing else I can do." Mia closed the file she'd been working on. If Jenny only knew the truth. Mia hadn't had a good night's sleep since the gala. The minute her head hit the pillow, her mind raced with every possible outcome from Ms. Blackman's request. "Let's go to lunch. I'll text Kyle to join us."

"Kyle?" Jenny's face flushed. "Why?"

"I thought it would be nice." Mia tilted her head, assessing Jenny. "Especially for you. Was I wrong?"

"No, I just could have used some warning. I look like death today."

"You look as pretty as ever," Mia complimented. "Go freshen up a little before we leave if that's how you feel."

* * *

"Honestly, we should all be worried about the jobs we have," Kyle stated before biting into a fried chicken sandwich. "Forget any kind of promotion."

It was the height of the lunch rush, and they were fortunate to find a table at the food court near their offices. Kyle worked for a men's health magazine, also owned by *Aris Publications*.

"What makes you say that?" Jenny asked, a small frown playing on her forehead.

"Word on the street is that there will be some major layoffs," Kyle continued, nodding his head knowingly. Leaning in conspiratorially, he dropped his voice to a whisper. "Rumor has it that some departments will be consolidating. As a result, staff will become responsible for the content on more than one magazine."

Mia rubbed circles over her temples. "Oh, my God."

"What is it?" Jenny asked.

"What if the reason Diana Blackman wanted my resume was to assess if I should be one of the employees cut?" Mia's eyes grew wide with concern.

"That's ridiculous!" Jenny assured her. "She was impressed with you," she argued, pointing her fork in Mia's direction.

"Totally ridiculous," Kyle echoed, finishing off the last bite of his sandwich. "If that was the case, she would be asking for each employee's resume."

Mia sighed. Plucking a fry from the parchment cone on her plate, she dipped it in a side order of truffle aioli. She dunked and sighed, dipped and thought, swirling the *pomme frite* in the sauce, unconsciously staring at it as it grew soggy.

"Either eat that or say something," Jenny demanded.

"I think you're wrong, Kyle," Mia said. "You're not a designer. Your job isn't in jeopardy. Apparently, mine is. You just said they're looking to consolidate creative teams."

"What about me, then?" Jenny asked.

"You have seniority. I'd go before you," Mia admitted.

"Only by six months!" Jenny laughed.

Mia froze when a ding on her phone alerted her that a work email had just come through. Tentatively, she opened it and sucked in a nervous breath.

"Well?" Jenny and Kyle asked in unison.

Mia wasn't sure she could get the words out without crying. Her throat went dry as she held back her tears. "I've been summoned to Human Resources," she whispered in defeat.

"When?" Jenny asked.

"There's no time like the present." Mia forced a smile. "My dad might just get his wish and have me back at home where he thinks I belong." She stood stiffly, snatching her bag off the arm of the chair.

"That's not going to happen," Jenny assured her.

"I'll see you guys later," Mia said nervously as she fled toward the food court exit.

"Come in, Ms. Andarakis." Averting her eyes from her computer, Nancy Williams gestured for Mia to take a seat.

"I'm sure you're wondering why I called you in today. I'll get right to the point."

Anticipating the Human Resource Director's next words, Mia held her breath. Her mind had already raced through all the things she would have to do in the coming days. The first order of business would be to look for a new job and a new roommate for Jenny. She'd never be able to afford the rent now. The second would be to beg her sister, Kally, to let her move in with her temporarily so she wouldn't have to go back home and hear her father gloat victorious.

Nancy interrupted her thoughts. "Over the next several months, all the publications will be going through some restructuring. We think your talents can be better served elsewhere."

Mia gripped the armrest. She wasn't sure if she was going to faint or lose her lunch. Both, maybe. This was really happening. Holding her breath, Mia tried to remain composed.

"Are you all right?" Ms. Williams inquired, looking at Mia in concern. "You've gone quite pale."

"I'm fine," Mia managed to choke out. "How long do I have?"

"Could you wrap up any pending projects by Friday? I'll schedule a meeting with your creative director immediately. She hasn't been informed of the change in her headcount yet."

Mia nodded. "Will that be all then?" She stood.

Nancy stared at her, perplexed. "Don't you want to know where you'll be assigned as of Monday?"

"Excuse me?"

"You'll need to know where to report to next week," she reiterated.

"I'm confused," Mia admitted. "Didn't you just lay me off?"

"Oh, my goodness, no," Nancy said with remorse. She removed her tortoise rimmed eyeglasses and massaged her eyelids. "I apologize if I didn't make myself clear. You aren't being let go. You're being transferred to another magazine."

Mia had never experienced whiplash before but she imagined this was what the emotional equivalent to that sort of blow felt like. Breathing out a sigh of relief, Mia processed what the woman was telling her. She still had a job. But as that thought passed through her mind, a thousand others flooded it. What if it was for a lesser position, or for less money? So many 'what ifs' clouded her brain. Forcing herself to conceal another wave of panic in front of this woman, Mia imperceptibly rolled her head, loosening her stiffened neck. As Nancy began to explain the nature of the transfer, Mia's clenched muscles began to relax, and she imagined the color in her cheeks had most likely returned.

"We're staffing a new magazine, and we need someone who has a wide range of skills. Due to budgeting constraints, our resources will be limited, but if all goes as planned, that could change going forward."

Wiping her eyeglasses with a lens cloth, Nancy continued, "Your resume speaks for itself, but once Diana Blackman recommended you, I didn't need any further information to make my final decision."

"Thank you. I don't know what to say." Mia extended her hand to the woman. "I appreciate the opportunity."

Nancy Williams nodded; a ghost of a smile barely concealed by her professional manner. She handed Mia a clasped packet with the *Aris Publications* logo stamped on the front. "I'll need you to look this over, sign it, and get it back to me right away. It outlines your new title and continuing benefits."

Still a bit dazed, Mia took the manila envelope. *This can't be happening.* Ten minutes ago, she thought her career was over. Now here she was, being offered a new opportunity. "Thank you. I'll get this back to you right away."

Mia stood in place for a beat, not wanting to leave abruptly or to seem unappreciative. She wasn't sure what to do next. Awkwardly, she began to exit. Their business had concluded and she didn't want to overstay her welcome. *Stop overthinking!* Turning, Mia waved goodbye, berating herself for her graceless exit.

Wide-eyed, Jenny stared at Mia when she plopped down into her desk chair. "Well?"

Mia barely registered Jenny's existence, much less her question or inquisitive stare.

"Mia! Say something!" Jenny demanded.

Mia looked up, smiling, shaking herself from her state of oblivion. "I still have a job! Just not here."

"Huh?" Jenny scrunched up her freckled nose. "What does that mean?"

"I've been transferred to another magazine. You were right," Mia admitted. "Diana Blackman recommended me."

"Wow! What magazine? So, you've been promoted? What's your new title?" Jenny rapidly fired questions that Mia realized she had no answer to.

"I don't know." She touched her fingers to her lips, stifling a giggle. "Once I realized I still had a job, my mind spaced out. I was just so relieved that I didn't think to ask."

Jenny rose from her seat, crossing over to Mia's desk and swiftly snatching up the packet she'd set down only moments before. "Well, this should tell you everything you need to know," Jenny said. "And if you don't open it, I will."

Mia motioned for her friend to hand the parcel over. "Ms. Williams said I'd be working for a new magazine," she said, pulling the papers out. "*Opul*, that's the name," Mia pondered.

She perused page after page while an impatient set of eyes stared at her, eager for any bit of information.

"It's a lifestyle magazine catering to high-end destinations, restaurants, events, and such."

"And . . . what else?" Jenny prodded. "What does it say?"

"The Editor-in-Chief is Penelope Aristedis." Her eyes flew up to Jenny's. "Creative Director—Nicholas Aristedis." Mia was speechless.

"OMG!" Jenny jumped from her seat and shook Mia by the shoulders. "Do you know what this means?"

"It means I'm in over my head."

"It means you'll be working with that gorgeous man every day!" Jenny exclaimed.

"And his wife! Don't forget that small detail, Jen."

"What else does it say?" Jenny asked.

"Well, the position comes with a salary increase, thank God!" Mia said. "I may be able to afford my apartment and eat dinner, too!" she joked. "And my new title is Associate Art Director. You'd better pinch me in case I'm dreaming."

"It's not a dream, and you deserve it," Jenny assured her. "Just remember the little people when you climb the golden ladder," she added with a playful glint in her eye.

Mia only hoped that ladder was on solid ground and that she would live up to the expectations of those who had put faith in her reputation.

"You can't depend on your eyes when your imagination is out of focus."
— *Mark Twain*

Chapter 4

Mia

Much to Jenny's chagrin, Mia didn't spend the weekend celebrating her new position by hitting the bars and toasting to her success. No, Mia holed herself up in her apartment, researching luxury lifestyle magazines. She learned everything she could about the demographic they catered for, the advertisers such a magazine would attract, and the types of features they leaned toward. Not that any of these decisions would be Mia's, but the information armed her with a sense of direction for design layout and art direction.

Diligence and preparation failed to assuage the angry swarm of bees warring in her belly on Monday morning as Mia headed into the offices of *Opul* Magazine. Just before reaching for the handle to the frosted glass entrance door, she brushed the coffee-colored strands of hair from her face and smoothed the fabric of her pencil skirt. Millennial pink—the trendy name for the color of her ensemble. She felt so far from a millennial in mind and spirit, but the pale hue was a feminine yet professional choice.

"May I help you?" a ruby-lipped receptionist asked when Mia entered.

"Yes, thank you. I'm Mia Andarakis."

Before she could explain why she was there, the young woman rose from her seat behind her Lucite desk. "Yes, I'll escort you in. I'm Suki, by the way."

"It's nice to meet you," Mia said politely. She followed Suki through a modern, open-designed office space. "Have you worked for *Aris Publications* for long, or are you new with the company?"

"I worked with Ms. Aristedis in the corporate office," Suki replied. "Here you go. This is your space. There's an itinerary for today's meetings on the desk."

"Thank you."

"Any time. Let me know if you need anything," Suki said with a smile as she turned, her pin-straight, hip-length hair swinging back and forth as she strode back to her desk.

Her cubicle, or rather workspace, as there were no distinguishing walls, was twice the size of her previous one. Promptly, she took her seat and dug into her schedule. The first order of business was a staff meeting in less than one hour. Spotting a beverage station across the way, Mia was delighted to see an assortment of tea selections. Opting for a ceramic mug rather than a to-go cup, she poured her tea, musing over the office's lack of movement and noise. But she reminded herself that the first issue hadn't even been brainstormed yet, much less set into production.

Mia tried to settle her nerves as she awkwardly waited in the conference room for the meeting to begin. Nicholas and Penelope had not yet arrived, and everyone had taken the opportunity to introduce themselves. She felt like an impostor, sitting in where she didn't belong. It seemed each individual had been pulled from another magazine owned by *Aris Publications*. Most, Mia noted, were more seasoned than she. With her hands resting in her lap, she clutched her knee to stop her leg from nervously swinging. After a few minutes of casual chit-chat, the door swung open. The energy in the room changed. At least for Mia it did, if the flutters in her stomach were any kind of signal. The room fell silent as Nicholas and Penelope entered.

"Good morning," Penelope greeted. "Nicholas and I would like to welcome all of you to *Opul*. Together, we'll build this magazine from the ground up. Now, you might ask yourself why, when so many magazines are folding or going strictly digital, we are venturing to publish a print magazine."

She looked about the room, waiting for comment, but the staff remained silent. "This magazine has been a brainchild of mine for quite some time. Nicholas and I have bounced ideas off each other endlessly on the type of content we'd like to include and the locations we'd feature." Penelope looked to Nicholas, smiling.

"Pavlos Aristedis is a believer in making our own way. Working from the ground up and knowing every aspect of a business before handing over the reins," Nicholas added. "It wasn't until now that my grandfather gave us the go-ahead for this project." An agitated expression momentarily crossed Nicholas' face as he glanced down the table to meet Mia's gaze.

She quickly looked away, wondering what had earned her the hard stare. He almost seemed bothered by her presence.

"Our staff will be minimal to begin with," Penelope continued. "We'll all have to roll up our sleeves and do what it takes to get the job done. Editorial and production will report directly to me. That's most of you here. Creative reports to Nicholas." She scanned the room. "Where is Mia?"

"Right here." Mia raised her hand timidly.

"You'll work directly with Nicholas. We've hired a junior designer to work under you, and we'll utilize freelancers if needed," Penelope stated. "Norah," she addressed the young woman three seats down. "As the Digital Art Director, you'll also report to Nicholas and monitor the Social Media Coordinator."

When Penelope finished addressing each team, Nicholas adjusted his tie and began to speak. "Each issue will focus mainly on one location or destination including the food, culture, attractions—on a high-end scale, of course. It will even feature a taste of its history.

My first thought was to jump right into Europe. However, this is an American-based magazine, so the inaugural issue will showcase the glamor and beauty of a destination in the United States."

Everyone in the room nodded in agreement.

"And after several issues, we can swing back around to another US location," Nicholas added. "For simplicity, we'll shoot the first issue locally in the Hamptons and East End of Long Island, including their beaches, towns, restaurants, and vineyards."

"Pitch meeting one week from today," Penelope added. "I want to be astounded."

Mia filed out of the room quietly while the others chatted among themselves as they bustled off to work on their respective projects. Nicholas unnerved her, yet Mia knew she'd have to set those emotions aside to succeed in this position. Her mind was already whirling with ideas. The East End of Long Island was as familiar to her as her own backyard. Mia had taken hundreds of photos there over the years to pull for inspiration. Still, she needed an angle that would impress Nicholas, if that were at all possible. The man avoided eye contact with her, and the one time he had met her gaze, it was accompanied by a scowl.

Then it came to her! A brainstorm! For the next three hours, Mia hunted for images, pulled from her own photo gallery, and created a preliminary layout for what she had in mind. Nicholas would either love it or think she was out of her mind, but it was a risk she was willing to take. Maybe. She didn't want to get fired or demoted back to her old position. The more she thought about it, the more Mia began to second-guess presenting the idea at all. Steeling herself, Mia gave her inner thoughts a pep talk.

Her finger hovered over the mouse on her computer. "Just press Send," she told herself. She blew out a shaky breath and, with one click, an email landed in Nicholas' inbox requesting a meeting regarding the attached folder. Nervously, Mia held her stomach, waiting for a reply. It was too late to back out now.

Nicholas' response was swift and surprisingly harsh. No greeting. No signature.

Now is a good time. Three hours ago would have been better.

Mia wasn't sure if she wanted to cry or throw something at the man. How was she to know he had wanted to see her right away? Her face heated, tears welling in her eyes. She was in way over her head. Rubbing circles at her temples, she took three deep breaths to compose herself and stood. Win or lose, it was time for Mia to slip into the role she was hired for.

Mia entered Nicholas' office after hearing a gruff, 'Come in!' in answer to her knock.

"Mr. Aristedis."

"Ms. Andarakis. Yes. So, you are the graphic wonder that has come highly recommended," he said with a touch of sarcasm. "Apparently, your creative talents have no bounds."

Mia opened her mouth to argue the point but Nicholas continued his reproach.

"So, why is it that it has been over three hours since the staff meeting this morning, yet only now have you asked for a meeting looking for direction from me?"

This was not the good-natured man she'd witnessed at the CCP meetings. That man had seemed kind and mentoring. This was like walking into an American Idol audition, thinking you were going up in front of the encouraging Lionel Richie only to discover Simon Cowell instead.

"With all due respect, Mr. Aristedis, I was placed in this position to work on a higher level, to concept ideas and layouts to present to you."

While Mia seemed to stand her ground, in actuality, her insides had contracted into a tight ball.

"That was my understanding, anyway," Mia continued, lifting her chin in defiance. "If you wanted to give me direction, I would have been more than happy to take it, had you called me in to discuss it with me."

Nicholas looked as though, at any second, he could lose his temper.

Mia's voice began to falter. "Since you didn't, I took it upon myself to come up with my own ideas," she quivered. Where the courage had come from, Mia had no idea.

For a fleeting second, she detected a gleam in his eyes. What it meant, she had no idea—annoyance? Amusement? Respect?

Steepling his fingers, he stared at her, silent, assessing. "Show me what you have," he demanded impatiently. "Hopefully, it wasn't a waste of precious time."

Mia nodded nervously. "I can pull it up on your computer. I sent you an attachment in the email."

Nicholas gestured for her to come around to his side of the desk. Coming up beside him, she leaned over the desktop, tapping away at the keyboard. The closeness of his body to hers caused a shiver to crawl up her spine. There was that electrical charge again, fogging her ability to think straight.

"Here," she said, shaking herself from the distraction. "I concepted this idea to show the dichotomy between the opulence of a destination and the less glamorous history of that location."

Nicholas frowned. "This is a luxury magazine. We are selling the opulence. Our target readers want to see high fashion, elegant parties, and exclusive hotels. They don't want to see the grittier side of life."

"I think you're selling your readers short," Mia argued. "They're intelligent people. Many are philanthropists. I think it would make interesting reading and the contrasting images are compelling."

Mia clicked through a series of photos she'd taken at the Hampton Classic a few years back. A collage of enticing images flashed across the screen: an array of eclectic hats, the faces of the wearers concealed by the large brims; signature drinks garnished with fancy accouterments; close-ups of riding boots and crops; and colorful ribbons laced between a horse's ebony mane. There was a young woman, proudly saddled English style, ready for competition. The next image was that of a Shinnecock Indian in a traditional headdress, mounted on his horse.

Mia clicked through a few more pictures of the annual Shinnecock festival, showcasing the Hamptons' indigenous people's heritage and the poor conditions where some of them dwelled.

"Mr. Aristedis, how many magazines are currently in circulation that caters to this demographic?" She didn't wait for him to answer. "Quite a few, right? This would make yours stand out."

"Do you, as a person at your income level, presume to understand the minds of the wealthy better than I, Ms. Andarakis?"

Mia was wrong. Simon Cowell was blunt and sometimes a little mean. Nicholas Aristedis was a condescending, cold-hearted, insensitive ass. He was Lucifer's spawn.

"My apologies. Someone like me would know nothing of the finer tastes of the upper class," Mia said with venom. "If you'll excuse me."

She bolted from his office, grabbed her bag off the back of her chair, and headed to the restroom. Nicholas was not the man she imagined him to be. From afar, he seemed as compassionate as he was beautiful. That was her unfortunate delusion. Pacing between the two sets of stalls and sinks, she frantically tapped a text to Jenny.

Mia: *I can't do this. The man hates me. I need to quit before I get fired.*

Jenny: *What? No!*

Mia: *I'm going to cry.*

Jenny: *Lunch. Meet me. Now!*

"He clearly hates me, and I don't know why," Mia said. "Even before today. He gave me the strangest glare at the gala."

"That doesn't make any sense," Jenny pondered.

"I just don't think I can work with him." Mia pushed her salad around with her fork. "Maybe I can get transferred back. I'll talk to HR, or to Mrs. Aristedis."

"Oh sure, what will you say?" Jenny asked Mia. "Your husband is a son-of-a-bitch to work for?"

"I'll figure something out. If I don't, I'm going to either have a breakdown, get an ulcer, or lose twenty pounds from stress."

"I'd like to lose at least that much. I'll trade you!"

"Trust me," Mia assured her, "you wouldn't want to put up with him."

After lunch, Mia quietly slipped back to her office. She went through her emails and messages, addressing each one. The last one was from Penelope Aristedis, requesting Mia to come to her office at four p.m.

Okay, that confirmed it. She was getting fired. Regardless, she was getting paid, even if it was only until the end of the day. Mia would go out with her head held high and mock something up along the lines of what she thought Nicholas had in mind.

Time ticked away painfully slow. It was as though she was waiting for a cup to fill from a leaky tap while watching the water drip, one drop at a time. Mia wished she could be more like her confident sisters—Kally, who took risks to follow her dreams, or like her little sister, Krystina, whose tongue cut like the sharp edge of broken glass when she had to defend herself. Or maybe she needed a bit of her brother, Theo's, cocky attitude instead. Anything other than her own willingness to retreat and slink away.

It's not that Mia wasn't sure of her skills. She was. Yet, insecurities rushed through her mind like an angry storm that never calmed or drifted to sea.

When it was time to meet with Penelope, Mia pulled a small mirror from her bag, checked her makeup, brushed her hair, and took a deep, calming breath. On shaky legs, she walked to her office and was summoned in upon knocking.

"Have a seat, Mia." Penelope smiled. "Would you like a cup of coffee?"

"No, thank you," Mia replied, her hands tightly clasped in her lap.

"Nicholas came to me and told me what had transpired between the two of you. He wasn't planning on discussing your concept with me. However, he wasn't proud of the way he spoke to you, and the rest came out in the details."

Mia didn't know how to respond.

"First, allow me to apologize on behalf of Nicholas for his behavior."

Mia's eyes flew up to meet Penelope's.

"I honestly don't know what came over him." Penelope shook her head. "He's never been difficult to work with, or for."

Mia's heart hammered in her chest. What did this mean then? Was it only she who elicited vehemence from him?

"I'm not saying his standards aren't high." She raised her hands. "Trust me, they are. But asides from today's inexcusable behavior, he's normally a reasonable man."

"I understand," Mia said. "He wasn't happy with the direction of my concept. I should have waited for him to give me some instruction."

"Well, no," Penelope disagreed. "You did exactly what you were hired for. Don't expect every pitch to be accepted, but I'm looking for fresh ideas and a new voice. I like your proposal."

"You do?" Mia stammered. Tension released from her ribcage. The death grip on her clasped fingers loosened. "But what about Mr. Aristedis?"

Penelope brushed her long, dark tresses off her shoulder. Mia noticed once more that her own vibrant, dark brown hair was of the same color. In an attempt to look more professional, she had cut her hair to a shoulder-length bob once she graduated from college. Yet this woman, with a mane that fell past the middle of her back, oozed a professional sophistication Mia believed she, herself, could never pull off.

"Don't worry about him. Can you pull up what you showed Nicholas?" Penelope gestured for Mia to come around to her side of the desk. "He explained it to me, and I love it. So much so that I want it to be the running theme. Honestly, I wish I'd thought of it myself."

"But he hated it," Mia said in a soft voice.

"No, he didn't. Upon further discussion, he agreed with me."

For the second time that day, she opened the folder to show Penelope her inspiration photos and the mocked-up layout.

As she clicked through image after image, Penelope commented enthusiastically. "You captured the essence of both these events." She leaned back in her chair. "The Hampton Classic is at the end of the summer, if I remember."

"Yes, the last week of August and into the first days of September," Mia replied. "And the Shinnecock Festival overlaps during Labor Day weekend."

"Perfect. Our first issue will be on the stands by October first. It will be a push, but if we have everything in place, we should be able to meet the deadline," Penelope said. "I'll set up a staff meeting for tomorrow. Great work, Mia."

Mia: *I'm not fired!*

Jenny: *Stone Street. Now! The Underdog.*

It was too pleasant an evening to hop in a cab. The Northeast rarely granted its citizens a spring season. April blew in remnants of March winds, and May often held onto a damp chill, penetrating right to the bone. Even early June could often be disappointing. But then, as if by magic, winter melted away as the sun aimed the full force of its rays down upon New York. And just like that, the city was alive again. Not that it ever slept. The crowds by the 9/11 Memorial and Museum were more densely populated than it had been two months prior, and far more pedestrians walked the streets of the financial district at this later hour of the day.

The gentle breeze tickling her face and the smell of the sea lingering in the air made Mia want to skip with giddiness. It was a silly thought, but it was how she had celebrated the first warm day of the season ever since she was a young child—skip outside, pluck a flower bud from a tree, and inhale its sweet odor.

Turning the corner onto the famed cobblestone street, Mia almost lost her footing trying to negotiate the uneven road in her high heels. The street, lined with long, market umbrella-covered tables, over-flowed with energetic millennials socializing after work. It was hard to tell where the seating ended from one pub and began for the next, but once she spotted Jenny, Kyle, and a group of others who worked in their building, she waved in excitement while weaving through the crowd.

"Finally!" Jenny exclaimed. "So, tell me what happened with his Royal Tight Ass."

Mia rolled her eyes. "I don't want to have to say this more than once." She waved Kyle over. "Come here."

"Hey! How was your first day?" Kyle asked as he broke away from a group of his co-workers.

"I'm about to tell you. Weirdest day ever," Mia admitted, exaggerating each word.

Jenny kept refilling Mia's wine as she relayed her interactions with both Nicholas and Penelope.

"Stop!" Kyle placed his hand over Mia's glass before Jenny could pour another glassful. "I'm ordering something for you to eat before you end up flat on the floor."

"I could eat a burger," Mia agreed.

"You got it." Kyle waved over the server.

"With mushrooms and Swiss cheese. And a side order of onion rings," Mia added.

"Anything else?" Kyle chuckled.

"A side salad with low-fat Italian dressing."

"Yes, that low-fat dressing will make all the difference," he laughed.

Mia gave him a playful shove. "Don't make fun of me. I had a rough day."

"What do you think he'll do tomorrow?" Jenny asked.

"I don't know," Mia sulked. "Hopefully, email me some directives so I don't have to see him face-to-face."

"So, am I to assume your crush is crushed? Over? Past tense?" Jenny inquired.

A cyclone of confusion brewed in Kyle's stormy-blue eyes. Stunned, he stared at the girls. "Mia? What is she talking about?"

Mia slapped her forehead repeatedly. "And I thought this day couldn't get any worse."

Kyle ran his fingers through his golden waves. "Excuse me," he said, disappointment evident in his tone.

Mia followed after him as he headed inside the restaurant. "I'm sorry. It was a silly crush from afar."

"That's why I never had a chance with you," he said. "How did I not pick up on it? I caught you staring at him a few times but I didn't make much of it."

"Kyle, whether or not I had any feelings for him, or anyone else, it wouldn't have mattered." Mia took a deep breath. The last thing she wanted to do was hurt Kyle's feelings. "You're my friend, and I never want that friendship to end. But I don't have romantic feelings for you, and it has nothing to do with Nicholas."

Kyle nodded, resigned. "I guess I just hoped."

"You're looking at the wrong girl," Mia reiterated. "Open your heart and your eyes," she advised.

When Mia finally made it back to her apartment at the end of the evening, she was exhausted. It had been an eye-opening day and she worried what tomorrow would bring. Thoughts of going into the office the next day unprepared kept her awake. Motivated, she opened her laptop and worked until she grew so tired she fell sound asleep on the sofa with her fingers hovering over the keyboard.

Chapter 5

Mia

Mia woke up the next morning disoriented. She never made it to her bedroom the night before. Her neck was stiff from falling asleep in an awkward position, and as she stood, she almost crushed her laptop below her feet. She had spent the better part of the night glued to her computer, designing several layout options for Nicholas to consider. God only knows what she had prepared in her weary state.

With only four hours of sleep, she was as exhausted as she was pale. Mia didn't have her sister, Kally's, olive complexion or Krystina's bronze glow. She was the fairer of the three sisters, and, right about now, she looked and felt like a ghost who had died a century ago. With her pinky finger, she dabbed a generous amount of under-eye concealer over her dark circles, hoping to bring her face back to life.

As a rule, tea was her beverage of choice. But on a rare occasion, today being one such instance, and in dire need of caffeine, Mia decided to drop into the Starbucks she passed along her way to the subway each morning.

As she brought the lidded paper cup to her lips, for what would be her third desperately needed gulp, a moppy-haired, teenaged boy on a skateboard whizzed by, knocking into her. Mia squealed as the coffee cup flew from her hands and hit the floor, the brown liquid splattering onto her open-toed pumps.

Infuriated, Mia stepped from the puddle, limping her way into a nearby bakery. Her frown held an expression containing a myriad of emotions, from anger and annoyance to frustration from the stabbing pain in her toe. She bit the inside of her lip, holding back her tears as she walked over to the counter and grabbed a handful of napkins. Her ankles were sticky, and her shoes were a mess. It was her second day on the job, and now she was going to be late.

A young woman wiping down tables spotted Mia. —There's a restroom in the back," she said, pointing in the direction of a narrow corridor.

"Thank you," Mia said. "Hopefully, this isn't a sign of how the rest of my day will go."

After she sufficiently cleaned herself up, Mia scooted off as quickly as she could, weaving past pedestrians to reach the subway station.

"No!" she exclaimed as commuters on the platform turned to stare at her. She'd arrived just as the train was pulling away from the platform. Mia paced the station while staring at the empty tracks as though a train would magically appear. When that didn't work, she checked the time on her phone and groaned.

"I'm going to be so late," she muttered under her breath, chucking the phone in her bag.

Stale, stagnant air invaded her lungs, agitating her further. Finally, after seven long minutes, the next train arrived, and she uncharacteristically pushed her way into the closest car.

Inhumanely overcrowded pigpens had more room than the train car and probably smelled a lot better. Finding herself nose to armpit with a tall, middle-aged man, Mia held her breath for as long as she was able to keep the pungent odor from invading her nostrils.

When the train stopped at her station, Mia rushed through the crowd and onto the street. Thankful to be out in the light of day and into the fresh air, Mia picked up her pace, only to be stopped by a tall, long-haired man buried under a stack of pamphlets. Shoving one in her face, he exclaimed, "The end is coming! Save yourself."

"I'll save myself by getting to work on time," she muttered, racing past him.

Breathing a sigh of relief when she entered her building, Mia quickly scanned herself in and raced to the bank of elevators. Harried and frustrated, she hit the up button several times.

"One of the elevators is broken," a woman informed her.

Mia nodded. *Of course, it is.*

"Hi, Suki," Mia greeted wearily.

"Bad morning?" Suki asked.

"You have no idea. Is Mr. Aristedis in yet?"

"He is."

"Mia groaned. "That's two days in a row I've made a bad impression on him."

"He's really a nice man," Suki assured her. "I'm sure it will be fine."

"Nice to you, maybe," Mia muttered. "I'll see you later."

It was nine-fifteen in the morning and Mia felt as though she'd walked through a battlefield. She was about to make herself a cup of tea and check her emails when her desk phone rang.

"Mr. Aristedis would like to see you in his office," Suki announced.

Blowing out a nervous breath, she knocked on Nicholas' door.

"Come in." He looked up, frowning at Mia.

"Good morning, Mr. Aristedis. I apologize for being a few minutes late."

"I suppose these things happen." He sat behind his desk, his eyes darting from her to his computer and back to her. "I've been told that two of your many attributes are your punctuality and your dedication to your work."

"I had an unfortunate chain of events on the way to work."

The crease between Nicholas' brows deepened. Was he waiting for her explanation?

"You see, I was walking to the subway and a boy on a skateboard ran into me."

Before she could say another word, Nicholas rose from his seat and was by her side in an instant. "Did he injure you?" he asked with concern. Taking hold of her forearms, he examined her. "Did you fall? Are you in need of a doctor?"

Astonished by his concern and the feel of his hands on her, she shivered. "No." Her eyes met his, and Mia thought she detected a flash of tenderness in them. "I may have a bruise on my arm at best, but I think it's my shoes that wore the brunt of it," she said in an attempt to lighten the tension between them.

Releasing his hold on her, Nicholas shoved his hands deep into his trouser pockets. He glanced down to inspect her nude-colored, spiked-heeled pumps, but not before raking the length of her lean legs with his gaze. "Your shoes?"

"My coffee spilled all over them. I had to clean myself up," Mia explained. "Again, I apologize for being late."

"That's not why I called you in." Clearing his throat, he continued, "It seems it is I who owes you an apology for my behavior yesterday. Your concept, although not what I had in mind, was a good one, and Penelope loved it when I presented it to her."

"I'm surprised you did," Mia murmured.

"Excuse me, Miss Andarakis?"

"It's just that you were so adamantly against it that I'd expected you to dismiss it, not present it." Mia swallowed her words, but before she thought the better of it, she continued, "After all, you reminded me that someone like myself couldn't possibly understand the discerning tastes of the upper class."

Mia had gone too far. Nicholas looked like a cork in a champagne bottle about to pop. His jaw tightened. Blue veins protruded from his neck but it was his eyes that frightened her the most. A rage brewed within the depth of those irises, murky and dark, swampy green and muddy brown, kicking up a storm. Lost was the dark honey hue she had admired in his hazel eyes.

"Do you purposely try to challenge me?" Nicholas asked through gritted teeth, slowly enunciating one word at a time. "Is it your intent to antagonize me?"

"No, sir." Mia hung her head.

"This is a small staff, and you are the one person slated to work directly alongside me." Nicholas moved around to his side of the desk, seating himself. Rubbing his forehead, he seemed to be collecting his thoughts. "I don't know how this situation is going to work."

Mia closed her eyes, willing back the tears. She would not cry in front of this man.

"You seem to bring out the worst in me, and it seems I have the same effect on you."

"I understand, sir," she choked out.

"Stop calling me sir," he barked. "I'm not my grandfather or an officer in the military."

Mia nodded. There was nothing more to say. Turning, she left his office, closing the door behind her. On the upside, she had only been here for two days. There wasn't much to clear out of her desk.

Suddenly, a floodgate of emotions broke from her. Covering her face with her hands, she silently sobbed, not only for blundering a rare career opportunity, but for also discovering that the Nicholas of her dreams was nothing but a delusional fantasy.

"Mia?" Suki asked, catching her distress. "What's wrong?"

"Mr. Aristedis said he can't work with me," Mia squeaked out. "I bring out the worst in him. That's what he said." She reached for a tissue and blew her nose. "I suppose it's true. It's all my fault. I said some things I shouldn't have."

"Oh, I can't believe that." Suki pulled up an empty chair from a nearby station. "And that doesn't sound like him. I can't imagine what's gotten into him."

"I don't know," Mia sniffled. "But it looks like I'm done here. I was just about to clear out my things."

"Are you sure you didn't misunderstand?"

"I'm sure." Mia wiped a tear from the corner of her eye. "I was up all night working on layouts to present to him today. A complete waste of time."

"Not necessarily," Suki said. "Email what you have to him. It couldn't hurt."

"You think so?" she sniffed.

"Yes, definitely." Suki rose and returned the chair to its original spot. Walking away, she gave Mia an encouraging thumbs-up.

Drying her tears, Mia tapped away at her keyboard, attaching the files to an email. When she was done, she wrote a brief note to Nicholas saying that she had a reputation until now for being a team player in her working environment. Mia apologized for her part in any difficulty. She hoped the material she forwarded helped him and his new Associate Art Director in some way.

With a heavy heart, she left her ID badge on her desk and left the building.

"Kally," Mia spoke into her phone. "Hi. I'm coming home for a few days. Can I stay with you instead of with Mom and Dad?"

Chapter 6

Mia

"Are you sure you didn't misunderstand?" Kally asked.

"How does one misunderstand, 'This situation won't work?'" Mia replied.

A symphony of chirping crickets drowned out the silence that fell between the sisters. Lilacs surrounded the perimeter of the backyard patio, their sweet scent carried by the soft breeze. Mia had run to safety, fleeing to a place where no one would think to look for her. Here, she could mourn the loss of her dream, hide the shame of her embarrassment, and cry in the arms of her compassionate sister. This was her sanctuary—untouchable, unreachable, protected.

"You can't just give up. You need to fight for what you want," Kally advised. There was a half-empty pitcher of iced tea infused with cinnamon sticks and lemon slices on the table between them. Kally refilled their glasses.

"This is so delicious," Mia said, gulping down half the glass. "Is there honey in here?"

"Mia? Are you avoiding the subject?"

"I can't be like you." Mia narrowed her eyes. "Actually, no! I've tried to be like you. I went out on a limb, stood up to him, defending my idea, and look where it got me."

"Sometimes, you just have to take the chance." Kally softly laid a hand over hers. "You did the right thing."

"No, that works for some people but not for me," Mia argued. "I'm better off just following instructions and keeping quiet."

"Then you'll never advance. If I had done that, I would still be working at Dad's restaurant instead of owning the café." Kally stood, taking Mia by the hand and dragging her to her feet. "Go sit in the lounger. I'll bring out a bottle of wine, and we'll watch the sunset."

Streaks of orange and yellow painted the sky as the sun slowly dipped behind the horizon. Shades of pink faded in, casting a rosy reflection on the descending globe. Lost in her thoughts, Mia only heard the whispers from the rustling leaves as a gust of wind blew by. She jumped when Kally approached her, wine glasses in hand.

"And where did your mind drift to?" Kally laughed softly, taking a seat on the lounger beside her. Emma, her Yorkie, jumped up, nestling herself between them. "So, tell me more about this boss of yours. Nicholas, is it?"

Mia accepted the proffered drink with a sigh. Not answering, instead, she swirled the crimson liquid around in the glass until it formed a whirlpool.

Kally snatched it from her. "Either drink it or talk to me," she ordered. "But don't play with it."

Pouting, Mia gestured for Kally to hand the wine over. Kally complied with a warning glare of admonishment.

Sipping appreciatively, Mia leaned back against the lounge cushion, a satisfied moan escaping her lips. "That's good." She finished a full glass of Pinot while Kally patiently watched her sister slowly relax.

"I think I need a little more," Mia said, holding her glass out.

Kally poured, stifling a giggle. "Be careful. You're already past your quota."

Mia waved her off. "How can someone be so beautiful on the outside and yet so equally ugly on the inside?"

"Okay, sweetie, who are we talking about?"

"Keep up, Kally! You asked me about Nicholas."

"So I did." Kally reached for the wine bottle. "I think I need more of this."

"I nearly fainted when I found out I'd be working for him. For months, I watched him from afar. Arrestingly handsome," Mia swooned. "Like someone I created from my imagination. And then, there he was right in front of me. Poof!" She waved her hand, spilling some of the wine on herself. "I'm so clumsy. Damn!"

"It's not a big deal." Kally handed her a napkin. "What are you saying?" Gasping, her eyebrows lifted in surprise. "Mia, is he the one you told Max and me about on New Year's Eve? The unobtainable man?"

"The one and the same," Mia said, regret lacing her words. "Lesson learned. Don't fall for a pretty face. Besides, the man is married. He was never an option. Just someone to swoon over."

"That, my sister, is what's known as a crush." Kally slid closer to Mia on the lounger. "It's okay," she cooed, stroking Mia's hair.

"Is it okay, though?" Mia covered her face with her hands, embarrassed. "Even with his obvious hostility toward me, his apparent lack of faith in my ability to do my job, and his harsh words, I still get that same feeling squeezing my heart every time I think of him?" She peeked through her fingers. "What's wrong with me?" she asked. "Now, on top of it all, I have to deal with a sick feeling of mortification for what is probably the end of my very short career."

"You need a good night's sleep. The morning has a way of clearing your thoughts. Stop overthinking," Kally advised. "You'll get through this and find another position. In time, he'll be a distant memory. Trust me." Kally helped her slightly drunken sister off the lounger and led her into the house. "Maybe tomorrow you'll come to the café and help me out. Baking always gets my troubles off my mind."

"I think I'd like that," Mia slurred as she fell into bed. "But you know, I'm terrible in the kitchen."

"I know," Kally sighed. "But I love you anyway."

"Surround yourself with only people who are going to lift you higher."
— *Oprah Winfrey*

Chapter 7

Mia

The last time Mia had been in Kally's café, The Coffee Klatch, was when Max, Kally's fiancé, proposed to her the month before. He had surprised her by restoring her café after it had been destroyed in a fire. Soon after, he rallied friends and family to witness the cutest and most befitting proposal for her sister.

Having no reason to get up at the crack of dawn with Kally, it was about ten-thirty by the time Mia strolled in. She walked into the café to find a long line of customers already waiting at the takeout counter and nearly every table occupied.

"Hey, Mia!" Krystina, her younger sister, called out. She pushed her way through the kitchen doors carrying an order of pastries. "Kally said you rolled into town last night. Taking a mental health day?"

"Something like that," Mia muttered. Heading for the kitchen, she pushed through the swinging doors.

"Ah! She lives!" Kally joked.

"You didn't really expect me to come in early? To do what? Proof yeast?" Mia mocked. "Trust me, that would have been a disaster!"

"What would you like to do?"

"Redesign your menus? Update your website?" Mia shrugged.

"So, anything that keeps you out of the kitchen." Kally crossed her arms. "Give it a go. It's like therapy." She cocked her head in the direction of their grandmother. "Here, put this on and go help *Yiayiá* with the *kataifi*." She tossed an apron at Mia, inscribed with one of her baking related quotes. This one read, 'Rise to the occasion,' the letters encircling a seven-layer cake.

As Mia sidled up to greet her grandmother, she tied the apron strings around her neck and waist. "*Kalimera, Yiayiá*." She kissed her grandmother on the cheek but the exuberant woman didn't settle for a quick peck. Grabbing her cheeks with the strength of a much younger woman, she pinched them affectionately. The ritual wasn't complete until the old woman kissed each cheek and drew her into a hug so tight, Mia thought her ribs would crack. At five-foot-one and seventy-five years old, she was a force to be reckoned with.

"*Efthymia mou*, no work today?" she asked.

"It's a long story," Mia sighed.

"And we have time. You tell me while we make the *kataifi*," *Yiayiá* said in her heavily accented voice.

"Oh, I don't know." Mia waved her hands in retreat. "I have trouble enough with regular phyllo. Shredded phyllo will be my ruination!" She leaned her elbows on the counter, resting her chin on her fisted hands. "I think I've taken enough hits for one week."

The old woman wisely remained silent, instead placing a portion of the finely shredded dough into her granddaughter's hands. With *Yiayiá's* guidance, together, they removed clumps, combing through them with their fingers.

With a pastry brush in hand, *Yiayiá* dabbed melted butter onto the phyllo before gesturing for Mia to add the mixture of walnuts and cinnamon.

"*Tóra kylíste*," she instructed. "That's it," *Yiayiá* encouraged. "Tuck and roll. Now place it in the pan and get another strip."

Soon, they had found a steady working rhythm. Mia's tension melted away as her grandmother told tale after tale, each one more amusing than the last.

"What about you, *Koukla*? What's going on?"

"Nothing that will amuse you." Mia lifted the baking tray from the counter. "Should I put these in the oven?"

"*Naí*," Yiayiá agreed, pulling out a fresh tray from beneath the counter. "I'll begin another."

"I told you I got a new position, right?"

Yiayiá nodded.

Mia went on to explain how her first days went, regaling her of the coffee spill, the broken elevator, and everything else that made her late to work. By the time she was done, they were both laughing so hard, they were gasping for breath.

"It wasn't funny at the time, but if I don't laugh, I'll cry!"

"And still, all morning you walk around with the long *moutra*." She mimicked the forlorn expression on Mia's face.

Dropping a spoonful of walnuts back into the bowl, Mia sighed.

"The man hates me, *Yiayiá*!" Mia exclaimed. "Everything about me. He can barely stand to look at me or be in the same room as me. And not only do I rub him the wrong way for some reason, but he hates my work too! It wasn't until the Editor-in-Chief said she liked what I showed him that he admitted it wasn't bad."

Mia bobbed her head around, searching for a tissue to wipe away the tears that were escaping.

"Is this what you're looking for?" *Yiayiá* asked, pulling a Kleenex from her apron pocket.

"Thank you," she said, accepting the tissue. Sniffling, she wiped her tears and blew her nose. "I idolized him, you know?" Mia said, her voice hoarse. "He represented everything I wanted to achieve."

"Handsome?" the old woman questioned, a gleam in her eyes.

Mia laughed. "Yes, *Yiayiá*, very. What does that have to do with any of this?"

She cupped her granddaughter's cheek. "I know you, *Koukla*." She pointed a wrinkled finger at her. "My body might have aged, but in my mind, I'm just like you. I remember it all so well."

"Life was simpler when you were young, *Yiayiá*." Mia truly believed every era had been better than today. Simpler. More romantic. Easier to meet and mingle when swing music and dance halls were all the rage. When couples met without the need for an app and social media didn't exist.

Life has never been simple or easy, *Efthymia mou*." Her grandmother lifted a tray of pastries, placing it into the oven. "Pour some tea, and I'll tell you a story." In the corner of the kitchen, a small, wooden table was pushed up against the wall. *Yiayiá* took a seat, patiently waiting for Mia to join her.

"Here you go," Mia said, setting the cup in front of her.

"I was born at the end of a world war. When your mother was born, Greece was in turmoil once again. You kids today complicate everything when you have more than any other generation before, and without ever having lived through peril."

"I can't disagree with that." Mia nodded.

"You say this man hates you? Ba!" She threw her hands up. "What is there to hate? Look at you!"

"That's not relevant here because he's mar—"

"Now you listen to *Yiayiá*," she scolded. "I won't hear any of this. Things aren't always what they seem. And men don't always show their true feelings."

"But *Yiayiá* . . ."

"Eh!" She lifted a hand, halting any further comment from Mia. "Do you think my Panayiotis took one look at me, got down on his knees and asked me to marry him?"

"That wasn't how it usually went back then?"

"No, *pethi mou*," she laughed. "Panos and I didn't get along at all."

Kataifi

Ingredients

3 cups walnuts or pistachio nuts, finely chopped

2 teaspoons cinnamon

½ teaspoon ground cloves

1 pound unsalted butter, melted

½ cup sugar

1 egg white

One package frozen kataifi dough, thawed

Method

Preheat the oven to 350° F.

In a bowl, mix the nuts, cinnamon, cloves sugar, egg white, and two tablespoons of the melted butter to create the filling.

Pull apart the shredded dough carefully, breaking up any clumps. Lay the dough out on a large cutting board and divide it into approximately 16 long pieces. Each piece will make one kataifi roll. Keep the unused dough covered tightly with Saran wrap to keep it from drying out.

Lightly butter a 9×13 inch baking dish.

With a pastry brush, brush a strip of dough with melted butter. Place a heaping tablespoon of the filling at one end of the strip and roll it up tightly to form a cylinder, tucking strands as you continue to roll.

Place the roll seam-side down in the prepared baking dish. Repeat the steps with all the remaining pieces of dough. Place the rolls close together, and brush generously with the remaining butter. Bake for 45 to 60 minutes, until golden brown.

While the rolls are baking, make the syrup.

Syrup

1½ cups honey

2 cups sugar

2 cups water

Orange rind

2 tablespoons juice from the orange

2 cinnamon sticks

Combine all the ingredients for the syrup in a pot. When it reaches a boil, lower it to a simmer. Simmer for twenty minutes.

Let the syrup cool before pouring it over the hot pastry, or cool the pastry and pour the hot syrup over it. Let the syrup absorb into the kataifi for one day before serving.

Chapter 8

Kalliope

Kalamata 1961

Magnificent splashes of orange bleeding into fuchsia danced around the descending golden sun. Like a kaleidoscope, the colors shifted positions, shapes, and hues. This was Kalliope's favorite time of day. Even when the seaside tavern was at its typical hectic self, time seemed to stop for those brief few minutes to take in the beauty reflected over the Messenian Gulf.

Her workday as a waitress began after *mesimeri*, the afternoon siesta. But seventeen-year-old Kalliope would have rather spent her time in the kitchen, baking up sweet treats or cooking up tasty *meze* while the taverna was closed. It took quite a lot of convincing, but eventually, her persistence and determination wore Demos, the taverna owner, down. He reluctantly agreed to let Kalliope assist his cook in the morning as long as she didn't make a nuisance of herself.

By the time the sun had set, she was growing weary. A lack of energy didn't exist in the fabric of the high-spirited townsfolk. Vibrant enthusiasm filled the air. Laughter competed with the sounds of the sea—boat sails whipping, anchors clanging, waves crashing to shore. Music played. Men sang. And the more they drank, the more they danced. Not that they had a dance floor. The aisles between the weathered, rectangular tables had to suffice.

Kalliope's thick, dark hair hung down her back in a tightly woven braid, accentuating her delicate, heart-shaped face. Long, dark lashes rimmed large, expressive eyes as black as olives. At seventeen, she was already a beauty.

Shy at first, Kalliope quickly learned the art of fending off advances with a wry smile and a cutting tongue.

"*Ella!*" a stocky, wiry-haired man clapped, summoning Kalliope. "Another round for everyone." She cringed when he ran his calloused finger down the length of her bare arm. "Get one for yourself and join us."

Fisting her hands at her sides, she contained her temper. "I'm working," she replied with no warmth.

A few minutes later, she returned, setting down each drink one at a time from a serving tray. Before she could step away, she found herself planted in the lap of the same patron who dared to touch her before. Grunting, she tried to get up, but the wretched man held her down by the waist. "Let go of me, *vlakas!*" Jabbing an elbow into his chest, Kalliope managed to extricate herself from him.

"The girl said to leave her alone," she heard someone bark from behind.

Kalliope didn't need to turn to know her defender was within inches of her. She could feel the power he commanded emanating from his body. Turning, her eyes traveled up his tanned, muscled arms, which were crossed against his faded t-shirt, and strayed up to the hard lines of an angry but handsome face.

"I can handle this, thank you," she assured him, meeting stormy, gray eyes.

Tipping his head in her direction, he stepped in front of her. "Touch her again and I'll slam you through the wall."

"I said I can handle it myself!" she shouted. "I'm not your problem."

"What's the problem here?" Demos asked, waddling over. He was a small man with bad knees and only a smattering of hair left on his head, yet he was fearless despite his age. "No brawls in my place, understand?" Demos buffered himself between the two arguing men.

"I was just having fun with the girl." The offender threw his hands up in surrender. "I didn't know she belonged to pretty boy over here."

"I don't belong to anyone!" Kalliope exclaimed.

"Keep your hands off her, or you'll have to deal with her father," Demos warned. "He'll cut your balls off and hang them up to dry with the octopus."

Kalliope's eyes glinted with satisfaction. Pivoting, she strode away, heading off to clear the table at the other end of the room.

"Can I help you with that?" her rescuer offered.

She had stacked her tray with soiled dishes and empty glasses. "I think I made it clear to you that I can take care of myself."

He blew out an exasperated breath. Raking his hand through his sun-kissed hair, he examined her critically. "Your disposition doesn't match your beauty."

"What is that supposed to mean?" She shifted the weight of the tray to her other hand.

"Give me that, for Heaven's sake!" Giving her no choice, he snatched the tray from her. "Stubborn," he muttered as he headed to the kitchen.

Kalliope stomped up behind him. "I asked you a question."

"And I tried to do a nice thing for you, and you bit my head off." He smiled smugly, leaning against the wall and crossing one leg over the other.

"What?" Kalliope threw her arms up. "Are you waiting for an apology?" Her exhale became a defeated groan. "Thank you, and I'm sorry. Okay?"

"That didn't sound sincere."

She looked up to meet eyes burning with mischief. "I need to get back. I don't have time for this. And by the way, what Demos said is true about my father. And that goes for anyone who even looks my way." She began to walk away.

"Don't you even want to know my name?" he called after her. "It's Panayiotis. My friends call me Panos."

"Goodnight, Panayiotis," she said, making sure to exaggerate every syllable of his full name.

* * *

Every evening for the next week, Panos stopped into the taverna on his way home. If his motive was to annoy Kalliope then he was successful, not that she'd let him know he affected her, by any means.

"What's this?" Kalliope asked with disgust after Panos slapped a package onto the bar, malodorous moisture seeping from its newspaper wrapping.

"For you. Fresh fish. I caught it myself."

"You smell like you caught the whole ocean." Scrunching her face as though she had just swallowed the worst-tasting medicine, she took a glass from the bar, using it to push the fish back in his direction. "My father doesn't allow me to accept gifts from men."

Outside the taverna, awning-covered tables were situated near the entrance. A terra-cotta planter stood on either side of the weathered, wooden doorway. The next afternoon, Panos snuck up behind Kalliope as she watered the brightly colored flowers.

"For you," he said, holding out a handful of purple blooms.

"For me?" She eyed them suspiciously. "For anyone, you mean. Those look like you got them off the side of the road."

"I did!" He grinned. "But I thought of you as I plucked them out of the dry dirt."

Kalliope set the pitcher down. "Why do you keep doing this? Haven't I made myself clear?"

"Very," he admitted. "How else would I have my fun if not to irritate you?"

"I'm fun for you?"

"No," he dragged out. "You're no fun at all. If anything, you're a killjoy and as cold as that fish I tried to give you."

A bilious rumble rolled from Kalliope's throat. Fisting her hands on her hips, she demanded, "Get out of here and leave me alone."

"Don't worry, I won't be bothering you again," Panos said with a scowl.

With a huff, she stormed inside, only to find Demos chuckling.

"He's harmless, you know," he told her, drying his hands on his stained apron. "Good-natured, despite his circumstances."

"Good-natured!" Kalliope repeated, incredulous. Removing her apron, she returned to the kitchen. "I'll be back after *mesimeri*," she told Yannis, the head cook.

Each morning, Kalliope's parents drove twenty kilometers from their village to work at one of the oldest olive groves on the Peloponnese Peninsula. The work was laborious, and it was up to their only child to prepare their main meal for the day.

As she left the taverna for the afternoon, Kalliope stopped at an outdoor fish market. Pointing to the *barbounia*, she held up two fingers. "*Thyo, parakoló.*"

For a moment, Kalliope entertained the thought that if she had accepted the fish from Panos, she could have saved money, but as quickly as it entered her mind, she brushed it away. Moving onto the vegetable cart, he popped into her thoughts again as she squeezed bright, yellow lemons and inhaled the fragrance wafting from potted basil plants. Loose, blond curls nearly covered his enigmatic, gray eyes. Eyes that were as soft and gentle as a kitten's fur until a hurricane of darkness swept through, overshadowing the fleeting kindness in their mystifying depths.

The two-bedroom house where Kalliope lived with her parents was tiny, nestled between other similar homes. The kitchen was located on the back end of the house with a door leading to a small patio for outdoor dining. As Kalliope unloaded her market bag, her mind once again drifted back to Panos.

No one who had ever come to her aid had such an effect on her, she thought, drizzling oil onto the fish. It was perplexing. Cutting two lemons in half, she squeezed the juice onto the fish. She hadn't asked for his help, yet he inserted himself at every turn. He was like a pestiferous gnat she had to keep shooing away.

Adding a generous amount of oregano and a few basil leaves was the last step before Kalliope placed the fish into the oven. "A killjoy," she muttered under her breath, throwing the pan into the oven with a bit too much force. A splash of oil splattered, and the stove sizzled. Picking up a rag from the counter, she dampened it under the faucet and wiped up the mess.

"A cold fish!" Slamming the oven door shut, Kalliope seethed. She wasn't about to give that contemptuous man another thought. She was glad to be finally rid of him.

Chapter 9

Mia

"*Yiayiá!*" Mia listened with rapt amazement. She held a forkful of *portokalopita* to her agape mouth but she had yet to take a bite. "You never told me any of this before! I thought it was love at first sight."

Just as Mia was about to ask her grandmother for the rest of the story, her cellphone rang. "Suki? Hi." Her expression changed, the brightness in her face disappearing, replaced by confusion . . . and maybe a drop of mortification.

"I don't understand." Mia listened, trying to keep up with the receptionist. Mia had only just met the girl but from what she had observed of Suki, she always seemed calm and composed—a person who takes a very Zen approach to whatever comes her way. This young woman was rambling in a frantic, run-on sentence, alarmed over Nicholas' reaction to Mia's empty desk this morning.

"Tell Mr. Aristedis that he did indeed fire me. I don't care what he is telling you now. Stating 'this won't work—'" Mia air-quoted, although Suki clearly couldn't see her "—is, in my understanding, an act of firing me."

Yesterday, Mia left dejected, beaten down by this man and feeling as though she were an abysmal failure. But she no longer worked for him. Upon Mr. Aristedis' orders, Suki pleaded with her to come back to the office. Still, Mia refused. Who did he think he was messing

55

with her head in this way? She was emotionally exhausted, and at this point, hadn't a thing to lose. She was done being made to feel inferior by this man, or anyone else for that matter. She was tired of shrinking quietly into the background, working her hardest, hoping someone would notice, and all for nothing.

"Sorry, Suki. Even if I wanted to come back, I'm out at Port Jefferson. It would take me over two hours to get back into the city."

Mia laughed at Suki's astonished response. "It's not the sticks! It's where I'm from. My sister owns a café in town. Right now, I'm drowning myself in an orange-flavored cake." She took a bite of the pastry, moaning her delight as she consumed a forkful of the syrup-drenched confection. "Have a nice day, Suki. Maybe we can do lunch soon."

When Mia ended the call, her confident veneer cracked. She covered her face with her hands, shaking her head. "What am I doing?"

"I think you're standing up for yourself. Like I did with my Panayiotis all those years ago." Her grandmother stroked affectionate circles on her back.

"It's not the same." She lifted her head, her hair flying in her face. "I need to punch something. Kally!" she called, stomping over to her. "Give me something to beat on. Pound cake! I can pound some cake!"

"What's got you all wound up?" Kally's friend, Egypt, asked. "Or should I ask, who?" She gyrated the lower half of her body in a belly dancer's hip-roll.

Mia humorlessly waved her off. "It's a work thing."

"Of course, it is." Egypt tied a Coffee Klatch logo apron around her waist. "What else would have you all hot and bothered? What is it with you Andarakis women? Krystina is forever hating on Loukas, Kally thinks about nothing but work—"

"Hey!" Kally chimed in. "Leave me out of this. I have Max."

"But how much arm-pulling did that take?" Egypt bobbed her head smugly.

"Put your snarky duck lips away. It all worked out, didn't it?" Kally glanced at the sparkling diamond adorning her left-hand ring finger.

"Back to me." Mia snapped her fingers. "I need to get my aggression out."

"You won't be doing that on pound cake, my epicureanistically deficient sister."

"That's not a real word," Mia complained.

"Yet, it describes you to a tee," Kally smirked. "How about whipping some egg whites for meringue. That should work out some of your anger."

"Here." Egypt threw an apron at her. It was one from a collection that Kally referred to as her mood aprons. This one read, 'Give me coffee and no one gets hurt.'

"Funny, but as you can see, I'm already wearing one." Mia chucked it back at her.

"This one's more fitting," Egypt said, flinging it back at her.

"If the two of you are done playing ping-pong in my kitchen, let's get back to work," Kally scolded.

A half-hour later, Mia set the mixing bowl and whisk down. With a cramped arm, stiff fingers, and white fluff streaked through her dark strands of hair, she was exhausted. "Why couldn't I have used the electric mixer for this?" she asked Kally.

"You could have. That's what I usually do."

"What? Then why did you make me do it by hand?"

"Because you needed to," Kally replied, plastering a fake smile on her face. "Apparently, it didn't help your mood though."

"Mia, Mia!" Egypt rushed through the doors leading from the main room to the kitchen. Setting down a tray of dirty dishes, she assessed Mia. "It's the quiet ones who always fool you." She narrowed her eyes suspiciously.

"What now, Egypt?"

"There's a man out front asking for you," Egypt sing-songed, flirtatiously twirling one of her golden-brown ringlets.

"Me?" she asked, completely flummoxed.

Kally came to her sister's side, wiping her hands free of excess flour.

"How is it the two of you manage to have the hottest men searching you out?" Egypt huffed.

"Hot?" One word at a time seemed all Mia could manage.

"Smoking!" Egypt exclaimed. "Well, in that proper, stuffed shirt sort of way. But still freaking gorgeous," she clarified.

"Stuffed shirt?"

"Did someone perform a lobotomy on you?" Egypt tried to shake her out of her stupor.

"Honey," Kally said softly. "What's wrong? Do you know who's out there?"

Mia shook her head. "No, it couldn't be him." She looked up at her sister in confusion. "Why would he come here?"

"Who?" Kally asked.

"Nicholas Aristedis. My boss. The only uppity, stuffed shirt I've met recently." She massaged her forehead. "My ex-boss," she corrected. "The one who fired me."

"Fired you?" Egypt bit out. "Fired you? I'm going out there to kick his ass! I don't care how hot he is."

Egypt stomped away, Mia on her heels, grabbing the edge of her apron and begging her to stop.

"Mia," Kally said, catching up with her. "He came all this way for a reason. The least you can do is hear him out." She took her sister by the hand supportively, urging her through the doorway. "Come on."

Oh, Lord, she thought. There he was in all his presumptive majesty, surveying his surroundings with a critical eye. While stiffly adjusting his shirtsleeves' cufflinks, Nicholas scanned the room until his eyes fell on her petite frame. Heat flashed across her face. Reflexively, she laid her hands on her roiling stomach, looking away the second their eyes met. In that brief moment, Mia detected a hint of something she couldn't quite figure out. Relief, perhaps, or maybe contrition. She didn't know Nicholas well enough to read the tales the mind allowed his eyes to convey.

"Ms. Andarakis, if you would grant me a moment of your time," Nicholas requested, edging a few steps toward her.

Mia stayed rooted to her spot. The Nicholas she'd come to realize stood before her. Not the kind, beautiful soul her imagination had conjured. No, in front of her was the imposing man himself—straight and to the point. An individual lacking warmth and emotion. Formal and all business.

Even so, the pounding of her thumping heart told Mia that Nicholas still affected her. At the very least, he intimidated and confused her. Mia couldn't understand why he'd bother to come all this way when replacing her with someone he hired himself would be the logical solution.

Mia nodded, gesturing for him to have a seat at an empty table.

With his lips pressed into a hard line, he raised a disapproving eyebrow. "Somewhere more private," he demanded. He lifted a hand in apology, as if suddenly remembering his manners. "Forgive me. Is there anywhere we can speak alone?"

Mia exhaled the breath she had been holding for far too long. "Follow me."

She led him through the set of swinging doors heading out the back. When they entered, all kitchen activity ceased. Nicholas halted, taking in the surroundings Mia assumed was unfamiliar, not to mention, unappealing to him. Had the pretentious man ever even seen the inside of a kitchen? She thought not.

Her grandmother was the first to take a step toward the couple. Mia glared at her in warning to not interfere. "This way," Mia said, ushering Nicholas into a back room.

Kally's office was not much larger than a storage room closet but it was tidy and private. It would have to do for whatever Nicholas had to say. The room afforded only two chairs—one behind Kally's desk and a folding chair propped up against the wall.

Nicholas' dilemma was written on his face, so Mia made it easy for him. "You may sit in my sister's chair," she offered, unfolding the other. It was almost comical. Almost.

Taking the proffered seat, he rested his elbow on the desk, uncomfortably rubbing his forehead. Nicholas peered up at her with a sigh. Mia waited for him to speak, and just when she thought he was about to, he raised his hand as if questioning himself.

Mia waited. The silence was unsettling. Blinking, breathing, swallowing—suddenly, she was self-consciously aware of each involuntary movement.

Finally, Mia broke the silence. "Why are you here, Mr. Aristedis?" she whispered. Mia dared not look up at him in case her resolve wavered. Instead, she kept her focus trained on her tightly clasped hands in her lap.

"I believe we've had an unfortunate misunderstanding."

Digging for a trace of courage, Mia met his gaze. "I understood you perfectly. You didn't see how we could possibly work together." She shrugged her shoulders. "It couldn't have been made clearer. Were you expecting me to wait for security to escort me out?" she asked, bitterness coating her words.

Running a finger around the rim of his starched collar, Mia noticed his jaw muscles clench and his neck reddening.

"Why do you do that?" he grated. She could see he was trying to maintain his composure. "Goad me when I'm trying to apologize," he clarified.

"I don't know," Mia said, determined to force back the welling tears. "Maybe because your apologies end up making me feel incompetent."

Nicholas closed his eyes and pinched the bridge of his nose. "It wasn't my intention. Penelope insisted I rectify this situation."

"Penelope," she repeated, her shoulders slumping. "I have the greatest respect for her, but, from what I hear you saying, Penelope liked what I pitched, not you, Mr. Aristedis. Penelope wanted you to come here. It wasn't your idea." Mia shook her head. "This was a dream opportunity for me, but if you have no faith in me, then I can't work directly for you. There are hundreds of designers who can easily replace me. You'll have no trouble finding one."

"Ms. Andarakis." He rose from the chair and walked around to stand by her. "Mia," he said, leaning his weight against the desk. "We—I don't want to look for anyone else. I am sorry. Truly," Nicholas said with sincerity. "I can't explain my behavior around you but I assure you it is not typical, and it won't happen again."

With Nicholas' six-foot frame hovering over Mia's diminutive stature, she felt overpowered by him. As if he sensed her discomfort, Nicholas extended his hand to her. She hesitated at first, but when she looked up at him, she saw a gentleness in his expression. She owed it to herself not to give up so easily on her career. And then there was that twisting feeling in her heart for this man. She wanted to believe him. Taking his hand, Mia rose to her feet.

"I have a car waiting outside to take me back to the city. I would like you to join me."

"Now?"

"Don't look so stunned." The corners of his mouth hinted at a smile. "There's still quite a lot of the workday left. That is, if you agree."

Mia nodded. "But I can take the train. I have to gather my things."

"The train is unnecessary," Nicholas insisted as he followed Mia out of the office.

"Excuse me! It gets insane back here," Kally apologized as she rushed past lugging a heavy sack of sugar, smacking into him.

"Can I carry that for you?" Nicholas asked politely.

"Thanks, but I'm dropping it right here." She plopped the twenty-pound bag onto the countertop. "My hands are a bit sticky," she explained, wiping them on her apron. "I'm Kally, Mia's sister."

"Nicholas. Pleased to meet you."

"And you already met Egypt, I believe," Kally said as Egypt whizzed by picking up a table order.

"*Kalós irthate*! Welcome!" *Yiayiá* shuffled over, a plate of pastry in hand for the offering. She set the dish on the counter, lifted onto her tippy-toes, and palmed both sides of Nicholas' face. She kissed one cheek and then the other before picking up the platter and handing it to him.

At that moment, Mia wished for an earthquake to split the café floor in half and swallow her. She had covered her face in embarrassment but, as she slowly removed one hand and then the other, she discovered nothing less than amusement reflected on Nicholas' face.

Mia's jaw fell agape as her grandmother engaged him in a light-hearted exchange. With his rigid propriety dropped, it was as though she was acquainting herself with the man for the very first time.

"*Teleiótita.* Absolute perfection," Nicholas moaned, indulging himself in a pastry. "Now this is home," he said warmly, cutting his fork into the honey-drenched *kataifi* for another bite.

"I can run to Kally's to get my things if you like while you stay here and let my *Yiayiá* ply you with more pastries," Mia joked. She had to give it to her grandmother. She had a knack for breaking the tension in just about any situation.

"As much as I'd love that, we really need to go," Nicholas said, shooting the pastry a look of longing.

Yiayiá held up her hand. "*Ena leptó!*" The small-framed woman scurried to the other side of the kitchen. Within minutes, she was back with a takeout box full of her offerings. She handed it to Nicholas. "Mia prepared the *kataifi*," she said, conspiratorially, winking at him.

Mia rolled her eyes. "I helped. You did most of the work."

Waving her off, *Yiayiá* kept her attention on Nicholas. "She's a beautiful girl. No?"

Before Nicholas could answer, Mia shouted. "*Yiayiá!*"

"You came all the way from Newy Yorky for my girl," she said knowingly.

Mia was officially mortified. Correction, first, you die of embarrassment, and then the mortification sets in. After that, you turn to ash—just cease to exist in any form whatsoever.

"Yes, he did, because I *work* for him." Mia's nostrils flared as she set her grandmother straight. "He's my boss, *Yiayiá*. Not a suitor. Just my very *married* boss."

Nicholas did a double-take. "No, I'm not."

"Not what? Not my boss?" Mia feared her grandmother had managed to get her fired again. Yup! She had scared the man away.

"No, I'm your boss, but I'm not married." He narrowed his eyes. "Is that what the tabloids are saying now?'

"Tabloids? I don't read them." Mia looked confused. "Penelope isn't your wife? But . . ." She pointed to the wedding band on his left-hand ring finger.

His lips curled up into a smile. "Penelope is my older sister."

Yiayiá looked back and forth between Mia and Nicholas, her eyebrows raised and a smile plastered across her face. Her hands were clasped under her chin as though she were in prayer, which she very well may have been.

"Where did you get the idea that she was my wife?"

"The CCP gala. You were introduced together. I just assumed."

"Ah, yes, I remember you." Tapping a finger to his chin, he lost himself in thought. "You were the young woman who checked us in."

"That's right."

"Yes," he pondered. "There was something familiar about you."

"From the meetings," Mia declared.

"No," he said dismissively. Circling back to the here and now, he checked his watch. "We need to go." He turned his attention back to Mia's grandmother. "It was a pleasure," he said with a smile, bending down to kiss her cheek.

This man was a paradox—formal and strictly business-like with her, Mia thought, yet warm and affable with her grandmother. "Love you, *Yiayiá*," Mia said, hugging her. Turning, she laughed humorously under her breath. Apparently, it was she alone who got under Nicholas' skin. Although she had no idea why.

Patrons now occupied every table in the café, and the line for take-out orders had grown. Mia waved to Kally and blew her a kiss goodbye.

"Hold on!" Kally slid a take-out cup carrier across the counter. "Three cappuccinos to go." She cocked her head toward the front window. "The third is for your driver. I presumed that's your car out there?"

"Yes, thank you. Darren will appreciate it," Nicholas said, accepting the tray. "Impressive place," he said politely, taking one last look around.

Mia, standing a step behind Nicholas, communicated silently with her sister. The language spoken through eye contact was all they needed to agree that this man was clearly out of his element here.

Mia leaned over the counter to embrace her sister. "Thanks for everything," she whispered.

"Any time." Kally eyed Nicholas warily as he began to head for the door. "I'm always here for you."

Mia haphazardly threw her clothing in her duffel bag. Nicholas had come here just for her. Something she was still trying to wrap her brain around. Despite that fact, she feared his impatience. It took less than ten minutes for her to emerge from her sister's domain. When she entered the car, he was on a call, so she quietly took a seat, pushing herself up against the door on her side of the vehicle, leaving plenty of space between them.

Now what? Eavesdrop on his conversation? That would be awkward. Pulling her iPhone from her bag, Mia popped a set of AirPods in her ears. Scrolling through her Spotify, she chose a playlist and was soon lost in the love ballads of the nineteen-forties. Just as she was beginning to feel her back relax into the plush leather of the backrest, Nicholas leaned over, irritation written on his face. Pinching his fingers together, he motioned for her to remove her earbuds.

Mia yanked them out, letting them drop onto her lap. Instead of the music pausing, it went to speaker mode. Mia's eyes flew up, expecting to meet Nicholas' irritation. She scrambled to shut it off but clumsily dropped the phone instead.

Rosemary Clooney crooned, 'Someone to Watch Over Me.' As if

the song evoked a memory, a hint of a smile crossed Nicholas' face. "You surprise me, Ms. Andarakis. I fully expected you to be listening to some pop tune by the likes of One Direction."

"I'm not fifteen years old."

"You're not eighty-five either," he retorted. "That was my grandmother's favorite song."

A glimmer of the man she hoped he was flickered in his eyes—vulnerable and sentimental. Everything about him softened, if just for a brief moment, until he once again regained his impervious composure.

"If it's agreeable to you," Nicholas started, clearing his throat, "I'd like to work late into the evening since we've already lost half the day."

Mia's every muscle tensed at his words. It was her fault they were behind schedule. The implication was clear. "Of course."

"I can order in dinner," he added.

She nodded shyly. "We can start now, if you like. I have my laptop with me."

"You might want to shut off your music first." Taking matters into his own hands, he picked up the device from the floor. "Why those songs?"

Mia tilted her head, eyeing him quizzically. It surprised her that he cared enough to ask her a personal question. "I can't explain it." She shrugged. "The music soothes me. The simplicity of those times appeals to me. At least, my perception of what life was like back then."

"An era riddled with war, death, and bigotry." His matter-of-fact yet reprimanding tone reminded her of a professor correcting an ill-advised student.

"Is that the cynic or the journalist speaking?"

"I'm just a realist. And I'm not a journalist. I leave that role to my sister."

The gold band on his ring finger caught her attention once more. "Can I ask you a question?"

Nicholas gestured for her to proceed.

"Why do you wear a wedding band?"

"It belonged to my father."

Mia looked at him with curiosity.

"He and my mother were killed years ago," he said in a low voice.

Mia gasped. "I'm so sorry. I had no idea," she said, restraining the urge to reach out and touch his hand.

Nicholas swallowed. "It's public knowledge," he said, staring out the window. "I'm surprised you didn't learn about it from a Google search," he lashed out bitterly.

Mia had no concept of what it was like to have her life under a microscope. "I don't Google celebrities or public figures."

Turning, Nicholas faced her. Now it was Mia who felt as though she was a specimen under examination.

"Twitter?" he asked.

Mia shook her head.

He furrowed his brow. "Facebook, then?"

"No," she stated emphatically. "Anyone I want to keep in touch with, I do so without the need of a social media platform."

"So, no Instagram either?"

"Yes, but only to post creative content." The mistrust in his expression was disconcerting. "You don't believe me. I can tell." She pulled her phone from her bag. "Here." Mia offered Nicholas her cellphone. "Check the apps."

He waved it away but she insisted. "No, I want you to look. One thing you should know about me is that when I say something, I mean it. I know nothing of your personal life, and I don't engage in gossip or have any interest in spending my time on social media. I don't imagine you do either."

"No, I don't," he agreed. "Your attitude isn't typical. I'm starting to see why you're drawn to those yesteryears."

They remained silent for the remainder of the ride. It was a bit uncomfortable as Mia wondered what was on Nicholas' mind. She stared out the window, watching the cars whiz by. Lost in her thoughts, she tried to unscramble all she'd learned about Nicholas today.

Chapter 10

Mia

August 2019

Rays of sunlight reflecting from Lady Liberty blinded interested onlookers. Thrilled tourists on joyrides shouted and laughed on roaring speedboats circling the monument, and the familiar smell of saltwater and bistro specialties lingered in the air just outside Mia's office complex.

Mia had missed her summer lunchtime ritual with her friends. The past few weeks hadn't afforded her more than a quick bite at her desk, but today, she just couldn't resist. It was one of those rare, warm August days, dry and pleasant. Often, at this point in the season, the humidity was so oppressive that locals either fled the city or remained in heavily air-conditioned spaces.

"How is it that you get to eat a grilled four-cheese sandwich with truffle fries," Jenny complained, "while I'm eating a garden salad with low-fat dressing?"

"It's all about choices." Mia tempted her friend, moaning her delight as she savored a bite of the gooey, buttery sandwich. Catching some of the excess dripping off the side with her fingertip, Mia didn't waste a drop. "No one stopped you from ordering one."

"My hips did," Jenny said, begrudgingly stabbing her fork into the plastic bowl of greens.

Kyle chuckled. "This is where I leave to get another soda." He looked to the women. "Anyone?" Both Jenny and Mia lifted their nearly full plastic cups. "Okay, then." Rising from the concrete steps overlooking the water, he strode away, disappearing into the food court.

"You need to stop doing that!" Mia admonished Jenny. "Stop insulting yourself in front of Kyle."

Jenny shrugged. "What can I say? Self-deprecation is my defense mechanism."

"Jen, maybe if you stopped making jokes at your own expense, he'd see you differently. Or do you feel safer in the friend zone?"

"Says the girl who goes about her workday with as little contact as possible with the big man himself."

"That's different," Mia defended. "I need to prove to Nicholas that I can take his direction while still working independently and taking the lead on day-to-day projects."

Kyle climbed down the steps, taking a seat just above the girls. "What are we talking about?" he asked, setting his beverage down.

"Mia's boss," Jenny replied, snatching Kyle's cup. She drank a long, satisfying sip from the straw and handed it back to him.

"You said you didn't want one," he complained, giving her the stink eye. Turning to Mia, he asked, "Is he giving you a hard time again?"

"No." She waved him off. "It's fine. He's actually been pretty . . ." She struggled to find the right word. " . . . cordial."

"Cordial!" Kyle almost choked on his soda. "How magnanimous of him."

"The truth is, he's working her into the ground," Jenny told Kyle. "She hasn't been home before eight o'clock any evening in the past two weeks."

"When I took the position, it was understood that there would be limited staff and long hours for the inaugural issue." Mia crumpled up her sandwich wrapper and stood. "Anyway, I need to get back."

Dreamily, Mia walked to her office. Lifting her face toward the sun, she let its warm rays wash over her before stepping back inside the overly air-conditioned environment. She always kept a sweater hanging over the back of her desk chair for that very reason. Reaching for it to quell her chill, Mia jumped, startled by a firm command when Nicholas summoned her.

"Coming," she swiftly responded. Standing in the doorframe to his office, Mia couldn't help but notice his shirtsleeves rolled up to the elbows, displaying tanned, muscular arms. His tie had also been loosened, atypical for his normally starched-up self. As Mia curiously examined his casual appearance, the slightest of smirks crossed his face.

"It's a hot day," he explained. "You're not the only one who stepped outside for lunch."

"I hope you didn't mind. I wasn't gone long. It was just such a nice day, and I thought a little fresh air—"

Nicholas held up a hand. "No need to explain. You may do whatever you wish during your break. Now, follow me to the conference room."

Nicholas led Mia to a wall of mocked-up sheets pinned to a board in a sequential magazine placement order.

"Penelope approved the layout," Nicholas explained. Rubbing the scruff on his chin, he scrutinized each page. "You confirmed with the photographer, I presume?"

"Yes, along with a small hair and makeup crew," Mia said. "There shouldn't be too much to do as far as background setup. I want the Hampton Classic and the Shinnecock Festival to be featured as unadulterated as possible."

"They'll be an opportunity for candid shots, and we can sift through those, but I want to focus on the opulence of the Hampton's event with carefully posed shots," Nicholas said.

"But for the Pow Wow, we need the reader to see the direct opposite," Mia argued. "The majesty of their rituals and, in contrast, the dire conditions in which they live can only be profoundly captured by a moment in time."

He sighed in defeat. "I believe my sister would agree with you."

But not necessarily him, she thought. Nicholas had never outwardly agreed with Mia. The approval came solely through his sister.

"Come back to my office so we can discuss logistics." Gesturing for Mia to step ahead of him, she complied.

"My car will pick you up Friday morning. Penelope will be coming out at some point, but later in the weekend."

"There's no need. I can go to my home on Long Island on Thursday night and meet you in the Hamptons in the morning," Mia said. "I figured I would be staying there for the weekend."

"And do what? Commute back and forth every day? With the Labor Day weekend traffic?"

Mia wanted to laugh at the expression on his face. Commuting must be beneath him, she imagined. It wasn't as though she was offering to travel back and forth to Mars every day.

"It will be more efficient for you to come with me. We have a house in Southampton. There are six bedrooms and a sizable home office. It will be far more convenient." Nicholas looked over at Mia and met her troubled gaze. "Unless you'd feel more comfortable in a hotel," Nicholas offered.

"No. You just took me by surprise," Mia said shyly. "It would make sense, and I don't want to cost the company any additional expense."

"It's settled then."

That was Mia's cue to exit but, as she began to leave, he called to her.

"One more thing. One of our advertisers is a sponsor for the Classic. They're hosting a cocktail party Saturday evening, and we've been invited."

"By we," Mia inquired, "you mean you and Penelope. Right?"

"And also, you."

"Okay," she shrugged off in what she hoped was a confident manner. Turning, she closed the door to his office. Palming her cheeks, Mia's face felt like she had just eaten a dozen habanero peppers. She needed to calm her nerves if she was going to get through this weekend. Meditation? Acupuncture? Hypnotism? She needed something.

Chapter 11

Nicholas

Seated at a table under a tent by the stables, Nicholas jockeyed his attention between his laptop, his phone, and the photo shoot. He was beginning to understand why Mia came so highly recommended. The girl who'd shrunk under his firm demands now directed every detail with authority. And although her beauty hadn't gone unnoticed, for the first time, he truly saw her as a colleague, an equal, a woman.

Earlier, as she instructed the photographer to capture elegantly dressed spectators, Nicholas noted that she could have been one of them herself. A navy and white polka dot sheath dress tastefully hugged her slim body. She had abandoned her coordinating wide-brimmed hat when it got in the way of her work, but at first sight, he thought she looked like a starlet from a bygone era.

"I'd like to go over today's schedule," he'd said to Mia in the car ride earlier that morning. It was his way of breaking the awkward silence.

"Of course," she replied, pulling her attention from the laptop she had immediately fired up. Her hat brim kept her face hidden from view but she tapped the keys and brought up the document outlining the day's schedule.

Pulling a pad and pen from her bag, Mia scribbled notes as Nicholas rattled off changes and additions to the itinerary. "Why not put that directly in the document?" he asked impatiently, irritated for some reason.

"I will." She peered up at him through a set of thick lashes. "I like to refer to my lists on paper."

Instantly, he regretted questioning her when she quickly shoved the items back in her bag.

That was only hours before, and now, Nicholas watched in amazement as Mia the meek became a queen bee before his eyes. A young girl proudly mounting an English saddle posed while Mia directed the photographer. Wasting no time, she set up each shot and then moved on to the next, making split-second decisions, gesturing with both the authority of a symphonic conductor and the grace of a ballerina. Nicholas observed Mia, unconsciously rubbing the scruff on his jaw.

At three o'clock, he called for a break, apologizing to the crew for the late hour. But Mia didn't head for the food. Instead, he found her gazing out over an open field.

"Mia," he interrupted her thoughts. "You need to eat something."

"I'd like to set up a few shots over here while the sun is setting," she mused.

"After you eat. I can't have you passing out on me." He pushed a plate into her hands, and she accepted it.

"Sliders. Mmm, with sautéed mushrooms." Closing her eyes, she moaned, savoring the flavors as she took her first bite.

Nicholas nearly choked on his own Adam's apple. The sight and sound of Mia feasting on his offering mesmerized him. When her tongue darted out to lick remnants of sauce off her lips, it almost brought Nicholas to his knees. As if she sensed his eyes fixated on her, Mia's gaze curiously met his.

And there it was again—that nonplussing mystery her eyes held. It had taken Nicholas by surprise the first time he noticed her on the night of the gala. He had yet to put his finger on what it was about Mia that evoked such a visceral reaction out of him.

"Well, I'll leave you to your thoughts." This girl rattled him. Never had he been at a loss for words with a woman before.

"Thank you." She held up the remains of the slider.

Nodding, he shoved his hands into the pockets of his ecru linen pants, ambling away.

Chapter 12

Mia

Blazing shades of orange blanketed the expanse over the horizon. The additional photographs had been taken before the sun completely disappeared behind the grandstand. It was quite possible these shots wouldn't even be included in the final layout, but what if they turned out to be the 'blue ribbon' of the entire series in the contact sheets?

By the time Mia crawled back into the car with Nicholas, they had been on location for over nine hours. They had arrived that morning straight from the city, and now, all she craved was a hot shower and a comfortable bed.

Mia opened her laptop to quell the silence, clicking through the untouched photos the photographer had immediately shared with her upon her request.

Nicholas, expelling a heavy sigh, glanced over to see what Mia was working on and frowned. Completing the text he'd been typing, he pressed send and dropped the phone on the seat between them.

"You've done enough for one day." Nicholas closed her laptop shut.

"I was in the middle of choosing photos for the relating articles to show Penelope." Mia reopened the flap.

"It can wait. You must be exhausted."

"And I'll rest when we get to the house," Mia retorted as she continued to type, not bothering to look up at him. "The only thing to do in this car is to use my time wisely and stay productive."

"You could just look out the window and enjoy the scenery," he suggested.

A quiver of a smile crossed her mouth. Turning her head in his direction, she pulled her fingers from the keyboard and closed her computer. "Rumor has it that you're a workaholic. Could rumor be misinformed?" she joked.

"I thought social media gossip was beneath you, Ms. Andarakis," he teased.

"I hear things," she countered, a playful lilt to her voice. Maybe it was time to relax her brain for the rest of the evening after all. Mia melted into the saddle-colored leather interior of the black, extended Audi A8. Taking Nicholas' advice, she peered out the window, though as the hour advanced, the moon's light bleeding through the night sky provided the only illumination.

The driver turned the corner, veering off the main road, and Mia perked up. "I know this place! The church is here." Turning to her right, looking past Nicholas, she ducked her head and pointed. "The Greek church," she clarified.

"I'm aware," he said, amused by her enthusiasm. "My grandfather is a benefactor."

Mia smiled. "One of my cousins got married here a few years ago."

They turned the corner onto a street Mia had driven down before. The homes that could be seen from the road looked very much like any other house in an upscale neighborhood, albeit a little larger. But the ones that caught her curiosity were hidden behind lush hedge fences and wrought-iron gates.

Her curiosity had been quenched the day she and her sisters had once explored a little further, driving down the long road. Abruptly, Mia had suddenly hit the brakes with great force. So much so that they might have been ejected from the car had they not had their seatbelts on. Perched over the garden barricade's view stood a stately structure beyond the scope of her imagination. The three-story home was more than just a house. Long Island was home to its famed Gold Coast Mansions, and Mia had visited several of them. This home was not of that grand scale, but in her eyes, it was a mansion all the same. French doors leading to second and third-floor terraces conjured romantic images. The open lawn was lush and green, carefully manicured, seemingly untouched by trampling feet. Her thoughts drifted to an era long gone. Mia envisioned men wearing knickers and women floating by in billowing dresses, smacking wooden croquet balls through hoops with their color-coded mallets.

Mia was jolted from her reverie when the car came to a halt at the gate. Looking up, she blurted in astonishment, "This is the house?" It was indeed the house she'd just been daydreaming of, not that Nicholas was aware of that. Embarrassed, she clamped a hand over her mouth.

"Of course, it is . . ." he snapped sarcastically. "I don't usually make a habit of invading other's homes."

And there it was again. Like a morning glory that had begun to bloom, Mia recoiled under his harsh tone just as the flower shriveled under the cool night air.

"I . . . didn't mean . . ." She lowered her eyes to the floor, shrugging off the rest of her explanation.

A sigh so loud it was almost a groan caught Mia's attention. Nicholas threw his head back and ran his fingers through his hair. "My apologies." He scrubbed his face with his hands. "I'm tired. But it's no excuse for bad manners."

She smiled at Nicholas but the gesture didn't quite reach her eyes. The excitement she'd felt only a moment ago had drained from her. She had been so excited at the idea that this was the same house. In giddy childishness, she'd wanted to call her sisters and tell them where she was staying for the weekend. Inconspicuously, she would have roamed the house, describing it to them in all its glory. But now, as the car came to a stop at the circular drive by the front door, all she wanted to do was slither away quietly, climb the stairs to whatever room she was assigned, and stay out of Nicholas' way.

"Is that you, Nicholas?" With a full glass of wine in hand, Penelope padded around the corner, donning a cropped t-shirt and wide-legged, white muslin pants. Her face lit up when she saw Mia hesitating at the doorway.

"Come in, Mia." Snapping her head around, Penelope glared at her brother. "Take Mia's bag up to the guest room."

"Which one?" he grumbled, taking the bag from her hands.

"I can do it," Mia said. "Just tell me where it is."

"Nonsense." Irritated, she waved her hand, ordering Nicholas up the stairs. "The last one on the right." Her sour expression shifted as she addressed Mia. "Join me for a glass of wine," Penelope said, leading her down the hallway. "Unless you're too tired and need to wash the day off first?"

"I'm fine. A bit sweaty from the heat though, and my feet are crying to be freed." Mia laughed. Penelope had a way of putting her at ease. At first glance, she looked intimidating. Like her brother, she was commanding and authoritative. Still, whereas Nicholas was mostly stern, at least Penelope exuded warmth.

She pushed a glass of white wine into Mia's hand and gestured for her to follow her out onto a stone patio. What Mia had admired from afar, she realized, was only the front lawn of the home. Beyond the veranda, pool lighting illuminated undulating ripples of water. Cushioned lounge chairs lined the perimeter, and a small pool house sat several feet behind the diving board.

Flames of blue and orange danced between glossy shards of fire glass recessed in a rectangular firepit Mia estimated to be about five feet long. Penelope directed her to the settee, strategically situated close enough to appreciate the tranquil atmosphere from the fire without becoming overheated. Together, they simultaneously expelled a satisfied sigh as they relaxed into the cushions.

Penelope tapped her wineglass with the tip of her manicured

fingernail. "I really don't know what's gotten into Nicholas. He's not usually like this." Furrowing her brow, she added, "His kindness will eventually shine through. You'll see. Once he's worked through whatever is eating away at him."

"He has a lot on his shoulders with this first issue." Mia didn't know what else to say.

"We both do, but Nicholas usually works well under pressure." She sipped her wine, contemplating. "No, it's something entirely different. He's a private sort but we generally confide in each other." Turning to Mia, she gently squeezed her hand. "Anyway, I don't want you to take it personally. I'll single-handedly beat the tar out of him if we lose you to some other magazine because of his attitude."

Mia blushed. "I appreciate your faith in me."

"Great work today. I saw the contact sheets."

"Thank you. I'm glad you were pleased. I was happy with them." Mia sipped her wine and stared into the flames lashing before her. "If I didn't thank you before, I want to do so now. I really appreciate this opportunity."

Smiling, Penelope lifted her glass, clinking hers with Mia's.

After a few minutes of small talk and an empty wine glass, Mia reluctantly stood. "We have an early call time tomorrow. Nicholas and I are heading to the reservation to take some portrait shots before the tourists begin to arrive," Mia explained, excusing herself.

Quietly, Mia tiptoed up the staircase and down the hallway, careful not to disturb Nicholas. She wondered in which room he resided and hoped it was at the opposite end from hers. The last room on the right, Mia reminded herself. When she stepped inside, she was struck by the scent of fragrant lavender. The room was cotton-white but for the palest of periwinkle accents. To her left, French doors led out to a private terrace. Opening the doors, she stepped out onto the balcony, a faint breeze brushing across her skin. Looking out at the cars passing below, Mia mused at how many times she had looked up at this very balcony, wondering about the people who dwelled here. Was someone looking up at her now, pondering over who she might be?

She rubbed at her shoulders, rolling her neck to relieve the stress and tension in her muscles brought on by a long day. What she needed was a bath—not a shower—a hot soak in a steamy tub. As if by magic, the connecting en suite to her room answered her prayers.

Mia marveled as she ran her hand over the sink vanity's gray and white marble, noticing the flooring under her feet was an exact matching stone. A glass shower with a circular, open-entry design was something she'd never seen before. But what dominated the space and her senses was the step-up garden tub illuminated by a low-hanging crystal chandelier.

"Ooh," she purred, hastily turning the faucet on to run the bath.

A tray had been set boasting an array of lavender-scented body care products. As Mia added a mixture of bubble bath and body oil to the water, she inhaled the fragrant vapor fogging the prismatic glass on the light fixture above.

After pinning her hair up and shedding her clothes, Mia climbed gingerly into the basin to acclimate to the temperature. It took mere seconds for her body to surrender to its warmth, marked by the small, gratified whimpers involuntarily falling from her lips. This rare indulgence had soothed her so. By the time she fell onto the bed and tucked herself into the crisp sheets under the lightweight duvet, she fell asleep without a single thought burdening her mind.

Chapter 13

Nicholas

Nicholas fastened the last button on his navy gingham dress shirt. From his chest of drawers, he chose a pale, yellow tie and matching pocket square. Expelling a weary sigh, his fingers mindlessly knotted the silk around his neck. Nicholas wasn't in the mood for a cocktail party. Still, when one of your largest advertisers invites you, declining isn't an option.

In an attempt to capture the land and its people's essence as it might have looked before Long Island was inhabited by settlers, Nicholas and Mia had started off at an early hour for the Shinnecock Reservation. By afternoon, an influx of tourists typically flooded the festival, which would have spoiled the authenticity.

Penelope and her editorial team were on hand as well to coordinate their interviews with the photographer.

Once again, Mia, in work mode, had been fascinating to observe. Her vision was concrete, creative, and she required little guidance. All day, she'd been an exemplary model of civility and professionalism, traits he rather admired in the workplace. Yet his inability to elicit a smile from her vexed him. Their conversation was limited to the task at hand. Nicholas wasn't quite sure why, but as he adjusted the pocket square to his very particular satisfaction, he thought of Mia and how she brightened when anyone else approached her.

With one last look in the full-length mirror, he buttoned his jacket and strode down the hallway. Penelope was waiting for him at the bottom of the staircase.

"I'll have to keep my eye on you all evening," Nicholas said. "Men will be throwing themselves at you."

Wearing gold, strappy, high-heeled sandals, Penelope met her brother's six-foot height. Her fashion sense had generally leaned toward a simple, tailored style, and tonight was no exception. Her one-shouldered, floor-length dress was free of embellishments, the soft, white material against her sun-kissed skin accentuating her exotic beauty.

"I can take care of myself, little brother," she warned. "It's me who usually worries for you in a large crowd of guests."

A knowing look passed between them—hers of understanding and concern while his held the anxiety he concealed from everyone but her. Just then, Nicholas slid his gaze to the top of the staircase as a vision in the palest shade of pink descended. Without thinking, Nicholas extended his arm, rushing forward to escort Mia the rest of the way down. With each step Mia took, a shapely leg peeked out. A slit cut from the side of her dress ran from her thigh down to the floor. Nicholas was captivated by her beauty. Glancing briefly at his sister, he caught the perceptive glimmer in Penelope's eyes. Ignoring it, he straightened his spine in denial.

"Mia, you look stunning," Penelope complimented.

"Thank you," Mia replied shyly. "That dress looks gorgeous on you," she said with admiration, returning the compliment. "And how do you manage to make a simple ponytail look so elegant?"

"Shall we, ladies?" Nicholas offered, looping their arms with his. "I must say, I'm a little offended," he declared, pouting as they made their way to the car. "Neither of you commented on my hair or perfectly manicured nails. I've been primping all day," he mocked, smirking.

Nicholas yelped when his sister smacked him playfully in the back of his head with her evening bag.

"You see?" Penelope slid into the car. "My brother can take the scowl off his face long enough to make a joke when he wants to."

Mia brought her hand to her mouth, stifling a giggle.

"Oh, and there it is!" Penelope provoked. "It's back," she teased, commenting on her brother's frown.

"Pia, enough!" Nicholas grumbled.

Mia titled her head in question.

"He couldn't pronounce my name when he was a toddler," Penelope explained. "Pia stuck but he usually keeps the nickname between the two of us." She reached across Mia's lap, tapping her brother gently on his leg. "I'm only having a little fun with you. You've been so stressed these past few days. I want you to have a nice time tonight."

"It's just another work obligation," he said, gazing out the car window sullenly.

"It's a party. Try to have fun."

Not twenty minutes later, the car pulled up to a circular driveway. Whereas the Aristedis Hampton residence had a Tuscan-style look to it, this house was more what one would expect to see from a waterfront home. Wide stairs opened onto a sweeping front porch, which wrapped around the house's perimeter, leading up to a raised deck around the back overlooking the water.

As they entered the home, they were greeted by waitstaff offering champagne from a silver tray. Nicholas handed a glass to Mia and his sister before taking one for himself.

Every room in the open-formatted home was occupied. The buzz from several conversations drowned out the background music. Acquaintances rallied for Nicholas' attention, some making friendly conversation, others wishing to discuss business. As long as they all didn't descend on him at once, he'd be fine. As soon as a room became too crowded, he moved to a quieter spot. But there was no escaping certain individuals from dishing out advice or showering him with their seemingly good intentions. Penelope, picking up his body language cues, rescued him when he wanted to extricate himself from an intrusive, middle-aged woman. She seemed to think he'd be a good match for her daughter. In turn, Nicholas did the same for Penelope when the most boorish man had trapped her in his one-sided prattle.

Finally, Nicholas led Mia and his sister onto the deck, where he felt the company might be more palatable. And it was. There, Nicholas could breathe. The rhythm of the waves crashing ashore lulled his mind to a peaceful state. Stars twinkled above, illuminated in sharp contrast to the midnight sky. The fruity taste of champagne on his tongue and the feel of his hand on Mia's silky skin at the small of her bare back as he led her outside aroused his senses.

"If you'll excuse me, I'd like to find the restroom," Mia said.

When she was out of earshot, Penelope turned to her brother. "She's a bundle of nerves around you. What have you done?"

Nicholas set his champagne flute down on a side table a little too roughly. "I'm her boss," he bit out. "What do you want from me? Why is it my fault that she's a nervous sort?"

"Only with you, brother. Only with you."

Nicholas waved a dismissive hand. "And you know this how? Have you made it your business to watch her moods and interactions with all the people in our employ?"

"No, but I watch you . . . watching her." Penelope stared at him, waiting for his reaction. "I see the way you look at her."

"While I'll admit she's attractive, it's of little consequence. We don't seem to bring out the best in each other." Although Nicholas kept the tone of his voice emotionless, the clipped way in which he spoke gave him away. Mia's allure agitated him, and so did their manner of communication—or lack thereof. Nicholas stared at his sister indignantly, his spine ramrod straight and his jaw clenched.

"Maybe you should get off your high horse," she said with amusement, patting his cheek.

"Like your standards aren't impossible to meet," he mumbled under his breath.

"That's unfair and below you, Nicholas," Penelope whispered softly.

Shaking his head, Nicholas closed his eyes. When he opened them, he took his sister's hands in his. "I apologize. Truly. I don't know what's gotten into me tonight."

The wounded expression left Penelope's face. "Don't you, though?" She raised an arched eyebrow and looked as though she was about to say something else. Instead, smiled smugly. "I'll leave you to your thoughts." She grinned, walking away.

"Finally!" a young woman said, coming up from behind just as Penelope had disappeared from his sight. "I was hoping to catch you alone."

"Hello, Cassandra." Nicholas forced a smile. This was yet another woman he had hoped to avoid tonight. Time after time, she vied for his attention, flinging herself at him shamelessly, to no avail.

"I wasn't sure if I'd see you tonight. Here's to hoping!" Cassandra exclaimed, snatching two glasses of bubbly off a tray from a passing waiter. Handing Nicholas one of the flutes, she leaned in to kiss his cheek, hugging him with her free arm.

Nicholas made no attempt to reciprocate the show of friendly affection. In fact, instead of embracing Cassandra, he dug his hand into his trouser pocket.

"Nicky." His name fell from her lips in an irritating whine. She planted her hand on his chest. Reaching for the knot in his tie, she gave it a tug. "I'm renting a summer cottage not too far from here. You could give me a ride home tonight." She pressed her expensively implanted D-cup breasts against him, just in case she hadn't made herself blatantly clear. Nicholas remained stone-faced.

"It's Nicholas," he corrected. "No one calls me Nicky." The name was bitter on his tongue. Before he had the chance to pry himself from her grasp, Mia came into his view. For the briefest of seconds, their eyes met. Quickly, she turned, disappearing into the sea of socialites.

"Could a greater miracle take place than for us to look through each other's eyes for an instant?" — Henry David Thoreau

Chapter 14

Mia

Why did she care? Mia's idealistic fantasy of Nicholas had already been shattered to bits. Now, for a reason beyond her rational sensibilities, additional fragments of her heart added to the mound of shards as she stepped back out onto the patio deck only to see a woman draped all over him.

Better to worship Nicholas from afar, like a poster of a celebrity pinned to a wall, taking in the physical beauty of sun-kissed skin, God-gifted features, and enigmatic eyes. But to be the object of his scorn for no apparent reason was nothing but cruel. Yet Mia hung onto fragments in time when his kindness and gentility occasionally emerged. Moments when the boy she imagined he'd once been forced his way to the surface through his sister's bantering or during a rare moment when she observed him alone and unhindered.

Stay away from his space and out of his personal life, Mia advised herself. You're nothing to him. The second she made eye contact with him, she turned away, hastening into the crowd. His eyes had widened at the sight of her, and the scowl on Nicholas' face made it clear to her that he was not happy with her intruding glare.

"Mia!" Penelope waved over the crowd.

Excusing her way through the guests, she made her way over to Penelope and a relatively handsome thirty-something man.

"There you are! I'd like you to meet Nolan Danville, the head of marketing at Perval Designs. One of our advertisers."

Mia extended her hand to the blond gentleman. He stood merely three inches taller than Mia's petite frame, clad in a mint green suit and donning a lavender bow tie.

"Very nice to meet you."

"Mia, you look awfully pale." Penelope placed her hand on the side of Mia's neck. "Let me get you a glass of water."

"Let me," Nolan insisted, excusing himself as he headed off in search of a waiter.

"Do you feel faint?" Penelope asked, looping her arm through Mia's for support.

Mia shook her head. "I'm okay, really. Please don't fuss."

"Do you happen to know where Nicholas is?"

Mia cocked her head in his direction. Penelope, standing on her toes for a better view over the crowd, groaned when she spotted the blonde fawning over her brother. The woman's coral dress looked to be two sizes too small, and her matching lipstick was, in Penelope's opinion, gauche.

"That girl is a viper. She's forever trying to sink her teeth into Nicholas."

"He's not interested in her?" Mia asked a little too hurriedly.

"Hell no! He's probably been trying to discreetly get away from her without causing a scene."

Penelope tapped her finger to her chin. From Mia's assessment, she seemed to be contemplating something. Patiently, Mia waited.

"For reasons I'd rather not discuss, my brother doesn't do well in overcrowded situations."

"How can that be?" Mia wondered. "He stands up in front of large groups and addresses them all the time. He manages entire work-forces." She shook her head in confusion.

"As long as Nicholas is in control of a situation, he's fine," Penelope explained. "Just keep an eye on him. If you see too many people storming him at once, he'll . . ." Penelope sighed.

"What?"

"We just can't let it happen." She braced her hands upon Mia's shoulders, her firm stare telling Mia all she needed to know.

Nolan strode over, a waiter by his side. Mia thanked him for the water, picking it up off the tray and taking a long, much-needed sip. Nolan had also replenished his and Penelope's drinks and, after accepting them, they clinked glasses.

"We should say hello to Nicholas. I need to save him from the blonde barracuda."

Nolan glanced over in Nicholas' direction. "Don't insult the barracudas. I find them rather fascinating, which is more than I can say for that teenager."

"Teenager?!" Mia repeated, her mouth agape.

"Okay, I exaggerate," Nolan admitted. "She's twenty-three but spoiled rotten."

"Follow me!" Penelope walked over to her brother, determination mounting with each step.

Mia stayed rooted to her spot until Nolan laced his arm through hers, guiding her in Penelope's direction. "Honey, you don't want to miss this show."

Angry eyes glared at Penelope when she tapped Nicholas' unwelcome companion on the shoulder.

"Excuse me, Carly, is it? I need to speak to my brother." With a condescending smile, Penelope slid her way between them, gently pushing her out of the way."

"It's Cassandra," she corrected, emphasizing each syllable.

"My apologies," Penelope said. The frost in her tone could have iced over the shoreline. "If you'll excuse us."

Nicholas stifled his chuckle into a hand-covered cough.

"Later, then?" Cassandra asked Nicholas sweetly, pressing a finger to his lips with a small pout. Mia curled a lip up in revulsion but felt decidedly pleased when Nicholas recoiled.

"I'm afraid that will be impossible," he declined. "As you can see, I'm otherwise engaged escorting these two lovely women home tonight. You already know my sister." Nicholas looked toward Mia. "And this is my . . ." He broke off.

Mia drew her eyebrows together. Did he have sudden amnesia where she was concerned?

Nolan encouraged her forward. "I'm his Associate Art Director," she clarified.

Cassandra eyed Mia up and down, her tongue darting out to lick her overly painted, collagen-plumped lips. Just as she was about to speak, Penelope cut in.

"So, if we're done here, I'm going to steal my brother away." Taking Nicholas by the shoulder, they turned, leaving Cassandra behind.

"Mia, Nolan," Penelope threw over her shoulder, extending her hand, "please join us."

Nolan pivoted, relishing in the look of fury ignited in Cassandra's deep blue eyes. Mia had made an instant ally in Nolan. Nudging her shoulder, she turned to see what he was snickering about. Her eyes widening in alarm, Mia quickly looked away, intimidated by the daggers of hate spewing from Cassandra. An image of a fire-breathing dragon popped into her mind. Latching onto Nolan's arm with both hands, she scurried away from the woman's withering glare.

"Let's get a bite to eat," Nolan suggested. "I'm famished."

"What about Penelope and Nicholas?" Mia asked as they stepped inside.

"They're fine." He removed his colorless eyeglass frames and held the lenses up to the light. "Salty." He pulled a lens cloth from his breast pocket, wiping his glasses clean. "Better. I need twenty-twenty just in case a certain someone sneaks up to attack us with her fangs."

"So far, she's been referred to as a viper, a barracuda, my own image of her as a fire-breathing dragon, and now you're suggesting she might be a vampire." Mia giggled. "Which is she?"

"All of the above. They all fit." Nolan handed her a buffet plate.

From the corner of her eye, Mia spotted Nicholas in the next room. He was involved in a friendly conversation with a man presumed to be a good fifteen years older than him. That was the Nicholas she'd crushed over at the CCD meetings— relaxed, approachable, his face free from that frequent grimace he seemed to save especially for her. This was the man whose every word she hung on. She had once longed to see that smile aimed in her direction.

"There you are!" Penelope exclaimed, breaking off her thoughts. Beside her was a well-dressed man in a blue and white striped seersucker suit. "Nolan, I don't think you're acquainted with David Stern."

Mia suddenly felt out of place as the three of them spoke of common interests and friends. To no one's notice, she slipped away. Spotting an unoccupied chair in the corner of the living room, Mia took a seat, finishing off her plate of mahi-mahi and kale salad.

"I can take that from you," a waiter offered, relieving her of her empty plate.

"Thank you," Mia said, rising. But now what? The carpet under her rose-gold heels had an interesting pattern. She expelled a shaky breath.

"You look bored."

Mia looked up to find the source of the cheerful voice. Although he didn't measure up to Nicholas' good looks, he was attractive.

"No-no," she stammered. "I just don't know—"

"Your first time at one of these things? I get it."

He pretended to snore and nod off, and Mia couldn't help but laugh.

"Bennett," he introduced himself, extending his hand.

"Mia."

Instead of releasing her hand, he held it, caressing her smooth skin with the pad of his thumb. Leaning in, Bennett whispered in her ear, "There are far more exciting parties around here than this one. Do you want to get out of here?"

Before Mia could answer, a masculine arm sliced between them. "She's with me on a work obligation." Nicholas' tone was as steely as his posture.

Mia's eyes darted back and forth between the two men. Staring each other down, it seemed either one could at any minute erupt. But Bennett's ire at Nicholas' interference was no match for Nicholas' rage. She equated the two men to statues, erected face-to-face—practically nose-to-nose, she noted. If Bennett was formed from plaster then Nicholas was carved of marble, every line on his face hard and defined.

"What is your problem?" Mia asked Nicholas as he took her by the arm, steering her away. "He seemed nice."

"He was hitting on you."

"I wasn't going to go with him." Mia shook herself from his grasp. "Not that it's any of your business if I did."

They walked back onto the outdoor patio. It was now twice as crowded as it was before.

"I'll remind you that we are at a client's home," he bit out. "Anything you do reflects upon the company."

"First, I've yet to meet this client, and second, if you are so embarrassed by lowly, little me then you should have asked me to stay back at the house." She met his glare, matching it with one of her own. "I need a drink," she said, breaking the tension and storming away.

Mingling guests blocked Mia's path to the bar. All she really wanted was water anyway. She poured a frosty glass of fruit-infused water from a dispenser on a rolling cart. As Mia stood on her toes searching for Penelope, her phone pinged. Removing it from her evening bag, she read the Twitter alert. A photo of two elderly men popped onto her screen. Much to Mia's surprise, one of the men was Pavlos Aristedis. The caption read, 'Merger agreement between two media giants.' Another headline stated, '*Aris Publications* and *Volpe Media* join forces.'

Flashes of light exploding near a cluster of guests caught Mia's attention. Aware that local press coverage of the soirée had been expected, she found it odd that they had suddenly imposed themselves so brazenly. Curiosity had her drifting closer to the commotion. What she saw concerned and confused her. Nicholas looked stricken as a crowd encroached upon him. He stood as motionless as a marble effigy, save for the terror reflected in his eyes. It gutted Mia to see this usually commanding man paralyzed with fear. Remembering Penelope's odd request to keep an eye on her brother, Mia flung into action, pushing her way through the crowd.

"Hey!" she shouted. "Give him some space!" Cameras flashed, reporters fired questions, and guests crowded Nicholas as they waited for answers. "This is a private party!" Mia elbowed her way through to Nicholas, shielding him with her small but fierce frame from the aggressive reporters. Wrapping her arm around him, she led him away from the line of fire. "Don't you dare follow us!" Mia's murderous glare equaled the venom in her bark. Fortunately, security was on her heels, breaking up the disturbance.

Without argument, Nicholas allowed Mia to whisk him away. *Without argument?* Nicholas was not himself. It was as though he was in a trance, or lost in an unpleasant memory, perhaps. Beads of sweat bubbled on his forehead as his breathing became increasingly labored. She guided him over to a less crowded section of the deck, by the steps leading down to the beach. Hastily, Mia poured a glass of water and snatched a napkin off the beverage cart—a challenging feat while supporting much of Nicholas' weight.

"Can you make it down the steps?" Mia asked. Receiving no response, she continued to pull him far away from the clamor of the crowd.

When they hit the bottom step, Mia realized she wouldn't be able to negotiate both the sand and supporting Nicholas in her four-inch heels. Kicking them off, she led him further down the beach, away from intrusion.

"Sit," she ordered, expelling a deep, exhausted breath. "Drink." She placed the now half-empty glass in his hand; the rest had spilled down the stairs.

Nicholas stared at her blankly as he gulped the water down. The rhythmic crash of waves failed to rouse him from the internal thoughts plaguing his senses. Mia brushed the sweat-soaked strands of hair off his face and patted his forehead dry with a napkin. Slowly, she could see some life returning to his eyes as the muscles in his face and neck relaxed.

They sat quietly, shifting to look out over the ocean. Mia was grateful that Nicholas had not rejected her assistance. Fearful of taking a step too far, she remained silent, granting him the solitude he apparently needed. Digging her bare toes into the cool sand, Mia looked up at the stars blinking in a Morse code-like pattern in the vast expanse of the sky, and she wondered if the universe was tapping out a message to her.

"Thank you," he whispered.

Nicholas laid his hand over hers. Turning, she was met with the eyes of a wounded child.

"I suppose you're wondering what happened over there," he murmured quietly.

Mia tilted her head. "You don't have to explain anything. I'm just happy I was able to help."

He waited for a beat before speaking. "My parents were killed when I was twelve." He looked up at her. "But, you already knew that."

Mia shook her head, no, but her eyes filled with sympathy nonetheless.

"Ah, yes, the woman who doesn't Google," he said. "They were vacationing in Amalfi after visiting my mother's family in San Gimignano."

Still clutching Mia's hand, Nicholas unconsciously played with the stack of rose-gold rings on her middle finger.

"She was Italian—my mother."

"What was her name?" Mia asked.

"Lucia."

"That's a beautiful name."

"She was a beautiful woman," Nicholas said. "Penelope looks very much like her."

Silence fell between them once again—Nicholas seemingly deep in thought; Mia leaving a page of questions in a book she was respectful not to open.

"My father loved speed." Nicholas continued eventually. "Fast cars, jet skis, speed boats . . ."

He looked up at her. From the light of the moonlight, Mia saw his eyes beginning to brim with tears.

"Have you ever been to the Amalfi coast?"

Mia shook her head. "No."

"The roads are very narrow and winding," he said solemnly. "It's hard to see what's coming around the bend."

Mia felt her own tears welling. Her throat tightened, making it hard to swallow. Nicholas held firmly onto her hand. Sliding in a little closer to him, she laid her free hand on top of his.

"They were riding on a Vespa when a tourist bus hit them head-on."

Mia gasped.

"Witnesses said the driver was also speeding and crossed over the line." Nicholas sighed deeply. "My father was killed on impact. My mother was still alive when she arrived at the hospital but she didn't make it through the night," he said in a sob.

"I'm so sorry." Mia wanted to take him in her arms to comfort him. Instead, she settled for stroking his hand.

"I hate people crowding in on me. It's suffocating."

Mia shifted her position, pulling a distance away from him so as to not encroach on his personal space.

Nicholas clasped her wrist, stopping her from moving further away. "That wasn't meant for you. Imagine you're a child, your parents are away, and your only sibling is away vacationing with a friend and her family. Think about how alone you'd feel."

"Where were you?"

"I was at my grandparents' summer home in Kefalonia. Most of my friends were back in New York. I had a few friends and cousins on the island but . . ." He shrugged. "My grandparents were hosting a party. It seemed like the whole island was invited. Everything about the night was perfect. The weather was pleasantly warm. Ideal for an outdoor gathering with music and dancing. And so much food."

Mia listened with dreadful anticipation as Nicholas became more transfixed by the memory.

"I remember the music coming to a sudden stop, and when it did, everyone froze in place. Silence shifted from a quiet hush to a rolling wave of shocked whispers. Grief-stricken, my grandfather sought me out, summoning me over to his side."

Mia brushed away the tears falling from her cheeks. Her mind envisioned a young version of the man before her receiving the most devastating news. The shock he must have felt . . . The desolation . . .

"At first, he didn't say a word, but from the ashen pallor of his face, I knew something was terribly wrong. He draped his arm around my shoulder, escorting me into the house." Holding his head in his hands, he looked down at his lap. "My grandmother was sobbing into a pillow on the sofa. I flung my arms around her, crying with her, though I still had no idea what had happened. When they told me, I didn't want to believe it. I refused to accept it. My parents were on vacation. They would come home, and all would be as it should. That's the only reality I wanted." A sob broke free as he paused, remembering that day.

Mia pictured three broken souls coming to terms with the unthinkable. She let out a long-held, shaky breath.

"As word spread, so did the flood of friends and relatives with good intentions. They encroached on me all at once, crowding me, spewing their condolences and advice." Nicholas looked up, meeting Mia's gaze. "I know this sounds terribly ungrateful, and they all meant well, but . . ."

"You'd just lost your parents."

He nodded. "I felt suffocated. Trapped. My heart pounded in my chest, and all I could see were the faces surrounding me, spinning around like a high-speed merry-go-round. The words coming from their mouths didn't make sense. I remember shivering uncontrollably right before everything went black."

"A panic attack," Mia murmured.

"Yes. The first of many."

"How often did they come?"

"The second one happened at the funeral, and others followed soon after, mostly at night after a nightmare. But now, they're rare. I can usually control my environment," Nicholas admitted. He cupped her cheek with the palm of his hand. "You pulled me from the vultures."

Mia closed her eyes, her face tingling from the softness of his touch. "I did. Someone had to."

"They all want a piece of me. Information. A story. Take, take. But not you." He sighed, staring deeply into her eyes, and Mia wanted to melt into those very depths. To pour her compassion into this man and erase the sadness plaguing him.

Mia didn't break the connection. *Let him peer into my soul.* If he was looking for answers, she'd give them freely.

She placed her hand over his chest. "You seem better now. Calmer. Your heart is beating at a normal rate." When Mia removed her hand, Nicholas took it in his, caressing it and pulling her to him.

He was intoxicating. The nearness of him. His scent of bergamot and sandalwood. His breath tickling her skin as he cupped her chin, drawing her lips to his and ever so tenderly kissing her.

Mia had imagined this moment in her dreams, the reality of it now leaving her breathless. Her mind went blank, save the image of his handsomely beautiful face. Heat blazed throughout her body as he pressed his lips to hers.

When Nicholas broke the kiss, Mia was frightened he'd come to his senses and regret it. But he surprised her, brushing away stray strands of her hair and tracing the outline of her face with his fingertips.

"You're so beautiful." He kissed her again, this time gently lowering her to lie beneath him on the warm sand.

This was the man Mia envisioned. The kiss she'd dreamed of and longed for consumed her. The intimacy between them bled into her very pores, seeping deep to the core of her being. Insecurity and fear gripped her heart like a vice but only for the briefest of moments. Mia intuited Nicholas felt as she did, having bared his soul, trusting her with his most private fears.

"I'm perfectly happy to stay here as long as you need but shouldn't you get back?" Mia whispered through their kiss, glancing in the direction of the gathering back at the mansion.

"Penelope is representing the magazine." Nicholas repositioned himself flat on his back and looked up at the stars. Mia followed suit. "I'm very content staying right here," he admitted, lacing his fingers with hers.

"I could look at the stars all night," Mia agreed. "It's hard to believe that somewhere, in another part of the world, others are staring at these same stars—that the sky is so vast and infinite." Mia pointed to a particular constellation. "Thousands of miles away, someone is reciting the legend of that cluster of light."

Nicholas turned on his side to face Mia. Propping his head up with his hand, he assessed her. "So, what's your story?" Nicholas inquired. "I told you mine. What's yours?"

"What makes you think I have a story?" Mia asked.

"Everyone has a story."

"That's not true," Mia argued. "My life is pretty ordinary. Mundane even."

Nicholas narrowed his eyes skeptically.

Mia laughed. "You don't believe me." She sat up. "Okay. I've lived in the same house my entire life until I moved into the city. My dad is still hoping I'll move back home because, according to him, that's where single girls belong. My parents are still married. My grandmother lives with us. My other grandparents live in Athens. I have two sisters and a brother. We're very average and ordinary." Mia shrugged.

"What's *your* story?" Nicholas asked again. "Not your lineage or your family dynamic. Your hopes, fears, heartbreaks?"

"Hmm. Hopes—to one day be a creative director, like you. Fears—I guess I have a few. I got bit by a jellyfish once. I don't want that to ever happen again. Heartbreaks—none yet."

"Ah, so you're the heartbreaker, then. I should have guessed."

"No. No great romances amounting to any broken hearts," Mia said on a sigh.

"That's impossible."

"No, it's not. I've just never dated anyone long enough to get that emotionally invested. Like I said, I've no story to tell." Mia preferred to shift the focus back to him. "And you? If you find it so hard to believe that I haven't had my heart broken, I assume you have?"

"That's a story for another time. Or never." Nicholas got up, brushed the sand from his trousers, and extended his hand to assist Mia. "What do you say we find Penelope and head home?"

Mia nodded, suddenly feeling awkward walking by his side. Wondering if this small stretch of time was an anomaly, never to be repeated, Mia was apprehensive over what the next day would hold.

Chapter 15

Nicholas

Nicholas woke up the next morning feeling completely wrung out. He was hungover. But this wasn't an alcohol hangover; he'd barely finished one glass of champagne at the party. No, this was an emotional hangover.

Draping his arm over his throbbing forehead, Nicholas rejected the idea of dragging himself from bed. He looked at the time on the alarm clock on his nightstand and groaned. Forcing himself to sit upright at the edge of the bed, he scrubbed his face with his palms.

Slowly, Nicholas got up and shuffled into the bathroom. Rifling through a drawer, he found a bottle of Tylenol, poured himself a cup of water from the tap, and downed three pills in one shot. He had less than twenty minutes to shower, trim the scruff on his face in an attempt to look at least somewhat presentable, and style the wayward hairs on his head.

In the shower, hot water rained down, loosening the tension in Nicholas' muscles. As the steam rose, so did the fog in his mind. It was all so clear. The panic that gripped him as too many bodies closed in on him. And the avenging angel who came to his rescue. Mia was in the forefront of his mind. Every image, like frames on a movie reel, was of this delicate beauty. She was compassionate. Understanding without judgment. Nicholas had revealed parts of himself to her he had only before shared with his sister.

He sighed, thinking of their kiss. He was in a vulnerable state. Opening his soul to another was an indulgence he hadn't allowed himself for many years, and he planned to keep it that way. Now, in the light of day, he knew he'd made a gross error. One he'd have to rectify.

Chapter 16

Mia

The next morning, Mia emerged from the guest bedroom, dressed and ready for their last day on location. First, they would head to Bridgehampton and, later on, at sundown, the Shinnecock Reservation.

"Cappuccino?" Penelope asked as Mia strolled into the kitchen. The elaborate contraption steaming milk while brewing espresso rivaled that of any found in a Roman café. Not that Mia had ever been to a café in Italy, but it's what she imagined one would look like.

"I'd love one. Thank you," Mia said. "I don't want to trouble you, though. I can do it. My sister has one like this in her café. Although this one seems more complicated than hers," she added.

"It's practically an antique," Penelope joked. She reached for another cup and saucer from the cabinet, setting them onto the counter. Turning to face Mia, her expression turned wistful. "It was my mother's. It belonged to her family."

"Oh." Mia didn't know what to say. "I'm so sorry. Nicholas told me what happened to your parents."

"About that," Penelope said, regaining her composure, "I heard what happened last night, and I want to thank you for being there for him."

"I did what anyone would have done."

"No," Penelope disagreed. She waited for a beat before continuing, staring at Mia as though she were trying to analyze her. "You instinctively knew what he needed. You did what I would have done—have done—you got him out of the situation and compassionately tended to him." She smiled softly before pressing a measured amount of coffee into a silver cylinder, tamping it down.

"Weren't you bombarded with the same questions, though?"

"I was, and as soon as I shot them down and walked away, I went looking for my brother. I knew what those reporters would do to him." Pulling the lever for the steamer, she waited for the noise to subside before continuing. "By the time I got outside and inquired about his whereabouts, you had already whisked him away. Here," she said, handing Mia a coffee cup clouded with white foam nearly spilling over the rim. "Croissant?" Penelope asked, guiding Mia to the island stools.

Mia nodded, placing one on a plate from the counter.

"I'm very protective of my brother, so naturally, I sought him out. I had to make sure he was okay. From a distance, I saw the two of you."

Mia's stomach lurched, wondering what it was she saw. The last thing Mia wanted was for Penelope to think she was taking advantage of her brother during a vulnerable moment.

"Why didn't you come over?" Mia tried to keep her voice from shaking.

"You didn't need me." Penelope laid a hand over Mia's. "You wiped his forehead and offered him a drink of water. He needed the calm, and you gave that to him."

"It's none of my business, so you don't have to answer, but . . . is there going to be a merger with *Aris Publications* and *Volpe Media*?" Mia wondered.

Penelope grinned, shaking her head. "That newsflash was based on nothing more than a photo of two old friends simply having dinner together. It must have been a slow gossip night."

"Good morning." Nicholas broke off their conversation, heading straight to the espresso machine, not even bothering to glance in the women's direction. From his back view, Mia watched him prepare his own beverage, admiring his tanned, muscular forearms peeking out from the rolled-up sleeves of his blue Oxford shirt.

"Well, I'm heading out," Penelope announced. "I have a meeting in a half-hour." Taking one last sip of her cappuccino, she set the cup in the sink. With a wink of approval and a nod of encouragement for Mia, Penelope dashed off.

Nicholas leaned against the kitchen counter adjacent to the island, sipping his steaming drink. He made no attempt to join Mia at the island counter, and she only sneaked fleeting glances, her view obstructed by the thick lashes of her downcast eyes.

Nicholas suddenly cleared his throat. "Mia," he started, his voice low and tentative.

"Yes?" Mia looked up at him shyly.

"I . . . want to thank you for last night . . . and I'll ask you to be discreet about . . ."

About what? The way his parents died? His panic attacks? The kiss?

"What I'm trying to say is that I don't want to give the public the impression that I'm a person who's not in control." He set his coffee cup down. Nicholas was about to say something, but instead, he rubbed at his forehead, frowning. "The last thing I need is for it to come out that I had a meltdown because some journalists closed in on me."

"If anything," Mia laughed, trying to make light of it, "they'll just think you have an insane, overly-protective assistant." She spiraled her forefingers by her head and made a silly face.

"Nice try, but seriously, I regard my privacy as extremely important."

"I know, and I am serious," she assured him. "I don't think they saw anything other than me getting you out of making a statement."

"Okay." He shuffled his feet.

"Okay." From the look on his face and how he was rubbing the back of his neck, she knew something else was on his mind. "Unless there's anything else, I think we should get going."

Nicholas nodded and began to exit the kitchen. Pivoting, he turned to face Mia and hung his head. "There is one more thing. What happened last night between you and me can't happen again. It was a moment of weakness, and it shouldn't have happened. I apologize if I was inappropriate."

Even if Mia wanted to respond, her vocal cords were suddenly incapable of producing sound. She couldn't even manage to squeak out a nonchalant reply. An imperceptible nod, as she forced the tears back, was all the response she could manage.

Nervously, he combed his fingers through his hair before disappearing down the hallway.

Fifteen minutes later, they were in the car on their way to the Hampton Classic. Mia busied herself texting the crew to make sure they were on time and instructing them where to set up.

It was nearly impossible to ignore the fact that she was sharing a backseat with a man she was more embarrassed to be near than ever before. She checked messages, sent emails, and consulted her calendar—anything to stay occupied.

Nicholas checked his messages before throwing his phone down on the seat between them. A few minutes later, he retrieved it and began scrolling again. Huffing his annoyance, Nicholas finally dropped the phone in his lap and turned to Mia. "Mia, would you please say something," he finally demanded.

Without looking up from her device, she asked, "What would you like me to say?"

"I'm not sure," he said with frustration. "But we have to work together, and I don't want this uncomfortable . . . weirdness between us." He angled his body to face her. "You're a beautiful woman, and there's no denying that I'm attracted to you. And there's something else about you, niggling in the back of my mind, that I can't quite put my finger on." He sighed. "It's almost as if I'm meant to know you," he said nearly inaudibly. Nicholas waved off his foolish comment. "I don't even know what I'm saying."

Mia sat stoically. While Nicholas' words sounded like compliments, the inflection in his voice told another story.

"But as much as there's something about you I'm drawn to," he went on, "you also aggravate me by constantly contradicting me and continuously twisting my words. And there's also the fact that I'm your boss. How would it look? Not to mention, that we come from two different worlds. I grew up with nannies and boarding schools. You had family dinners and small-town summers."

Mia raised an incredulous eyebrow at his assumptions.

"Still, I can't deny my desire to kiss you again. No one other than my sister has ever done for me what you did last night."

Nicholas went to take her hand but Mia snapped it away. "Do you have any idea how much you've insulted me?" she scolded. "What's wrong with you? One minute you were thanking me for my help and kindness, and the next you're saying last night was a mistake." Rage was building inside her. If he fired her for speaking her mind, so be it. "Now, you have the gall to say you're attracted to me for some unexplainable reason but . . . but, oh, this is rich!" She fisted her hands. "Rich boy is too good to lower himself to be with a commoner." She bowed to Nicholas mockingly. "From now on, I'll address you as your Royal Highness."

He let out an exasperated sigh. "And this is what I mean about you twisting my words. That's not what I meant."

"It doesn't matter. You're my boss, as you've just clearly reminded me." Mia crossed her hands over her chest. "What will people think? Well, I'll tell you what I know," she growled. "If you were the last eligible bachelor on Earth, I wouldn't even date you, much less kiss you again. You are the most disagreeable man I've ever had the displeasure of meeting."

"Did you just Elizabeth Bennet me?"

"Only after you Darcyed me, you pompous snob."

Fuming, Mia snapped her head around to stare out the window. Bending, she fished through her bag for her earbuds. Anything to avoid speaking to him. This conversation was over.

Chapter 17

Mia

Mia slipped into the Uber's backseat, giving the driver the address of the Southampton house. She and Nicholas had worked professionally and civilly all day, speaking only when necessary. It was far more exhausting for Mia to hold up a cold and indifferent exterior than it was for her to be amiable and pleasant. By the end of the day, her aching muscles craved the luxurious bathtub in the guest bedroom en suite, but that was not to be. She'd made a decision, and when Nicholas was temporarily called away to deal with another matter, Mia was able to put her plan in motion.

The photographer had finished shooting before Nicholas arrived back at the Shinnecock Reservation. After dismissing the crew for the night, Mia called for an Uber to pick her up. When she arrived at the Aristedis home, she asked the driver to wait for her. Gathering her belongings quickly, Mia returned to the car, giving the driver a Port Jefferson address. Then she tapped out a text to Penelope.

Mia: *I took an Uber back to the house. Please let Darren know I won't be needing a ride.*

Penelope: *Okay. See you later.*

Mia: *Actually, on my way to Port J. Staying with my family for the rest of the weekend. Thanks for everything. See you Tuesday.*

Penelope: *Have fun.*

"Anyone home?" Mia called out as she let herself into her childhood home.

"Mia!" Krystina shrieked, grinning. "What are you doing here? I thought you were out east for the weekend."

"We wrapped up early, so I thought I'd stay here for the rest of the weekend."

Mia dropped her overnight bag to reciprocate her sister's hug. "I tried to call Kally to see if I could stay with her but she didn't answer."

"That's because she probably can't hear her phone over the sound of fireworks going off."

"Fireworks?" Mia wasn't aware of any celebrations this weekend.

"She and Max took Athena to Disney World."

"Oh, I completely forgot. I could use a little fairy dust myself right about now," she said, sounding a bit forlorn.

"Rough week?" Krystina asked.

"You could say that. I'm starved." They walked into the kitchen, and Mia headed directly for the refrigerator.

"Everyone's outside, and there's plenty of food," Krystina said.

"Great. Let's go. By the way, who's manning the café while Kally is away?"

"Egypt, me and . . ." Krystina rolled her eyes. "Loukas," she added with disdain.

"You really need to give that boy a break."

"No, I do not," Krystina said definitively, flipping her sandy-brown hair off her shoulder.

A clamor of excitement erupted when Mia stepped onto the back patio. Her mother hadn't expected her, and nothing made Melina Andarakis happier than having her children home. Once she had practically stolen Mia's breath away from the force of her embrace, double-cheek kisses were exchanged by aunts, cousins, and finally, her *yiayiá*.

After greeting his daughter with a quick peck on the cheek, George shoved a loaded plate of food in Mia's hands. "Eat! It doesn't look like you're doing much of that in the city."

"I eat plenty, Dad," Mia argued. "But I am so hungry," she conceded, taking her first bite before reaching her seat.

"When you move back home, you can have meals like this *káthe méra*," he said, swapping between Greek and English as he often did.

Mia's shoulders slumped. It was the same thing every time she came home, which was why she preferred to stay at Kally's house. "For the last time, I am not moving back to Long Island. I'm perfectly happy in my little apartment in the city."

Pointing a set of BBQ tongs in her direction, he said, "*Tha deíte*! When you get married and have babies, you won't want to be wheeling a stroller around on those dirty streets."

"Well, since there's no fiancée or even a boyfriend, much less a baby on the way, I'm not too concerned," she replied, her voice taking on an edge.

"*Yióryios, afise tin*! Leave her alone," Melina scolded. "My girl has important things to do," she stated proudly.

He waved his wife off with a grunt and poured himself a shot of ouzo.

"Mmm. This is so good," Mia moaned between bites of thinly sliced, marinated flank steak. "My favorite."

"Everything is your favorite," Krystina laughed. "How long are you staying? Can we do something together tomorrow?"

"Don't you have to work at the café?"

"Only until three."

"I have to look at the train schedule. I don't want to get back too late. I have to work on Tuesday. What did you have in mind?" Mia asked.

"I don't know? Shopping, the beach, paddleboarding?"

"We can go shopping on a rainy day. The other two sound great. I haven't had much time for any of that this summer, and I could use a distraction."

"Do you want to talk about it?" Krystina asked.

Mia shook her head. Once she began to speak, she was sure the tears would follow. But her sister immediately noticed the tears welling in her eyes.

"Hey," Krystina consoled Mia, embracing her. "It can't be all that bad."

"It's the man I work for. I love what I do at the magazine but dealing with him is like an exercise in mental gymnastics."

"Try not to take it too personally," Krystina said, pulling away. "Let's make our day together a mini vacation. It will be fun."

* * *

Around six-thirty p.m. the next day, Mia and Krystina pulled up in the driveway. They unloaded the car of beach blankets, a cooler, and their semi-inflatable paddleboards.

Before changing out of their bathing suits and cover-ups, they went out back, lured by the aroma of herb-scented grilled meats.

"Hungry much?" Krystina teased Mia when her stomach grumbled louder than a growling puppy.

"Famished! That was more exercise than I've gotten in weeks." Mia pushed her way through the back door, wasting no time in grabbing a plate.

"Did you have a nice day, girls?" Melina asked. She lifted a finger to silence them at a chiming sound. "I think that was the doorbell."

"Are you expecting someone?" Mia asked.

"Just Loukas, but I don't know why he'd be ringing."

"Because he doesn't live here," Krystina complained, dropping her fork.

Her mother shot her that same reprimanding glare each time she uttered an unkind word about the boy. He was her late friend's son, and the boy's father had never recovered from his wife's death. In fact, it seemed as though Loukas was a painful reminder of her, and therefore his father treated him unnecessarily harsh.

"Be nice," Mia warned when her mother disappeared into the house to answer the door. But it was not Loukas who stepped onto the patio. The person standing before her family had Mia dropping her own fork along with her jaw.

Frozen, Mia locked eyes with Nicholas, his expression unreadable. What on Earth was he doing here, and how did he know where to find her?

Meanwhile, Melina was beaming. "This is Nicholas. He came for our Mia."

Mia wanted to die. Closing her eyes, she covered her face with her hand.

"Holy shit," Krystina whispered, kicking Mia under the table.

Their brother, Theo, who hadn't said a word or paid anyone mind—he was busy texting some girl—suddenly decided something of interest might be happening. "It's always the quiet ones," Theo snickered under his breath. "I didn't know you had a secret life in the big city," he said sarcastically.

Mia shot him a look of warning.

But it was Mia's father who strutted over, puffing out his chest. "You're here for my daughter?"

"Yes, sir, I am."

"George," he said, extending his hand.

"Nicholas. It's nice to meet you. May I have a word with your daughter?"

"Are you Greek?" he asked.

"Oh my God," Mia said under her breath. She wanted to disappear.

Theo chuckled, and Melina shot him a warning glare.

"Yes, yes, I am," Nicholas replied. "Well, half Greek."

"What's your last name?" George was going into full interrogation mode.

"Aristedis."

"You're Greek then," George said, his accent thickening.

Mia jumped from her seat. "Dad! Nicholas is my boss, not some would-be suitor for you to cross-examine. Please, stop."

She rushed over to Nicholas, ushering him into the house. "What are you doing here?" she seethed.

"I came to drive you back to the city," he said stiffly. "I find myself constantly having to track you down. You really should have stayed at the house. It would have been far more sensible."

"I can get myself back home just fine, thank you." Mia fisted her hands on her hips. "I'm sorry you were so inconvenienced but I didn't ask you to search me out. I stayed at your home strictly for business, and our business, for now, has concluded."

"Don't act like a child."

"*Ásto diáolo!*" She wished him to hell.

Nicholas threw his head back and laughed. "Do you always curse in Greek? Do you think it sounds more or less impolite?" He said mockingly. "Just wondering."

"You can leave now."

"No, you can get your things, and we'll go together. Darren is waiting in the car."

"You're relentless."

"Agreed. You and I have much to discuss. First on the agenda is to clear up any misunderstandings between us so we can figure out a way to work together. I've kept my eye on you this week, and I have no intention of losing a talented employee."

Mia looked at him with apprehension. "Thank you. My reputation means everything to me. However, I believe you might have been right from the beginning."

"To what are you referring?" Nicholas asked impatiently.

"You said you didn't see how you could work with me," she explained, her eyes downcast.

Sighing with annoyance, he rubbed his forehead. With a steely glare, he asked, "Is this a position you wish to retain? If not, let me know now. If you do, let's move on like two professional adults."

Mia stared into his cold eyes. Even if she was able to reply, Mia was certain she'd only manage to croak out an embarrassing sob.

"I'm waiting." He gestured for her to respond. "Do you want to work for *Opul* or not?"

"Yes," Mia confessed.

Relief washed over him. "Now that we've cleared that up, we need to concept the photo shoot for Athens. We'll be leaving in three weeks, and I'd like to go over the preliminary sketches with you."

"Athens? Three weeks?" Mia's heart began to race.

"Why do you look so surprised. You know the magazine's focus is destination-driven."

"I know." She looked down at what she was wearing, embarrassingly aware that she was in a see-through cover-up. With windblown, salty, sundried hair and not a trace of any cosmetics on her face, she must have looked a fright. "I can't leave. I need to shower. I'll see you at the office in the morning."

"I'll wait," he insisted. "I'll join your family, if it's not an imposition," he said, raising an eyebrow.

"As long as you don't hold me responsible for what they say or do," Mia said, heading toward the stairs.

"Duly noted," he chuckled.

Chapter 18

Nicholas

That girl! Never in his life did a woman frustrate him as she continually did. Nicholas leaned his head back against the headrest of the car, rubbing his eyes with the heels of his palms. It had been a long day, beginning with another misinterpreted discussion with the ever-defensive Ms. Andarakis. Of course, he didn't help matters.

He had that evening and the following day to make it right—for the two of them to come to an understanding without hostility, and, he had to admit, his verbal fumbles. But no! Instead, she takes off without a word.

When Nicholas arrived back at the house, he found Penelope on the back porch with a glass of wine. Flames danced on a bed of fire glass by a chaise lounge where his sister stretched out in a tank top and silk pajama bottoms.

"Hi." Wearily, he took the seat across from her.

"Hi." Penelope sipped her wine. "You look beat." She lifted the opened bottle of Pinot, offering it to him.

Sighing, Nicholas nodded. He pulled a glass from the patio bar and poured himself a generous amount of wine. Returning to his seat, he swirled the crimson liquid in his glass and took a healthy gulp.

"Did you know Mia wasn't coming back to the house tonight?" Nicholas asked.

"She texted me earlier. Why?"

"No reason." Nicholas downed half his glass in one gulp. "I just assumed she'd head back with me when Darren came to pick us up, that's all." He tried to come off as though it was inconsequential. "I thought she'd stay until tomorrow, and we'd all head back into the city together." He tried to conceal his disappointment.

Penelope eyed him suspiciously. "She said she was spending the rest of the weekend with her family." Setting down her goblet, she sat up from her lounged position. "It did seem a bit sudden. Nicholas? What did you do?"

"What makes you think I did something? Really, Pia!"

"Because, with Mia, it wouldn't be the first time. Seriously, Nick. What is it? I see the way you look at her when you think no one is watching. But all you do is snap at the girl."

"I don't know," Nicholas groaned.

"I think you do." She raised an eyebrow. "You're not a stupid man, and don't take me for a sister who's blind to your faults."

He spread his arms wide. "Have at me with your psychoanalysis," he said sardonically.

"Don't do that," she reprimanded. "You know I always have your best interests at heart." She rose from her seat, joining him on the settee. She placed her arm around him, willing him to look at her. "It's been a long time. Jumping from woman to woman works for a while. Keeping them at arms-length when you're not invested is fine. But eventually, it gets old . . . especially when someone special comes along."

"You make me sound like a man-whore. I'm far more discerning than that," Nicholas said defensively. "Special is overrated anyway," he grumbled. "Discussion closed."

Nicholas drained his glass. "I'm going to bed," he said, rising abruptly. "Goodnight."

The next day, Nicholas made it his mission to track Mia down. He wasn't about to walk into a feud with her at the office on Tuesday morning. No, he was calling the shots and, if he had it his way, they would straighten this mess out on their way back to the city today.

He went for a run to clear his head then decided to play a round of golf. It wouldn't be fair to descend upon her too early. After all, she was visiting her family. With minimal effort, he was able to find her parents' address on the internet.

His mind was riddled with visions of Mia in that body-hugging dress, her slender leg taunting him as it spilled out from the side slit. Her compassionate smile, her sweet lips. He tried to shake her from his thoughts but his sister's words wouldn't allow it. He had to figure out a way to maintain a professional relationship with her. That's all he had to offer her.

* * *

Nicholas' gaze lingered on Mia as she climbed the stairs. Through her sheer cover-up, he could see the outline of her slim figure immodestly covered in a magenta bikini. But it was her toned, bare legs that once again captured his attention.

Slowly, he ambled his way to the backyard, wondering what new questions would be fired at him.

"Excuse me," Nicholas addressed Mia's family. "Mia is changing. My driver will be taking her home tonight." He waved to *Yiayiá*, and she smiled back at him, nodding her head.

"Sit down," Melina offered. "I'll make you a plate."

"I don't want to trouble you." But George had already dropped two oregano-crusted lamb chops on his plate. Melina took care of the rest, adding roasted vegetables, rice pilaf, and a generous helping of *Pastitsio*.

"So, Theo? Right?" Nicholas asked the boy sitting adjacent to him.

"That's me." He looked up from his phone.

"Are you in college? Working?"

"I just graduated. I'm taking this semester off, working with my dad, and then leaving for London to work on my masters."

"What's your field of study?" Nicholas inquired.

"Hotel and restaurant management."

George took his seat at the head of the rectangular teak table. "I tell my son, why not go study in Greece? What's London going to do for him when we own a Greek restaurant?"

From the corner of his eye, Nicholas caught the agitation in Theo's expression. "Well, since he is already familiar with the Greek food and experience, it might do him good to broaden his scope of knowledge." He turned to Theo. "I went to university in London. I think you'll like it."

"Thanks, man." Theo smiled. "I think I will too."

"Where are your people from?" George asked Nicholas.

"My father was from Kefalonia and my mother from a town in Tuscany. San Gimignano."

"Was?" Melina asked.

"They both passed away."

"*Panayia mou*, they must have been so young." Melina crossed herself.

Nicholas simply nodded. It wasn't something he liked to talk about. "What part of Greece are you from?"

"I'm from Athens," George said proudly. "My wife's family is from Kalamata."

"You don't have a trace of an accent, Mrs. Andarakis. Were you born here?"

"I came here when I was three years old with my mother."

Melina placed her arm around the old woman's shoulder. Up to now, she had remained quiet. But the old woman had been observing Nicholas intently. He could feel her eyes trained on him from the moment he stepped onto the patio.

"Just the two of you?" he asked Mia's *yiayiá*.

"My husband sent us ahead," *Yiayiá* said, adding to the conversation for the first time. "For safety."

"The country was in turmoil. My . . . father," Melina began bitterly, "felt it was more important to embroil himself in political battles than to stay with his family."

"Panayiotis fought for the people of Greece," *Yiayiá* defended. "He was driven by his conscience."

Nicholas sensed a point of contention between mother and daughter, yet he wanted to learn more without instigating additional tension.

"May I ask what year we're talking about here?"

"It was the late sixties," Melina replied. "When the monarchy was overthrown."

"Ah!" Nicholas said, as if all had been made clear to him. "If I'm not imposing, when did your husband finally join you?" Nicholas had gone too far. He could see it in the old woman's mournful expression. "I'm so sorry. I didn't mean to bring up painful memories. I'm sorry for your loss."

"He's not dead," *Yiayiá* insisted. "He's out there, somewhere. I just know he is."

Melina rolled her eyes. Shaking her head, she clarified, "We have nothing to suggest he's alive. It's my mother's . . . wish."

Nicholas had the distinct impression Melina held back what she was really thinking. He thought it best to drop the subject and take it up with Mia at a later time. Something told him there was much to be unearthed here.

"I'm ready," Mia said, sliding the glass door open. "I apologize for taking so long."

"Not at all," Nicholas assured her, relieved to have the tension broken. "We've been having a nice chat." He gestured to his plate. "All the while being well-fed."

Nicholas tried not to stare at Mia. The girl was positively glowing in a romper imprinted with bright-colored lemons, accentuating her newly sun-bronzed skin. Less than an hour ago, Mia was covered in salt and sand. Now, she looked as though she'd been dipped in golden honey.

Nicholas stood, addressing Mia's father first. "Mr. Andarakis, thank you for your hospitality." Turning to Theo, he said, "Good luck in London. I'll have Mia forward you my email address. If there's anything I can help you with, let me know. I have many friends and contacts in the UK. And you . . ." He made his way over to Mia's grandmother. "I can't remember the last time I've enjoyed the company of such a charming woman." Bending down to kiss her cheek, he smiled. She was nothing like his own grandmother, yet in essence, they were very much the same, and it tugged at his heart.

"You are welcome back any time, Nicholas," Melina said.

"Thank you." He kissed her cheek in farewell. "You won't have to twist my arm with meals like this."

Mia made her rounds, hugging each member of her family. Without another word, together, Nicholas and Mia slipped into the backseat of the car.

After several minutes of disquieting silence, Nicholas spoke. "You have a lovely family. You're very fortunate," he trailed off.

"I would have thought they'd be too provincial for you," Mia said nearly inaudibly.

But Nicholas caught the remark and wasn't sure whether to interpret it as snide or defensive. Running his fingers through his hair, he turned to her in frustration. "Can we please start fresh? No bickering or insults? Mia, I believe we have the potential to work well together if we can just move past this rough start. Can you do that? Because I'd like to try."

She closed her eyes, pressing at her temples with her fingertips. "Yes, of course. I apologize."

Nicholas sighed with relief. "Good. Now, moving on, when I asked you what your story was, you told me you didn't have one."

"That's right," she agreed hesitantly.

"But you do. A long-lost grandfather whose whereabouts are unknown?"

"That tale belongs to my *Yiayiá*, not to me."

"Nonetheless, that is one fascinating family history."

"Yes, and a bone of contention between my mother and grandmother."

"I sensed that."

"Mom is resentful and feels they were both deserted. *Yiayiá*, on the other hand, insists something has prevented them from being together for all these years."

Nicholas cocked his head to one side, trying to process what Mia was suggesting. "She couldn't possibly think he's still alive."

"She does. She said if her husband was no longer in this world, a part of her soul would die, and she'd feel it. She'd know."

Nicholas was stunned by the faith of the old woman. "How old would he be?"

"Eighty," Mia said. "Not old by Greek standards," she joked. "But if you take into consideration that he might have been imprisoned and tortured, it's doubtful he survived."

"Has anyone tried to find out?"

"My sister, Kally. She went to Greece last spring and searched for any information she could find out about him."

"And?"

"And she was making progress until she hit a roadblock."

The ride to Manhattan flew by. Nicholas was intrigued by this mystery. So much so that an idea sprung to his mind.

"Mia?"

"Yes?"

"I wanted to go over some preliminary concepts I had for the Athens shoot. Originally, I had in mind to contrast the light and dark aspects of Greek mythology. The beauty of Aphrodite as opposed to the deformity of the Cyclops. The tragedy of Oedipus in contrast to the love of Psyche and Cupid."

"That sounds wonderful." Mia pulled out her laptop. "I'll pull up some inspiration."

"Hold on," Nicholas said. "I've changed my mind. Maybe mythology has been overplayed. I now want to go into a more recent history. Your grandmother's story inspired me."

"But I love the images I'm already conjuring in my mind." She sounded disappointed.

"But the elegance of the royal family in their day, followed by their unseating and then the destructive aftermath of it all ... Now that's a story."

"True. I can't disagree. But is there some way we could still add in your original idea?"

Nicholas contemplated the thought, ideas running through his mind. "Let me talk to Penelope and see how much print space we have."

The car came to a halt.

"Well, look at that! We managed to have a productive meeting without killing each other." Nicholas grinned. "Kudos to both of us." Darren began to exit the car but Nicholas gestured for him to stay seated. Instead, he exited, walking around to open Mia's door and escort her out.

When he retrieved her bag from the trunk, Darren patted him on the back in a fatherly fashion. "Don't let this one slip away," he whispered. "Trust me."

Nicholas shook his head and grinned. The older man often had a bit of advice to offer or an opinion to spout. He had been driving Nicholas since his teenage years, and no one other than his sister and grandfather knew him better.

Nicholas slung Mia's bag over his shoulder, expecting to walk her to her door. "I'll keep that in mind. She's a good employee."

"You know that's not—" Darren's argument was interrupted when Mia came around the back of the car.

"I've got it," she said, taking her bag from Nicholas. "Thank you for the ride, Darren."

"It's always my pleasure," he responded.

"I'll see you in the office tomorrow. Goodnight, Nicholas."

"Goodnight then," he said, watching Mia as she walked through her apartment lobby door.

Darren clapped his hand over Nicholas' shoulder. "You should have insisted and walked her to her door," he advised. "You could have squeaked out a few more minutes rather than staring at a closed door."

Nicholas slid into the backseat. "It's nothing like what you're suggesting. I wanted to make sure she got in safely, that's all." At least that's what he kept telling himself.

A low chuckle rumbled from Darren's chest. "Whatever you say."

Melomakarona

1½ pounds unsalted butter, softened

16 ounces vegetable oil

4 oranges, juice and zest

2 egg yolks

1 cup sugar

2 teaspoons cinnamon

½ teaspoon ground cloves

4 teaspoons baking powder

5 pounds of all-purpose flour

Whole cloves for decoration (optional)

Method

Preheat oven to 350° F.

Mix sugar, cinnamon and cloves in a bowl and set aside. In another bowl, mix half of the flour and all of the baking powder. In a large bowl, cream the butter and sugar. Beat the egg yolks, orange juice and zest together and then add it to the butter mixture. Add the oil and mix on medium speed. Add the flour and baking powder mixture, blending thoroughly. *Slowly add more flour until a soft dough forms. Shape each cookie into a diamond shape. Prick the tops gently with a fork. (This helps the syrup to absorb). Press a whole clove in the middle of each cookie.

Place the cookies onto a parchment-lined baking sheet and bake at 350° F for 35 minutes. Drench in warm syrup after the cookies have cooled. Sprinkle with finely chopped walnuts.

Syrup

32 ounces sugar

24 ounces water

1 cup honey

2 strips orange peel

3 cinnamon sticks

Bring all the ingredients to a boil. Simmer for 20 minutes. Remove from heat. When cookies have cooled, soak in syrup for thirty seconds on each side. Remove and sprinkle with chopped walnuts.

The cookies can be frozen but only before the syrup is added. Soak in syrup as needed after thawing.

Yields approximately 120 cookies

*Baking is usually measured out in exact amounts. Cookbooks and chefs have repeatedly stated that while cooking is an art that lends license to experimentation, baking, although also an art, should be treated as a science. But the amount of flour to be used in some of my mother's recipes, has been vague. A 5-pound bag of flour may not be used in full, yet this is what she'd written down. I learned from watching her. Knowing how the dough feels in your hand and recognizing the correct consistency is key. With practice and time, I've learned the texture required for achieving cookies almost as perfect as hers.

Chapter 19

Mia

September 2019

The last days of summer were not to be taken for granted. Mia had worked tirelessly to prepare for the next magazine issue, and in two days, she was scheduled to leave for Athens. A quick respite with her sisters was a welcome break.

Without a care in the world, Mia sunned herself on the front deck of a fifty-foot yacht. Along with the other boats pulling out of the harbor, it motored slowly into the Long Island Sound. Max, Kally's fiancé, had borrowed the vessel from his father, who was away on business for the week.

"Do you girls want a bite to eat?" Kally asked Mia and Krystina from the cabin window.

"I thought we were eating out east?" Krystina asked.

"We are, but I thought we could use something to tide us over."

"I could eat," Mia said, rising.

"Shocking!" Krystina laughed.

They made their way to the deck on the boat's stern, waving to Max and his friend, Leo, standing at the helm. Loukas was also keeping company with the men, fascinated by whatever he was viewing through a pair of binoculars.

"Can I help you carry anything out?" Mia asked, stepping into a cabin so large it would rival her NYC apartment. She slipped her cover-up over her head and padded into the kitchenette.

Kally handed her a chip 'n dip set loaded with pita chips and a Mediterranean bean spread. "Are you coming outside, Athena?" Mia asked of the child sitting on the U-shaped sectional.

Athena, Max's daughter, contently played with Kally's Yorkie, Emma. "No, thank you," she said politely as she stroked the puppy.

Kally pulled out a bowl of watermelon and feta salad from the refrigerator and followed Mia through the glass doors. Krystina had already joined Egypt by the deck bar and was watching her blend a batch of frosé.

After serving up four stemless wine goblets of the frozen beverage, the four women slid into the semi-circular bench-style leather seating situated around the outdoor deck table.

"Mia, are you excited?" Egypt asked. "Only two days, and you're off!"

"Excited, nervous, ambivalent."

"Ambivalent?" Egypt questioned. "For what?"

"You've got this," Kally assured her sister.

"She does!" Krystina agreed. "Let's toast on it."

All four women raised their glasses.

"To the most beautiful woman to set foot in Athens this summer," Krystina toasted, clinking glasses.

Mia rolled her eyes. "That's the last thing on my mind." But Mia supposed that for a seventeen-year-old who uploaded Instagram photos of herself every chance she could, appearances were a priority.

"To doing a kick-ass job on the November issue," Egypt added, raising her glass once more with her own toast.

"Now that's more like it." Mia nodded.

"And . . ." Kally raised her glass. " . . . may you impress the boss in more ways than one."

Egypt set her glass down too quickly, the contents spilling over the rim. "You're holding out on me, girl. Let me have it. Every detail." Her sage-green eyes grew wide, and she leaned forward eagerly.

"I'm afraid you'll be sorely disappointed. I have nothing to report."

"Ha! So not true!" Krystina argued. "They have a love-hate relationship." She leaned in conspiratorially. "One minute, they're flinging insults at each other, and the next, he's kissing her."

"Really?" Egypt narrowed her eyes.

"No, not really. My sister exaggerates," Mia corrected. "It was one kiss in a moment of weakness and distress on his part."

"Distress?" Egypt frowned. "Was he drowning? Drunk?" She snapped her fingers. "I got it! He died and needed true love's kiss to bring him back to life!"

"Very funny." Mia was not amused.

"Touchy." Egypt dipped a pita chip into the bean spread and popped it into her mouth. "Moving on . . ."

"Egypt," Kally warned.

Egypt raised a palm. "Hold on. I have to get to the bottom of this. So why do you and Bossman have trouble seeing eye to eye?"

"Because she likes him," Krystina answered for Mia.

Mia placed her hand over her head, her arms hiding her face. She groaned in frustration.

"Now we're talking." Egypt's face lit up. "If I remember, he was pretty hot."

Krystina whipped out her phone faster than a cowboy drawing his gun from a holster. After a few taps, she flipped the phone around to show Egypt a Google image of Nicholas.

"Damn!" Clad in nothing but soaking wet bathing trunks, his defined abs were on full display.

"Are the two of you done now?" Mia asked.

With her elbows resting on the table, Egypt fisted her hands under her chin, her eyes laser-focused on Mia. "You know, for as long as I've known you—and that's a long time—you've never come to blows with anyone."

"I never said I came to blows with him."

"True, but you're usually very agreeable."

"Because fighting doesn't get me anywhere, and, in the past, I haven't had anything to fight over."

Mia met Egypt's eyes. In an unspoken language, Egypt understood not to challenge her on that point. And Mia knew she wouldn't. Egypt had proven that to her long ago.

"Until now," Kally pointed out.

"Exactly," Egypt agreed. "He's important. He gets under your skin, and I'll bet my profit from this month's jewelry sales that you get under his skin too."

"I think I'm just an annoyance to him. Someone his sister wants on his staff who he has to put up with."

"Loukas, up there," Krystina said, flicking her head up in his direction, "is my biggest annoyance. You don't see me kissing him."

Mia slid out from the bench seating. "I'm going to sunbathe on the lounger. Alone." Nicholas was a sensitive subject, and she wasn't ready to talk about him. She must be a glutton for punishment to still have strong visceral feelings for a man who outwardly barely tolerates her.

The days following the weekend in Southampton had gone well, at least on a professional level. Nicholas treated her as a colleague and had dropped his gruff exterior, finally trusting her unique perspective and creative talents.

On Mia's part, she had to conceal emotions brimming on the edge of spilling over. Anything could betray her true feelings—the lilt in her voice, the language of her eyes, the heat emanating from her every time Nicholas was near. She tried to force it down, reminding herself of his past offenses, but it was to no avail. Why is it that, with the most minuscule character flaw, she'd dismiss a man as not even worthy of her interest, yet, with Nicholas, none of it seemed to matter? She couldn't shake him from her consciousness, though it was precisely what she needed to do.

Molding her body into the plush lounger cushions, Mia sprawled out, closing her eyes and soaking in the warmth of the sun. Drifting off to sleep would erase the visions of Nicholas from her thoughts. Or so she'd hoped.

But then an image of a woman popped into her brain. The very same one she'd noticed him dancing with at the gala. Confident and dominant, like a lioness on the prowl, she stalked her way to Nicholas' office, the tap of the spikes of her heels warning of her approach. Mia was instantly jealous. No, it was more than that. She was dispirited, crestfallen, resigned. She wanted to look away but she pushed herself to face reality. At first, Nicholas seemed puzzled by her unannounced appearance, irritated even, and Mia felt a spark of hope. But alas, that hope was dashed when Nicholas smiled as he planted a kiss on each cheek. Not on the lips, Mia noted, relieved, although she had no right to be.

Just when Mia thought the jungle was safe, the red-headed vixen pounced on her prey, pulling him in at the neck, startling him with a full-blown display of PDA. Mia quickly averted her eyes, praying Nicholas didn't see her as a nosy voyeur. But their eyes had met for the briefest of seconds. Mia would not have exaggerated to say she detected a hint of apology on his face before he quickly ushered the woman into his office. Ten minutes later, off they went. Together. On a date? Mia sucked in a breath, holding back the tears she refused to let fall.

"Well, sun-napping isn't working," Mia muttered. She reached inside her canvas bag for her iPhone and tapped the Spotify app. 'Sing, Sing, Sing,' by Benny Goodman, always put her in a positive frame of mind, reminding her of the simplicities of an era she idolized. It took merely seconds for Mia to horizontally shimmy and shake to the rhythm of jazz, relaxing at last.

* * *

Later that evening, at the Andarakis home, Mia found herself sipping tea at the kitchen table with her mother and *Yiayiá*. Patting a hand over Mia's, her grandmother examined her thoughtfully, the wrinkles at the corners of her eyes deepening as she squinted at her. Without a word, she rose, padded over to the counter, and plucked a pastry from a platter.

"I made today," the old woman said in her heavily accented voice. She placed the syrup-soaked, diamond-shaped cookie topped with crushed walnuts in front of Mia. "You eat, and tell me why your heart is heavy."

"I'm fine, *Yiayiá*." But the unconvincing half-smile gave Mia away.

Taking Mia's face between her aging, compassionate hands, *Yiayiá* whispered, "The eyes don't lie, *koukla mou*."

Absently, Mia broke apart the corner of the moist *melomakarona* with the tines of her fork. "I'm a little nervous, that's all."

"About what?" her mother asked. "Your job? The trip to Athens?"

"Both." Mia exhaled a groan. "I'll be with my boss the entire time."

"Nicholas?" *Yiayiá* flashed a bright smile. "He's coming to see me tomorrow."

Mia did a double-take. "What?"

"I have a date." She shimmied. "You snooze, you lose!"

"*Mamá!*" Melina laughed, playfully throwing a potholder at her. "He's looking for more information about the story she told him."

"Oh, yes," Mia said. "That makes sense now. He wants the Athens' magazine issue to focus on the royal family and the turbulent times when the monarchy was overthrown." Frowning, she added, "It's odd he'd go directly to you instead of coming through me though." She sighed. "Or not."

Melina sipped her tea, her watchful eye observing her daughter over the rim of the cup. "Is he difficult to work for? He was very charming, from what I could tell."

"He has high expectations," Mia answered. "As he should. At first, I felt as though my very presence irritated him, and I think I overreacted. I'd snap at him defensively, and we'd butt heads."

"That doesn't sound like you," her mother probed.

Lifting her eyes upward, Melina rubbed her chin with her forefinger. Mia waited and watched, wondering what her mother was thinking.

"Mom?"

"Yes?" Melina said, stretching out the word.

"What is that mind of yours conjuring up?"

"I did warn you that Greek men are a pain in the ass, did I not?"

"He's my boss, not my husband," Mia clarified. "And lately, we've come to an understanding and have been getting along a little better."

"*Psémata!* Lies!" *Yiayiá* waved a wrinkled finger in her direction. "When that boy came to this house, it was to bring you back with him." Her eyes widened. "Eh?" She stood, leaning over the table for emphasis, her fisted hands pressing into the wood. "I saw the way he stared at you when he thought no one was looking." She walked to Mia's side and kissed her forehead. "And you don't fool me, *engoní mou*. Your heart is an open book."

Mia covered her eyes in embarrassment. "Only open to you, I hope. I've succeeded at working side by side with Nicholas these last few weeks. It was easy for me to stay strictly professional if I kept reminding myself of his past rudeness and cutting remarks."

"But . . ." her mother prodded.

"A woman showed up the other day to see him," Mia said somberly. "She was everything I wasn't. Sophisticated, confident, and fully in control." Mia laughed humorlessly. "She clearly demanded his attention, and, from what I could tell, she had it." Mia dabbed at the corners of her eyes. "It upset me, even though I have no right to be. And now, in less than two days, I have to travel to Europe with him and keep pretending he has no effect on me."

"Rest your mind, *pethi mou*," *Yiayiá* ordered. "All will fall into place as it should."

Mia wasn't sure if it was wisdom or mischief she detected in her grandmother's expression, but she had a feeling she was about to find out.

"Those who love deeply never grow old; they may die of old age, but they die young." — Benjamin Franklin

Chapter 20

Nicholas

If Nicholas was truly honest with himself, Mia's grandmother's history wasn't the main reason he trekked out to Long Island. For reasons he'd rather ignore, he had set out to see Mia herself. In fact, he reminded himself, it was his sister who hired the writers, and they were responsible for worming out the information detailing each article.

But Mia had awakened a chord in Nicholas that he'd buried long ago, and he found it almost impossible to shake her from his mind. She unexplainably captivated him at first glance, something no one had done in years, if ever. But despite his best efforts, his stern behavior, his only defense to keep her at bay, wavered a time or two during rare, weak moments of vulnerability, and he had chided himself for it. Yes, the girl pulled at heartstrings he didn't know still existed. Or had they only hardened into a protective shield? Perhaps they had never entirely disappeared at all? He didn't know anymore.

Those emotions, he'd vowed, were forbidden to poke through his armor. A puncture in his metaphorical breastplate would jeopardize his once-injured heart. He won't and can't allow it. Yet, as if by a force beyond his control, he was unnecessarily about to enter Mia's family home.

"Come in," Melina greeted Nicholas with a warm smile after he rang the doorbell. "It's nice to see you again."

"Thank you for having me."

"My mother is in the kitchen."

Following Melina's lead, Nicholas' gaze automatically drifted to the top of the staircase. Passing from one room to the next, he peered in, hoping to catch sight of Mia. The house was quiet but for the clatter of dishes.

"*Nikólaos!*" *Yiayiá* exclaimed. "*Ella!*" She waved him over, rushing to his side, her arms outstretched in welcome.

A chuckle rumbled from his chest as he greeted her with a double-cheek kiss. This woman had little in common with his own grandmother, yet her warmth and caring nature reminded him of her. Nicholas was struck with a pang of melancholy. He missed the comfort of his grandmother's embrace and the smell of his favorite mouthwatering foods he'd find her lovingly preparing in the kitchen.

"Come." She took him by the hand and led him to the dining room. A variety of pastries were resting in the center of a table set with four place settings.

"Where is everyone this evening?"

"George and Theo are at the restaurant. Krystina is at a friend's house," Melina answered.

"He doesn't care about them!" *Yiayiá* threw her hands up. "Efthymia is upstairs. I'll get her."

"No," Melina stopped her mother. "I'll tell Mia that Nicholas is here. I believe she's taking a shower. But he came to speak to you, *Mamá.*"

"Finally! I have you to myself," *Yiayiá* joked as Melina walked away. There was a mischievous gleam in her eyes. "It's been a long time since I've had the attention of a handsome man." She sighed. "You're almost as beautiful as my Panos," she said, her tone turning nostalgic.

Nicholas liked this woman for so many reasons. She was amusing for one, but that wasn't all. It was her optimism, faith, and hope. In the face of loss, she had all three, whereas he'd possessed none of those qualities in his own times of despair. He admired her resolve, and at the same time, felt oddly ashamed at his own weaknesses.

"*Kyria Kalliope*, would you trust telling me what happened to your husband?"

"Ah, if I knew what happened, he would be here with me now." She patted Nicholas' hand sadly. "I have little information but I do know what he was involved in."

"Mia brought me up to speed. Apparently, her sister was able to learn of his whereabouts up to a certain point."

Yiayiá looked past Nicholas and smiled. "*Efthymia*, come sit with us."

Nicholas turned, craning his neck to get a full view of the lovely creature descending the staircase. Clearly, blush pink was her favorite color. The pale-tinted, asymmetrical tunic snuggly fit over her skinny jeans, accentuating her slender figure.

"*Nikólaos* was just asking about your grandfather."

Nicholas stood politely, offering Mia his chair.

"Please sit, Nicholas," Mia said, smiling. "I'll take another."

"Before you do," *Yiayiá* began, "go to my room. On my nightstand is a wooden box. Bring it to me."

Mia nodded, heading for a room on the main floor her father had extended to the house several years back. Returning shortly, Mia handed her grandmother a weathered, honey-colored, wooden box barely larger than a recipe box.

Gingerly, *Yiayiá* opened the lid and removed three yellowed papers. "This was the letter I gave to my Kally before she left for Athens." She handed it to Nicholas. "It led her to a baker in Kalamata. Panos had the woman mail the letter to me so it couldn't be traced back to him."

"And like I told you," Mia said, turning to Nicholas, "that was the last she heard from him after he left for Athens."

"What I didn't think to give Kally was this." She handed Nicholas a frayed flyer.

Nicholas furrowed his brow. "*Seeds of Prometheus?*" he read aloud.

Newly blooming flowers served as the logo of the titled publication. "Gardening?"

"No. It's written in code," *Yiayiá* explained. "This was his way of letting me know where he was headed. This publication, unlike the one Panos worked on in Kalamata, was based in Athens. This is how the resistance communicated."

"Were you able to decipher the messages in this flyer?" Mia asked.

"No. Panos only sent me this copy along with the one letter I'd received. I only know what I do because he was doing the same type of work in Kalamata. He'd often expressed that he felt he could be more effective in Athens, so it was no surprise that he ended up there."

"Odd name for what this is," Nicholas pondered.

"The flyers were handed out in plain sight without arousing suspicion . . . as far as I know anyway." She looked down, stroking the precious box containing what little she had left of her husband's memory.

Nicholas' eyes flew up to meet Mia's. At that moment, he knew they both harbored the same fear. What if Panos had been caught? What if the Junta was on to him?

Mia gasped. Nicholas placed a finger to his lips in warning so as not to alarm the old woman.

"May I hold onto that for a while?" Nicholas asked. "I promise to return it."

"Do you know the legend behind Prometheus?" *Yiayiá* asked, handing over the paper. She didn't wait for a response before continuing, "Craftsman worshipped him. Zeus decided to hide fire from man but Prometheus, through his clever mind or trickery, stole it back. Do you see a parallel here?"

"I think so," Mia said. "The trickery is the code in the flyer."

Her grandmother nodded.

"That's not all," Nicholas added. "The craftsman represents the people, and Zeus is the tyrant ruler."

"Exactly," *Yiayiá* confirmed. "However, Zeus punished Prometheus and tied him to a rock, letting the eagles peck away at his liver mercilessly."

"Ew!" Mia pulled a face of revulsion. "So if the ones running the paper were caught, they would have been punished," Mia stated, thinking out loud.

"That's the fear," her grandmother admitted. "But Prometheus' liver grew back each day. Don't you see?" she said, with hope in her voice. "He persevered until one day, finally, Hercules came to rescue him."

Nicholas was astounded by her faith, yet worry gnawed at his stomach that her hopes would be shattered. It had been fifty years since she'd heard from the man. There was no possible way he could still be alive, and Nicholas had no words to comfort her. Taking her hand, he lifted it to his lips and respectfully kissed the old woman's hand.

"I think you just found your tie-in to the monarchy, Junta, and mythology," Mia pointed out.

"I think you might have something there," Nicholas said. "I'm heading back into the city, and I'd like to offer you a ride. Maybe we can discuss it on the way in?"

"I'd like that. Thank you," Mia replied. "I'll need a few minutes to gather my things."

"Take your time. I have this ravishing young woman to keep me occupied." Nicholas winked at *Yiayiá*.

Mia raised an eyebrow. "Well, now you've done it!" Mia placed her hands on her hips. "You've just given her license to . . . " She waved him off. "You'll find out. Don't say I didn't warn you." Mia giggled as she climbed the stairs.

"*Kyria* Kalliope," Nicholas stared her down in mock disapproval. "What was Mia referring to?"

"Bah! My granddaughter has no sense of humor. Make a few jokes and she shakes her finger at me!" *Yiayiá* leaned in and whispered, "S-E-X."

Nicholas' eyes widened. Stifling a laugh, he repeated, "S-E-X?"

"*Mamá!*" Melina reprimanded, coming down from the second floor with a basket of laundry. "What are you telling the boy?"

When had Nicholas become a child again? At the age of thirty-two, he'd long since passed the age of boyhood.

"*Áse me na eímai.* Leave me be!" She waved her daughter away.

Melina just shook her head and continued down the hall.

"*Nikólaos*, I need a favor." From the old box, *Yiayiá* removed another paper. "Take this with you too. It's a letter I wrote to my husband."

"I don't understand."

"I never mailed it. It was too risky," she explained. "I was saving it for a safer day, or for when he came back to me."

"What would you like me to do with it?"

"Hold onto it, and if by some chance, through *kalí týhi*, you find my Panos, give it to him."

Luck. The woman was now banking on luck. His heart broke for her. Nicholas took her hands in his, gazing upon her with sympathy. "If I find out any information on what happened to your husband," he said, careful with his words, "it will be due to investigation, not luck." He didn't want to give her false hope but no hope at all might prove harmful to her spirit. "I'll do my best."

With doubtless gratitude, *Yiayiá* flung her arms around him. Nicholas hesitated a beat, thrown off by the contact, before returning the embrace. She felt so small in his arms, just like his own grandmother. For a brief second, he remembered what it was like to hold her, and he savored the memory until his thoughts were broken by Mia's return.

"I leave you for ten minutes, and you hit on my boss," Mia joked, setting down her overnight bag.

"If you were smart, you'd be . . . what do you kids say? Jumping his bones," her grandmother declared, shaking an admonishing finger at Mia.

Mia slapped a hand over her face. "Okay, it's time to go."

Nicholas laughed. He couldn't remember the last time he'd been so entertained. "*Kyria* Kalliope, it's been a pleasure."

"Mom, I'm leaving," Mia called out.

Melina scampered into the hallway. "*Kaló taxídthi*," she said, wishing her daughter a good trip. "Make sure you see your grandparents."

"I will," she said, kissing her mother goodbye. "*Kalínychta, Yiayiá.*" Mia hugged her grandmother tightly.

As Nicholas opened the passenger door for Mia, he commented, "You warned me. She's something."

"You have no idea. My grandmother is the definition of a paradox. Just last night, she lectured me on the pitfalls of avoiding confession."

Nicholas swung around to the driver's side and got behind the wheel.

"No driver tonight?" Mia asked.

"I do know how to drive, and I like to get this baby on the road when I can."

Living in the city afforded Nicholas little time to take his sports car out for a test run, especially with his hectic work schedule.

"This car should grace the Autobahn, not the Long Island Expressway. It wasn't designed for speed limits," Mia commented.

An awkward silence fell between them.

"Nicholas, I'm so sorry," Mia murmured in apology.

"It's fine," he said, glancing quickly at her. "Trivia question," Nicholas added, changing the subject. "Who, other than me, drives an Audi R8?"

"I have no idea. Your sister? The CEO of Google? It's not something I keep track of."

"Iron man."

"Like, Robert Downey Jr.?" she asked.

"No, like Iron man. Not the actor who plays him."

"Superman's car would have been more fitting for you." She slapped a hand over her mouth to shut herself up.

Nicholas stopped at a red light. Turning, he could make out her silhouette in the shadow from the street lamps. "Why?"

Mia didn't answer at first but when he kept his eyes trained on her, waiting for a reply, she sighed in defeat. "It's just that with your glasses on, you look like Clark Kent."

"Huh!" Nicholas thought about this for a bit. She was checking him out, he noted. "Do you have a liking for superheroes or just that one in particular?"

He could swear she was blushing. Even in the dark chamber of the car, he could see the flush across her face. When she didn't answer, he tried a different tactic. "Tell me, am I the Christopher Reeves Superman or the Henry Cavill variety?"

"Neither," Mia was quick to answer. She squealed as Nicholas suddenly picked up speed, merging onto the Expressway. "George Reeves. The original Superman of the 1950s."

"I should have known." He grinned. "Which reminds me, I found a Spotify station that I think you'll enjoy. Pressing a control on the steering wheel, Nat King Cole's voice crooned 'Unforgettable.'

"I love this song. But this car and your advanced speed call for something more upbeat." Mia pressed the options on the app button until she found what she was looking for. "I bet you thought I only listen to old music."

"This is current? You are aware that this song was recorded over thirty years ago?"

"Abundantly," Mia replied, happily tapping her foot to the beat of the Go-Go's.

Chapter 21

Mia

"While that was the most luxurious plane trip I've ever taken, it was also the most boring flight," Mia informed Nicholas as they deplaned the aircraft.

Together, they walked with the masses, following signs written in both Greek and English, heading to the baggage claim area. Passengers whizzed by in a rush, wheeling overnight bags as though the building was on fire.

"It was, after all, a red-eye," Nicholas reminded her. "Sleep was all that should have occupied you. Am I to believe that you might have actually missed my company?" He smirked.

"Come to think of it, waking up without a stiff neck was nice," she admitted, giving him the side-eye. She waited for a beat before relenting. "But it would have been nice to have someone to talk to."

"That's the benefit of first-class. Quiet and private."

Instead of standing by the carousel, Nicholas escorted Mia to the line of waiting chauffeurs.

"*Kalimera, Kyios Aristedis.*" The driver tipped his hat to Mia, addressing her politely. "*Despoinídtha*, this way to the car. I'll come back to wait for your luggage."

Once settled in their seats, Nicholas asked Mia when she'd last visited Athens.

"I haven't been here in years," Mia replied. I was twelve years old, to be exact."

"Really?"

The look of disbelief on his face made her laugh. "Why do you find that so implausible?"

"That was a long time ago," he explained. "You have grandparents here. I would have thought your family visited more often."

"Well, as you once pointed out, we come from different worlds." There was a touch of bitterness in her tone. "My father can't leave his restaurant unattended, and my mother works for the county. Their lifestyle doesn't afford the time off for long visits to Europe."

Nicholas closed his eyes, breathing in deeply. "Please don't throw my words back in my face. I regret them." He looked at her with sincerity brimming in his hazel eyes. "I'll make it my personal mission to set aside time for you to see your grandparents."

Mia didn't know Nicholas well, yet she was quickly learning how to read him. The warm honey in his eyes had dulled, and the small crease at the corner of his mouth told Mia he was upset. There was an imperceptible underlying sadness creeping over Nicholas. Mia could feel his melancholy wash over her like a stain. Her stain. Mia wished she could take back her words.

"That's very kind of you, considering we are here strictly for business."

"Family is important," he said, lost in his thoughts. "You never know how much . . ." Nicholas paused, glancing down at the floor. " . . . or how little time you have with them."

Mia sympathetically placed her hand over his. Turning away, Nicholas stared out the window. "We're here," he said blankly.

Mia's recollection of Athens was spotty at best. Most of her memories included family dinners, days at the beach, and walks to the market. They had dined at local tavernas and visited some of the historical sites. Still, at that age, an appreciation for ancient ruins had not yet been formed.

Now, with her chance to soak in every glorious moment as she entered the city of her heritage, she hadn't paid it any mind. It was Nicholas who had captured her attention. But once she exited the vehicle, Mia gasped. Across from where she stood, Evzones were standing vigil, still as statues, guarding the parliament building. High atop the structure, formally known as the Royal Palace, the flag of Greece proudly waved. She'd been here before, vaguely recollecting a walk through the adjoining Royal Garden on a scorching summer day.

Nicholas escorted Mia, guiding her by the small of her back, into the Hotel Grande Bretagne. She had known her position with *Opul Magazine* would allow her to travel but this was on a scale beyond her dreams and comprehension. The lobby alone screamed of old-world opulence. Floors covered in earth-toned marble and ornate rugs stood out amongst the inlay-paneled walls and ceilings.

"It's exquisite," Mia breathed, taking it all in.

"You haven't seen anything yet." Nicholas smiled, his mood lifting as he led her to the reception desk.

Mia wandered while Nicholas checked in. Her eyes roamed appreciatively like a child discovering a secret room filled with candy. Circular sofas covered in burgundy velvet sat regally in the center of the lobby. She edged her way over to the plush seating and ran her hand over the material. Everything about this place was rich and lush. Even the curtains looked as though they belonged in a palace. She crossed the room to take a closer look at the detail, her heels echoing as she strode over. Beyond the floor-to-ceiling windows, Athens' streets were bustling with speeding cars and strolling pedestrians. Mia couldn't wait to explore this city.

Mia placed her hand over her mouth to cover a yawn. Her grumbling stomach, however, was not as easily concealed.

Nicholas hinted at a smile. "I could use a good meal too," he said. "Would you prefer to freshen up first?"

"If that's okay with you."

"Of course," he agreed politely.

Mia never knew what to expect with Nicholas. He was back to his formal manner again, as if they were strangers meeting for the first time. One step forward and two back. That's how it went with him. On the rare occasion that a sliver of his sensitive side emerged, it quickly disappeared as though he'd made a gross error.

Silently, they walked to the bank of elevators. Self-consciously, Mia rode up to the seventh floor, apprehensive of looking in his direction. If Nicholas was even aware of her discomfort, he made no attempt to ease it. In fact, he seemed as uncomfortable as she.

"We have adjoining suites," Nicholas informed her as the elevator stopped on their floor. "If a half-hour will suffice, I'll come for you then," he said, stopping in front of her door.

Mia nodded. "It's fine." Shutting the door, she wondered why he had once more grown so stiff-necked toward her. Her mind was so muddled with confusing thoughts of Nicholas that, at first, she didn't even look at her new surroundings.

"Wow!" she exclaimed, scanning the palatial suite. Cream and taupe hues touched with soft gold adorned the room. A floral-printed, tufted headboard framed the king-sized bed. Her luggage had already been delivered and was resting on a wooden rack by the armoire. Mia opened her bag searching for her toiletries, and headed to the bathroom.

"Oh, my!" Mia did a double-take. If this was a dream, she didn't want to awake. A marble, freestanding bathtub dominated a room more massive than any she'd ever seen in a hotel before. A stall shower of glass and marble large enough for an entire family beckoned to her. The ivory marble floor contrasted with the charcoal tub and matching sink vanity, adding an extra touch of elegance.

Mia had been in her clothing for almost twenty hours. It only took her mere seconds to peel them off. Two hours of soaking and pampering would rejuvenate her muscles and do wonders for her spirit. That's all she wanted. But Mr. Iceberg had only bestowed to her a paltry thirty minutes.

* * *

As it turned out, a half-hour proved to be just enough time for the steaming hot water running down her back to revive her. Quickly, she touched up her makeup, pinned her hair up, and slipped into a white linen dress that fell just above her knees.

When Mia opened the door to her room, she discovered Nicholas in the hallway leaning against the opposite wall waiting for her to emerge. Immediately, he straightened up, the heat of his stare not lost to her as he followed the straps of the crisscrossed neckline on her dress and the tendrils of hair grazing her bare shoulders.

Mia concealed her smirk. If Nicholas thought she missed his reaction, he was wrong. His quick intake of breath as his eyes were drawn to her bare skin told her all she needed to know.

Nicholas cleared his throat. "You look lovely," he said, finding his composure and forcing himself to look her in the eyes before averting his attention to the elevator.

That didn't kill you, Mia wanted to say, but instead, she held her tongue. What was it about him that made her want to start a confrontation? No one had this effect on her. Imagining herself taking in a deep, cleansing breath, she refrained from any retort and smiled politely.

"Thank you." They strolled down the hall to the elevator. Inwardly, Mia vowed not to repeat the awkwardness from before. "Do you usually stay at this hotel when you're in Athens?"

"Yes, unless I stay with friends. We have a family home in Kefalonia, and I have a moderate place in Mykonos." Nicholas led the way as the doors opened. "Have you been to the islands?"

"No. I had only come to Greece that one time when I was small, and we didn't venture far beyond Athens." She stopped short, staring in awe at the room beyond the elevator. Mia was overcome with emotion at the beauty beyond the rooftop restaurant. She felt a connection to this ancient, architectural structure proudly elevated atop the Acropolis. This was part of her heritage, her people's history. And although she remembered reluctantly climbing the steps to reach the Parthenon so many years ago, Mia had never appreciated it the way she did at this very moment.

"*Kalimera, Kyrios* Aristedis," the hostess greeted him. "We have your table waiting for you."

Mia and Nicholas followed the woman to a table by the balcony. "This is breathtaking." Mia pointed to Lykavittos, the mountain to the left of the Parthenon. "I have a vivid memory of being terrified riding up on the cable car."

Nicholas placed his napkin in his lap. "Do you have a fear of heights?"

Her eyes widened as she nodded. "Yes," she admitted emphatically.

"So, no London Eye for you."

"Definitely not. And not something I need to worry over, as we are nowhere near that death contraption."

Nicholas chuckled. "But it may be at some point in our travels," he challenged.

"I hardly think going on a Ferris wheel is part of my job description."

"Unless I insist." There was a mischievous sparkle in his eye.

"Insist?" she threw back at him. "That might be grounds for my resignation." She picked up her glass of water, casually taking a sip.

Nicholas raised an eyebrow. "If I ask you nicely, maybe you'll venture up there again." He gestured to the high-peaked mountain. "There's a nice restaurant with an incredible view up there. And after all, you're a big girl now."

A server came by and placed a bread basket on their table. Nicholas ordered a bottle of wine and an appetizer enough for two to share.

She was trying to figure this man out. Was he playing with her?

"If you had to describe yourself in one word, what would it be?" Mia asked suddenly.

An odd expression flashed across his face. "Conflicted."

"Not the answer I was expecting."

"What were you expecting? Or should I ask, what word would you have chosen?"

"Moody," she blurted, slapping a hand over her mouth for her brash faux pas.

He laughed. "And you, Mia, are a bit bellicose."

She closed her eyes, embarrassed. "Not usually. I apologize. You seem to bring out the worst in me."

"I suppose that's partially my fault," he said regretfully.

The wine came, interrupting their futile conversation. Mia kept her eyes trained on Nicholas as the sommelier poured wine in his glass, waiting for his approval. Nicholas swirled the crimson liquid before bringing the glass to his nose. After breathing in the bouquet, Nicholas nodded his approval, and the sommelier filled both their glasses. Mia was about to speak, but thankfully, the appetizer came, interrupting her already muddled thoughts.

She looked up and caught him staring at her pensively. If she had to guess, it was as though he was making a decision about her. Nicholas had a dimple on his right cheek, and when he concentrated over something, it deepened. Mia had noticed this on several occasions. Nothing about Nicholas escaped her.

Finally, he asked the question on his mind. "Why did you ask me to describe myself?" Nicholas spread creamy burrata on sourdough bread and drizzled a stream of olive oil over it. He waited for her response.

"I suppose I was trying to figure you out. To see how you view yourself." The last thing she wanted was another argument with him. Why couldn't she just keep her thoughts to herself around him? But apparently, she couldn't, because her mouth suddenly had control over her mind. "I never know which Nicholas I'm going to come in contact with from day to day, and it's off-putting." Mia gulped down more wine than she intended. Maybe if she got drunk, she'd pass out and shut up.

Nicholas massaged his fingers over his brow. With a long exhale, his shoulders slumped. "I am sorry for that. You are off-putting as well, and that's why I'm conflicted."

"I don't understand." Her tone was pleading. Unconsciously, she clutched a pendant Egypt had crafted from a drachma coin Mia had been given during her last trip to Greece.

"You wouldn't," he said softly. "Some of us have demons to contend with. You wouldn't know about that."

"Don't be so sure about that," Mia muttered, the napkin in her lap becoming the focus of her attention.

Nicholas reached his hand across the table, lifting her chin with his forefinger. "You claim to have no story. Yet each day, I unearth a pebble of information that tells me otherwise."

"It looks like our entrées have arrived," Mia said, relieved for the distraction. "I'm famished."

"You always are." Nicholas grinned. "That's one thing I know for sure."

After they finished dining, Nicholas suggested a walk in the National Gardens located across the street from the hotel before heading to the Acropolis to discuss the shot list for the shoot.

Mia stopped to observe the Evzones guarding the parliament building. "Why not shoot some models here emulating royalty?" she asked. "It was the palace at one time."

"Permission is not easily granted, and I don't have time to deal with Hellenic bureaucracy."

"Too bad," she said. "I did pull some historic photos of the royal family."

"We could utilize the gardens," Nicholas suggested. "After all, they were commissioned by Queen Amalia."

"Lead the way!" Mia recalled strolling through the park many years ago. Her mind had already begun racing with ideas.

Silently, they walked, side by side, down narrow labyrinthine paths, Mia soaking in the natural beauty of the foliage. But when they reached a particular statue, Mia suddenly halted. Seated in the middle of lush greenery, an angel bowed her head. She couldn't take her eyes from the stone figure, yet it wasn't her beauty that mesmerized her. No, it was something altogether different.

"Mia? Are you feeling ill?" Nicholas asked. "You have the strangest expression on your face."

"I-I've been here before," she said as though it were a shock to her system.

"Yes, you mentioned that."

"This is where I got lost," she muttered.

"Lost?"

"Yes." Mia turned to face Nicholas. "I was twelve years old; it was the one and only time we visited my grandparents. We had come here one morning after breakfast. Krystina was in a stroller, and my mom and dad were chasing after Theo. They didn't notice when I stopped to look at the angel. I was so taken with her. I couldn't help but wonder why her head was bowed in such a sad way. By the time I took my focus from her, my family had walked away without realizing I wasn't following behind."

"That can be worrisome in a place you're not familiar with."

"That's an understatement. I panicked," Mia admitted. "I didn't see my family anywhere, and I had no idea which path to take. I ran to a slightly elevated bridge overlooking a pond, thinking I'd have a better view of the area, but too much foliage blocked my sight. I stood there, deciding what to do next, trying to calm myself. I could have either wandered around, taking the chance I'd spot them, or I figured if I stayed in one spot, hopefully they'd find me by retracing their steps."

Nicholas peered into Mia's eyes as if he was seeing her for the first time. "There's a bench over here. Let's sit for a while," he said with concern. "How long were you parted from your family?"

"I'm not sure—a while," she pondered. Mia sat beside Nicholas as she recalled the day. "As I nervously peered in every direction, an older boy approached me, asking if I was okay. When I told him that I was lost and needed to find my family, he stayed with me and guided me through the garden as if he knew it well."

Nicholas shook his head in disbelief. "Mia," he whispered.

She smiled. "He was very kind and promised not to leave me." Mia clutched at her pendant. "We walked around for a while until I finally spotted my parents talking to a park employee. They were so relieved."

"But the boy was a little sad to lose his companion, and so were you."

"Yes." Mia frowned. That was quite perceptive of him to realize, she thought. "Before we parted, he gave me this." Mia held out the coin dangling from her chain for Nicholas to see.

His eyes flew up to penetrate hers. "His mother's coin."

"What? How would you know that?"

Nicholas reached into his pocket, pulling out a golden one-hundred drachma, identical to the one she wore around her neck. "I was that boy." Nicholas looked as stunned as she felt.

"You?" Mia was speechless. "Did you know from the start?"

"No. I'm as surprised as you are. Your recollection resonated with me. I remember helping a young girl who was lost on the bridge find her family. It could have been a coincidence, but once you showed me the coin, I was sure."

"Why did you give it to me? I never understood. The coins were important to you. And I was a stranger."

"Yes, they were, and that's why I still carry this one around. My mother gave me the coins dated with my birth year when I turned twelve years old." He shrugged. "I wanted you to have something to remember me by. It was an impulse but you need to know that I wouldn't have just given it to anyone."

"That was incredibly sweet, and, as you can see, I took good care of it."

"I knew from the first second I laid eyes on you there was something familiar about you. Something I couldn't quite figure out, and it's been gnawing at me since," Nicholas admitted.

He cupped her cheek, and she closed her eyes, leaning into his palm. "You might have been the one who was lost but it was me who was all alone," Nicholas whispered.

"You were sad."

"And the way you're looking at me now is exactly what stayed with me after we parted. Those tender, caring eyes, and the maturity and wisdom of a girl beyond your young age." He took her hands in his. "No one other than my sister truly understood me. Maybe because she was going through it also. But somehow, you did."

"This is unreal. I can't believe that boy was you!" Mia exclaimed. "I've wondered about him . . . you . . . over the years, and hoped that a newfound joy eventually washed away your grief."

Nicholas stood, extending his hand to Mia. "It did . . . for a while. But somehow, the hits kept coming."

Mia didn't pry. As she had all those years ago, she listened. Only learning what Nicholas offered. That night on the beach, when he told her of the circumstances behind his parents' death, the story didn't bring the boy she met in the garden to mind. Back then, as a boy, he'd only told her his parents had been killed four years prior in a tragic accident. That was enough to shatter any child's world. But if that wasn't enough, he had shared that he'd then only recently lost his beloved grandmother too, a woman who had lovingly cared for him since his parents' deaths. She had seen the grief shadowing his eyes. Yet he'd set his own troubles aside and come to her rescue. Unconsciously, she smoothed her finger over the pendant, as she so often did.

With his sister and grandfather as the most influential figures in his life, Mia wondered what hits he referred to. But Nicholas remained quiet until they approached a small bridge.

"This is it." He led her onto the wooden, arched bridge overlooking a small pond. "This is where I first saw you. Alone, frantically turning in every direction. It didn't take a genius to figure out you had lost your way." He rested his arms on the railing, entranced by the soft ripples of water and long-ago remembrances.

Mia recalled how forlorn young Nicholas was back then. She hated to watch him revisit that dark place now.

"What do you say we find the ideal spot for some photos," she said enthusiastically. "You know this park better than I do. Any thoughts?"

Turning, a broad smile lit up his face as he pulled himself back to the present. "Yes. I have just the place. It may not be the old palace but it's stunning and impressive, and it will make quite a regal backdrop for our purposes."

Nicholas took her by the hand, quickening his pace as he pointed in the direction of where he was heading. "This way."

"Are we leaving? I was hoping to plot some shots by the foliage."

"Your angel and our bridge. I've already decided," he said definitively.

After a brisk walk, Nicholas stopped in front of the Zappeion building. The eight towering Grecian columns at the entrance were just as Nicholas had described—regal, majestic, and absolutely perfect. Mia could see the scenes of the past in her mind's eye. Flowing gowns of taffeta and silk, their trains draped around columns or creeping down the stone steps; bejeweled headpieces, the sun reflecting off the prism of the gems.

"You're right," Mia said, her inflection laced with awe. "This is it."

Nicholas beamed. "With that settled, let's head over to the Acropolis. We'll be shooting before the park opens to visitors but we will only have three hours."

* * *

Once they had settled the business for the day, Mia and Nicholas meandered the Pláka's streets and alleys. Mia stopped by a food cart piled high with rings of sesame coated *koulouri*. She ordered two of the crunchy bread rounds and handed one to Nicholas.

"We can stop at a café for a bite to eat if you like," Nicholas suggested when Mia stopped by another vendor grilling *souvlaki*.

"This is more fun," Mia said, reaching into her bag for some cash.

"I've got this," Nicholas insisted.

Mia nearly hummed her pleasure with each bite of marinated meat she picked off the skewer. Along the way through the narrow streets, she stopped to browse at teaser items shop owners displayed by their store entrance.

"What on Earth?" Mia sputtered. She could feel her face flush with embarrassment. A storefront showcasing racks and racks of wooden penises were out in open view. Dark wood, light wood, ones in many colors adorned with brushstroke flowers. Huge ones, tiny ones attached to keychains, and . . . No, it couldn't be, she thought. But indeed, it was none other than a pair of salt and pepper shakers. Mia could think of a few people who would get a chuckle out of receiving one of these but she could never bring herself to pick one up and pay for it.

Nicholas tried to suppress a laugh. "I guess you never saw one of these?"

Mia choked on words that never made it past her throat. One of what? she wondered. A penis? By now, she must have gone from pink to purple.

"Tourists love them. Especially the Australians. Just about every souvenir shop carries them."

"Why?" Mia asked the question as though the whole country had lost their mind.

"It goes back to the ancient tradition of festivals for fertility and honoring the phallus," he explained.

"Okay." She looked away, embarrassed. "On another subject, my grandfather has his store somewhere around here."

"Do you have an address? Let's stop by to see him."

"I'm not sure he'll even be there. He only goes in for a couple hours a day, according to my sister. Kally came here over the summer to help out when my grandfather broke his hip." Mia spied a pastry shop, and her taste buds navigated her in that direction.

"Oh, no!" Nicholas reached for her, steering Mia away from the confections. "I made a reservation for dinner. At this rate, you won't be hungry."

"I can assure you that I will be."

He flashed a glance at his wristwatch. "It's getting late. Let's head back to the hotel."

Chapter 22

Mia

Athens, Greece 2004

Mia dragged her feet through the National Gardens of Athens, following a few paces behind her family. This was the most boring summer of her life. While her friends back home were walking into town for ice cream, going to the beach, and having sleepovers, she was stuck with elderly relatives visiting broken-down buildings.

"Why couldn't I have gone with Kally?" Mia whined. "It's not fair. They're my cousins too."

"When you're eighteen, you can go off on your own too," her mother said as she struggled to keep hold of her six-year-old son. "Theo!" Melina scolded as he broke away from her. "Get back here!"

"Let the boy run," George said, pushing Krystina in a stroller. "We're in a park. How far can he go?"

"Here," Mia said to her two-year-old sister, handing her the stuffed monkey when it fell from the carriage.

"That's covered in dirt now!" Her mother snatched it from Mia before Krystina could take it from her. "What were you thinking?"

Mia made a face behind her mother's back, rolling her eyes defiantly.

She shuffled along, hanging back far enough to pretend she was on her own.

Every night it was the same thing. Dinner at home with all the relatives. They would laugh and sing, eat and drink, talk and dance. There was no one her age. No one at all.

During the day, they'd sometimes sightsee. How many ruins were there to visit? And the churches? They all look the same. Yet her parents had to step into each one they passed.

Mia had come all this way, and there was no plan to visit Santorini, Mykonos, Corfu, or any of the hundreds of exotic islands surrounding the mainland. Instead, she was stuck here, bored to tears.

If she really wanted to take a close look, the foliage was pretty, and it was a nice place to enjoy a stroll with nature. But Mia wasn't in the mood to give in to the temptation until she came upon a statue that captured her attention.

Surrounded by a bed of greenery sat an angel, her wings pulled back, her head bowed down. The stone figure didn't seem to represent a celestial deep in prayer, or one brimming with joy. No, this young seraph was sad.

"I'm with you," Mia muttered to the statue. "I want out of here too." But as she fixated on her, she wondered why the artist had created her this way. Most angels reflected a peaceful, content aura. She stared at her for so long that, by the time she looked up, her family was nowhere in sight.

Mia's heart plummeted as the adrenaline kicked in and her feeling of panic escalated. She spun in every direction looking for them, calling to them.

"Mom! Dad!" she shouted, cupping her hands by her mouth to increase the volume of her voice.

The park was unusually empty, the only visitors she saw were at a distance. Spotting a small bridge overlooking a pond, she ran to it, thinking she might see her family at that slight elevation. Again, she pivoted in every direction, but it was no use. Too much greenery blocked her view.

Mia hung her arms over the rail, contemplating what to do next. She could wander around and get further lost, or wait for her parents to find her. Nervously, she took another look around when a boy, a little older than she was, approached her.

"Are you okay?" he asked, his hazel eyes watching her with concern.

"I'm lost," Mia croaked. "I got separated from my family and I don't know my way around."

"I'll help you find them," he offered. "I know my way around here pretty well."

Her eyes met his, and she witnessed something sad in them. "That's very nice of you."

He shrugged, his mop of dark hair falling in his face. "I don't have much else to do." He led the way down a path. "You have no idea which way they went?"

"No. I stopped to look at a statue, and I wasn't paying attention. They were too busy with my younger siblings to worry about keeping track of me."

They meandered down an area lined with canopied foliage. She may have walked this way earlier in the day, but now, with this thoughtful, cute boy guiding her, the trees had come to life. Everything seemed greener and the air sweeter.

"You're not here with anyone?" Mia asked.

He shook his head slowly, his eyes downcast.

"Do you live around here?"

"No. But when my grandfather comes here on business, I wander around while he's working."

"Oh." That statement could lead to so many questions but something told Mia not to pry.

He cocked his head, looking at her pensively. "Curiosity is written all over your face."

"Is it?" Mia pressed her hands to her cheeks. "Please ignore it."

"Does any of this look familiar," he asked as they turned a corner.

"I guess, but it doesn't mean I'll find them here. Is there a lost and found for people?" she joked.

"If only," he said, his voice laced with sorrow.

These little hints of emotion made Mia feel as though this boy wanted to unload something from his mind.

"I really want to thank you for taking me around to find my way. I'd be terrified without you," she admitted. "I wish I could return the favor," Mia said, planting a seed.

"You're a nice kid," he said, smiling at her. "How old are you?"

"Twelve," Mia muttered, already feeling like she'd been dismissed as a child.

"I'm sixteen," he said matter-of-factly. "You're cool for your age."

"Thanks," she said in a deadpan tone, not sure if that was a compliment or not. "Can I ask you something?" She didn't wait for a reply. "Do you like traveling with your grandfather on business? Because I wish I had stayed home with my friends for the summer."

"It's not that I mind it." He shrugged, sucking in a deep breath. "I just miss what it was like before."

"Before . . . what?" Mia asked hesitantly.

He flipped his hair off his forehead. "Let's take a break from the sun." He pointed to a shady spot by a large tree and took Mia by the hand.

Mia felt the heat rising to her cheeks. This must be what butterflies fluttering in her stomach felt like. This older boy had no idea the effect he had on her, and Mia was grateful for that.

When they sat down on the grass, Mia's companion rested his back against the trunk of the tree. Mia, with her legs crossed, faced him. He closed his eyes and scrubbed his face with his hands as though it would erase the tension.

"When I was your age," he started, dropping his hands, "my parents were killed in a tragic accident."

Without thinking, Mia reached for his hand. "I'm so very sorry." She inched closer to him, shedding a tear. "I can't begin to imagine what that must be like." Now she was a bit ashamed of herself for wishing she hadn't been forced on this trip with her family.

"No, you can't," he agreed. "But others think they can," he said bitterly. "My *pappou* is a busy man. It was my *yiayiá* who watched over me after . . ." he trailed off. "She'd cook and I'd watch her while spilling all my news . . . or emotions." He kept hold of Mia's hand, fiddling with a silver ring she wore on her middle finger. "She was affectionate and understanding. She was always there when I needed her."

Mia's eyes flew up to his. She was afraid to ask the question. It was written all over his stricken face.

He answered her with a nod before confirming, "She died a few months ago." His voice cracked with emotion.

"You've lost way too many people for someone of your age," Mia sympathized. "You'll always feel their loss, I'm sure, but hopefully, in time, all your good memories will help you through. I've never lost anyone. The closest I've come is to having a grandfather I never met, but that's not the same, so maybe I don't know what I'm talking about."

"You really are a sweet girl, and smart for your age," he said. "Honestly, I'm tired of people telling me it's time to move on. People close to me. Ones who should comfort me and . . . love me."

Mia had the impression he was thinking of one particular person. Whoever it was, he hoped this boy wasn't in for another heartache.

"I think everyone handles grief in their own way," Mia stated. "That, I can tell you, I've witnessed firsthand."

"Thanks. I think we better track down your parents before they call the police."

Mia laughed. Standing up, she brushed blades of stray grass off the back of her shorts. "If they've even noticed yet. My brother can be quite a handful!"

"Let's head to the front entrance," he suggested. "They might be waiting for you there."

As they walked side-by-side, their conversation took on a lighter tone. They chatted about common interests and their friends back home. Soon, they were at the front gate. The moment Melina spotted Mia, she ran to her, simultaneously sounding relieved and accusatory. "Where did you run off to?"

"Nowhere." Mia pulled away, embarrassed when her mother grabbed her face to examine her. "I stopped to look at something and when I turned around, you were all gone."

"And you made a friend." Melina eyed the boy suspiciously.

"Yes. If it wasn't for him, I would have never found my way back."

"Thank you, young man." Melina turned to Mia. "Say goodbye to your new friend. Your father is waiting with the children, and they're getting very restless."

"Okay, Mom. Give me a minute." When her mother didn't move, she implored, "Please?"

Melina narrowed her eyes and sighed. "Two minutes." Turning, she walked away.

"Thank you," Mia told the boy, sad to leave him. She knew it would be the last time she'd probably ever see him. "Getting lost with you was the most fun I've had this whole trip."

"It's me who wants to thank you," he said. "There aren't many people I find easy to open up to," he admitted. He reached inside his front trouser pocket and held out two coins. "I always keep these with me. I want you to take this one to remember me by." He pressed one of the coins into her palm.

"A Greek coin?"

"They hold a sentimental value for me," he explained. "My mother gave them to me on my birthday . . . just before she was killed."

"Oh, I can't accept it!" Mia exclaimed, handing it back to him.

But he wouldn't take it back. "I really want you to have it. I still have the other." He dropped it back into her hand and curled her fingers around the golden memento. "Take care." He gave her a quick peck on the cheek.

"You too," Mia said, softly touching her cheek. "I'll never forget you."

Chapter 23

Mia

Athens, Greece 2019

After returning to the hotel, Mia showered and reapplied her makeup, all the while pondering what an odd day it had been. She still couldn't wrap her brain around the idea that Nicholas was the boy she had met all those years ago. He had revealed some deep wounds that day, yet they oddly had never exchanged names. She was still a child then, about to embark on her teen years. He had impressed her with his generosity and open heart, and the pendant she wore was a constant reminder of him.

Mia rifled through her wardrobe mindlessly. Her thoughts kept drifting back to Nicholas—the boy she'd met by sheer fate. If ever she should believe in destiny, it was now. Over the years, she'd elevated him to a demi-god. Every boy was measured against him, or at least the image she'd created in her mind. Nicholas! The only man to make her heart beat faster and make her stomach flutter.

She chose a simple, black pencil dress with a sweetheart neckline and cap sleeves. A long strand of knotted pearls, turned to hang down the open back's deep cut teased her skin with the slightest movement.

Something had changed between them. Nicholas had softened to her. Or had she simply mistaken his confusion for stern glares?

160

Whatever the case, she was happy to not be on the other end of his wrath for a change and hoped it stayed that way.

Nicholas stood as soon as Mia stepped up to the hostess podium. It was as though he was keeping watch for her. Once again, they had been seated at the rooftop's edge with a view that was more breathtaking than the travel photos had suggested. The Parthenon, bathed in golden light, stood majestically, reigning over all of Athens. It was as if the gods conducted their celestial duties here while humans foolishly thought they controlled the fates.

Aware that Nicholas was raking his eyes over her, Mia's heart skipped a beat. Or was it because she was doing the same to him. Wearing a crisp white shirt adorned with platinum, monogrammed cufflinks, his charcoal, double-breasted suit dripped of sophistication. But this man could have been sporting a worn-out t-shirt and a ten-dollar pair of slacks and still look like he belonged on the cover of a fashion magazine.

"You look stunning, Mia." Nicholas pulled her seat out for her.

"Thank you. I like the way you look too." *Seriously?* "I mean, I like what you're wearing." Embarrassed, she expelled a nervous breath.

"Just your basic suit and tie," he said dismissively.

His lopsided grin was meant to put her at ease. Basic. Nicholas was anything but basic. Krystina threw around that word. 'That place is basic. Her outfit was basic. That dude was basic.'

"You were right," Mia said shyly. "The view was worth another look at night."

"It certainly was," he agreed. But Nicholas wasn't staring out into the night, at the temple erected for the goddess Athena. It was Mia who had his full attention.

"We should review the final schedule for tomorrow," Mia said, circling back to business.

"I think we have it cemented." Nicholas cocked his head to one side, his eyes penetrating hers. "It's a beautiful night. Let's forego any discussion of business. You're in Greece, and here, once the workday is over, we enjoy the beauty before us." Nicholas lifted a glass of the champagne he had already ordered to the table. Gesturing for her to do the same, they clinked glasses before taking their first sip.

Just as Mia was about to speak, a woman called out to him, waving in his direction. The lioness. First the gala then the office. Now here. She must be his girlfriend. Why else would she be here? The bile in Mia's stomach churned. She was about to be sick. She couldn't bring herself to meet Nicholas' eyes. What a fool she was to think he'd have any interest in her. Why? Because of a childhood chance meeting? She should've known better. If Mia didn't leave quickly, embarrassing tears would fall.

"Nicholas! There you are!" Confident and domineering, the throaty voice coming from this woman dripped with seduction.

Nicholas stood. "Renata? What are you doing here?"

"What kind of greeting is that?" Ignoring Mia, she planted her hands onto Nicholas' shoulders, pressing a crimson kiss to his lips. "I wanted to surprise you."

Suddenly, Mia felt invisible. Neither looked her way as they carried on their greetings.

"This is a business trip, not a vacation," Nicholas affirmed.

"But you do come back to the hotel at night," she whispered in his ear, just loud enough for Mia to hear.

This was too much for her to bear. Mia rose from her seat. "I'm going to head back to my room."

"No." Nicholas raised his palm, halting her. "We haven't had dinner."

"I'm not hungry and . . . Renata, is it? I'm sure she wants your undivided attention."

"That's right," Renata said, her voice laced with fake sweetness. "Assistant duties are over." Shooing her away, she said, "You can run along now."

"Mia." Nicholas shook his head. She wasn't sure if the expression on his face meant he was apologetic or guilt-ridden. Either way, it didn't matter. She couldn't dash away fast enough.

Chapter 24

Nicholas

"Sit down," Nicholas demanded, wiping the remnants of Renata's lipstick off his face with his finger and pointing to the chair that Mia had occupied only moments before.

"You don't look happy to see me," the redhead pouted.

"It's time we cleared this up once and for all. I've tried to be a gentleman. I've been politely trying to convey my lack of interest in you but there's no getting through to you." He leaned forward, his hazel eyes darkening dangerously. "We are not a couple. We are not dating," he stated sternly. "You need to stop insinuating yourself into my personal life."

"You had no problem insinuating yourself into my panties." She raised an arched eyebrow.

Without moving a muscle, he shot her a murderous glare. Renata didn't really care for him. She was just like all the others. Nicholas was a prize, and she would stop at nothing to come out the victor. He was sure of that now. Nicholas had been around her kind before, and it was one of his greatest regrets.

"One time," he admitted. Nicholas kept his composure, but his patience was wearing thin. "I made it clear upfront, that it wouldn't lead to anything. But you keep coming around, showing up every place I just happen to be." Nicholas leaned forward, his fists digging into the table. "It stops now. I'm not a man to be toyed with or manip- ulated. Go find someone who wants to play." Abruptly, he got up from the table, threw a few bills down, and walked away.

Pulling out his phone, Nicholas tapped out a text.

Nicholas: *You didn't eat dinner. I hope you ordered room service.*

No response. Ten minutes later, he tried again.

Nicholas: *I'm heading to my room. I'd like to speak to you.*

No response. In the elevator, Nicholas began to formulate another message. Erasing it when he found himself in front of Mia's door, he rapped on it softly instead. Nothing. He rapped harder. Still, she didn't answer.

"Mia, if you're awake, I'd really like to speak to you."

He sighed, relenting. It was late and had been a long day. They had an early call time in the morning, so he presumed Mia had fallen asleep. But a disturbing gnawing crept through his mind. He prayed Mia wasn't about to flee on him again.

* * *

The next morning, Nicholas knocked on Mia's door to escort her to breakfast before heading to the first location shoot. A chime on his phone indicated a message, and he groaned. Mia had already left with the crew, stating that she had details to discuss with them on the way.

Nicholas had hoped to speak privately with her during breakfast. Renata had wreaked havoc on their evening, and he needed to clear up exactly what she was to him. Or rather, what she wasn't.

When he arrived at the Acropolis, the crew was set up and ready to begin. Mia bounced back and forth between the photographer and the models, speaking rapidly and dishing out directives, barely shooting him a glance.

"I see you have everything under control," Nicholas said, sidling up to Mia. "May I have a moment of your time?"

Briefly, Mia looked up from her clip-boarded checklist, offering a pleasant smile. "Good morning." She flipped up to the next page. "The two of you on the right." She pointed. "If you could switch places . . . Great! Thank you." She turned to Nicholas. "Unless there's something you'd like done differently from what you see here, we have no moments. The clock is ticking, and I'm already stressing we won't get this done in three hours."

"Mia." He rested his hands on her shoulders. "Take a breath. We have this covered."

With a steely glare, she peeled his hands off of her. She refused to look up at him for a reaction but heard his low, frustrated groan. Too damned bad, she thought.

"This is new to me. I'm used to having much more time than this." Mia didn't look his way as she spoke. She ran over to the photographer, leaning into him as they conferred.

Nicholas followed on her heels. "We're going to run into this situation many more times," he said. "It's not like booking studio time. You'll adjust."

Mia ignored him.

Finally, Nicholas called her over sternly. "Mia. A word."

She stomped over to where he waited and glared at him. "Well?" she challenged. "The clock is ticking."

"Last I checked, I'm still your boss. I expect you to communicate with me."

"Last I checked," she snapped back, "I answered you each time you spoke. Now, if that's all, time is money."

By nine o'clock, they had successfully gotten through the shot list and packed up for the next location. Once again, Mia headed to the van with the crew, but Nicholas had other ideas.

"You're coming with me," he insisted.

"It's not a good use of time," she argued. "You and I already made all the decisions. I want to go over it with the crew on the way."

"Are you avoiding me?" he asked.

She smiled up at him. "No, not at all. What reason would I have for that?" She crawled into the vehicle, signaling for the driver to take off.

* * *

"I love it!" Penelope exclaimed, coming up behind her brother.

"Pia!" Nicholas embraced his sister with a double-cheek kiss. "I wasn't expecting you this early."

"I happen to love this spin on the issue. I wanted to check it out for myself."

Nicholas pulled up the photos from the morning shoot on the laptop. "Take a look at these."

"Nice." Penelope looked over to Mia. "It looks like she's in her element."

Nicholas glanced at Mia with admiration. "She's incredible. At her work," he added quickly. "Very organized and creative."

A knowing smile crossed Penelope's face. "It's about time, brother."

He furrowed his brow, puzzled.

"I've been waiting for you to fall. I've seen this coming but now it's written all over your face."

His shoulders tensed. "I don't fall," he said defensively.

"She's not Devalina. The complete opposite, I'd say."

"Enough!" Nicholas barked. "Discussion over."

"Tabled until I can speak to you alone," Penelope demanded. "If you think I'm going to let that social-climbing, self-centered bitch ruin your chance at finding the woman truly meant for you, you're delusional." Penelope turned her head around. "Ah! And here she comes. The woman of interest."

"I'm warning you, Pia."

"Let's break for lunch and pick up in an hour," Mia said as she directed the crew over to the building plaza corner where catered food had been brought in.

"Penelope!" Mia came over to greet her.

"I'm impressed, Mia."

"Thank you. Did Nicholas happen to show you the contact sheet from this morning?"

"He did," she answered enthusiastically.

Together, the trio walked over to the craft service table, filled their plates, and found a seat.

Nicholas leaned over and quietly asked, "Maybe we can talk over dinner this evening?"

"I'm visiting my grandparents tonight." Mia looked away. "Besides, I think your evenings are spoken for."

Nicholas let out a heavy sigh. "You won't need to worry about Renata. She's not—"

"I'm not," Mia cut him off sharply before continuing. "I mean, I'm not worried about her because your personal life is not my business." She turned to Penelope. "How long will you be here for?"

"Only a few days. I have to get back," Penelope said regretfully. "But feel free to take a little extra time while you're here."

"Oh, I don't know. We have the next issue to plan."

"And I'm the boss," she pointed out. "If need be, you could always work from here."

"Thank you. That's a nice offer." Popping the last bite of food in her mouth, she declared, "Well, back to work!"

* * *

That evening, as Nicholas and Penelope dined at Spondi, an elegant French restaurant, he willingly regaled her with tales from the previous day's happenings. She had always been the one person in his life he could rely on for a sympathetic ear or honest advice. He told her how he'd discovered that Mia was the girl he'd met many years before, and then of Renata showing up unexpectedly, presumably giving Mia a twisted view of their relationship.

"Stalker!" Penelope sing-songed. "At least you finally got rid of her. Now, my dear brother, what are you going to do about Mia?"

He groaned. "I attempted to pull Mia aside all day but she never gave me the chance to speak to her privately." He picked at an artfully plated seafood appetizer, decoratively garnished with herbed oils. "Honestly, maybe it's for the best."

"No, it is not!" she scolded. "I know you better than anyone else on this planet, and I've never seen you look at anyone the way you look at her."

He eyed his sister skeptically.

"You think I didn't notice?"

"I'm glad you believe yourself so enlightened. Mia is an attractive woman, and I'm a man, after all. But I have my reasons for remaining uninvolved. Devalina is only one part of it."

Penelope reached her hand out to clasp his. "I lost them too." Her voice cracked as she held back a sob. "I miss them, and I hope one day to find the kind of love they had."

Nicholas looked away. "It's easier this way." When he looked up, catching his sister's gaze, he sighed heavily. They were having this heart-to-heart, whether he wanted to or not. "At least they went together and didn't have to mourn for each other. You see what it's like for *Pappou*. He's broken. I refuse to put myself through that. A woman hasn't been born for me to love so much as to destroy me."

Penelope curved her lips into a smile. "We shall see about that." She fell silent for a moment. "Do you believe in destiny?"

Lifting his hands, palms up, he shrugged. "I don't know? Destiny," he spat. "A word people throw around to explain nonsense. Like we have no control over our lives."

"I don't believe you're that cynical." Penelope forked her salad. After biting into the crispy romaine lettuce, she pointed her empty utensil in his direction. "How else but by destiny do you explain that the very girl you had a happenstance meeting with over fifteen years ago turns up in another country working for you? A girl that you offered a sentimental possession to?"

"Coincidence," he said matter-of-factly. "And when did my pragmatic sister start entertaining all these romantic notions?"

"I call it as I see it." Penelope grasped her brother's hand. "Open your eyes. True love is a treasure, a rare discovery. Not to be taken for granted or mishandled."

"What about you?" Nicholas challenged. His sister shouldn't dish out advice she wasn't willing to follow for herself. "Why haven't you searched for it?"

"It's not something you search for. Love finds you at its own pace. I learned that the hard way." Sadness shadowed her face before she concealed it with a smile. "You see!" She perked up. "I am pragmatic. We both need to be, or else the fortune hunters will prowl at our door once more. Jonathan showed his true colors before it was too late, and I suspect the dozens throwing themselves at your feet want your wealth as much as your body."

He laughed humorlessly. "Devalina did, until she discovered working factored into my lifestyle."

"Mia is not Devalina."

"Mia isn't relevant. She barely tolerates me."

"Whatever you say, little brother," she laughed.

* * *

Nicholas called for a separate taxi to take Penelope back to the hotel. Her eyes narrowed with suspicion but, before she had a chance to ask what he was up to, Nicholas shut the passenger door, bidding her goodnight.

When he slipped into his own cab, Nicholas gave his driver the address of a taverna for a street he was not familiar with.

When they arrived, the driver looked him up and down with a scowl. "You sure?" he asked, pointing to a rundown, graffiti-covered building, the sign, which should have read, *Taverna Eleftheria*, instead, due to missing sign letters, said *verna theria*.

Nicholas nodded, paid the driver, and headed into the seedy establishment with a small amount of trepidation. Scanning his surroundings, he saw nothing alarming other than the condition of the place. Everything was old, or maybe merely well-worn. If the patrons noticed, they weren't bothered by it. Old posters hanging by thumbtacks were so faded it was hard to make out what they had once advertised. Background music was only second to the chatter and zealous debates from the four or five occupied tables.

Nicholas strode over to the bar. "I'm here to see Kostas Laskaris."

"Aristedis?" the man pouring drinks asked.

Nicholas nodded.

"He's in the back," he said, pointing to a rickety door. "He's expecting you."

Nicholas knocked as he entered. "Kostas?"

The elderly man stood, limping as he made his way around the scratched-up metal desk. "Yes," he said, extending a hand.

The missing finger on the proffered hand was not the first disfigurement Nicholas noticed. Hair no longer grew where a scar ran from his forehead to the side of his head above his ear.

"What brings you looking for Panayiotis Nikopoulos?" The hard lines of the man's scarred face looked at Nicholas with suspicion.

"I'm a friend of his granddaughter," he explained. "Her grandmother, Panos' wife, is still alive and living in the United States."

Kostas kept his eyes suspiciously trained on Nicholas. "Panos spoke of her constantly. It's what kept him going."

"She's convinced he's still alive. My sources tell me you might know what happened to him."

"We were friends, and . . . we were imprisoned together." Kostas fell silent. "I speak of those times rarely." Lumbering over to a shelf, he grabbed a half-empty bottle of Raki and two glasses. Without a word, he set the glasses on his desk, poured a generous amount in each one, and motioned for Nicholas to sit. "I will tell you what I know, but I'm afraid it won't lead you to the answers you hope for."

"He is a man of courage who does not run away, but remains at his post and fights against the enemy." — Socrates

Chapter 25

Kostas

November 1, 1968

"Papandreou is dead!" Kostas ran down the narrow stone steps leading to a poorly lit basement. Grabbing Panos by the collar, he exclaimed, "News is spreading in the streets but that scum won't announce it on the radio."

That scum, of course, was the current dictator, George Papadopoulos, leader of the Junta, who had overthrown the monarchy and parliament of which Georgios Papandreou had once been Prime Minister before he was forced into house arrest. And now he was dead.

In the lower recesses of a flower shop, the owners and several others ran an underground newspaper sending messages to the resistance. On the surface, it seemed innocent enough, with its articles on floral arrangements and helpful gardening tips. But they were in the thick of a dangerous game, up against an evil and brutal government who would stop at nothing to punish their betrayers.

"Did they kill him?" Panos asked.

"No. He's been sick for a while. It was some sort of blood clot that led to a stroke that killed him."

A young woman around nineteen years old holding a bucket of

daisies descended the stairs. From the flower-stuffed container, she drew out a folded paper, handing it to Kostas. "The funeral is in two days," she whispered, her eyes round and alert. Turning, she scurried away, clutching the cylinder containing her parents' wares.

Kostas and Panos read the instructions carefully before getting to work, printing a special edition of the encrypted newspaper, *Seeds of Prometheus*. They were to gather the masses in protest to honor a man they respected while voicing the citizens' intolerance of the oppression they faced under the current ruler.

"If we don't draw a huge crowd, the result will be disastrous," Kostas warned.

"And if we do, we'll succeed in making them look weak in the eyes of the world."

Kostas cupped his friend's shoulders. "They don't care what the world thinks of them, my friend."

* * *

Kostas, Panos, and the rest of their posse were a small group compared to the mourners who flooded Athens' streets on the day of the funeral. Over three hundred thousand people paid their respects to the 'Old Man of Democracy.' Kostas believed they had made a considerable contribution to the crowd's size, as they had distributed the paper all over Athens, asking everyone to 'buy their flowers.' But the majority of mourners came on their own, walking in procession behind the car transporting the casket through Syntagma Square to the church.

It was a slap in Papadopoulos' face. Kostas grinned. The people were speaking out. No! They were shouting out—thousands of voices as one. The resistance had rallied the chant and, like a contagion, it could not be stopped. "Democracy! Down with the Junta!" they roared. "The people will win! Freedom!"

Kostas, Panos, and the other protestors incited the chants through a megaphone. There had to be over fifty members from their organization urging on the protesters. But the Greek people, who had fought and clawed their way back to independence many times throughout history, would stop at nothing to do it once again.

"Spread out," the leader ordered. "They're watching us."

The military police surveyed the situation, refraining from taking action, yet ready to interfere at any given moment should violence break out. Restraint was not in their vocabulary. Dragging citizens off for expressing anti-Junta opinions or being struck with a pipe for blatantly singing a song by a banned artist had become an everyday occurrence.

Forbidding mourners from paying respects to the dead would have angered the Greek Orthodox Church and create more dissension. That would only make matters worse and would be used as a trump card to rile up the masses. The resistance was well aware of this.

"We'll be no good to the cause if they arrest us," Panos said. "Disappear into the crowd," he told Kostas.

"We can't leave everyone behind," Kostas argued.

"They'll start identifying us if we remain in a cluster, and our cover will be blown."

But the police had grown agitated. As the resistance began to disperse into the crowd, screams began to replace the chants. MPs closed in, swinging batons, unconcerned if they caused severe bodily injury. One woman was dragged by her hair, lifted off her feet, and arrested. Others were struck at the knees and hauled away. Later they would learn over forty people had been arrested, many from their own faction. With democracy snuffed out like sand shoveled over a campfire, there would be no trial—only punishment.

* * *

Almost an entire year had passed since the funeral protest. They had lost some key players on that fateful day and many others during smaller demonstrations.

"What are we doing here?" Panos asked, slumping his body against a large piece of equipment. The collating machine began spitting out page after page. Panos positioned himself to catch the papers as they flew out, stacking them neatly in a pile. "We've accomplished nothing," he complained, his cigarette angrily bobbing from his lips as he spoke. Frustrated, he threw the butt on the floor, stamping it out with the toe of his shoe.

"I understand your frustration but we knew this was going to be a test of patience and fortitude." Kostas grabbed Panos by the face. "Don't give up now."

"I miss my wife. My daughter is being raised without me." Panos hung his head. "She won't even know who I am."

"She will. She will! You'll send for them when a restored Greece emerges."

"*Styn patrítha!*" A mop-haired man in torn jeans came barreling down the stairs.

"To the homeland!" Kosta repeated. "What's the news, Manolis?"

"The plan is set, and I'll need the two of you to create the diversion," Manolis said.

"What plan?" Panos looked to both of them.

"My team created a bomb large enough to blast the entire parliament building. I'll need the two of you to distract the military police with a smaller explosion several blocks away."

"The old palace?" Panos shook his head vigorously. "No. That's a historic building."

Manolis laughed. "It's not the Parthenon or the Temple of Apollo. It's not even two hundred years old, much less two thousand. Our aim is not the building but to rid ourselves of as many in the regime as possible."

Kostas slapped Panos on the back. "You won't be doing the bombing. Don't let that concern you."

"All you need to do is lead the police away from parliament," Manolis said. "It's all set for tomorrow morning."

Panos grabbed at his hair, shaking his head in disagreement. "This doesn't seem right to me."

Kostas braced his friend by the shoulders. "Look at me," he ordered. "Have I ever steered you wrong? No one is getting hurt here, Panos. Just a few falling bricks."

Manolis slid a bookcase away from the wall. Behind it was a gaping hole in the concrete. He reached in and pulled out a duffle bag. "Here are the explosives for the diversion. Inside are the instructions for the exact location and the time to set them off." He handed them to Kostas. "Everything you need to know is in there." Manolis raced halfway up the steps and halted. "Don't disappoint me," he warned, his eyes trained on Panos before he retreated, climbing the staircase two steps at a time.

* * *

The next day, Kostas and Panos spent the early hours delivering flowers. They planned their route to arrive at the designated location at exactly nine forty-six in the morning.

Kostas was revved up and excited; energy emanated from him like a missile about to launch. Panos, on the other hand, was fraught with nerves. He didn't like the whole idea and told Kostas so.

"It's a foolproof plan. Nothing to worry about. Manolis has it all covered," Kostas assured his friend.

Their last stop was a hair salon about four blocks from Syntagma Square. Next to it, the abandoned storefront with its windows covered by large sheets of paper was the targeted address.

While Panos delivered the flowers to the receptionist, Kostas cut the window glass and entered the failed and now empty café. In unison, they exited the doors, ran into the florist's van, and began to ride away just as the thunderous rumble from the bomb sounded. Kostas drove ahead but Panos looked back at the destruction and cried out in anguish. Bits of concrete erupted everywhere like volcanic lava. But that wasn't the worst of it. The bomb was meant to only have enough power to take out a fifty-five-square meter space. Either Manolis miscalculated, or he lied. Instead, the explosion also struck the establishments on either side of the abandoned store. Panos, riddled with guilt and remorse, thought of the salon where he'd just delivered flowers and the sweet girl who'd accepted them at the front desk.

"Kostas!" The bellowing cry rumbled from deep within Panos' soul.

"That wasn't supposed to happen," Kostas shouted, slamming his fist to the steering wheel. There was panic in his voice.

"They're running out!" Panos panted, relieved as he looked out the rear window of the van. "I pray they're all safe. We need to go back and help."

"Are you crazy? We need to get out of here and fast!"

But that was not to be. As Kostas sped down the street, the van was blockaded by military jeeps. Kostas frantically threw the car in reverse, but it was a futile move. They were surrounded in both directions.

"We need to run," Kostas shouted.

"To where?" Panos asked with resignation. "It's over, Kosta," he declared, succumbing to his fate.

Just then, several military men marched over and banged at the vehicle windows with their rifles. Kostas and Panos protected their faces with their arms as shards of glass rained down upon them. The officers reached inside, unlocking the doors and yanking them open.

"We'll deliver you dead or alive," one of them shouted as he dragged Panos from the van. The other knuckled Kostas in the face before pulling him out and throwing him on the ground. They were cuffed, laughed at, spit upon, and kicked in the stomach several times. The last thing Kostas remembered was being lifted into a military vehicle before receiving a blow to the head.

Chapter 26

Kostas

October, 1969

The damp surface of the concrete floor chilled Kostas' sore bones. When he dragged himself up, propping his back against the wall, his head throbbed, and he felt as though lead bricks were pressing on his chest.

The room was dark. Only slivers of light bled through the steel bars barricading a small window. It was difficult for Kostas to survey his surroundings with blurred vision in one eye and the other swollen shut.

The fluid on the floor, he discovered, was not moisture from the dampness seeping through the wall cracks. It was urine and blood, pooled around him, beneath him . . . all over him. Visions flashed before his eyes. Sadistic and demonic. For the moments when he'd remained conscious, the humiliations he endured was nothing in comparison to the excruciating pain.

Kostas feared that this was only the beginning. The clanging of keys, loud voices, and the creaking of a heavy-sounding door terrified him. A limp body was flung against him like a rag doll, followed by a harrowing groan. Startled, Kostas wondered if he could live through another round of torture. When a string of obscenities was aimed in his direction before the slamming of the door, Kostas knew he was spared additional abuse . . . for now.

With what little strength he had left, Kostas rolled the man off his own bruised body. Barely able to make out the man's face, Kostas gasped when recognition struck. He choked out, "Panos?"

"Kostas? Is that you?" Panos groaned.

"It's me, my friend." Kostas couldn't believe his eyes. Had Panos endured even more than he had? One eye was cut and swollen, and that wasn't all. His left ear was missing. "What did they do to you?"

"Do I need to tell you? It looks as though you've suffered the same punishment."

"I still have all my body parts," Kostas said, laboring to speak. "At least I think I do."

"They sentenced us to eight years in this hell," Panos told him. "They stomped on my chest with the heel of their boots when they told me."

"Sentenced," Kostas spat weakly. "As though we had a trial. They should just kill me and get it over with."

"That would be a mercy their worm-infested hearts would never grant." Panos coughed, the simple act causing him shooting pain. "They asked for names," he whispered.

"I know." Kostas nodded. "Me too."

I spit in their face," Panos said proudly. Lifting his hand over what little was left of his ear, he said, "My punishment."

* * *

Days went by, then months, until Kostas could no longer keep count. He surmised summer had come as the nights he and Panos shivered in their cell had finally passed. There were weeks when they were left untouched, only seeing guards momentarily when meager amounts of food were pushed through the door. At other times, they became objects of sport or entertainment. Kicked around like a football or pounded at like a punching bag.

Listening to constant screams of terror was almost as bad as the physical beatings—insidious torture on the psyche. At first, listening to another's torment was unbearable, until relief set in that, this time, it wasn't him. The longer it went on, and it often did throughout the night, the deeper the horror crept into his mind, controlling every thought and fear. Wondering, wondering when they would come for him next.

And they did. Many times, and after what he estimated to be two years of incarceration, he and Panos endured another cruel and sadistic game at the hands of the Junta.

"Strip down, you two," a guard ordered as he entered their cell. "Everything. Now!"

When they did as he asked, their captor tied a black blindfold over their eyes. With a rifle pointed to their backs, he pushed them forward. Neither dared to say a word or ask a question. Kostas began to breathe heavily, and he could tell Panos was also nervously gasping for air.

When they reached their destination, a courtyard within the prison walls, the guard lined them up, along with several others. Kostas could not surmise how many, but from the shuffling of feet dragging across the gravel, it had to be more than a dozen men.

"If you're the praying kind, I'd say one now," a guard shouted to the sightless prisoners. The laugh that followed held a tremendous amount of sinister pleasure. "Men," he addressed his firing squad. "Take aim. Shoot on my count of five."

Kostas trembled. He never honestly expected to come out of this prison alive. Still, faced with the reality of it at that moment, he was overcome with a myriad of emotions. Terror, for what he'd suffer when the bullet hit. Regret, for ever thinking he could fight an unbeatable monster. Deep, deep sadness for a life snuffed out too soon. He wasn't sure what came next. He'd always thought the afterlife was the human delusional idea for immortality. With his end looming just seconds away, he now felt doubt and confusion. He wanted to cling to the belief that paradise did indeed exist. Otherwise, what was the point of everything they had endured?

Slowly, the sadistic barbarian counted off. "*Ena, thyo . . .*" He paused. Walking over to the lineup, he addressed the prisoners. "Should I let one of you live?"

They knew better than to dare and answer.

He walked away, shouting out, "*Trea.*"

Kostas wished he would get it over with already. His heart hammered so hard in his chest; it could have broken a rib.

"*Téssera.*"

One more number and his hell would end.

Nothing. Kostas waited and waited. The anticipation was soul-crushing. Fear gripped him like a sharp-edged vice penetrating every layer of flesh.

"Guns down," the guard ordered. "Take these pathetic weaklings back to their cells."

Kostas didn't dare break down. The lone man that did, falling to his knees, sobbing, was shot on the spot. Somehow, through that exercise of mental torture, he found the strength to wait until his jailer shut the door behind him and had marched away.

Kostas and Panos looked to one another, traumatized. Panos held out his arms and the men embraced, quietly crying as they comforted each other.

"I wish they had done it," Kostas confessed. "I can't take it anymore."

"We have to survive," Panos said, desperation and a large dose of determination urging him on.

Kostas knew what drove his friend. His family. Kalliope and Melina were all he thought of. But Kostas had no one to live for.

Little did they know that it would take another four years for the regime to fall apart at the hands of their own missteps. It wasn't until that victorious day that Kostas, Panos, and the rest of the prisoners were finally set free.

Chapter 27

Nicholas

Nicholas scrubbed his hands over his face. He was emotionally drained and imagined Kostas was more so after reliving the torment through his telling. And Nicholas suspected this was only half the horror. Did he even want to know how the scar on his head came to be? He glanced at the missing finger on the old man's left hand and shuddered.

"I was lucky," Kostas said when he caught Nicholas staring at the missing digit. "They threatened to cut off the whole hand."

"Lucky?" Nicholas said with incredulous disgust. He swallowed nervously, his Adam's apple bobbing in his throat. "I knew of the dictatorship on an academic level, of course. But to hear . . . this." He took a deep gulp of his drink. "My grandfather doesn't speak much about that time. His family left Greece right before the coup. It was as though he predicted what was coming."

"Some fled while others stayed to fight." There was no judgment in Kosta's words. "Wise or idealistic. What was the better choice?" He used his hand to mimic a balancing scale. "In the end, our efforts and protests didn't matter. The regime crumbled from within."

"If I may, what happened to Panos? Is he still alive? If so, do you know where I can find him?"

"So many questions." Kostas attempted a smile. "The answer is, I don't know. We parted ways shortly after our release. I suppose it was too painful a reminder for both of us to stay in touch."

"Did Panos say whether he was planning to return to his wife?"

"Trust me, if Panos was able to make his way back to Kalliope, he would have." Kostas pursed his lips, hesitating. Pressing his fingers to his forehead as though smoothing out the wrinkles, he contemplated his next words. "You must understand, neither one of us came out of that hell the way we went in. Much had been taken from us, physically and psychologically. In many ways, Panos fell victim to the worst of it."

Nicholas nodded solemnly. "I'm sorry. For what you endured and for making you relive the memories."

"It was a long time ago. A lifetime." Kostas slapped his hand on Nicholas' back. "It's my turn to ask the questions. "Kalliope? You said she's alive. Is she well?"

"Yes, she is. I've only met her a few times but she's a remarkable woman. I've never met anyone with such faith. She's convinced her husband is still alive and would come to her if he could."

Kostas nodded. "I'm certain that's true. He was a man in love. But why go to such lengths for an old woman you barely know?"

"I'm acquainted with her granddaughter and . . . "

"And . . ." Kostas prodded, a sparkle in his eyes.

"And it's a fascinating story."

"Right," Kostas laughed.

* * *

Nicholas began the next day fatigued from lack of sleep. All night he mulled over the information he'd learned from Kostas. The only news to report back to Mia's grandmother was that her husband had been imprisoned and brutally tortured. He had no evidence that Panos was even still alive, yet found no record of his death to give the woman closure. All he could offer were second-party accounts that would wound her soul.

But Nicholas suspected Kostas had omitted information that could lead him to the missing man, and he was determined to find out what that was and why Kostas had kept it from him. One way or another, he would find out what happened to Panayiotis Nikopoulos.

Nicholas remained silent in the car on his way to the set location. He couldn't bring himself to look at Mia. Offering a gruff morning greeting, he slipped into the backseat of the car alongside her. He pretended to concentrate on incoming emails, keeping his eyes trained on his mobile phone.

"Have I done something to upset you?" Mia's voice quivered.

Nicholas looked up from his phone. "No. Not at all. I apologize." He smiled, but it didn't reach his eyes. "I have a lot on my mind." He didn't have the heart to tell her what he'd learned. He had spent half the night detailing an email to the private investigator who'd found Kostas. Something Kostas said might give him another lead.

"Anything I can help with?" she asked.

"No, not yet." Mia went full-on Hellenic today, he noticed. She wore a lightweight, long-sleeve, cotton dress with a Greek key design at the neckline and hem. The length could be mistaken for an oversized shirt rather than a frock, but he wasn't complaining as he admired her legs from thigh to ankle.

"Forgive my manners. How was your visit with your grandparents?" Nicholas inquired.

"It was wonderful to see them. Thank you for asking." She closed her laptop. "I haven't seen them since—"

"Since you were twelve years old," he interjected. "I know." Nicholas examined Mia's face, wondering how it was that he hadn't recognized her. She was older, a woman now. More beautiful but her features remained very much the same. And those eyes . . . Those unmistakable eyes dripped with the same compassion she had held for him all those years ago. Even when she was cross with him, the essence of her soul bled through.

The rest of the day went relatively smoothly except for one maddening photographer. He continually eyed Mia throughout the day, flirting with her at every opportunity. Other than that infuriating display, the models cooperated, and so did the weather. They even wrapped up for the day earlier than expected, which prompted the damned photographer to shamelessly ask Mia out for drinks.

"She has other plans," Nicholas snarled, stepping between them. A physicist would say that fire and ice in the same space was an impossibility. But there it was. Flames lashed from Nicholas' eyes while his demeanor remained frozen. "And we leave now." Taking Mia by the arm, he dragged her away.

"That was rude!" she blurted.

"He's an old lech," he retorted. "Would you have really taken him up on his offer?"

"He's hardly old."

"Too old for you." He ran a hand frustratingly through his hair. "Would you have accepted?"

"No! Not that it's any of your business." Mia whispered something under her breath.

"What? I didn't quite make that out."

She looked up at him, her eyes wide. "I said, I learned long ago never to take drinks from strange men." She drew her gaze to the ground. "I'll meet you in the car," she grumbled, stomping away.

Nicholas, shaking his head at his overreaction, followed her into the vehicle. But for his sighs, he remained silent. For a girl who claimed to have no story, Nicholas was discovering there was so much more to her than she let on.

"I'm sorry," Nicholas apologized. "I was out of line."

"You must think very little of me if you think I'd go off with some guy nearly twice my age."

"On the contrary. I think very highly of you," Nicholas admitted. After a pause, he took a chance. "You accepted a drink from me."

"What? Oh," she said on a sigh. "You're a strange man, Nicholas Aristedis, but you're not a stranger." A hint of a smile crossed her lips.

He supposed his behavior toward her would be regarded as rather odd.

"I have an appointment this evening," he blurted.

"A date, you mean?" Mia pried.

"About that. We need to clear up a misconception. Renata is not my girlfriend. I'm not involved with her in any manner," Nicholas explained.

Mia's brows drew together in confusion. "She followed you to Athens."

"Exactly. Subtlety hasn't worked, so I, unfortunately, had to make myself brutally clear, and thankfully, she's now gone." Nicholas waved the subject away. "Anyway, Penelope would like you to join her for dinner. I'll meet you both afterward, if you agree."

"I'd like that. Thank you."

Nicholas wasn't ready to share who he was meeting with that evening or why. If all went as he'd hoped, maybe soon he'd have news to report to Mia and her family.

Chapter 28

Mia

"You just got here! You're leaving already?" Mia couldn't imagine flying across the Atlantic only to stay for two days.

She and Penelope were seated at a little, out-of-the-way taverna, frequented mainly by locals. String lights hung overhead, connected by the awning to street-lined trees. Magenta bougainvillea crept up the stone wall while clay pots holding geraniums lined the restaurant entrance walkway.

"I need to get back, but I wanted to take the opportunity to come on location and, while I'm here, visit a friend or two," Penelope explained. "It's not unusual for me to hop on a plane for a quick visit."

Mia savored a bite of food as if it were a religious experience. The fish was broiled with lemon, garlic, and oregano. So much oregano. It was fragrant and delicious, and she'd never had seafood as fresh as this.

Penelope rested her hands under her chin, watching Mia's ecstasy over the food with amusement.

"Well, if I have to get on a plane for any longer than three hours, I'm going to make it worth my while." Mia raised her glass as though making a toast.

"Then don't hurry home," Penelope said. "I suggested to Nicholas that the two of you stay a little longer."

"That's very nice of you, but why? We have the next issue to brainstorm."

"And you have your laptops," Penelope pointed out. You can certainly work from here while also enjoying yourselves."

Mia leaned back in her chair. "I don't know. Your brother can barely stand my company for too long. Just this morning, we rode to the set location in silence. What makes you think he'll agree to this?"

Penelope raised an eyebrow. "He already has," she said smugly. Crossing her arms over her chest, she stared at Mia, deciding what to say next. "You have my brother all wrong. He's not been himself lately, and it's mostly because of you."

Mia's eye's flashed with alarm.

"I can't explain away all his odd behavior but I know he likes you. He told me the two of you discovered you'd met before." Penelope lifted her hands, palms up. "What are the chances?"

"We were kids. It doesn't mean he likes the adult version of me."

"Oh, but he does," Penelope assured her. "You need to trust me on this. I can't say too much. It's not up to me, but Nicholas has been working on something that involves you, and it didn't work out as he'd hoped. That accounted for his mood this morning."

Mia was more confused than before. How can someone say so much and, at the same time, offer nothing substantial? Just as she was about to attempt prodding Penelope for more details, Nicholas strode over, taking a seat beside her.

"I was just telling Mia that the two of you are free to stay on for several days longer."

"I don't—" Mia began.

"It's all been arranged," he told his sister. Turning to face Mia, he said, "Since you'd mentioned that Athens was the only part of Greece you got to see on your last visit, I thought it would be nice to take you elsewhere."

"That's very nice of both of you but I'm ready to go home and get back to work."

"We can work here just as well. It's all settled," Nicholas stated. "We leave for Mykonos tomorrow afternoon."

* * *

If Mia's face was pressed up against the car window any harder, her features would have been permanently reshaped. This was the Greece she saw in travel ads and magazines. Athens had a charm of its own, rich in history and ancient structures. But it was still a city, noisy and overcrowded. Mykonos looked like it was created from a magical, mystical realm. The reflection from the sun danced like diamonds sparkling above the waves in the vivid, crystal-blue waters. She'd always assumed, as only a person in her industry would, that the images she'd admired of the whitewashed buildings against the Aegean backdrop had to have been retouched. Not so, she discovered, and it astounded her.

But for appreciative sighs along with exclamations of wonder, Mia made no comment, nor was she aware of Nicholas' amusement over her enthusiasm.

Finally, just before they pulled up to his home, he spoke. "Clearly, we need to have you travel more often."

"I've always wanted to," Mia answered. "My vacations have been limited to the States."

When they stopped in front of a coastally situated home in Tourlos, an area less than ten minutes away from Little Venice by car, Mia's eyes widened.

"I thought you said you kept a modest home in Mykonos?" Mia asked, turning to face Nicholas.

"There are others here that are much larger than this one," he said. "Ten or twelve bedrooms. This one only has five."

"Only?" she laughed. "Wow, it's a shack then."

Nicholas came around to her side of the vehicle, escorting her from the car. He asked the driver to bring their luggage into the house while he showed Mia around.

The house was bathed in white. Not only the exterior but the inside as well. White walls. A white, winding staircase. White furniture but for some sand-colored accents. Panoramic windows and glass doors lead to the veranda, overlooking a luxurious infinity pool, giving off the illusion of a waterfall spilling into the Aegean Sea.

"This is the most beautiful house I've ever seen." Mia wanted to pinch herself to make sure she wasn't dreaming. "Do you spend a lot of time here?"

"No, not as much as I'd like to," Nicholas admitted. "Let me show you to your room." As they walked up the stairs, he asked her, "Would you prefer to go into town to eat tonight, or would you like to stay in and watch the sunset while we dine here?"

"I'm dying to see all of Mykonos but that can wait. I'd love to see the view from here."

"I was hoping you'd say that," Nicholas said. "A quiet evening after traveling would be my preference too." He opened a door, gesturing for Mia to enter. "This is your room. Please make yourself at home."

A soothing shade of washed-out beach-blue accented the predominantly white room. Periwinkle hydrangeas in sand-colored ceramic vases and a delicate chandelier hanging over the bed added feminine elements to the space. But what drew Mia's attention were the French doors leading onto a small balcony. She practically skipped over to them like a child excited by a playground.

Opening the doors, Mia stepped out and gasped. "I said I wanted to see all of Mykonos, and I think I can from right here!"

Nicholas came up alongside her. "It doesn't take much to please you, does it?"

She turned to look at this most handsome, confusing enigma of a man. One minute, Nicholas was cross with her, and the next, he was offering her the world.

"This," she said with awe, "this is everything." Gripping the guardrail,

Mia closed her eyes, lifting her face to feel the warm breeze brush over her skin. She drew in a deep breath, taking in the pleasant scent of salt and sea, committing it all to memory. Nicholas was close. So close, in fact, that she could almost feel electrically charged ions ricocheting between their bodies. He stared down at her, and when Mia looked up at him, her breathing grew shallow. Nicholas brought his hands up to caress her face, but he let his arms fall before touching her.

"I'll meet you on the veranda," he said abruptly, digging his hands into his trouser pockets before walking away.

Mia's nose followed the tantalizing aroma of what she was sure had to be a dish that included truffles. The rest of the ingredients didn't matter was because if truffles were presented to her on a sheet of cardboard, she'd most likely eat it, savoring every last bite.

She'd freshened up and slipped into a white piqué sheath dress. Her pale rose teardrop earrings swayed as she walked in her matching blush-colored high-heeled sandals.

Mia found Nicholas on the veranda, his back to her as he peered out over the horizon. Even from behind, he was attractive, she thought. Impeccably dressed in ecru linen trousers and a crisp white shirt, she admired his lean yet muscular form.

Mia caught his attention with the click-clack of her heels hitting the chalk-colored, travertine patio. Turning, he smiled and pulled out a chair in a gesture for Mia to join him at the elaborately set table.

"Wine?" Nicholas asked as he poured, not waiting for her response. "Thank you."

A spinach salad garnished with pomegranate seeds and pine nuts and topped with manouri cheese was placed before her.

"A toast." Nicholas raised his glass. "To sharing sunsets and successful photo shoots."

Mia's soft laugh revealed her shyness as she focused on the clinking of their glasses rather than on Nicholas.

Nicholas made small talk while the sun slowly began to dip into the sea. As he served Mia a generous helping of pasta with truffle sauce, her mouth watered from the aroma alone. She wasn't sure what she appreciated more—the dish she was about to devour or the explosion of pinks and oranges before her, creating a kaleidoscope of color in the sky.

"Before the sun is completely swallowed up," he said, standing, "let's get a better view." Nicholas extended his hand, and Mia took it, letting him guide her past the infinity pool and down a set of stone steps leading to a private beach.

"I've seen some beautiful sunsets but nothing as stunning as this," she raved.

Nicholas, his attention solely on Mia, said, "And I've seen some beautiful women but none as lovely as the one standing before me."

Mia didn't know what to make of his compliment. Her stomach flip-flopped, and her heart skipped several beats. This was the man who had once told her he was attracted to her against his will. Time and time again, he'd been harsh with her. Mia didn't dare trust his words.

"Why did you bring me here?" There was trepidation in her question.

Nicholas seemed puzzled. "You've been working hard, and we've traveled all this way. It seemed a shame if you didn't have a few days to enjoy yourself."

Mia looked down at the shoes she had discarded in the sand. Maybe she was reading too much into his motives. There was a time when her nature had been far more trusting. She bent down to retrieve her shoes and head back to the house, but Nicholas stopped her. He ran a hand through his hair, his expression looking as though he was warring with his emotions.

"That's not it," he admitted. "No, it is. You do deserve a few days off. But the truth is, I want to spend time with you. There, I've said it."

"There, I've said it?" Mia repeated. "It's that painful for you to like me?"

"Yes." He groaned. "No! I haven't done this in a long time, and I vowed I never would."

"Never would what?" Mia was utterly confused.

"Never get emotionally attached."

Mia drew her eyebrows together. "To anyone? What about all the women you've dated?"

He shook his head. "None were serious. None were what I'd call a relationship. Not in a very long time anyway."

"How long?"

"About ten years," Nicholas said.

"Why?"

"I have my reasons."

Mia scooped up her shoes and began to walk away. "That's not an answer."

"Wait!" Nicholas pleaded. "I'll explain. But can we do it sitting down face to face?"

"Yes, of course."

Nicholas took her by the shoulders. "But that will require you answering some of my questions too."

"That's fine. I'm pretty much an open book."

He laughed. "Not so. I have to pry the pages of your metaphorical book open bit by bit."

Gently, he took her hand, kissing the inside of her palm. Mia shivered at the unexpected contact.

"Before we go up, I need you to understand my sincerity and regard for you," he whispered.

"Okay," Mia said nervously.

Nicholas pulled her in by the waist, closing the space between them, hoping to evaporate the tension and uncertainty he had created. Looking deeply into her eyes, he uttered not a single word. Instead, he ran a finger softly along her jawline before leaning down to finally claim her lips.

The first time he'd kissed her was born from gratitude and his urgent need for comfort. Regardless, she still tingled from the memory of his mouth on hers every time she thought of it. This kiss was different— passionate yet brimming with longing. It held a sweet promise while dominating without forcing her to relinquish control she wasn't ready to give up.

The sun had disappeared as a crescent moon rose. The sky darkened as the kiss lingered and deepened. Mia didn't want the moment to end. But they had much to discuss, and she had a feeling it would be a long night.

Pomegranate Spinach Salad

Salad ingredients

6 ounces fresh baby spinach

½ cup pomegranate seeds

¼ cup pine nuts

4 ounces manouri cheese

Salad dressing

½ cup olive oil

½ cup sherry

1 tablespoon rice wine vinegar

2 teaspoons pomegranate balsamic glaze

2 teaspoons honey

A dash of salt & pepper

1 teaspoon dried tarragon

Method

Remove the seeds from the pomegranate by slicing it in half. Hold one of the halves in the palm of your hand, face down. With a heavy utensil, whack the pomegranate repeatedly until all the seeds fall out. Set aside.

With a fork, break apart the manouri cheese into small chunks and set aside. Manouri is a semi-soft, creamy cheese produced mainly in Northern Greece. You can find it in Greek, and often Italian, grocery stores, as well as specialty cheese shops. Ricotta salata, from Italy, is very similar and can easily be substituted.

Place spinach in a large bowl. Carefully drizzle just enough of the dressing to lightly coat the salad. Add the pomegranate seeds and pine nuts and toss. Top with the manouri cheese. Garnish with additional seeds for a burst of color.

"Nothing is more noble, nothing more venerable, than loyalty." — *Cicero*

Chapter 29

Nicholas

Summer 2009

At twenty-two years old, Nicholas didn't expect to have his life planned out already. Most young men his age about to graduate from college looked forward to years of unencumbered adult freedom. But Nicholas wasn't like most young men. Losing half his family at the tender age of twelve had a profound impact on him. Further devastation hit when his beloved grandmother passed away a few years later. Nicholas craved a sense of security. He longed for that one person to count on—a partner—a person with whom to build his future. Devalina was that woman. Born of an Indian mother and a British father, they met during their sophomore year at the University of the Arts in London. He instantly fell head-over-heels for her beauty, wit, and positive outlook on life. Along with his roommate and best chum, Ian, the three became inseparable.

Ian was an intelligent student; however, he focused more on his social life, whereas Nicholas was quite the opposite. He'd often forgo a campus soiree to work on a project or practice his design skills. Devalina toed the line between her work/fun balance and would often head out on her own, leaving Nicholas to his studies. At the time, he never gave it a thought. His girlfriend wanted the full college experience while Nicholas preferred to focus on his education.

With a week away from graduation, Nicholas had formulated a plan—one he had not yet proposed to his girlfriend. He and Devalina would marry, work their way up in his grandfather's publishing company, and eventually become a powerhouse duo in the magazine industry. They had discussed their career paths many times in hypotheticals, had both even fantasized about taking the industry by storm. Now, he would officially ask her to be his wife and make it all happen as they'd both dreamed.

With this in mind, Nicholas hopped on a plane to Athens to meet with his grandfather's friend, a prominent jeweler. After selecting a classic, round two-carat diamond solitaire, Nicholas couldn't wait to get back to London. With the ring burning a hole in his pocket and his love for Devalina searing his heart, Nicholas took an earlier flight back than he'd initially planned. The result of that decision changed the course of his life in a way he'd never expected.

For about the hundredth time, Nicholas patted the box bulging in his front trouser pocket, checking obsessively for the engagement ring. He was excited to show it to Ian and tell him what he was about to do.

"Hey, Ian. Are you in?" he asked as he unlocked the room to their dorm.

"Fuck," Ian gasped, pulling the bedsheet over his companion's head.

"Oh! My apologies," Nicholas exclaimed. "I didn't know you had someone in here."

"It's okay, man," Ian sputtered nervously.

Nicholas was about to exit until something odd registered in his mind. Pivoting around, he asked, "What's Devalina's bag doing here?"

"Ugh, is that hers?" Ian asked. "She must have left it behind."

Nicholas' face hardened. "From last weekend?" Bending down, he lifted a shoe off the floor. "And this?" he asked. "She left her shoes too?" Rage began to simmer from within. He hoped to God there was a good explanation before his temper erupted. "Ian? Who's under the covers?"

"Nick, come on."

"Ian, who is in bed with you?" Nicholas demanded. The answer was in Ian's silence. Nicholas stomped over to the bed, yanking the sheet away. Devalina shot up, draping the sheet around her bare body. She looked up at Nicholas, her honey-topaz eyes apologizing through a fearful expression.

Nicholas balled his hands into tight fists until his skin turned bright red. He remained stiffly frozen in place. His breathing labored, Nicholas looked as though he was about to explode.

"Nick," Devalina whimpered.

That's all it took to rouse Nicholas from his stupor. He picked up the first thing in his sight, a laptop, grunting loudly as he tossed it across the room. Turning, he stormed out of the room, kicking everything in his path.

"Oh, Nicky," Penelope cried over the phone. "My poor brother. I'd hop on a plane right now if I could."

"I'll be okay," he said. He had gotten used to burying his hurts. He'd just push this one aside too, as best as he could manage. "I'll see you at graduation."

"Get a hotel for the next week, or better yet, throw Ian out and tell him to stay with that whore."

"Pia, she's not a whore."

"Don't defend her! I'm looking out for you. I don't owe her any consideration, and neither do you."

Later, after Nicholas had roamed the campus, torturing himself with questions on what had gone wrong, he had returned to his room. Ian refused to meet his gaze. His suitcase was on his bed with a pile of clothing haphazardly thrown in it.

"I'll be out of your way in a few minutes," Ian said quietly.

Nicholas glared at Ian. "Are you staying with her?" He shouldn't care. But for Nicholas, this was a double betrayal. Ian was his best friend.

"I'm bunking with James."

"Why?" He had to know. How could the love of his life and his best friend do such a thing? What had he done wrong?

"Why?" Ian sneered. "Get your head out of your ass." He dumped the contents of a dresser drawer into a suitcase, zipping it shut force-fully. "You're a bore. The girl was looking for a little fun." He pushed past Nicholas, knocking his shoulder on the way out.

Nicholas sat at his desk chair, staring blankly at the black screen of his computer monitor, mulling over Ian's accusations. Was it a crime to take his studies seriously? And a drag to plan for the future? To work hard to reach a goal? He'd been doing it for both himself and Devalina, who, he believed, was on the same career path as he was. He felt like such a fool. Nicholas pounded his fist on the desk, knocking his books to the floor. He didn't even hear the knocking on his door.

"Nicholas?" Devalina called out, rapping harder.

"Go away!"

"We need to talk," she begged.

"I think your actions spoke loud and clear."

"Open the door, Nick."

Nicholas shuffled across the room. Opening the door, he blocked the entrance with his body.

Devalina sighed in exasperation. "I'm not having this conversation in the hallway."

"Fine. Enter." He swept his hand, reluctantly inviting her in. "Explain away your betrayal after I devoted three years of my life to you."

"Devoted?" She laughed humorlessly. "The definition for devoted is to be very loving and loyal. And you are. Devoted to your ambition, but not to me."

"That's not fair," Nicholas defended himself. "I thought we were on the same page. We had plans—goals."

"You had plans, mapping out our entire future. I've barely entered my twenties, and you know what? I'm looking for some fun and adventure."

"And I could have given that to you."

"Really? What have we done together this year except for working on class projects?" Devalina asked. "How many times have we been out together? How many parties did I go to on my own?"

"On your own but not alone," Nicholas accused.

"I'm sorry, Nick. I truly am." She placed her hand on his forearm, and he flinched. "I didn't mean for it to happen. It just did, and this wasn't the way I wanted you to find out." Unconsciously, she twirled her thick mane of her dark ponytail around her finger. "Look, I didn't take a gap year after completing school but I intend to after graduation. I don't want to jump right into a life of responsibility. Ian feels the same."

Nicholas ruffled a hand through his hair. "You'll take a gap year together?"

"Seems so," Devalina said. "We want the same things, and he can give them to me."

"I could have given you everything." Desperation coated his words. "Why do you think I worked so hard? I sacrificed now for the life we wanted later." He ran his hand through his hair. "Do you think I don't like to have fun? You were my escape from the stress, the work, the exams."

"I'm twenty-one," Devalina pointed out. "I can't get these years back. When I'm forty and tied down with responsibility, I don't want to have regrets."

"You should have spoken to me. An honest person doesn't sleep with her boyfriend's best friend." The memory of their betrayal stabbed him deeply, and he imagined it would for some time. "She breaks it off gently before picking it up with the other guy," he said with disgust, glaring at her.

"Nicky . . ."

"Don't call me that," he barked. "You lost your right to use endearments."

He strode over to the door, opening it forcefully. "You're not at all who I thought you were. Please leave."

Devalina looked at him sadly, remorse shadowing her features. "I am truly sorry, Nicholas. I never meant to hurt you."

Nicholas shut the door behind her and fell onto his bed, emotionally wrung out. This was probably the last time he'd ever see her. His Devalina. No! Not his Devalina. She never belonged to him. It was all a lie. If there was one thing he was now sure of, it was that he would never, ever trust any woman with his heart again.

Chapter 30

Mia

"Oh, Nicholas," Mia said with sympathy. "That was awful of both of them. The worst kind of betrayal, I think."

Nicholas had lit the glass-encased, double-sided fireplace. The temperature had dropped almost twenty degrees since sunset. He'd thrown down two oversized white pillows on the area rug where they had made themselves comfortable for what Mia knew would be an uncomfortable discussion for Nicholas.

"We've all had heartbreaks and disappointments though. That one breakup turned you off getting involved again?"

"No, I think that was just the last hurt I decided to endure," Nicholas explained. "You have to understand, I lost my parents and then my grandmother. She was my main caretaker after my parents were killed. I was sixteen years old when she died, and living day in and day out with my grandfather's grief was more painful than acknowledging my own."

They were lying face to face on the pillows by the fire, their heads propped up on their hands. Mia reached over with her free hand, cupping his cheek with her palm.

"I had a girlfriend at the time," Nicholas continued. "She was sympathetic at first but she soon tired of my moods, and we argued about it. 'Life goes on,' she said. 'You need to move on.'"

Mia frowned. There was so much she could comment on about that but she chose not to interrupt him.

A smile crossed his face, and Nicholas tenderly brushed a strand of hair from Mia's face. "My grandfather had business in Athens, and he took me with him. While he worked, I roamed the streets, observing happy, whole families, friends enjoying a lighthearted day out, and lovers walking arm in arm." He closed his eyes, remembering. "And then the most fortuitous thing happened. I came across a young girl who seemed to be lost."

Nicholas ran a finger down the length of her nose, and Mia giggled.

"If you can believe that a brief encounter with a twelve-year-old girl could have a major impact on me, then trust that I mean it."

"How?" Mia finally interjected. "I mean, I never forgot you because I was twelve. And not only did an adorable and hot, I have to add, older boy help me find my way back to my parents, but he spent time talking to me like I was his equal."

"Hot, huh?"

"Yes, very," Mia confirmed. "But what about me impressed you? I was just a kid."

"A very sweet kid. One who listened to me like no one else had," Nicholas said. "It was strange but, for some reason, I felt connected to you from the start. Like I could tell you all my inner thoughts and fears without criticism."

He took her hand in his, caressing it.

"You were exactly what I needed at that very moment. It made me realize that Lily, my girlfriend," Nicholas clarified, "and I weren't right for each other. She didn't get me and was growing impatient with my moods."

"The test of love is how a couple deals with the challenging times," Mia said. "It's easy to be supportive when everything is as it should be."

"Exactly!" Nicholas agreed. "If a girl I'd only met for an hour could give me more comfort than the one I'd called my girlfriend for over a year, then something was terribly wrong. So I broke up with her."

"Wow, I didn't see that coming."

"I knew I'd made the right decision when she took it in stride. No waterworks or yelling. Just an uneventful parting of ways."

The death of his parents and two breakups had caused Nicholas to reject the idea of future entanglements? That seemed extreme to Mia.

"I can tell by the way you're looking at me that you still don't completely understand."

"No, I don't."

"My grandmother died sixteen years ago, and my grandfather hasn't been the same since. She was the love of his life, and he's a shell of a man without her." Nicholas sighed. "The public sees a powerhouse businessman. Work is the only thing driving him. But once he sheds his suit, the inconsolable grief is evident every time I look at him."

"That's so sad," Mia whispered.

"I've already dealt with enough sorrow for a lifetime. It's much easier to stay detached than to end up like him."

"Is it, though?" Mia asked. "Loss, and pain, and grief are all heart-rending emotions. But going through that makes you appreciate the opposite emotions all the more. Love, comfort, affection. Humans are designed to yearn for all three."

"Not me," Nicholas disagreed. "Not until you walked across my path, challenging my resolve."

"You mean your true nature," Mia corrected. "A long time ago, I met a kind, compassionate boy."

"However you want to label it, I tried to fight the inexplicable pull you have on me."

"Lust?" she joked.

"Sure, of course." Nicholas ran the pad of his thumb over the seam of her lips. "You're beautiful. But I think we both know it's so much more than that." Still lying face to face, Nicholas pulled Mia even closer, pressing his body to hers and kissing her, over and over, tenderly and deeply, devouring her very soul. Mia's head spun. Happy atoms danced throughout her entire being, bouncing off every cell in her body like an old-fashioned pinball machine.

Contrary to what Nicholas admitted, Mia didn't know what this was—what they were, or what 'so much more' meant to him. Right now, she was in bliss, and she prayed this unpredictable man's mood stayed rooted in place. She liked this Nicholas. Disagreeable Nicholas made her nervous as hell.

The fire warmed Mia's bones but the heat running along her skin came from her response to Nicholas—the way he grazed his fingers tenderly up and down her arm. The intense manner in which his eyes locked with hers. The sensual kisses he mapped along her bare shoulder.

Nicholas pinned her underneath him. "Now that I've confessed my deep, dark secrets, it's time you did the same."

"Protecting your heart is hardly a dark secret," Mia whispered. "Although taking that road can sometimes lead to more sorrow, not less."

"Are you speaking from experience?" Nicholas sat up, pulling Mia onto his lap.

"What would make you think that?"

"Well . . ." Nicholas flipped her around at the waist so she was straddling him. Meeting her eye to eye, he theorized. " . . . You say you've had no serious relationships and claim to have no story, which I don't buy."

He raised an eyebrow. Nicholas didn't sound combative or even forcefully nosy. Even the raising of the eyebrow, which could be a sign of suspicion, didn't come off that way. In this case, it was a playful gesture. 'I'll tell you mine if you tell me yours.' This was a side of Nicholas that Mia wasn't used to.

Her mind was racing with conflict. There was a reason Mia was reluctant to date and kept only a few in her trust. What she was about to tell Nicholas, and she hadn't made up her mind whether to do so yet, no one else knew, other than her sister's friend, Egypt. No, not even Kally knew. Mia had sworn Egypt to secrecy.

Nervously, Mia looped her hand around Nicholas' neck, running her fingers through the hair on the back of his head. She sucked in a deep breath.

"A while ago, on my eighteenth birthday, to be exact, something happened. Almost happened. It would have been a much bigger deal if it wasn't for my sister's friend, who pulled me from a bad situation."

Nicholas unlocked Mia's clasped fingers around his neck, lifting them to his mouth and brushing his lips across her knuckles. "Mia, take your time, and tell me what happened."

Mia nodded. "Egypt, you met her."

"Yes," Nicholas said. "She's quite . . . interesting."

Mia stifled a laugh. "She has a lot of energy. Egypt is also the most trustworthy and loyal person you'll ever meet. Anyway, she insisted that I had to go out on my birthday. I agreed and was hoping Kally would join us. Oddly, I'd been spending more time with her friend that summer than she was. Kally worked so many hours but, on her time off, she seemed to disappear."

"Disappear?" Nicholas furrowed his brow. "To where?"

"I didn't know until years later but Kally was having a secret relationship with a man she knew our parents would disapprove of. Only Egypt knew."

"What was there to disapprove of?"

Mia shook her head. She picked the reasons off with a show of fingers. "He wasn't Greek. He was considerably older. He came from the 'wrong side of the tracks,' no matter that he was successful. And he had long hair and rode a motorcycle. Oh! And he had tattoos."

Nicholas took Mia's face in her hands. "You, my dear Mia, are like an artichoke."

"What?" she asked, flummoxed.

"You keep telling me you have no story. Then I find out about missing grandfathers, half-brothers, of which I still don't know the details, and a sister with a secret liaison. Now, I'm not-so-patiently waiting to hear about what almost happened to you," he said in what sounded like one long-breathed, run-on sentence.

"And what does that have to do with artichokes?"

"You peel off a leaf," Nicholas started, playfully mimicking the motion. "Scrape off what little you can from it, and then peel off another. After a while, you get to the heart, tender and protected by all those tough outer layers."

"You have an interesting mind, Mr. Aristedis."

"The artichoke symbolizes many things in different cultures. In some, it represents peace, prosperity, and the hope for love. In others, it symbolizes the spirit of transformation. It reminds us not to choke back our feelings. To let go of the tough exterior and let the heart shine through."

"That's very profound," Mia said. "You continue to surprise me. So, tell me now, if I'm an artichoke, what vegetable are you?"

The corners of Nicholas' mouth lifted in amusement. Narrowing his eyes, he said, "Tell me your story. We can discuss produce later."

Chapter 31

Mia

2010

"Mia, girl, get your face away from that computer and go have some fun." Egypt bounced her way into Mia's bedroom.

"Hey, Egypt. If you're looking for Kally, she's not home."

"Nope! I came for you, birthday girl. I'm taking you out tonight," she informed Mia. Walking over to the closet, Egypt rifled through Mia's wardrobe, commenting on each garment. "Too prim," she said of a floral dress. "Boring," was her critique on a striped shirt dress.

"Do you like any of my clothing?" Mia asked.

"You're eighteen. Spice it up a little." Egypt pulled out a ruffled cotton mini-skirt. "This will do." After rummaging further, she found a form-fitting halter top to complete the ensemble.

"I appreciate your effort to take me out with you but I can't get into the places you go to."

"But you can go to Shafer's." Egypt made a face. "You'll be limited to soft drinks but it will still be fun." She grabbed Mia by the wrists, pulling her up from her desk chair. "I'll treat you to dinner and cake, of course, and then we'll go upstairs. You never know who you might meet," Egypt said, wiggling her eyebrows.

Mia threw her head back and laughed. "We're only going a half-mile from home. The only people we'll see there are the ones I've gone to school with my whole life."

"Is this all necessary?" Mia asked.

Egypt scrunched Mia's dark hair into soft beach waves. A cloud of aerosol hairspray nearly suffocated her in Egypt's attempt to get the curls to hold.

"Yes, it is." Egypt was deep in concentration, smudging black kohl liner at the base of Mia's lashes to give her eyes a sultry, smoky look. "Eighteen is a rite of passage, and we need to celebrate."

Mia stood and looked in the mirror. "I look . . . good, I guess. Not entirely like me, but it's fine. More mature." She wasn't sure but maybe it was time for a change.

* * *

The loud buzzing from cicadas only added to the other everyday sounds of a Port Jefferson summer. Day and night, the streets were crowded with locals and tourists shopping, strolling the pier, and dining at one of the many eateries. Come sunset, music escaped from lively restaurants and echoed from outdoor bars.

Mia and Egypt exited the car after circling a number of times for a parking space. As they walked past the tennis courts, Mia stopped for a minute to say hello to a friend she spotted playing doubles.

"Why did my sister say she couldn't make it tonight?" Mia asked as they headed toward the restaurant.

"She was working and then after had previous plans already set for this evening." Egypt stepped up to the hostess desk, asking for a table. She didn't elaborate on Kally's whereabouts, and Mia decided to drop the subject. After all, they were out to have some fun.

They decided to order an assortment of appetizers to share instead of full meals. Afterward, Egypt had the server bring Mia a slice of cake with a candle for Mia to make a birthday wish.

"Hopefully, you wished for a hot as sin man to materialize."

"Egypt!"

"Well, that's what I always wish for."

"Then you must blow out a lot of candles because you go through guys faster than the speed of light," Mia joked.

"Are you ready? Let's go up," Egypt said with a laugh. She stood, swinging her hips. "I want to dance."

They climbed up to the rooftop bar. The music was deafening, and the crowd hopping. Mia recognized quite a few faces. Some were huddled in a group, chatting with drinks in their hands. Others were dancing. Meanwhile, people of all ages stood by the bar.

Egypt took Mia by the hand, dragging her along. She pushed their way through the crowd until she reached the bar.

"A Long Island Iced Tea and a Coke, please," Egypt ordered.

As they sipped their drinks, a couple of Egypt's friends waved to her, weaving their way through the crowd toward her. Egypt introduced Mia to her acquaintances, explaining that she knew Kara and Jeanne from a yoga studio. After chatting for a while, as best they could over the pulsating music, Mia noticed a friend of her own on the other side of the outdoor deck. She excused herself and walked over to speak with her.

"Maddie!" How are you?" Mia asked.

"Mia!" she exclaimed, hugging her. "I haven't seen you since graduation. Where have you been?"

"I've been interning at a local TV station and working on some tutorials in graphic design," Mia said. "What have you been up to?"

"You know. Hanging around. Going to the beach. Buying stuff to fill my dorm for college."

Just then, from the corner of her eye, she spotted a couple of guys heading their way. Mia's stomach flipped like a gymnast tumbling back handsprings. She'd had a secret crush on Trevor for the past two years, but they were only casual friends. He'd been steadily dating another girl for three years. Still, they had many classes together and were often paired for group projects. He was fun to be around and always worked hard on the projects alongside her.

As Trevor and Bradley wove their way through the sea of people, Maddie shared a tidbit of gossip with Mia. "Look who's on his way over." She flicked her head in the boys' direction. "Did you hear? Trevor and Tricia broke up."

"Really?" Mia was surprised. "They've been going out forever."

"Forever is a long time." Maddie wiggled her eyebrows. She spoke fast before they approached. "They're going to different colleges," she blurted out. "Read between the lines."

"Hi, girls," Bradley greeted. "You're both looking pretty fine tonight."

"Always the flirt," Maddie said.

"How've you been, Mia?" Trevor asked. "I haven't seen you around."

"I'm well, thank you. I've had a busy summer," Mia replied. "What have you been up to?"

"This and that. Working at the country club. Getting ready for Dartmouth," Trevor said.

"Congrats on getting into that school, but I have to say, going any further north than here is not for me. I hate cold winters."

He smiled at Mia admiringly then leaned in to whisper in her ear. "It's so loud and crowded. I can barely hear you. Why don't we take a walk where it's a little quieter?"

She shook her head. "I'm actually here with another friend," Mia explained. "She's way over there." She pointed. "I should probably get back to her."

He took her empty glass from her hand. "Not until I've refreshed your drink and had a chance to catch up with you. Okay?" he begged with a cute, pleading face she just couldn't resist.

Mia giggled. "Okay."

He stepped away, heading to the outdoor bar. Turning, she discovered her other classmates were gone, but soon, Trevor was back at her side with a Coke for her and a Jack Daniels for himself.

Mia thanked Trevor for the drink, eyeing his glass of amber fluid.

She took it from him, lifting it to her nose and sniffing. "How were you able to get that?" Mia asked, returning it to him. "I'll stick to soft drinks," she said, taking a long gulp from the one he handed her.

Trevor grinned smugly. "Fake ID. You're such a rule follower, Mia." He planted a kiss on her cheek. "It really is adorable."

"Whoa!" Mia said. "Sorry. Head rush," she explained as she fell into him. "I feel so lightheaded all of a sudden. You didn't order this with alcohol, did you?"

"Scout's honor," Trevor said, raising two fingers. "There is no alcohol in this Coke."

Everything began to spin. "I feel sleepy all of a sudden," Mia said. "I told Egypt I was too tired to go out," she slurred. "I was on the computer all day."

"Come on," Trevor insisted. "You need to sit down someplace, away from all this noise."

Trevor escorted Mia down the stairs, practically having to carry her. But to where he took her, she didn't know, because the next thing she remembered was waking up in Egypt's bed.

* * *

"Is your friend feeling okay?" Kara, Egypt's friend, asked.

"She's fine. Why?"

"I just saw her go down the steps with some guy, and she seemed to be a little out of it."

Alarmed, Egypt spun around, looking for any sign of Mia. "Excuse me," she apologized, rushing over to the girl Mia had been speaking with. "Hi, I'm Mia's friend. We came together, and I'm looking for her," she explained. "Where did she go?"

"She wasn't feeling well so Trevor took her to find someplace quieter for her to sit," Maddie said.

"Not feeling well, how?"

Maddie shrugged. "She was a little lightheaded. That's all."

212

Egypt could feel the golden-brown ringlets on her head winding tighter. Something wasn't sitting right with her, and her instincts rarely failed her.

She narrowed her eyes. "What type of car does Trevor drive?" Egypt said the boy's name as though it was the filthiest profanity.

"Black Mazda Miata," Bradley said.

"Do you know where he parked?" Egypt asked impatiently.

"Sure," Bradley said, confused. "We came together. Down by the baseball field."

Egypt groaned. She'd have to sprint in four-inch heels. "Thanks," she said before running off.

Kara and Jeanne called to her. "What's going on?" Kara asked.

"I think Mia might be in trouble."

"We're coming with you," Jeanne called after her.

They ran out of the restaurant, cutting across Chandler Square to the poorly lit back parking lot. Kara almost fell, tripping on the curb as they passed by Rocketship Park.

Egypt peeked into every black car diagonally parked along the ball field. Frustrated, she banged on the hood of a Honda, setting off its alarm.

"Egypt!" Jeanne called out. "Over there. The last car. That's a Miata." Jeanne confirmed.

Like an episode of *Charlie's Angels*, the three badass women stormed over to the vehicle. What Egypt saw enraged her. Her adrenaline level reached a point when she was sure she could flip the little bastard's car over. The passenger seat was entirely reclined, and the little shit was all over her best friend's little sister. Mia's halter top was pulled down and her skirt hiked up. Worse was that Mia didn't seem conscious of any of it.

Egypt banged on the window. "Get off her, you little fucker," she shouted. Thankfully, the moron didn't think to lock the doors. She yanked it open, startling Trevor when she punched him in the face.

"Crazy bitch," Trevor screamed.

"You haven't seen anything yet." She grabbed a fistful of his hair, pulling until he yelped. "Unless you're not particularly fond of your balls, you'd better get out of the car now before I brutally rip them from your body."

Trevor rolled off Mia, exiting from his side of the car. But he wasn't getting off easy. Kara and Jeanne jumped into action, blocking him from running away.

Egypt laughed. "You think pretty boy would leave his car behind?" She came around to his side. "You never know what might happen to it. What did you give her? Do I need to take her to the hospital?"

"No!" He panicked. "Just some Ambien. I swear."

"No Ecstasy?" Egypt asked. "The truth," she demanded.

"No!"

Egypt dug into her pocket for her keys. She threw them to Kara. "My car is parked by the tennis courts. Please bring it around for me."

"Sure, but before I leave . . ." Kara walked over to Trevor. "I videoed the entire thing. If I come back and you've touched one hair on any-one's head, I'll go straight to the police."

Egypt and Jeanne helped Mia out of the car. "I'll let Mia decide if she wants to press charges once she's conscious," Egypt warned. Now, get the hell out of my sight."

Trevor jumped into his car and tore off, leaving Egypt and Jeanne supporting Mia's weight on the darkened street. Minutes later, Kara pulled up. Helping bundle Mia into the car, she thanked her friends and took Mia home.

* * *

"If I could have spared you the details, I would have," Egypt told Mia as the girl sobbed. After waking up, Egypt had explained everything.

"I can't believe he would do something like that to me," Mia cried. "I always thought he was a decent guy." A horrific thought came to her. "Egypt, do you think he . . ." Mia couldn't finish the sentence.

"No," Egypt assured her. "I caught him in time. If I thought he had, I would have taken you to the hospital."

Mia closed her eyes, breathing in a sigh of relief.

"If I had found you a few minutes later, it might have been a different story though. My first instinct was to call the cops and have him arrested but I thought the better of it," Egypt said. "If it were up to me, I wouldn't hesitate. But it isn't my call to make."

"You did the right thing," Mia assured her. "I don't want anyone to know about this. Not the police, or my sister, and especially not my parents. They'd never let me out of the house again."

"You might want to consider that if he's done this to you then he's probably done it to other girls and will continue to."

"I don't want anyone to know." The thought of coming forward and the case going to court petrified Mia. "I can't bear to see his smug face when he gets off scot-free. And you know he'll probably get off."

Egypt held Mia's hands between hers. "But he'll continue to if something isn't done."

"Please," Mia implored. "I just want to forget this ever happened."

Egypt promised her silence but, like a ghost creeping about, what Trevor did to her haunted Mia. She could bury the trauma in the recesses of her mind, or at least pretend to, but the damage had been done. Innocent trust, benefits of doubt—they no longer existed save toward a precious few people closest to her.

Chapter 32

Mia

Nicholas stared blankly at Mia. There was no other way to describe how he was looking at her, and she didn't know what to make of it. Mia feared how he would now view her. One night out and she couldn't manage to take care of herself. Her throat burned with the bitter tears she refused to spill.

Mia had repositioned herself upright when she began relaying what had happened to her all those years ago. This wasn't a story to tell lying relaxed by the fire as though she were reading a romantic fairytale.

She drew in a shaky breath, averting her eyes to focus on anything but Nicholas' steely face. "I knew I shouldn't have told you," she whispered into her lap. "There's a reason why I've never shared it."

The expression on his face changed. "I am trying my hardest to keep my composure right now," Nicholas said, his tone monotone.

Just then, she noticed what she hadn't a moment ago—his hands balled tightly at his sides.

"The idea of you or my sister being disrespected or assaulted in any manner is not something I can let go of."

"Has she been . . ."

"No." Nicholas was quick to say. "Not in a sexual way. But she's been disrespected and used in other ways, and it tore her to shreds."

Mia didn't understand, and it showed on her face.

"Money can be a curse. You never really know who to trust. Or who to love."

"Oh, poor Penelope," Mia said as understanding struck.

Nicholas stretched out his arms, relief washing over Mia at his invitation. She slid into his lap, letting him engulf her in his comforting arms.

Nicholas pressed a kiss to her temple. "I would never lay a hand on you without your permission."

"I know," she said softly. "I trust you."

"Why?" he asked. "When you trust so few people, and especially men, why have I been granted this grace?"

"I just know," she replied. "I've known from the first time I laid eyes on you that you were a man of integrity and kindness." She laughed. "Even when your words were cutting and you scowled at me, I could tell deep down there was good inside you."

"I only scowled to keep myself from falling under your spell," he said, tracing the lines of her face. He looked earnestly into her eyes. "I'm not looking to get hurt again, either."

Mia cupped his face. "We all harbor wounds and insecurities." She rested her head on his shoulder. "I—" she stopped short of telling him she loved him. What started as infatuation had become so much more. Even during Mia's angry protestations toward Nicholas and her tears of frustration, he'd somehow managed to seep into her heart, penetrating her soul.

"What?" Nicholas asked. "Tell me what's on your mind."

"It was nothing," Mia said. "I was just going to say that I'm very loyal to those I care about. That's all."

"That's everything," he emphasized. Trailing kisses along her neck, he pecked his way to her earlobe, sucking on it along with the delicate pearl earring piercing her lobe. He made his way to her mouth and ran his tongue along the seam of her lips. Mia moaned as she opened for him, and Nicholas deepened the kiss, making it last long enough to send Mia into a state of euphoric bliss.

When Nicholas pulled away, there was a serious expression on his face. Half desire and half contemplation. His lips curved up into an imperceptible smile. "It's late," he said reluctantly. "Why don't we call it a night, and tomorrow, I'll take you on a tour of the island."

"I'd like that." When she stood, he followed, walking Mia to her bedroom. Ever the gentleman, Nicholas kissed her, yet he made no attempt to step inside. It took all of Mia's restraint not to ask him in. Instead, she closed the door behind her and leaned against it, wrung out with emotion. She had not expected to share such confessions with Nicholas, or he with her.

* * *

Moonlight filtered in through the narrow slats of the window blinds. Mia lifted her phone off the nightstand to check the time. Three-fourteen a.m. Almost exactly an hour since the last time she checked. But it wasn't her own story racing through her mind and keeping her awake. It was everything Nicholas had shared. He'd endured so many levels of heartache, and she wanted nothing more than to wash away those painful memories for him.

And she couldn't help but think about what she had told him. Mia second-guessed every word she had said. She wasn't a stupid girl and wasn't one to put herself in precarious situations. She wanted him to understand that she'd done absolutely nothing to encourage Trevor's behavior.

But what really occupied her mind were the passionate kisses and tender caresses Nicholas had showered upon her. Her skin tingled and her belly flipped just thinking of it. The memory of his body pressing so close to hers would be forever imprinted on her soul.

It was no use. Mia kicked the sheets off and hopped out of bed. Walking over to the window, she twisted the Lucite rod and raised the window blinds. The view was breathtaking; a golden glow illuminated the houses dotting the shoreline and winding up the mountain. Even the water looked as though thousands of candles floated in the darkness under some kind of reflective sorcery.

Mia was restless. The house was much larger than she'd initially expected. Nicholas had told her he owned a modest home in Mykonos. She supposed, like beauty, modesty was in the eye of the beholder. But in her assessment, five bedrooms, an open-design living room boasting more square footage than her parents' entire first floor, and a veranda that could easily host fifty guests, was far from average.

She tip-toed from her room so as not to disturb Nicholas. Maybe the night air and the quiet, soothing sounds of nature would make her drowsy. Mia headed to the glass doors leading out onto the veranda, only to discover it was already occupied. With his hands clasped on his head, Nicholas paced slowly. He wore nothing but a pair of low-slung, navy pajama bottoms. Mia had never seen him unclothed before. With his back to her, even from where she stood, it was evident Nicholas had the body of a man who worked out religiously. His narrow waist made his shoulders appear broad, and she noticed his biceps flexing, fraught with what Mia surmised was tension.

Nicholas dropped his hands and gazed out at sea. Mia wondered what had kept him from his slumber. Had stirring up the ghosts of his past upset him? Or did hers now invade his spirit as well?

Making a split-second decision, she padded toward the patio, opening the sliding doors gingerly. If privacy was what Nicholas preferred, she'd walk away. Mia wasn't sure how to navigate whatever was happening between them, and she wasn't sure if he'd welcome her intrusion.

"I see you couldn't sleep either," she said softly, flattening her palms on his bare back. She was about to rub away the tension in gentle circles but Nicholas grasped her small wrists, wrapping her hands around his waist.

Mia hugged him from behind, pressing a kiss to his back. Turning, he faced her, his hair standing up in every which way. Mia smiled and ran her hands through his mess of hair. Even disheveled, he was the most handsome man she'd ever seen.

"What's kept you up?" she asked.

Nicholas cupped her chin. "You," he replied simply. "I will never let anything happen to you, even if I have to guard you personally," he vowed.

"It was a long time ago." Mia shook her head. "Why don't we leave the past behind with our earlier talk and move forward now. I don't want to be emotionally chained to something I couldn't control, and neither should you." Mia stroked his face. "What that girl did to you was her indiscretion, not yours." She flicked her head toward the doors. "Ready to get some rest?"

"No," he said, his eyes smoldering as he pulled her close. "You asked me what kept me up? I'll ask the same of you."

"I . . . was thinking of . . . you," Mia admitted.

"Thinking of me as in how I kissed you? Like this?" Nicholas bent down, claiming her mouth.

"Yes," she breathed.

"How can I sleep when only a wall separates us and all I can think of is how much I want to make love to you," he said, his voice thick with emotion.

"Why don't you then?" Mia asked, emboldened.

Nicholas rested his forehead against hers. "Are you sure?"

"I trust you," she said.

"There's that word again," he said. "The single most important word in your vocabulary."

"One of them, anyway," she agreed. "So, what's holding you back now?" Mia stared at him, wide-eyed.

"Not a damn thing." Startling her, Nicholas lifted her off her feet and carried her to an upholstered lounge chair large enough for two. Setting her down, Mia kept her hands threaded behind his neck, jolting him down on top of her when she didn't let go.

Earlier, Mia had wished upon a star, and now that very same mystical bolt of fire, light-years away, winked back at her conspiratorially.

The warm night air glided along her skin as Nicholas peeled her garments off tenderly, slowly, casting them aside. Mia, in turn, slid his bottoms down, admiring the contours of his muscular form.

Nicholas paid worship to Mia's body as he used his fingers, mouth, and tongue to explore every inch of her creamy skin. She discovered erogenous zones she never knew existed—electricity coursing through Mia's veins at his touch. For the first time in her life, she gave herself over completely to a man, this man—body and soul. This is what it was like to float on a cloud, her mind drifting to an unknown realm where nothing mattered but the mind-blowing sensual sensations fusing with her spirit. Nicholas groaned out her name as he rhythmically glided in and out of her, languidly, yet not lacking intense passion, savoring the connection between them.

Without breaking contact, Nicholas pulled Mia up into a sitting position. She wrapped her legs around him as he placed a hand on each of her hips, guiding her stroke for delicious stroke.

Mia looked deep into his eyes, trying to decipher what she read in them. His lips grazed hers, and she could feel his warm breath on her face as he panted out his pleasure. "I need to see you fall to pieces for me."

"Falling," Mia moaned. "Been falling since the first second you touched me."

Her words put him over the edge, and Nicholas picked up his pace, fevered by his urgency. When he met his peak, he thrust into her, unraveling what was left of her control. Entangled as one, the rapture had overtaken them, neither attempting to move when they returned back to Earth. Sated, Mia and Nicholas looked fixedly into one another's eyes until Mia sunk her face into the crook of his neck.

Pushing fallen strands of hair from his face, she asked, "Do you think you might be able to fall asleep now?"

Nicholas answered her with a kiss. Lifting Mia off the lounger, he said, "Only if you're beside me."

Mia could live with that, she thought, as Nicholas carried her to his bed.

Chapter 33

Mia

Considering the hour Mia had finally fallen asleep, she awoke energized. Still, she didn't want to move a muscle so as not to disturb Nicholas from his slumber. With his arm resting over her back, his hand cupping her naked bottom, Nicholas wasn't a quiet sleeper, she had discovered. He didn't snore but the sound coming from him hummed like melodic, soft sighs.

Gingerly, Mia began to slide out from his hold but, like a bear's claw, Nicholas gripped her butt cheek tighter. "Stay," he ordered.

"You were asleep a second ago," she said, astounded. "You were snoring."

"I don't snore."

"Maybe not snoring then. But making little noises in your sleep like a baby," she clarified.

He pulled her on top of him and kissed her. "I was dreaming of you."

Mia smiled. "I'm going to take a shower, and then, if you like, I can make breakfast."

"I have a better idea," he said. "Have you seen my shower?"

She laughed. "Yes. You could throw a party in there. It's bigger than my bedroom."

"Uh-huh," he said with a sly smile. "We can shower together." He wiggled his brows. "Then, I take you for a breakfast that you and your never-ending appetite will never forget."

"Somehow, I don't think sex in the shower is as alluring as they make it look in the movies," Mia said. "All that water pelting at you."

"You have to know the right moves so that doesn't happen," Nicholas said, his voice dripping with seduction. Rolling over and pinning her under him, he explained, "First, I get the water steaming hot, and you let me lather every inch of your body." Nicholas trailed kisses down her neck to the hollow of her collar bone. He didn't stop until he reached her breast, allowing his lips to linger there. "And I mean every inch." He ran his tongue along the nub of her nipple, licking and sucking until he elicited a moan from Mia.

"And then?" Mia groaned.

"I take you to the other side, out of the stream from the shower jets. That's where I bend you over the built-in marble bench and have my wicked, wicked way with you."

But before the couple had a chance to live out that fantasy, Nicholas was already making love to her. Breakfast would have to wait, she thought happily. There weren't many things Mia would give up food for, but two courses of Nicholas before she had her coffee was a dish she'd gladly choose.

* * *

"Car or Vespa?" Nicholas asked, stepping into the garage.

"Based on the way those Greeks were driving when we arrived yesterday, definitely the car."

"Those Greeks!" Nicholas chuckled. "As if you don't speak their language."

"Not maniac car-speak!" she exclaimed. "I value my life."

"Truth is, I don't generally use the Vespa. Penelope does," he said. "I avoid it for obvious reasons."

Mia placed her hand on his arm. "I'm sorry."

Nicholas took her hand, lacing their fingers together. "I'm glad you're here with me."

"Me too."

The Myconian Kyma Hotel was a five-star luxury resort, the likes of which Mia had only seen on magazines' travel pages. Nicholas escorted her to NOA, the resort restaurant with a menu only to be rivaled by its view.

Wide-eyed and breathless, Mia soaked in every detail like a baby observing the world for the first time. Modern and tasteful. Simple, with its predominantly white décor, the splashes of color accenting the space only adding vibrancy to the atmosphere.

Once again, they were escorted to a table with a prime view. The indoor seating could easily be described as open-air as the floor-to-ceiling windows contained no glass.

Mia nearly jumped for joy. Bringing her hands to her mouth, she squealed, pointing. "It's the windmills!"

Nicholas chuckled, amused by her uninhibited enthusiasm. "We can go there after lunch if you like."

"Yes!" Mia agreed. "If you can drag me away from this view."

"Nicholas," a woman said as she approached their table. "I noticed your name on the reservation list this morning."

Nicholas stood politely. The tall, leggy blonde leaned in, kissing each cheek while running her hands over his biceps.

Mia's irises were brown but she was seeing green at that moment. Why is it that every woman Nicholas knew exuded an air of supreme confidence and sensuality?

"It's good to see you back on the island." She winked at him. "Make sure you look me up before you leave."

Nicholas cleared his throat. "Ariana is the restaurant manager," he told Mia, returning to his seat.

"It's a beautiful restaurant," Mia responded civilly, with an edge to her tone that only another woman would detect. Mia had no intention of befriending her.

"Ariana, this is Mia, my girlfriend."

"Girlfriend?" Ariana parroted back. The startled expression on her face only angered Mia.

"A pleasure," Mia said, extending her hand.

If Nicholas noticed the unspoken war of wills happening before his eyes, he didn't let on. Mia simply eyed Ariana with venom. The days when women like this made her feel small were over as of this minute. She was tempted to suggest she lift her jaw and close her mouth before a fly made its home in there and laid eggs. But she kept it classy.

"I think I'd like to order now," Mia told Nicholas.

"I'll get your server," Ariana said, retreating.

"Warn me now. Am I going to have to fend off a woman every place we go?" The question was posed in jest but, she was truly beginning to wonder.

Nicholas reached across the table, taking her hands in his. "There's no need to fend anyone off. I see only you."

It took biting her tongue not to ask him why. Why, when he could have any of these stunning women, is he interested in her?

After lunch, Nicholas drove to the windmills just as he'd promised.

"Do you know how many fashion shoots have been located at this very spot?" Mia asked, not expecting an answer. "I thought for sure the photos were retouched. But no, this place is actually real."

"We can do our own shoot if you like."

"For *Opul?*" That would mean she would be able to come back here again. "A future issue?"

"No, right now." Nicholas pulled his phone from his pocket. "This one isn't for the magazine. It's only for me."

"No," she laughed, covering her face. "Why don't we just take a selfie."

"We'll get to that." He took her hand as they walked toward the whitewashed steps leading to the windmills. "Sit down."

Mia lowered herself to a sitting position approximately halfway up the steps. Thin straps tied into bows held up her 1940's style sundress.

Pleated cotton, cinched at the waist, flared when she spread the full skirt around her like a fan. The tulip pattern, shaded in soft pink hues, stood out against the stark-white structures behind her.

Mia played with some different poses. She leaned back to feel the warmth of the sun on her face. Resting her hand under her chin as though in deep contemplation, she held a thoughtful expression for her next pose. Finally, she outstretched her arms, beckoning Nicholas to her.

They ambled up the steps leading to the windmills. Nicholas snapped a series of pictures until Mia snatched his phone from him, turning the tables. A pair of middle-aged women, entertained by the couple's lighthearted antics, approached them.

"I'd be happy to take a picture of the two of you if you'd like," one of the ladies offered.

Mia gladly handed the phone over to the woman. "Thank you, that's very kind of you."

She handed the phone back after taking three snapshots. One with Nicholas' arm around Mia's waist. Another of the two of them in profile, staring into each other's eyes. And in the last one, Nicholas kissed the inside of Mia's palm. They thanked the women before strolling away in the direction of Little Venice.

Nicholas shook his head, laughing at her as they walked along a narrow path. "Most women weave in and out of every shoe shop and clothing boutique."

Instead, Mia stopped at each spice store, cheese shop, and gelato stand they passed. The only thing she purchased were pastries, very much like the kind her sister, Kally, made for her café.

"I'm eyeing those too," she said. "But I'm content just window shopping."

Lazily, they meandered the narrow, stone alleyways. It was like a picturesque maze Mia could get lost in and never find her way back. Each turn looked very much like the last. Whitewashed buildings with bougainvillea clinging to the walls surrounded them. Aegean-blue shutters uniformly framed the windows. Pretty little storefronts displayed a sampling of their wares hanging on racks and tables outside their doors. Bistro after bistro, each with water views. Charming. Magical. Otherworldly. There wasn't a description Mia could think of that would do justice to this place. It felt very familiar to her to hear the chatter of pedestrians speaking a language that had surrounded her all her life. Still, she had never stepped foot on this ground before and would not be able to negotiate her way around alone. Despite that, Mia felt a connection to this corner of the world. Suddenly, she was overcome with emotion.

"Hey," Nicholas said, wiping a lone tear from the corner of Mia's eye. "Is something wrong?"

"No," Mia replied. "Not at all." Embarrassed, she waved it off.

"Tell me."

"I'm having a wonderful time. It's just so beautiful here." Mia gestured with a wave at her surroundings. "I never want to leave. This whole trip has been so unexpected."

Nicholas motioned for her to sit at a table for two outside a café. "And me? I suppose I'm unexpected as well after our rocky start."

Mia looked shyly down at the lacquered, blue table.

Nicholas looked at the sign on the wall. "Frappé?"

Mia beamed. "I'd love one. Extra sweet."

Minutes later, Nicholas came back with two tall glasses brimming with the frothy iced-coffee beverage.

"About that rocky start," Nicholas said.

"Can we forget about that?"

"I know we talked about that last night, and there's no excuse for my past behavior." Nicholas ran his hand through his hair. Mia could see he was searching for his words. "We all have walls, Mia. For one reason or another. I haven't let myself become emotionally connected to anyone in a very long time. I . . ."

"Don't want to get hurt again?" Mia asked. "Some hurts are unavoidable and, I suppose, frighteningly, inevitable." Mia wanted to lighten the mood. "As my *yiayiá* would say, 'If Adam and Eve hadn't eaten that damn apple, we'd all be running around paradise naked, and no one would ever have to die.'" She mimicked her grandmother in her heavily accented voice.

Nicholas laughed. "That sounds like something she would say," he said.

"I can only promise you that I would never hurt you intentionally," Mia vowed. "But from what I've witnessed, there's a long line of women waiting for their chance with you."

"You're doing it again," he pointed out. "Making jokes to avoid a serious discussion."

"And I thought I was the insecure one."

"Mia," he warned.

"Nicholas, I'm not that girl who ran off with your friend. I share your same work passions, so I don't find you boring." Mia shook her head. "What a twit!"

She rotated her glass, wiping away some condensation from the iced drink. Exhaling, she pondered how to phrase what she wanted to say without using the 'L' word.

"I care about you. Just you," Mia started. "You could lose your magazine, the incredible house you own on this lovely island, and all of that luscious hair on your head that I'm always tempted to run my fingers through, and it wouldn't change how I feel about you."

Nicholas closed his hand around hers, giving it an affectionate squeeze. His expression softened.

"Whatever happens, good or bad, we'll work through it together because . . ."

"Because you trust me," he said, finishing her sentence.

Accurate as that was, it wasn't the word Mia was holding back on the tip of her tongue. "Yes, trust is requisite in a relationship."

"Let's go home so I can trust you out of that dress."

"Now who's making jokes?" Mia laughed.

"I'm not joking. *Páme.*"

Chapter 34

Nicholas

Mia had claimed a cozy seat under a shady spot on the veranda. Nicholas watched her from behind the glass doors, her concentration solely focused on her laptop. Right now, Mia was utterly oblivious to her surroundings. With the opportunity to stare out onto the stunning landscape, take a walk on the beach, or dive into the heated pool, Mia chose to immerse herself in her work. Nicholas admired her work ethic and sense of commitment.

Those qualities only made Nicholas' feelings for Mia grow stronger. This was a difficult admission for him, even if he only acknowledged it to himself. His heart hammered in his chest at the thought. Thump, thump. The pounding hindered his breathing, or was that his anxiety causing his breathlessness?

Nicholas inhaled slow, deep breaths and then exhaled just as slowly. He couldn't—wouldn't—let the fear crush what his heart was telling him. He had to believe Mia was nothing like Devalina, with her warped sense of entitlement—out for what she could get, never considering what she might give. If she wasn't having fun, Devalina grew bored, and that's what drove her into the arms of an equally rich but more social man.

On the other hand, Mia was a woman pieced together by integrity, loyalty, hard work, and empathy. She asked nothing of him, and for that reason, Nicholas wanted to give her the world.

Nicholas slid the door open and strode over to Mia, taking the seat beside her. "This is your last morning in Mykonos and you spend it working?" he asked.

"As I believe you were," she answered. "I have to stay on my toes, or my boss will fire me."

He ran a trail of kisses up her neck. "That would be awfully foolish of him."

Mia angled the computer to face Nicholas. "I'm getting a jump on the next issue." She clicked through some images. "What do you think?"

"Impressive," Nicholas complimented. "Very impressive." He closed the laptop. "If you'd like, we can work on the plane. But for now, I'd like to enjoy our last day here."

"What did you have in mind?"

"Hmm, there are so many ways I can answer that," he teased. "But for now, let's take a walk by the water. I have something I'd like to talk to you about."

Mia furrowed her brow. "That sounds serious. Is something wrong?"

"No, not exactly," Nicholas said. "I need to tell you about something."

Nodding, Mia stood and placed an aqua, large-brimmed hat on her head. Nicholas laced his fingers with hers, and they headed down the winding stone steps leading from the veranda to the beach.

The sun was more intense than usual for October. Without a cloud in the sky to alleviate the heat, Nicholas was grateful for the continuous breeze drifting by. Silently, they ambled down close to the shoreline, refreshed when the ebbing water flowed close enough to splash their feet.

"Why don't we sit," Nicholas suggested.

Mia lowered herself strategically, where her bottom could stay dry but her outstretched legs could be cooled by wet sand.

"When I came to your family's home and spoke to your grand-mother, she gave me some useful information for one of the subjects I'm featuring in an article."

Mia scrunched her nose. "What information?"

"The news flyer. The one that was encrypted as a gardening publication. If you remember, she let me hold onto it."

Mia nodded.

"She hoped that maybe through the information I gathered for the feature, something might be uncovered about her husband's whereabouts."

"Are you saying that you came across something?" Mia asked.

"Not exactly." Nicholas swallowed nervously. He wasn't sure if she'd find what he had done intrusive or if it was something she'd appreciate. Mia had said his behavior toward her was unpredictable. Well, he could say the same of her. "I hired a private investigator to locate your grandfather, or at least find information on what happened to him."

"Why?" Mia seemed utterly bewildered by this.

"There's something about your grandmother that tugs at my heart." He smiled, thinking of the old woman. "But mainly, I did it for you."

"Me?"

Mia's tone came off as incredulous, and that struck him as odd. Was it that unfathomable he'd want to do something nice for her family? Nicholas wondered.

"We weren't together. I didn't think you even liked me very much."

It was true. Nicholas and Mia weren't together at the time. Still, her statement tore through him like a knife gutting his insides. "I've already explained myself," Nicholas said a bit too curtly. "I've always cared for you. Maybe my subconscious forced me to feel what I tried to deny by insinuating myself into your family affairs."

"I'm sorry," Mia said. "I need to let go of my own insecurities." She leaned into him, pressing a kiss to his cheek. "I'm assuming you wouldn't be telling me this if you didn't discover something," Mia said.

"He's dead, isn't he?" she asked, staring at her feet as she buried her toes in the sand.

"I don't know," he admitted. "Like Kally, I hit a wall, but I have my man still on it."

"What did you learn?"

Nicholas drew her close to him, keeping a firm grip on her hands. He told her everything he'd learned from Kostas. As much as he wanted to, he didn't hold back. Not from telling her of the beatings or violations to her grandfather's body. Not of how long the men rotted in that dictator's hell. And not of the fact that he made it out of there alive. In what condition, Nicholas did not know. The road ended at Kostas' taverna.

Mia's tears ran down her face; intermittent sobs rumbled from deep within her. "Those poor men," she cried. "My grandfather. A man I know only through my *yiayiá's* memories. Though her eyes and her splintered heart."

Nicholas wiped away her tears with the pad of his thumbs.

"Kostas didn't keep in touch? They went their separate ways?" Mia asked. "You would think what happened to them would bond them for life."

"Or be too painful to keep reliving," Nicholas suggested. "Maybe for your grandfather, looking at his friend was like seeing the darkness in his own soul. You can't go through something like that and not come out branded by that evil."

"But if he was still alive, why didn't he come for my grandmother?"

"That is what I'm trying to find out," Nicholas said. "Something isn't adding up. Kostas knows more than he's saying. I'm sure of it."

"What would his motive be to hide the truth?" Mia wondered.

"I don't know, but I think your grandmother deserves answers. Even if they aren't the ones she hoped for."

But as Nicholas pondered the ramification of truths and long-awaited-for information, he wondered if some mysteries were better left unsolved. The last thing he wanted was to cause Mia's grandmother any additional anguish.

After walking back from the beach solemnly, Mia and Nicholas went into town for one last meal before their flight back to New York. This was not the way he'd intended to end their little respite. It had been a joyful few days—the best Nicholas had experienced in years. Still, he had no choice but to tell her what he'd learned. For him, a melancholy mood had been cast on the day. And if that wasn't enough, now they had the burden of deciding if and when they would tell her *yiayiá*.

Standing in the foyer, the door open, waiting for their ride to pull up to take them to the airport, Nicholas watched as Mia rifled through her carry-on for about the sixth time, checking nothing was left behind.

"What are you looking for that wasn't there the other ten times you checked?" Nicholas chaffed.

"I always get nervous that I'll forget something important, and I won't be able to board the plane." She pulled her passport from her bag. "Like this!"

"And there it is. Stop stressing." He rubbed his hands up and down her arms. "Relax." Nicholas reached for a package on the console table. "I wanted you to have something to remember this trip by."

Mia looked at him in awe. "That's so sweet of you. Coming here was more than I could have dreamed of. I'll never forget it."

"We passed a jewelry store a couple of times, and I noticed each time we had, you admired this in the window display." He pressed the small, white box in her hand.

Mia untied the navy-blue ribbon. When she lifted the lid, a tiny squeal of delight crossed her lips. "Nicholas! This is too much."

"Not at all," he insisted. "Can I put it on for you?"

Mia nodded, and Nicholas removed the cross from the box. It was a traditional-style Byzantine gold cross with an intricate filigree design. Mia ran her fingers over it admiringly once it was clasped around her neck. She still wore a long chain around her neck, the coin Nicholas had given her so many years ago dangling from it.

"Now, both of these are from you." Mia rubbed the coin between her fingers. "Do you know why I kept looking at this cross?"

He shrugged. "It's pretty?"

Mia laughed. "Yes, it's lovely. But it's exactly like the one I lost. Identical," she exclaimed. "It was my baptism cross, and I'm pretty sure it came from my grandparents' jewelry store. I was working at the Greek festival our church sponsors every August, and, of all places, I must have lost it on church grounds."

"Then I'm glad I bought it for you. Although it's not quite the same as finding the original."

"But just as special." Mia stood on her tip-toes and kissed Nicholas. He pulled her in by the waist, deepening the kiss until the sound of a car pulling up the drive interrupted them.

"Back to reality," Mia said. "Goodbye, heaven on Earth. I'll miss you."

"We'll be back again. I promise," Nicholas whispered in her ear.

Chapter 35

Mia

"I want every juicy detail," Jenny said excitedly.

Mia had returned to her apartment, jetlagged yet exhilarated from the past few days she had spent with Nicholas.

"How did you go from barely tolerating 'Grumpy Pants Bossman' to being swept away to paradise by 'Greek Prince Charming?'" Jenny's eyes were as wide as saucers.

Mia told Jenny most of what happened between yawns and her struggle to keep her eyes open. "I really need sleep," Mia said. "I have work tomorrow."

"I'm sure your boyfriend will give you the day off," Jenny squealed.

"Let's not jump to conclusions," Mia said. "He's still my boss, and although we had a wonderful time together, I'm not completely clear on where I stand with him. Boyfriend might be a stretch."

Jenny flicked Mia's arm. "Wake up, girl. A man doesn't take a woman to his private home on a faraway island unless she's his girlfriend."

"It wasn't that far away. We were already in Greece for business," Mia clarified. "But . . . he did introduce me as his girlfriend at a restaurant he frequents."

Mia knew that would elicit a reaction from Jenny. Ducking, she dodged the pillow Jenny threw at her even before she flung it.

"Don't get too excited," Mia warned her friend. "He only said it to fend off one of his many admirers." She said this only to keep her friend's imagination from running wild but, in the back of her mind, Mia wondered if there was some truth in that declaration.

* * *

The next morning, Mia strode into the office wearing a taupe 1940's style coatdress with padded shoulders, her matching peep-toe platform shoes granting her an extra four inches of height.

"Welcome back, Mia," Suki smiled, greeting her warmly as she passed the reception desk. "How was Athens?"

"Amazing." Mia beamed. "The shoot went off better than I'd hoped, and being in Athens felt like going home for the first time. I even had a chance to visit my grandparents a couple of times."

"I'd love to hear all about it. Maybe lunch today?" Suki asked.

But before Mia could agree, Nicholas rounded the corner. "Not today, Suki," he said. "Mia and I have an important business lunch to attend."

Mia had no such lunch on her schedule that she recalled. She glanced over at Nicholas in question but he made no attempt to offer details. Turning to Suki, Mia said, "Definitely tomorrow then."

Nicholas escorted Mia down the hall. "Who are we meeting with today?"

"No one," he confessed. "I'd just like you to myself."

"We have a lot of work to do to get this issue out and the next one started," Mia pointed out.

"I'm already on it," Nicholas chuckled. "I'm beginning to wonder who works for whom. Come to my office, and we can map out the next issue," Nicholas said. "Oh, and mark yourself 'out of office' starting November eleventh. We leave for Florence that evening."

Mia followed him into the room, shutting the door behind her.

"That soon?" It was already late October, and they had just arrived home.

"We need to get it in while the weather is still pleasant. And with the holidays coming up, I want to get a jump on it." Nicholas swept Mia into his arms and kissed her.

Mia's candy-apple red lipstick left a dark stain on Nicholas' mouth. Mia wiped it away with her fingers, smirking. "We can't have the staff talking." She giggled nervously but she wasn't joking. The last thing she needed was for her coworkers to think she was given preferential treatment.

"Nice outfit," Nicholas admired, running his hands down the length of her body. "Only you can make a seventy-year-old dress look like the latest style."

"It's not a seventy-year-old dress." She rolled her eyes. "It's a new dress with a retro look."

Nicholas seated himself at his desk chair. Crooking a finger, he gestured for Mia to join him on his lap. "What is it about the 1940s that has you so interested?"

"I don't know." Mia laced her hands behind Nicholas' neck. "Everyone dressed so nicely back then, even just to go to a movie or a ballgame. People seemed friendlier, and life was slower and not as complicated."

"In the movies maybe," Nicholas pointed out. "You do realize there was a world war going on during that era, right? Food rations and military death notices, not to mention the horrific atrocities that happened throughout Europe."

Mia pouted. "Why do you have to burst my bubble? Just let me have my fantasy."

"So you are aware that life wasn't as perfect as they painted it?" he asked.

"I'm not ignorant," Mia defended. "I'm also aware that there were a lot of unfair practices back then."

"Every era is unique in its own way. Some aspects are charming, and others are pretty awful," Nicholas said. "I can understand why you're attracted to the fashions and the swing dancing. It sure does beat jumping around aimlessly on the dancefloor." He laughed. Pausing for a beat, Nicholas examined Mia thoughtfully, tenderly stroking her hair. "What happened to you happened to women back then too. It was just spoken of only rarely."

Mia closed her eyes and buried her face in Nicholas' chest. When she picked her head up, she asked, "How can you know me for such a short amount of time and yet read me so well?"

"I pay attention to what's important to me," he whispered. "Would you like to know which era I'm most partial to?" Nicholas asked. He didn't wait for her to answer. "This one, because I'm living it with you."

Mia ran her hands playfully through his hair. "Me too. I couldn't have handled worrying about you going off to war if we lived back then." She gave him a peck on the cheek. "But I'd still like to convince you to take swing lessons with me. My sister promised me a few Benny Goodman tunes at her wedding." Mia froze, stumbling on her words. "I didn't mean to imply . . . or assume . . . that you'd be my date."

"Why are you so nervous?" Nicholas asked. "Unless you're planning on asking someone else, of course, I'd like to escort you to Kally's wedding."

"Someone else!" Mia laughed, poking him in the chest. "There's no one else, or I guess I can see if that photographer is still interested."

"The old lech," Nicholas grumbled. "When is the wedding? I'll make sure not to schedule a shoot for that week," he said.

"February fifteenth. The day after Valentine's Day. It's a Saturday," Mia said. "Now, I think it's time I got back to work. You just gave me a deadline for the Florence shoot that's going to need every minute of my attention."

The next day, Nicholas and Penelope attended a board meeting. That freed up Mia to have lunch with Jenny and Kyle, and she asked Suki to join them.

"It's nice to see you, Mia, my elusive roommate," Jenny said in jest. "You're home so infrequently these days that I almost forgot your face."

Mia stuck her tongue out at Jenny and giggled.

"The magazine has her traveling around the world!" Suki said. "I'm envious."

"Right." Jenny grinned. "That and hottie Bossman keeping her occupied," she added, wiggling her eyebrows.

"Jen!" Mia warned.

"You and Mr. Aristedis?" If Suki didn't close her mouth, she might be in danger of swallowing a fly, Mia mused. "I had no idea."

"That's a good thing," Mia said. "Let's keep it that way. I'm not ready for the rest of the staff to know." Mia felt she had to offer some explanation. "It's new . . . and it turns out that by a stroke of coincidence, we had met once before, many years ago. I think that encounter has factored into making our professional relationship more personal."

Kyle pushed his food around on his plate. Stone-faced, he offered nothing to the conversation asides from a couple of judgmental grunts. Jenny not-so-inconspicuously elbowed him.

"Kyle? Is there something you'd like to say to me?" Mia asked.

"Nope," Kyle said in a clipped tone.

"Kyle, please, I'd like us to remain friends," Mia pleaded. She looked crossly at Jenny. "I didn't mean for you to find out this way."

"A guy like that will keep you around until he either gets bored or thinks you're getting too serious," Kyle said bitterly. "Then what?" He rocked his pointer finger between himself and Jenny. "We get to watch you fall apart." He pushed his chair back from the table. "I'm done. I've had all the lunch I can stomach for one day." Kyle threw down his napkin, leaving without so much as a goodbye.

"What on Earth?" Mia always considered Kyle to be even-tempered. She'd never seen him quite so agitated.

"I need to learn how to keep my mouth shut," Jenny berated herself. "You and I both know he's got a thing for you. Throwing Nicholas in his face was thoughtless on my part."

"He would have found out sooner or later," Mia said. "I just didn't want it to be today."

"Is there always this much drama at lunch with the two of you?" Suki asked, aiming for levity.

"No, I'm sorry, Suki," Jenny apologized. "You must think we're off the wall."

"Not at all," Suki assured Jenny. "But let me see if I have this straight." She leaned in on her elbows. "Kyle likes you," she addressed Mia. "But you don't romantically like him and have never reciprocated his feelings." Before Mia could answer, Suki turned to Jenny. "And you like Kyle but he is completely clueless."

Both Mia and Jenny were impressed by her intuitive assessment.

"How and where did you pick that up in the conversation?" Mia asked.

"I'm very perceptive." Suki patted herself on the back. "It was your body language," she told Jenny. "And the fact that I've been in your position more times than I want to count."

"I'm sorry," Jenny said. "It sucks, doesn't it?"

Suki laughed. "Yes, but the moral of the story is that men are dumbass blind. They don't see what's in front of them."

"Oh, they see it if they choose to," Mia added.

"If it's meant to be, it will happen," Suki said. "If not, it's his loss and someone more suitable is out there waiting to meet you."

"I completely agree," Mia said. She looked at the time on her phone. "Right now, the only thing 'meant to be' is for me to get back to my desk," she said as a text from Kyle came through.

Kyle: *I was out of line. I'm sorry. Still friends?*

Mia: *Of course. Always.*

"See you later, Jen." Mia dropped her phone into her bag and slung the strap over her shoulder.

"It was great to meet you," Suki told Jenny.

"You too! Text me for a lunch date any time," Jenny said. She cocked her head in Mia's direction. "I have a feeling this one will be otherwise engaged."

"Although the world is full of suffering, it is also full of the overcoming of it." — *Helen Keller*

Chapter 36

Mia

The following weekend after Mia and Nicholas had arrived home from Greece, they reluctantly took the ride out to Long Island to speak with Mia's grandmother.

Mia was unsure about this decision. What if it caused her *yiayiá* more anguish? Without realizing it, Mia had been sighing on and off during the hour and a half drive.

Nicholas, steering with one hand, held hers with his other. He gave it a reassuring squeeze. "Stop worrying."

"What if we tell her and she has a stroke or something?" Mia asked. "I'll never forgive myself."

"She's the strongest woman I've ever met," Nicholas reassured her. "Must I remind you, she asked me to tell her if I found out anything?"

"True, but I'm sure, in her mind—in her dreams, you'd find my grandfather and bring him home to her."

"She'll have plenty of support. I suggested to your father that he gather your family," Nicholas said, glancing quickly at Mia. "That way, we only have to go over the story once, and she'll have everyone she loves beside her."

Mia hesitated before saying what was on her mind. "Considering what you told me . . . you know . . . about how you found out about

243

your parents, I'm surprised you think it's a good idea to have so many people around."

They were less than a mile from the house now. Instead of continuing up the road, Nicholas pulled over.

Stupid, stupid, Mia berated herself. She'd upset him. How could she be so insensitive?

Nicholas put the car in park and turned to Mia calmly. "This is a completely different situation. I was a twelve-year-old, blindsided by the most devastating news. Your grandmother has been living with her husband's absence for decades. Any news, good or bad, is at least something."

Mia exhaled. "Okay."

"Besides, no one will be looking to close in on me. If anything, they'll rally around your grandmother. She'll need the extra support."

"You're right," Mia agreed.

"Ready?" Nicholas asked. Taking her face in his hands, he brushed a soft kiss to her lips.

Mia nodded, and Nicholas put the car in drive. Moments later, they pulled into the Andarakis driveway.

Krystina ran to the door the moment she heard Mia call out to announce their arrival.

"Why are there so many cars in the driveway?" Mia asked Krystina.

"Thank him!" Krystina pointed to Nicholas. "When you asked to have the family together to hear what you learned, you had no clue what you were bargaining for," she warned Nicholas.

"I meant your parents and siblings," Nicholas clarified.

"And Mom took that to include Aunt Rhea, Aunt Thalia, Uncle Markos, their children, and of course, Max. Oh, and now that Max is part of our family, she asked his grandfather to come too," Krystina said, rattling off everyone she could think of.

"Don't forget me!" Loukas said, coming up behind Krystina.

Loukas rested his hands on Krystina's shoulders, and she

immediately shrugged them off. "Hands off me!" She sneered. "I don't even know why you were asked to come."

"Because he's part of the family," Mia said, swinging an arm around Loukas' shoulder. She shot her sister a disapproving glare. "Lead us to the wolves, Loukas."

As they stepped into the dining room, conversation ceased for maybe three seconds until an explosion of greetings befell Mia and Nicholas. Melina hopped over chairs to stand by her daughter, kissing her from cheek to cheek.

"Mom," Mia whispered. "Nicholas meant for this to be only for the immediate family."

Melina waved her off. "Why tell it over and over again." She turned to Nicholas. "We're anxious to hear what you learned. Sit, *pethia*."

Nicholas and Mia took a seat beside *Yiayiá* at the dining room table. George poured him a glass of wine, and Thalia made him a plate of *meze*, pushing it in front of him.

Yiayiá stared at Nicholas with trepidation. So many emotions could be read in her eyes—anticipation, hope, and fear. Mia took her grandmother's hand between hers, squeezing it in comfort.

"The flyer you gave me proved to be very helpful," Nicholas started once everyone had fallen quiet. "Once I got to Athens, I hired a private investigator."

A chatter of approval rang around the room. The family was impressed that Nicholas would go to such lengths and expense for one of their own family members.

"He led me to a taverna owner. A friend of your Panayiotis," he told *Yiayiá*. "*Kyria Kalliope*, this friend, Kostas, was part of a resistance group, along with your husband. They were the ones who printed and distributed the flyers—just like the one you gave me—*The Seeds of Prometheus*."

Crossing her hands over her heart, *Yiayiá* gasped. There was a question in her eyes, urging Nicholas to continue.

"I'm sorry to tell you that the Junta arrested and imprisoned both of them for approximately five years," Nicholas said solemnly.

"But this Kostas made it out," *Yiayiá* said. "What about my Panos?"

"He made it out too," Mia interjected, putting her arms around her grandmother.

"He wasn't killed by them." *Yiayiá* crossed herself three times, whispering *Panayia mou, voithisé me*—Most Holy Mother, help me. "Did this friend know where he is?"

Nicholas clasped his hands together, bowing his head as if in prayer. He took a deep breath and looked up at her. "No, they parted ways after they were released," Nicholas said. "It was a horrific time for both of them, and although they were bonded by their experience, it was too painful for them to remain in touch."

The room was silent. A grim heaviness hung in the air.

"Tell me," she demanded.

"*Yiayiá*," Mia pleaded.

Her grandmother didn't often give her 'the look,' but when she did, Mia didn't dare argue.

"Tell me what my Panos endured."

The tension in the room was palpable. Mia didn't want her to hear it, and she could tell by the muscles tightening in Nicholas' jaw, these were details he wanted to leave out. *Yiayiá* didn't waver in her determination to hear all of it, her eyes imploring him to continue. Nicholas relented.

"Panos and Kostas were subject to torture, both physical and psychological," Nicholas said, taking her shaking hands in his. "There's no reason to upset you with the details."

A sob erupted from the other end of the table. Melina buried her face in her hands and wept. George embraced his wife, pulling her into his chest and allowing her to mourn for the father she never had a chance to know.

"I'm sorry, *Mamá*," Melina cried.

"For what, *manoula mou*?" her mother asked.

"For hating him all these years. I accused him of abandoning us."

"I knew he didn't," *Yiayiá* said.

"But we have to wonder," Thalia spoke up, "why he didn't come to find you when he was released from prison."

Mia looked at her grandmother. She saw, for the first time, the old woman's confidence wavering. Mia signaled to Nicholas, and he instantly understood her message. He nodded, and Mia was struck how, once again, he seemed to read her thoughts.

Nicholas squeezed *Yiayiá's* hand affectionately. "Kostas told me that Panos loved you. You and Melina were all he talked about. Please don't doubt that."

Yiayiá nodded as tears spilled from the corners of her eyes. Nicholas pulled out a handkerchief and wiped them away.

"He also said that if your husband could have found his way back to you, he would have."

"That must mean he's dead." *Yiayiá* shook her head. Pounding her chest with her hand, she said, "I was so sure I'd feel it in here if he was."

"Don't give up hope quite yet," Nicholas said. "Something in Kostas' story didn't add up. I suspect he left some information out. I agree. It doesn't make sense that your husband wouldn't come looking for you. It's also not sitting right with me that he wouldn't stay in touch with the only man he shared such a traumatic experience with—the only other person who understands what he went through."

"What are you saying?" Melina asked.

"That I'm not done investigating. I still have my man on it," Nicholas answered. "I am going to do my best to find out what happened to your father after he was released from the prison," he told Melina.

"You're a good boy, Nikkos," *Yiayiá* said.

Nicholas looked at the old woman fondly. "My own grandmother used to call me that."

George stood, breaking the somber mood. He raised his glass. "A toast. To my father-in-law. A brave man who sacrificed everything for his family and country. And to our health. *Yamas*!"

"*Yamas!*" everyone around the table echoed.

"And for hoping," Mia added. "*Yia elpída!*"

As the family became distracted with side conversations while they picked on appetizers, *Yiayiá* requested Mia's and Nicholas' attention. "Can I speak to the two of you privately?"

"Of course," Mia agreed. "Let's go into the living room."

Yiayiá took a seat in a wingback chair. With her hands resting on the arms of her chair, she looked as regal as a queen upon her throne.

Mia and Nicholas took a seat on the sofa across from her. "What's on your mind?" Mia asked.

"First, is there anything you didn't want to say in front of every-one?" *Yiayiá* asked.

"Other than details that no one needs to hear, no," Nicholas said.

"Don't you think I have the right to know what happened to my husband?"

"*Yiayiá*, how will it help you to hear such things? It will only give you nightmares," Mia said.

"Nightmares my Panos lived through while I lived here in comfort," she uttered.

"I'd hardly say that when you worried about him every day for decades," Mia argued.

"It's not the same."

"You're stubborn," Mia declared.

"Ha!" Her grandmother laughed. "It's in the blood. You are too, *koritsaki mou.*"

"Are the two of you done playing verbal ping-pong?" Nicholas asked.

"Are you going to tell me what I want to hear?"

"*Kyria Kalliope*, he was beaten repeatedly. The Junta used many forms of torture. Much of it was more mental than physical. That's all I know," Nicholas said. "A person can't go through that without being scarred, on the inside as well as the outside. He may not be the man you married. You need to be prepared for that if he is still alive."

"Thank you for your honesty, Nikkos. That's all I ask," *Yiayiá* said. "You get to a certain age and people treat you as though you're frail. I can assure you, I am not." She pointed to the dining room. "I've been through more than everyone in there put together," she stated.

"Okay, I'm sorry, *Yiayiá*," Mia said. "I wanted to protect you, that's all. Let's go back inside with everyone now."

Mia stood but her grandmother gestured for her to sit once more. The woman was apparently still holding court.

"I'm not done," she said. "I told you that was only the first thing I wanted to discuss."

Mia and Nicholas looked at one another with raised eyebrows. Mia stifled a laugh.

Yiayiá's face softened. "Tell me, *pethia*, what is going on between the two of you?"

"What . . . what do you mean?" Mia stuttered.

Nicholas took Mia's hand. "It's not a secret," he whispered.

"I only had to look at you to know," *Yiayiá* said. "I'm happy you figured it out. I knew before the two of you realized it yourselves. Now, don't screw it up!"

Mia and Nicholas burst with laughter. "We'll do our best," Nicholas grinned.

"Unfortunately, we have to leave," Mia announced, escorting *Yiayiá* back to the dining room. "This will be a working weekend for us."

"You're heading back to the city already?" Melina sounded disappointed.

"No, actually, we're headed to my house in Southampton," Nicholas said. "We'll work from there, and this evening, we'll be dining with my grandfather."

Mia turned to him with a look of bewilderment. "You didn't tell me that," she said under her breath, concealing her irritation with a smile.

Mia took a turn around the table, kissing each person goodbye. Nicholas waved to the crowd, and they left the room.

"Why didn't you tell me?" Mia asked. "You can't just throw this on me at the last minute."

"He only got in last night," Nicholas explained. "Penelope has been pumping you up, and he's anxious to meet you."

"As if this afternoon hasn't been stressful enough!" Mia exclaimed.

"He's going to love you." Nicholas kissed her as they headed out the door. Onto the next adventure of the day.

Chapter 37

Mia

Pavlos Aristedis was working in his study when Mia and Nicholas arrived at the Southampton home. The elderly gentleman peered over his computer as the couple entered the room.

"*Pappou*, I'd like to introduce you to Mia Andarakis," Nicholas said.

Pavlos rose from his desk, smiling. Even with the few steps he took to reach her, Mia sensed his command and power by his straight posture and unreadable countenance.

Pavlos greeted Mia with the customary double-cheek kiss. "Nicholas told me what an asset you've been to the magazine but he didn't mention you were an *Ellinítha*.

"I guess my name gave me away." Mia grinned. "It's a pleasure to meet you, sir." The familiar sense of intimidation, the same kind she had when she'd first formally met Nicholas, came flooding back to Mia. Mr. Aristedis was an imposing man, tall and slender, with an elegant air about his stature. His hair was white as freshly fallen snow, and she'd bet her favorite pair of shoes the man hadn't lost even one strand of it in all his eighty-two years.

"I had dinner catered in," Pavlos said. "Get settled and join me in the dining room."

Nicholas and Mia excused themselves and padded up the stairs. When Mia stopped in front of the door of the room she'd previously stayed on her last visit, Nicholas blocked the way. "Where do you think you're going?" he asked.

"The guest bedroom," Mia answered as if it had to be spelled out.

Nicholas shook his head. "This way." He pointed in the direction of the room just beyond where they stood.

"I can't stay in there with you!" Mia exclaimed. "What will your grandfather think?"

"His room is on the other side of the house but I imagine he wouldn't think anything of it."

"You imagine?" Mia speculated. "What has he allowed in the past?"

"Do you really want to have this discussion in the hallway?" Mia detected a hint of annoyance in Nicholas' tone. "I thought I made myself clear regarding my past dating status."

"You did, but I'm assuming I'm not the first girl you've brought here," Mia said. She waved off the subject when Nicholas frowned at her. "In any case, all I can say is that if we were staying at my parents' home, they'd send you to the other side of the house to sleep." She smirked. "Probably the basement."

"Let's plan never to stay there then," he joked. "Now, we need to get downstairs pronto because, if I know my grandfather, he's already seated and impatiently waiting for us."

Dinner was unusual, if not a little uncomfortable for Mia. The formality was a bit unsettling. Pavlos and Nicholas discussed business as though they were at a board meeting while Mia listened intently, trying to keep up.

After a while, all she could focus on was the filet mignon in champagne sauce, baby roasted potatoes, and grilled asparagus on her plate. She would have taken a bath in the creamy gravy if she could have; it was that delicious. Instead, Mia coated each bite of steak, soaking up every last drop. She barely noticed when Pavlos turned his attention to her.

"Tell me about yourself." Coming from Mr. Aristedis, the request sounded like an order. Under the table, Nicholas took Mia's hand reassuringly. She had to admit, that one small gesture gave her the comfort and courage she needed to speak.

Mia began to tell him about her father's restaurant and what her mother did for a living. She talked about her siblings and her grandparents in Athens, who she just had the pleasure of visiting.

"Is it okay if I share your grandmother's story and what we've been up to?" Nicholas asked.

Mia nodded and addressed Mr. Aristedis. "My *yiayiá*, my mother's mother, lives with us. She came here when my mother was three years old."

Mia went on to tell Nicholas' grandfather the entire story as she knew it. Nicholas interjected with the information they'd learned during his investigation, and Pavlos contributed with his own recollections of the time.

When Nicholas' iPhone vibrated, he pulled it from his pocket and frowned. "I need to take this, excuse me," he said, leaving the room.

An awkward silence ensued until Pavlos set down his fork, taking a hard look at Mia. "This a quite fortuitous," he said to Mia. "I wanted the chance to speak to you alone."

Mia smiled politely, hoping the elderly man didn't pick up on her discomfort. He could intimidate with a simple glance.

"I love my grandson very much."

The pronouncement warmed Mia's heart. "He loves you too. Nicholas speaks of you all the time."

Pavlos remained stoic, seemingly unmoved by Mia's admission. "His sister and I are all Nicholas has in this world. We are both fiercely protective of him."

"As you should be," Mia agreed. "I feel the same toward my family."

"Penelope endlessly sings your praises, and her approval doesn't come easily." Pavlos steepled his fingers, narrowing his eyes. "Still, I'm not so quickly won over. I need to learn more."

Mia felt internal heat rising from inside her chest, spreading up to her neck, as a flush intensified across her face. Someone must have cut her tongue out because, suddenly, she was struck mute.

"I'll get to the point," he said. "The women Nicholas has dated in the past came from families who were, shall we say, financially sound, for lack of a better expression."

Mia closed her eyes, trying to keep the composure she was sure to lose. "You mean wealthy," Mia challenged. "Let's not mince words," she said with false sweetness. They were only thirty seconds into this conversation, and Mia knew she would crumble to pieces before their discussion had ended if she didn't dig way down deep to find the strength to defend herself.

"Yes, wealthy," Pavlos agreed. "Unfortunately," he said with a sigh, "none of these women were significant to Nicholas, but had they been, I had little concern in their motives stemming from financial gain."

Calmly, Mia lifted her wine glass, sipping slowly as she pondered. "I don't know if that's an accurate statement. Some women, no matter how wealthy, want it all—the man, the money, and the empire."

Pavlos leaned forward. "And what is it that you want?" he asked, glaring at Mia as though he could read her innermost thoughts. "Nicholas and Penelope stand to inherit a fortune. You're a woman of average means from a modest family. What do you expect to gain?"

"Gain?" Mia was incredulous. The gall of this man! "Nicholas is my boss, and yes, we've begun to date," she admitted with a shaky tremor to her voice. "But that's all it is—dating. And we only started recently."

Mia inhaled deeply, trying to quell the trembling in her voice. Every part of her was internally quivering. Exhaling, she said as firmly as she could, "Nicholas is a grown man and makes his own decisions about who he wants to spend time with."

"I watched Penelope fall apart after the man she was to marry loved her money more than her. Nicholas also fell under the spell of a young woman who preferred a jet-setting lifestyle to hard work." He pounded his fist on the table. "I will not watch either of my grandchildren go through that again. If you marry my grandson, you will have to sign a prenuptial agreement, and I'll make sure it's not a generous one."

Mia's nostrils flared as she glared at the old man in vexation. "First of all," she said, her tone harsh, "Nicholas has not asked me to marry him, nor has the subject even remotely come up." She put her hand up to halt him, fully aware that the same gesture offered to someone in Greece meant 'F' you. "Second, I hate the idea of prenups. Marriage should be based on love and trust, meant for a lifetime. A contract such as that prepares for the demise of the marriage before it begins. But," Mia continued, softening her voice, "I get it. You need to protect your grandson and his assets. I would gladly sign it because I know if I entered into a loving union, it would be forever. However, I would insist on one thing."

"Ah! The one thing," Pavlos chided. "And what would that be?"

"That the contract states, I leave the marriage with nothing other than what I entered into it with."

She'd thrown the man off his game. It was written all over his face. Check and checkmate. "You see, I don't want a thing from your grandson except his . . ." Mia wanted to say, love. She cleared away the emotion in her throat. "I just enjoy his company."

Pavlos leaned back in his chair, massaging his jaw thoughtfully. "Mia, do you love my grandson?" His voice was no longer stern.

"Those are not words that have been spoken between us. If and when that time comes, Nicholas will hear it from me first," Mia said.

"Fair enough."

"Now, if you'll excuse me, I'm going to lie down." Mia pushed her chair back from the table. "I'm building a headache. Please offer my apologies to Nicholas. Goodnight, Mr. Aristedis."

Standing politely, Pavlos said softly, "Goodnight, Mia."

As she headed toward the staircase, Mia noticed Nicholas in the study, still deep in conversation on his mobile. She crept up the stairs and decided to rest in the guest bedroom instead of Nicholas' room. Weary, she peeled off her dress, crawling into bed wearing only her undergarments. Within minutes, Mia was fast asleep.

Filet Mignon in Champagne Sauce

4 1-inch-thick filet mignon steaks

8 large stuffing mushrooms, whole. Stems off

3 shallots, sliced

5 tablespoons butter

½ cup champagne

1 cup heavy cream

Salt & pepper to taste

Method

Sprinkle meat with salt & pepper. Melt four tablespoons of butter in a large skillet and pan-fry the steaks on both sides until cooked to your preference. Flip the meat to the other side. Add the shallots and mushrooms. When the steaks are done, remove from heat and set aside on a platter. Cover to keep warm. Place the cooked mushrooms on the platter with the steaks.

Add the champagne to the pan and bring to a boil. Add the heavy cream. Lower the heat and simmer for two minutes. Remove from heat and stir the last tablespoon of butter into the sauce. Add the steaks and mushrooms back into the pan. To serve, pour the sauce over the steaks and garnish with two mushrooms.

Chapter 38

Nicholas

"Sorry about that," Nicholas trailed off as he came into the dining room. "Where's Mia?"

"The girl wasn't feeling well," Pavlos said. "She went up to her room."

Nicholas took one glance at his grandfather, and he knew he was up to something. "When did she go up?"

"About five minutes ago."

"What did I miss in my absence?" Nicholas asked. He only hoped the old man had put on his grandfatherly hat rather than the ruthless businessman headgear.

"We were getting acquainted."

Nicholas muttered under his breath. His grandfather was intentionally vague. He was sure of it. "What, specifically, did you talk about?"

"Nothing to concern yourself with." Pavlos seemed put off by the questions. "We came to an understanding, in the end."

Nicholas placed his elbows on the table, scrubbing his face with his hands. "What did you say to her?" He looked up at his grandfather. "Tell me you didn't interrogate her." Nicholas' tone rang of accusation.

"I had to know her motives," Pavlos said, pointing at Nicholas. "If you think I'm going to stand by and watch someone take advantage of you . . . well, I'll go to my grave first."

Nicholas groaned. What was he supposed to say to that? His

grandfather's methods were slightly dictatorial but his intentions were good. "*Pappou*, I can take care of myself and my own love life. Your interference will only prove to hurt me in the long run."

Apology marked his grandfather's face. "She genuinely cares about you. Mia is a good girl."

"Let's hope she isn't up there calling an Uber right now," Nicholas sighed. "It wouldn't be the first time," he muttered. "If you'll excuse me, I need to go to her."

"Of course. Goodnight, *agori mou*."

When Nicholas entered his bedroom, he found it empty. A burst of adrenaline pumped through his veins, sending a message of panic straight to his heart. Looking for any sign of her, Nicholas relaxed when he spotted Mia's overnight bag sitting in the corner of the room beside his. She wasn't gone. Nicholas was more relieved than he wanted to admit.

He peeked inside his connecting bathroom, finding no evidence of her. It didn't appear that she had showered or even set out her toiletries on the sink vanity. Nicholas couldn't imagine where she'd gone. Then he had a thought. Quietly, he lurked down the hallway to the next room. Mia was sound asleep in the guest bedroom. Poor girl. His grandfather had, most likely, put her through her paces.

Nicholas looked about the room. Mia's heels were haphazardly strewn in the middle of the carpet and her dress discarded carelessly onto a chair by the window. Light filtered in between the panels of curtains, illuminating slivers of light on her angelic face, her bow-shaped lips still stained with berry gloss. Nicholas rolled down the duvet just enough to spy on what she was wearing, discovering nothing but sheer blush lace. He groaned inwardly.

Nicholas wasn't about to disturb her slumber; still, he wasn't about to crawl into his own bed without her either. He stripped down to his boxer briefs and slipped under the covers beside her.

The next morning, Mia stretched out her arms and screeched when she realized she wasn't alone.

"It's just me," Nicholas warned.

"Why aren't you in your own bed?" Mia's voice was gravelly.

"You weren't in it."

"Nicholas." Mia turned on her side to face him. "This isn't a good idea."

"What isn't?"

"All of it," Mia said. "My being here. Me and you. Your grandfather disapproves, and I know how much you love and respect him."

"I do, but he doesn't get to tell me who to be with."

"That may well be but it's not something I can live with. I can't stay here. The man hates me."

"I can assure you that he doesn't," Nicholas said.

"You didn't hear the things he said to me."

"No, I didn't, and I'm sorry for that," Nicholas apologized. "He was completely out of line. But as my only parent figure, he thinks he's justified." Nicholas brushed away the stray strands of hair falling across Mia's face. "He likes you." Nicholas smiled. "He said, and I quote, 'She genuinely cares about you. Mia is a good girl.'"

"Really?" Mia questioned.

Nicholas chuckled. "Don't sound so skeptical. Those were his exact words. He's a tough nut to crack, but once he decides he likes someone, he can't do enough for them."

"I don't know," Mia said dubiously. "I got the sense that he'd like me to slither away like an undeserving slug who has no right to be slinking up his pristine walkway."

"Where do you come up with this stuff?" Nicholas laughed.

"Don't make fun of me!" Mia slapped his arm playfully. "I'm serious. I was going to leave first thing this morning."

"Now, why doesn't that surprise me?" Nicholas asked, not expecting a reply. "When are you going to stop cutting out on me?" He held onto her, shifting Mia so her back was pressed against his front. Nicholas kissed the tip of her shoulder, smiling into it when goosebumps rose on her flesh. "You like me," Nicholas teased.

"Just a little," Mia murmured.

* * *

Nicholas had to prod Mia down to the first floor of the house.

"I'm not ready to face your grandfather," she admitted.

"Come on," Nicholas said. "Do I have to pick you up and carry you myself? Trust me, his bark is worse than his bite."

"Ah, *pethia!*" Pavlos, grinning from ear to ear, stood in the foyer. "I've been waiting for the two of you to come down. I have a splendid idea." Dressed like an old sea admiral, Pavlos was decked out, no pun intended, in white slacks, a navy blazer, and a sea captain's cap.

Nicholas sauntered down the stairs, his arm looped in Mia's. "Pappou, hasn't anyone told you there's a rule against wearing white after Labor Day?" Nicholas ribbed his grandfather.

Pavlos waved him off dismissively. "It's springtime in the southern hemisphere."

"I see. Is that like when someone says 'it's five o'clock somewhere?'" Nicholas bantered.

"Exactly! I have champagne on the boat, and it's ready to go," Pavlos declared. "It's a rare day in late October when it's seventy degrees. Let's go for a little ride before I have it sent south for the winter."

Nicholas looked at Mia. "What do you say?"

Before Mia could utter a word, Pavlos took her hand. "I would very much enjoy your company today. Please join me for a day on the boat. I know I was harsh with you, and I'm truly sorry," Pavlos apologized. "I love my grandchildren, and I can't stand the thought of them being hurt or used in any way."

"I understand," Mia said.

"Thank you. Nicholas practically threatened to never speak to me again."

Nicholas cocked his head and shrugged when Mia looked to him for confirmation.

Pavlos opened his arms to Mia, embracing her with a double-cheek kiss.

I know what it's like to have Greek grandparents," Mia grinned, letting Pavlos off easy. "If anyone dared to hurt me, my *yiayiá* would probably curse them with *the máti*," she laughed.

Nicholas handed Mia one of the two champagne flutes he was holding. She was seated at the semi-circular sectional on the flybridge deck, her hair blowing in the wind as the boat motored along.

"Your grandfather said we were going on his boat. I've been on Max's father's boat. It's fifty feet long," Mia said. "Already more than most boaters dream of owning. Mia waved her hand around in awe. "But this is not a boat. It's a cruise ship."

"It's a yacht," Nicholas corrected, amused. "Cruise ships are more than ten times this size."

"Don't be so literal." Mia sliced off a chunk of cheese and filled a cracker. "A yacht with a hot tub on the deck? That spells cruise ship to me." She popped the cracker in her mouth, licking the excess cheese off her lips with the tip of her tongue.

An imperceptible growl reverberated in his throat. Leaning in, he kissed her.

"Was that to stop me from contradicting you?" Mia giggled.

"That was because your lips are irresistible." The woman had no idea of the effect she had on him.

"It's such a lovely day," Mia said, leaning her back into his chest as she admired the view. "I'm not looking forward to when the cold weather sets in."

"I'll be happy to keep you warm," Nicholas promised, sliding his hand under her top.

"Will you?" Mia pretended to think about it. "This sweater is doing a pretty good job shielding me from the wind," she mused. "And I have a set of toasty footed pajamas for super cold nights."

"Sexy," Nicholas said in a disdainful tone. "Are you testing my sense of humor?" He loved seeing this playful side of Mia come out.

"You have one?" Mia asked wryly. She slid onto his lap and rubbed the stubble on his jaw against her soft cheek. "You know I'm only teasing you."

"It's good to see you at ease enough to do so with me," he said. "For a while, I only seemed to make you tense." Nicholas couldn't blame her.

"You were an ogre." She gave him a peck on the cheek. "Talking about ogres, where did your grandfather go?" She held her hands up in surrender. "I'm kidding. He totally redeemed himself this morning."

"He's talking to the captain."

An hour later, the yacht pulled up near a waterside restaurant as they waited for a courtesy dinghy to take them to the dock. The wind had picked up, so Nicholas requested a table indoors by a large window overlooking the water.

Pavlos asked Mia about this grandmother of hers who went around giving the evil eye to anyone who looked at Mia the wrong way. In turn, Pavlos spoke of his wife and their many happy years together.

Without even looking at him, Mia sensed the shift in Nicholas' mood. She reached for his hand under the table, caressing it tenderly. She was the only one other than Penelope who instinctively knew when to comfort him or give him space to breathe. More and more, Nicholas realized that he didn't want space, or even a wisp of air, between himself and Mia. A tumble of emotions barreled through him—some filling his soul with a joy he had never felt, and others overshadowing that sense of happiness with abject fear.

By the time the boat returned to the yacht club, the sun had begun to set. Mia voiced her dismay on how the shorter days were yet another sign of winter on the horizon.

"Are you ready to leave?" Nicholas asked Mia.

"Sure. I'm just taking in all the colors as they fade from one hue and darken to the next."

Nicholas stood behind her, wrapping his arms around her waist. The height difference between them allowed Nicholas to rest his chin on the top of Mia's head. "It's peaceful out here. Sometimes I'd come out in the evening alone and sit on the deck." Often it was during times of sad contemplation but Nicolas omitted that grim truth.

"I'm heading back home," Pavlos interrupted." I'll see you there."

Mia smiled and Nicolas waved as the old man ambled down the dock.

* * *

"Thank you for a lovely day, Mr. Aristedis," Mia said, standing by the front entranceway. Their bags were already loaded in the trunk of the car.

"It was my pleasure. I'm leaving for my island in a couple of days," Pavlos said. "I need to check on the house, and I like to spend this time of year there, but I look forward to seeing you when I get back."

Nicholas grinned, content that no lingering animosity existed from their initial conversation. Affectionately, he threaded his fingers with Mia's.

Mia smiled. "*Kaló taxídi.*" She reached up, offering a double-cheek kiss to Pavlos.

Nicholas was quiet on the ride back to the city. He found himself lost in thought over the events of the past few days. It had been quite a weekend. Telling Mia's grandmother the news they had learned, followed by the explosive encounter Mia had with his own grandparent, had left him feeling somewhat drained. This woman had taken his simple, drama-free existence and turned it upside down. Normally, this would make him run far, far away from a woman. But Mia had quite the opposite effect on him. He was beginning to wonder how he ever existed without her.

Chapter 39

Mia

Mia stamped her feet and shrieked like a child who'd just received her favorite toy from Santa Claus. She and Nicholas had just arrived at their suite in Florence, Italy. Immediately, she ran to the balcony to check out the view. It didn't disappoint. High above all the clay-topped roofs, the Duomo proudly stood as the life-force of the cultural city. Mia could only imagine what evening looked like as the sun set behind the holy monument.

"If you like this view, wait until you walk through the city," Nicholas said as he came up behind her.

Turning, Mia looked at him in awe. "Do I thank Penelope for hiring me or just thank God that you didn't fire me after my first week?"

Nicholas brushed the hair away from the side of her face. Trailing a string of kisses down her neck, his voice was muffled. "It's me who's grateful you didn't quit for good."

Mia could quickly get drunk on Nicholas' caresses but she pulled herself back to sobriety. She was in Florence! There was so much to see!

"Come on, let's go!" Mia tugged at Nicholas. "We only have today. I want to see as much as we can."

"There's an outdoor café in the *Piazza della Repubblica* that I think you'll enjoy," Nicholas suggested, laughing at her excitement. "Then

I've arranged a tour of the Uffizi and tickets to see the inside of the Duomo. After that, you'll be hungry again, if I know you."

Mia clapped her hands. "I'm ready! Just pump me up with some of that coffee the Italians obsess over, and I'll be set to go."

Florence, or *Firenze*, as it was rightfully named, Mia learned, was not like any other city she'd ever been to. Nicholas had advised she trade out her heels for a pair of sensible riding boots. Wisely, Mia had listened. With a language translation book in one hand and a city guide in the other, Mia tripped over the uneven cobblestone path more than once, even in her flats.

With the absence of modern skyscrapers in this renaissance city, Mia imagined everyday life here had not changed drastically over the last hundred years. Residents didn't race around town in a frenzy. Pedestrians strolled about in deep, animated conversation, a gelato in one hand and often, a parcel in the other. If taxis existed, Mia saw no evidence of them, except on the main highways or occasionally in front of a hotel.

"Forget the guide," Nicholas insisted, snatching the pamphlet from her clutches. "Look around you. Listen to the rhythm of the language. Smell the aroma wafting from the *trattorias*."

"I don't want to miss anything," Mia said.

"You can't know *Firenze* in a day," he forewarned. "And you certainly can't experience it looking at a map."

Soon they arrived at an open square surrounded by centuries-old buildings. Mia's face lit up when she spotted an operating carousel.

"I thought you'd like it," Nicholas proclaimed. "The café is over there," he pointed out.

The weather had remained mild for November, but when Mia approached Caffè Gilli, she couldn't decide whether to eat indoors or out. Outside, Mia could watch passersby and observe riders on the carousel as it turned around to the music. But stepping inside the café was like being transported to another era. Rich wood, marble table-tops, and plush, upholstered chairs furnished the main dining room. Beyond that, as Mia explored further, she discovered a section dedicated entirely to confections in all colors, shapes, and sizes—flowers and fruits; animals and geometric shapes—and chocolates replicating monuments and masterpieces.

Mia was astounded by the detail of each creation and the beautiful aesthetic in which they were displayed.

"I have to bring some home for my sisters!"

"We can purchase them later tonight so they don't spoil," Nicholas suggested.

They found a table and ordered. While the couple waited for their food, Nicholas pulled out Mia's guide, spreading it out on the table.

"We have a very early call in the morning," Nicholas explained. "An hour before sunrise, the crew will be setting up in front of *La Cattedrale Santa Maria Del Fiore*. The *Duomo*," he clarified, pointing to the location on the map. "We'll also shoot at the *Loggia dei Lanzi* at *Piazza Della Signoria*." Nicholas circled the area on the map. "The archways are stunning, and I want shots of the models next to the statues in wide-angle views." He looked up at Mia. "Are you listening to me?"

"Oh, yes," she said dreamily. "When you speak Greek, to me, it's the same as listening to English. A familiar language I've heard all my life." Mia's breath came out in a swoony sigh. "But when you speak Italian, it's so sexy my insides get all jittery."

"Is that so?" Nicholas smiled. He lifted her hand. Kissing the top of it, he said, "*Sei l'unica donna con cui voglio passare i miei giorni e le mie notti facendo l'amore.*"

"Dreamy," Mia said, her eyes heavy-lidded. "I don't know what that means, and I don't care."

"I said, you are the only woman I want to spend my days and nights making love to."

Nicholas had a way of knocking the breath from Mia. The feather-like sensation of his lips grazing over her skin sent chills through her. And his words sent shivers right to the core of her soul. Mia drew her eyes from his, shyly, praying this dream would never end. Yet her insides fluttered with nerves. Soon, someday, Nicholas would tire of her and move on to someone else. He'd professed only his desire for her, not his love. For now, though, these waves of insecurities would have to be brushed aside. Mia was in Florence, and she intended to soak up the art, history, and yes, the romance of it all.

* * *

The next morning, the photo shoot finished without incident. In fact, Mia thought it had gone extraordinarily well. Models, emulating the powerful Florentine Medici family, posed by the centuries-old structures, each a testament to their influence and contribution to their city during the renaissance. In contrast to the extravagance of the times, the darker tones of the era were also addressed. Penelope's team was assigned to write articles on the devastation of the black plague and what segment of the population it mainly affected. To highlight this, Mia had suggested recreating a scene depicting the inequity and affliction on the citizens. Nicholas loved the idea. They hired additional models and found a dingy, narrow alley for the set location.

Nicholas came up behind Mia, discreetly rubbing her shoulders. "I kept you up too late last night," he whispered in her ear. How the man was able to sound both worried and proud simultaneously, Mia would never understand.

"I'm not tired," Mia answered. But she was trying her hardest to stay focused. Her mind drifted off to their late-night hand-in-hand walk to the *Ponte Vecchio*, leading to a long kiss on the full moon-illuminated bridge. Sigh . . . A ride on the carousel after dark and dinner for two at a rooftop restaurant overlooking the enchanting city had finished off a magical evening out.

What came after they'd returned to the hotel left an indelible mark on Mia's body, and even more so on her heart. The Greek side of Nicholas was sensual, but in Italy, when that side of his DNA emerged, he was erotically and deliciously carnal. Mia shook the ridiculous thought from her mind. What was she thinking? Nicholas' sexual prowess had nothing to do with geography.

Mia clasped her hands together, lifting them high above her head in a stretch. What she wouldn't do for some coffee right now! The pistachio-rimmed latte she enjoyed the night before at the *pasticceria* near the Duomo would have been a godsend at that moment.

"For you, *la mia bella ragazza.*"

Nicholas, as if reading her mind, handed her the very beverage she'd just been dreaming of. Mia took it greedily, thanking him. In the States, her takeaway would have been in a disposable cup. Here in Italy, coffee was revered like gold bars protected in a fortress. "How did you manage this?" Mia asked of the glass latte mug.

"It will be returned," Nicholas said.

"Kally needs to add this to her menu."

"Two more shots and it's a wrap." Nicholas looked at the time on his iPhone.

"Yup," Mia said with regret. "And then we leave. What time is our flight?"

One side of Nicholas' mouth curved up in a knowing smile. What wasn't he telling her?

"Two days from now."

"What is two days from now?"

"Our flight. I wanted to surprise you," Nicholas said, waiting for her reaction.

"That's . . . amazing! But I have nothing to wear. I came with an overnight bag. Enough clothing for only two days."

Nicholas smacked a kiss on her. "I doubt that. But if you're concerned, we can go shopping."

Mia had seen some lovely boutiques she'd not had a chance to explore.

"There's something else." Nicholas took on a serious expression. "Tomorrow, I'd like to visit my grandparents in San Gimignano. Would you join me?"

"Oh." Mia's eyes grew wide. "That would be lovely. How far is it from here?"

"It's a little over an hour away," Nicholas said. "But very scenic. I think you'll enjoy it."

* * *

"Tell me what to expect." Mia was honored to be asked to meet Nicholas' grandparents. Still, she was nervous. She worried about how the day would leave Nicholas and wondered if it would drudge up too many memories for him.

Nicholas rented a car, and he seemed in good spirits when they set off to visit Domenico and Francesca Innocenti.

"They're very down-to-earth people," Nicholas said. "My grandfather is over eighty years old and still works the vineyard."

"Vineyard?"

"I guess I forgot to mention that part. It's been in their family for generations."

"Your family too," Mia said.

"Yes," he said sadly. "My uncle and his children run it now. My mother left the vineyard when she married my father. I find winemaking fascinating but it's a lifestyle, and I was only exposed to it a few times a year growing up."

"How did they meet? Your parents?"

Nicholas took his eyes off the road momentarily to glance at Mia. It took only that quick moment for Mia to read the sweetness of nostalgic memories and the melancholy of a long-ago loss simultaneously reflected in his expression.

"They met at the vineyard." Nicholas shook his head, laughing to himself.

"What?" Mia asked with a smile, wondering what he was thinking.

"Penelope recently asked me if I believed in destiny," he answered. "I thought it was a strange question coming from my pragmatic sister. But my parents met their destiny more than once," he said on a sigh.

"Nicholas," Mia whispered, her tone gentle. She placed her hand over his.

"It's fine," Nicholas said. "I enjoy visiting my grandparents, even if it stirs up too many emotions for me."

"Think of the vineyard as the place where your parents fell in love," Mia said. "From what you told me, they were so happy together."

"They were. My grandparents had taken my father to Italy for a vacation. They were only in Tuscany for a few days. They could have chosen any vineyard to visit," Nicholas continued. "There are dozens of them. But they chose Innocenti for the view and the highly-recommended wine tasting luncheon on offer."

Mia could picture it in her mind. She tried to calculate the year. The early eighties, perhaps.

"My mother, Lucia, welcomed them, seating my father and his parents at the outdoor patio overlooking the landscape." Nicholas gestured to his right. "The view was very much like what you see out there."

"It's stunning," Mia said with admiration. "So lush. What are those trees called? I've never seen evergreens so tall and narrow."

"Italian cypress," Nicholas said. "They stand quite regally, don't they?"

Mia agreed. They were nature's statues, not carved, but grown only for this land, she thought nostalgically. "Tell me the rest." Mia relished in a good love story.

"As my father explained it, he was captivated by my mother from the moment he saw her. He wasn't normally nervous around girls, but with my mother, he was a mess." Nicholas chuckled. "He didn't even realize that she was just as tongue-tied around him. My father and his parents stayed at a hotel in Florence. The next day, my father took the car, and instead of touring the sites of *Firenze*, he drove back to the vineyard."

"But then he had to go home. What then? How did they keep in touch?"

"The old-fashioned way. There was no social media or cell phones. But there were letters. They wrote almost every day. Three months later, he went back and asked for her hand in marriage."

"That's the most romantic thing I've ever heard," Mia swooned.

It wasn't long after he finished his tale that Nicholas turned onto a long dirt road lined by tall cypress trees just like the ones she had admired. Beyond the evergreens, rows and rows of grapevines dominated the land on either side of the path leading to the Innocenti home.

"I thought you said it was a small family vineyard?"

The centuries-old home that appeared into Mia's view was grander than she'd expected. It boasted the trademark paprika-colored clay rooftop like most of the buildings throughout Tuscany. The front door archway was lined in stone blocks but the walls were a pale, buttery hue. Despite its imposing size, the building was charming.

Nicholas pulled up near the entrance to the house. Mia wasted no time exiting to get a better view of the surroundings.

"So, right here," Nicholas said, framing out the center of the home with his fingers, "was the original structure. It was built in the early eighteen-hundreds." He took Mia's hand, guiding her to the right of the building. "This wing was added on after my parents married. You see, guests were brought into the private home for wine tastings and luncheons during inclement weather."

"That sounds quaint," Mia said.

"It had an appeal tourists enjoyed. But my father's family offered them the funding to expand. They added a tasting room and a dining room. It was designed as an extension to the main house to maintain the homey atmosphere patrons had come to enjoy." Turning, Nicholas guided Mia to the other side of the house. "This addition was the other phase, constructed a few years later. Let's go in."

Mia looked around the room, observing the wine shop. Bottles stacked in rows on dark wooden shelves were neatly arranged. Wine glasses etched with the vineyard name sat on glass tables. And a sampling of gift items unique to the region was displayed decoratively throughout the space. The Tuscan-gold paint and low-hanging light fixtures gave the area a warm, inviting charm.

"Is that you, Nico?" A middle-aged woman came from behind the counter to greet him.

"*Ciao, Zia Lena.*"

With her hands outstretched, the tall, slender woman ran to embrace her nephew. They exchanged double-cheek kisses, which the salt-and-pepper-haired woman repeated on Mia once Nicholas introduced them.

A couple juggling several bottles of wine set them down on the counter by the cash register.

"*Scusa.*" Lena patted Nicholas as she scurried to the patrons. "Go see your *nonna.*"

"She's adorable," Mia said as they exited the building. "I bet she was stunning in her youth."

"She was," Nicholas confirmed. The old, wooden entrance door to the main house was as heavy as it was weathered. Nicholas pushed it open, gesturing for Mia to enter first. "Lena and my Uncle Ciro were childhood sweethearts."

Nicholas nudged Mia when they found his *nonna* in the kitchen. He put his fingers to his lips, signaling for Mia to remain quiet. *Nonna* sang to herself as she chopped garlic, stuffing it between the leaves of extra-large artichokes.

When Nicholas began to sing the words along with his grandmother, the old woman turned in surprise. Dropping the weighty vegetable onto the counter, she wiped her damp hands on her apron before raising them to the heavens. "*Il mio bel ragazzo!*"

After peppering her grandson with kisses, *Nonna* took Mia's face between her wrinkled and surprisingly strong hands. The old woman had an unreadable expression on her face, and Mia didn't know what to make of it. *Nonna* examined Mia closely. She spoke no English but what she said sounded sadly affectionate to Mia, which made no sense. Mia turned to Nicholas for translation and saw unshed tears filming over his eyes.

"She said you remind her of her daughter," Nicholas croaked out, his voice gravelly with emotion. "My mother. Especially around the eyes, she said."

Nonna nodded, understanding that Nicholas had translated her words. The woman, who stood a few inches shorter than Mia, lovingly kissed each side of her face as though she were one of her own.

"Thank you for taking me to meet them," Mia said in the car on their way back to the hotel.

Aside from not being able to understand a word his grandparents spoke, it was a perfect afternoon. The patio's view overlooked hills and vineyards, and from a distance, Mia had been able to see the town's rooftops beyond. The wine was some of the best she'd ever tasted, and the meal exploded with a flavor that would linger in her mind forever. Mia had picked off the leaves of one of the artichokes his grandmother had prepared. As she sucked out the garlic and lemon juice, Mia almost laughed out loud, remembering when Nicholas had once compared her to the multi-layered vegetable.

"You've met all of my relatives, yet you didn't ask me along to visit your grandparents in Athens." Nicholas pretended to be offended.

"If I recall, you were off on some mysterious mission that night," Mia retorted.

"And who was I looking for?"

"Okay, you win this one." Mia grinned.

When they pulled up to the hotel entrance, Mia stepped out of the car, looking about. "I'm going to miss this city," she said on a mournful sigh. Turning, her eyes grew wide. "Let's not waste this last night. I want to go for a walk, eat gelato, and then get a cappuccino."

Nicholas placed his hands on his hips, feigning exasperation. "What? No *bomboloni?*"

"Oh, yes!" Mia exclaimed. "Those, too!"

Nicholas handed his keys to the valet. "Come on." He took Mia by the hand, threading his fingers with hers. "But when we get back, I'm throwing you over my shoulder, carrying you up to bed, and having my way with you. That is, if you haven't eaten your weight in ice cream and donuts first," Nicholas smirked.

Chapter 40

Nicholas

"I don't know if I'm more nervous or excited," Penelope told Nicholas. They were meeting in her office, discussing the inaugural issue of *Opul*. The first of December was soon approaching, and the very first copies of the magazine would be on the stands any day now.

"What you and Mia have accomplished on the creative side was beyond even my own vision." Penelope leaned back in her swivel chair. "The two of you make a great team . . . in more ways than one."

When Nicholas stared at her blankly, giving nothing away, she frowned.

"She's your lobster."

"My what?"

"Your lobster. The one meant for you." She threw up her hands, frustrated he didn't get it. "It's a reference from *Friends*. The TV show?"

"I never watched it." Nicholas intentionally appeared uninterested. He didn't live under a rock. Of course, he'd watched an episode or two.

"I'm not surprised. Your sense of humor disappeared long ago."

"Pia, back to the matter at hand, please," he insisted before his temper flared. He cared for Mia but he didn't want to think about 'the one' or ridiculous lobster analogies. He certainly wasn't discussing it with his sister. She knew better than anyone that he had no interest in such things.

"Sure," she said. "The launch party—everything is arranged. All you have to do is show up. Will you be escorting Mia?"

"She'll be there."

"That's not what I asked. Did something happen between the two of you? You are still seeing her, aren't you?" Penelope asked.

"Yes, we are, but we keep our personal life and work life separate," Nicholas explained impatiently. "Mia prefers to rise on her own merits and not have the staff think otherwise. I happen to be in agreement with her."

"I hope that's all it is." Penelope reached her hand across the desk, covering his affectionately. "I don't want to see you miss out on a chance at happiness. Do you love her?"

"Pia," Nicholas groaned, rubbing his forehead with his fingertips. "It's not like that. We enjoy each other's company. I don't even know how she feels about me."

"Seriously? You don't? *Vlákas!* You're a fool!" she barked.

"Alright, I know she cares about me. Mia is a good person. That's the way she is with everyone though. It's not as if she had told me she loves me."

"Men are idiots!" Penelope waved him off dismissively. "Get out of my office."

* * *

Mia had unexplainably made herself less available in the past week since she and Nicholas had arrived back from a two-day shoot in Charleston. Nicholas was perplexed. Once again, they'd spent every moment together while there, both during the workday and after hours. There wasn't time for sightseeing but they'd hit a couple of excellent restaurants, and he'd made a point to take Mia to the famed Rooftop Bar atop The Vendue, Charleston's Art Hotel.

Thanksgiving was only a few days away, and Mia hadn't shared her plans with him. He assumed she'd head back to Long Island for the weekend. His plans had been arranged by Penelope and their grandfather. The holidays weren't particularly exciting for Nicholas. Watching families celebrate together and enjoying each other's warm company only made him miss his parents and grandmother even more, accentuating what was with what is. It was during these times he found he steeled his heart even further—affirming his resolve that he'd already lost too much and wasn't willing to put his emotions through any more hurdles. It saddened him to think about it—the contrast between then and now. Dinner at a Michelin star restaurant as opposed to his mother's home cooking. What was the point of pretending to celebrate?

The Saturday following Thanksgiving, Nicholas donned his Armani tux and had his driver take him to The Pierre for the *Opul* launch party. It was a big night for him—one he'd anticipated for months. So why was he so miserable? He'd checked his phone continuously for days, to no avail. Mia hadn't called or even sent a text. Not that he had typed a text her way either. The truth is that he had, several times, but Nicholas just couldn't bring himself to press the send button.

When he arrived at the venue, the room was already buzzing with guests. The ballroom was set for a cocktail party. A combination of high-top tables and standard round ones, each with seating for four, were arranged throughout the room. Floral arrangements of calla lilies in long, glass cylinders adorned the tables. An elaborate champagne wall dominated one side of the room, while white-gloved waiters offered hot *hors d'oeuvres* to guests.

Nicholas spotted Mia in the crowd and, without a second thought, weaved his way over to her through the sea of guests. Engaged in conversation, she was unaware he was behind her until Mia's companion acknowledged him.

"Mr. Aristedis," the young man greeted formally.

Mia turned, seemingly surprised to see him standing in front of her.

"If you'll excuse us," Nicholas said, "I need a moment of Ms. Andarakis' time."

With a nod, the man politely slipped away.

"It seems you have an admirer." Nicholas' tone was laced with jealousy.

"He's a coworker of my friend, Kyle, who I've seemingly lost track of." Mia glared at him. "If you'll excuse me."

"Mia." Nicholas reached for her arm.

"Enjoy your evening. It's an important night for you," she said before walking away.

Nicholas scanned the room with intense scrutiny. He spotted his sister speaking to an editor from one of their other magazines. Pavlos was seated at a table in conversation with a friend, sipping a cocktail. Nicholas pressed his lips together in a hard line, looking from person to person. Mia had disappeared into the crowd, and he wondered where she had gone.

Huffing out a frustrated breath, Nicholas walked over to the bar and ordered a scotch. "Make it a double." He drew out a five-dollar bill from his pocket and placed it in the tip jar.

"You don't look happy," a leggy blonde said, coming up beside him.

Nicholas smiled humorlessly into his glass. "It's launch day." He lifted his glass as if making a toast. "I'm celebrating. How have you been, Brenda?"

"I'd be better if I'd heard from you," she complained, pouting.

"I've been busy."

Brenda leaned into Nicholas. Resting her hands on his shoulder, she whispered, "If you're not busy tonight," she purred, "I can heighten the celebration." She planted a kiss on him, leaving a dark red lipstick mark on his cheek.

Nicholas pulled his face from her. Before he managed to turn the woman down, Nicholas was rendered silent at the sight of Mia standing at the top of the ballroom entranceway, escorted by her friend, Kyle, who had his other arm looped around Jenny's.

Even from a distance, Nicholas and Mia were able to meet each other's eyes simultaneously. As if by radar, he could pick her out in a crowd of thousands. Mia was a vision wearing delicate, white lace over nude fabric, and as no one had ever done before, she took his breath away. But her naturally warm expression was absent from her face. Instead, she looked past him to the woman draped over his shoulder. He shrugged Brenda away and pulled a handkerchief from his pocket to remove the stain from his face. Mia quickly averted her eyes. With her friends by her side, she purposefully strode over to the other side of the room.

Chapter 41

Mia

The butterflies in Mia's stomach felt more like angry hornets swarming around her insides as she walked toward the ballroom of The Pierre with her friends. When it had become apparent that Nicholas made no attempt to escort her, Mia asked Penelope if she could invite two of her close friends who also worked for *Aris Publications*.

Since Mia and Nicholas had returned from Charleston, their interaction, or lack thereof, had been confusing. She racked her brain, going over the two days they'd spent in the historic city, trying to figure out if she did or said something to cause a rift between them.

Mia looked about the room. The space was stunning in its garden-like motif, the floral balcony wall mural adding to the illusion. The carpeting was a work of art, threaded with intricate designs in Santorini blue and desert sand, the hanging crystal chandeliers above complementing the room with an air of elegance.

Nicholas or not, she was here now and was going to make the best of the night. She'd arrived with Kyle and Jenny but the room was so crowded that they were soon separated, and Mia was left chatting with Kyle's friend. He was nice enough but she was distracted as she attempted to discreetly look for Nicholas. When she turned to find him right behind her, and suddenly now requesting her time, Mia was annoyed, dismissing him to find her friends.

Pushing her way through the crowd, she climbed the ballroom steps and paced the corridor.

"We've been looking for you," Jenny said.

"Same here," Mia replied. "I don't know how we got separated."

"Are you ready to go back in?" Kyle asked, offering his elbows to both women.

"Ready." Mia drew in a deep breath.

When they reached the staircase, Mia hesitated. From her vantage point, Mia's eyes only took an instant to seek out Nicholas standing across the room by the bar. Her intake of breath was involuntary, the small gasp that fell from her lips only loud enough for her escorts to hear. Jenny, glimpsing the cause of Mia's distress, placed a supportive hand on the arm exposed by Mia's one-shouldered evening gown.

Stoically, Mia averted her eyes from the cause of her upset and led her friends to the other side of the room.

"I'm sure there's a logical explanation," Jenny said.

Kyle opened his mouth to comment but Mia shot him a steely look. "Not a word. If you say, 'I told you so,' Kyle Mathews, I swear I'll . . . I don't know what I'll do, but I'll think of something."

"What a threat!" Kyle laughed, and Jenny and Mia followed suit.

Kyle wrapped his arms around Mia, rocking her side to side. "I was going to suggest we all get a drink. That's all," Kyle said.

"Thank you." Mia gave him a peck on the cheek before walking to a bar set in the far corner of the room.

Mia was barely three sips into her Moscow mule when Nicholas approached.

"May I have a word?" Nicholas asked. His tone was formal and clipped.

Jenny pulled Kyle away, which Mia wished she hadn't done.

"No need. I got the message," Mia said snidely. "But I believe Marilyn Monroe over there is looking for you." She waved him away. "You wouldn't want to keep her waiting."

"Mia," Nicholas started. There was indignation in that one word. Before he could go on, the event planner came over, interrupting him.

"You're wanted at the podium, Mr. Aristedis," she said.

"Now?" he asked in a tone that startled the woman.

The poor woman looked like she wanted to disappear but she regained her composure and stated, "Ms. Aristedis asked me to find you."

"Yes, of course. I apologize," Nicholas said. Turning his attention back to Mia he said, "When I get back, I expect you to be right here where I can find you."

"Is that an order from my boss?"

"Don't act like a child."

"Then don't bully me." Mia crossed her arms over her chest, standing her ground.

Mia watched as Nicholas shook his head, turned, and briskly weaved through the crowd. Penelope and Pavlos were already up on the elevated platform. When Nicholas joined them, a waiter hurried over, handing him a flute of champagne.

With her glass in hand, Penelope approached the microphone.

"Thank you so much for coming tonight to celebrate the launch of *Opul*. My brother and I have dreamed of publishing a magazine together since we were teenagers." Penelope lifted her glass in Pavlos' direction. "And although our dear grandfather could have indulged our whims, he insisted we learn the business from the ground up."

Pavlos nodded, bowing his head in acknowledgment.

"We couldn't have created this inaugural issue without our talented and dedicated staff. Nicholas and I look forward to a long relationship with you in the workplace."

At that last statement, Mia glanced up at Nicholas. Their eyes locked, and he seemed to be trying to convey a message to her.

"Nicholas, would you like to say a few words?"

"Just enjoy the evening. It's been my extreme pleasure to work with our incredible staff thus far. I look forward to seeing what we accomplish in the future." Nicholas' attention was focused solely on Mia.

This mercurial man, Mia thought. He had her head spinning in confusion. "I'm going to the restroom," Mia told Jenny. Turning, she made her way through the crowd and up the three shallow steps leading to the corridor.

With no inclination to return to the party, Mia planted herself at a bank of chairs and stared into the mirror. This night hadn't turned out as she'd expected at all. It should be a joyous event, celebrating an accomplishment she'd had a role in. Now, all Mia wanted to do was go home and crawl into bed.

After ten minutes of watching women wash their hands, fuss with their hair, and reapply lipstick, Mia exited the restroom. Leaning against the opposite wall, Nicholas waited.

Mia caught a glimpse of him in the corner of her eye and continued walking, pretending she hadn't noticed him.

"You can't avoid me forever." Nicholas rushed to her side, circling his fingers around Mia's small wrist to halt her. "Please." He nudged her over to a quiet alcove. "Let's not do this around prying eyes."

"What do you want from me, Nicholas? You confuse me. I never know where I stand with you."

"I could say the same," Nicholas accused.

"How? It's you who's been strange since we came back from Charleston earlier this week." Mia began to raise her voice but then lowered it to a whisper. "You seduce me with your Italian words of how you want me day and night but you didn't invite me to come with you tonight or even so much as ask me what I was doing for the holiday."

"You were the one to suggest not announcing our relationship to the staff." He pointed an accusing finger at her. "I was trying to respect your boundaries."

"How very convenient for you."

Nicholas planted his hands on his hips, his tux jacket flailing behind. "Why is it you women always expect the man to lay it all out? You're not exactly forthcoming either. You could have mentioned your plans to me. Maybe suggest we spend at least part of the day together."

Mia looked down at her strappy sandals. Her insecurities had crept back into her psyche. Nicholas was right, of course. Mia was as guilty as he was.

"I wasn't sure you'd want to," she said, not meeting his gaze.

Nicholas lifted her chin with his fingers, forcing Mia to look at him. "Of course, I wanted to. While I was dining in a restaurant with Pia and my grandfather, all I did was imagine what it was like at your home."

"I had no idea," Mia whispered. "I'm sorry. You didn't miss much unless you like loud, chaotic family gatherings."

Nicholas backed Mia up against the wall, bracketing her between his arms. "I like you. I want to be with you. That's all that matters," he said, his voice raspy. He waited for a beat, taking her in from head to toe. "You look stunning." Nicholas ran his nose down the length of hers until his mouth found her lips. "The room grew illuminated the moment you stepped inside it," he breathed into her mouth.

Nicholas pulled Mia in at the waist, leaving not even a millimeter of space between them. He reclaimed her mouth, his kisses laced with passionate desperation. "How did you get here tonight?" Nicholas whispered when he took a breath.

Breathless, Mia managed to murmur, "Uber."

"I'll send a car for your friends. You're coming home with me."

Mia didn't refuse.

"Come with me," Nicholas said as they walked toward the ballroom. When they landed at the entrance, Nicholas surveyed the room until he found who he was looking for.

"Brenda," Nicholas called out, lifting a hand. "I'd like you to meet someone. This is Mia, my girlfriend," he said smugly.

The woman looked as disappointed as she was surprised. Brenda smiled, but Mia read a different emotion in the woman's eyes. She wanted to shrivel like a fading flower. The woman was another of Nicholas' voluptuous predators, and it was apparent that she was a worthy opponent.

"It was good to see you." Nicholas turned to walk away. Turning back around, he added, "And if you happen to talk to anyone else in your social circle, feel free to mention that I'm unavailable."

Mia covered her face with embarrassment. "You didn't have to do that."

"I did, and if by the end of the night everyone else knows it too, that's fine with me."

* * *

With the holidays fast approaching, the staff at *Opul* was busier than ever. The office was slated to be closed between Christmas and New Year's. Every last detail for the next issue had to be completed before they went on break. Mia worked extra hours, grabbing lunches and dinners on the fly. By the second week in December, she wasn't feeling well. Lethargy set in. Unusual for Mia, as she normally had boundless energy.

At her desk, Mia stretched her legs and rubbed her arms. Every muscle in her body was sore, especially her neck. Mia surmised the reason for that was the angle at which she kept her head perched while looking at her monitor for extended periods.

Oddly, Mia had no appetite. She managed to swallow a spoonful of dry cereal in the morning but even the smell of coffee made her nauseous. Weakly, she stood, ambling unsteadily to the beverage bar. She pulled a can of ginger ale from the refrigerator and returned to her seat. After drinking two sips of the carbonated drink, Mia sprinted, as quickly as she could in her current condition, to the restroom before being sick.

"Mia!" Suki wiped her hands on a paper towel, glancing at her hurried entrance in concerned surprise.

"Go." Mia waved her off, her head over the toilet. The violent sounds erupting from deep within her belly would have awoken the dead.

Suki refused to leave. Instead, she dampened towels and handed them to Mia to wipe her mouth with. "You're shaking," Suki observed when she laid her hand on Mia's back.

"Chills," was all Mia could say before she heaved again.

"I'll be right back," Suki promised.

It was probably only a minute later but it felt as if an hour had passed before Suki returned. But Suki wasn't alone. Nicholas rushed through the door of the women's restroom, calling to Mia.

"Don't-want-you-to-see-me-like-this," Mia labored. She was still hovering over the commode.

"This is no time for vanity," Nicholas said. "Do you still feel as though you need to vomit?"

"I-don't-think-so. Weak."

Nicholas picked Mia up off the floor. She was deathly pale and shaking. He carried her out of the restroom and into his office, setting her down in his chair.

"Cold," Mia said almost inaudibly.

Suki, who had followed Nicholas out of the restroom, rushed to Mia's desk, taking her sweater off the back of her chair. She handed it to Nicholas, and he draped it around Mia.

"Suki, call New York-Presbyterian. Tell them Nicholas Aristedis is bringing a patient into the emergency room, and that he wants someone to see her immediately. Give them any information they need," Nicholas added as he punched in a speed dial. "Darren. Get here as fast as you can. Mia needs to get to the hospital. It's an emergency."

"What's going on?" Penelope rushed into Nicholas' office soon after with Suki close behind.

"Help me put her coat on and get her downstairs." Nicholas tried to remain composed but his face was pale.

"The layout," Mia whispered.

"That can wait," Penelope said. She felt Mia's forehead and neck. "She's burning up. Suki told me she had the chills."

"Hot now," Mia said.

Once again, Nicholas picked Mia up, this time carrying her to the bank of elevators. Penelope ran ahead, hitting the down button repeatedly, as though the door would open more quickly by assaulting it.

"Call me as soon as you know something," Penelope demanded.

Mia mumbled incoherent words, her face pressed close to Nicholas' chest.

His expression grave, Nicholas nodded. "I will."

In the car, Mia leaned against Nicholas. "No hospital. Home," she begged.

"We need to find out what's wrong," Nicholas insisted.

"Take something for fever and sleep," Mia managed to slur. "Maybe ER crowded. Don't want to wait."

"You won't. They're expecting us," Nicholas said.

"Doesn't work that way," Mia argued weakly. "Bed."

"We're almost there. We'll get you in a bed right away," Nicholas reassured her. "I promise. My grandfather made a large donation in my grandmother's name. They will treat you right away."

Just as he'd ordered, a wheelchair was waiting at the ER entrance for them when they arrived. Nicholas gave triage all the information he knew, rummaging through Mia's wallet for her identification and any medical card that might warn of possible allergies.

"Place my last name on her chart beside her own," Nicholas ordered. "I want it to be clear to anyone who tends to Mia that she's to be treated with the utmost care."

"She will be, Mr. Aristedis, but her chart must reflect her legal name," the admitting nurse pointed out.

"Put it in parentheses then, or 'in care of," he snapped impatiently. "Just make sure it's done."

Mia was taken to a curtained-off section in the ER and helped onto a bed. She changed into a hospital gown, and when another bout of sickness struck, Mia shooed Nicholas away with embarrassment.

Soon after Mia was hooked up to an IV, a doctor entered her room to consult with her.

"Hi, Efthymia?" A slim, middle-aged man wearing a white jacket came to her bedside. "I hope I said that correctly. I'm Dr. Yang. Can you explain your symptoms?"

"She had the chills and then was running a fever. She's weak and can't keep anything down," Nicholas answered the doctor's questions before Mia had a chance to.

"If you don't mind waiting outside," Dr. Yang interjected, "I'd like to examine the patient."

Nicholas looked as though he was about to argue but he took one look at Mia and relented.

When Nicholas stepped out, the doctor continued his inquiry. "Aside from the vomiting, are you suffering diarrhea?"

"On and off, yes," Mia said.

"Muscle aches and weakness?"

"Yes."

"Any sharp stomach pains?"

Mia nodded. "More spasm-like."

"I'll order a CT scan, stool culture, and bloodwork," the doctor said. "I want to rule out a few things to be safe but I suspect you have a bacterial infection."

"Can I go home after that?"

"No. You're dehydrated. You'll be staying the night." Dr. Yang opened the curtain to find Nicholas pacing on the other side. He turned back to Mia. "Did you eat anything unusual? Raw fish? Anything that might have tasted off?"

"I've been busy," Mia admitted. "I've been grabbing food off street vendors." She shrugged, trying to recall what she'd eaten over the last few days. "I had a hot dog, an empanada, and some fruit. Nothing out of the ordinary. Yesterday, I bought some fried chicken from a food truck."

"If that chicken wasn't cooked all the way through, that could be it." He made a note on the portable computer, wheeling it out as he left the room.

"You ate all that crap?" Nicholas was incensed. "If you were too busy, I would have ordered decent meals into the office for you."

"Please, Nicholas, I don't have the energy to argue," Mia pleaded. "I didn't want special treatment. Everyone in the office was slammed."

"If they don't take you to a private room in the next ten minutes, I'm going to the hospital administrator," he fumed.

"No, you're not." Mia was firm. "You do realize people are dying in this hospital, don't you?"

Thankfully, Nicholas fell silent. At least for the time being.

Much to her relief, it wasn't long before Mia was indeed transferred to a private room. God must have answered her prayers. Nicholas was about to get everyone fired if they didn't move quickly enough for his liking.

"Go back to work, or go home," Mia insisted. "There's nothing to be done here. They gave me something to bring my fever down, plus an anti-nausea medicine. Everything else will take time."

Mia was pale and weak. She felt only marginally better than when she had arrived at the ER, but she put up a front for Nicholas' sake. And, admittedly, his hovering was driving her crazy.

"I'm not leaving you."

"I'm here to take Efthymia down for her CT scan," an orderly interrupted.

"Go," Mia implored Nicholas as the orderly helped her into a wheelchair.

* * *

A little over two hours later, Mia was back in her hospital bed. The technician promised the radiologist would read the images right away and come up to see her.

All Mia wanted was to sleep. Her body ached, and she felt feverish again. As her lids grew heavy and she began to drift off, another doctor entered the room, calling her name.

"Efthymia?" he asked.

Drowsily, Mia opened her eyes to answer. When she saw who it was standing by the doorway, her eyes snapped open.

"What are you doing here?" There was terror in her voice. Mia sat up, finding the strength to push herself back up against the headboard, hugging her knees tightly against her chest."

At first, the young doctor seemed startled by her extreme reaction until he took a better look at her. "Mia?"

"Get out!" she shouted. "What are you doing here?"

"Calm down." He lifted a palm. "I'm the radiologist reading your scan."

"I don't care." Mia breathed heavily. "I want another doctor."

"I didn't recognize the name," he admitted. "I didn't know it was you."

"Get out. Don't come near me."

"What's going on?" Nicholas rushed in, a bouquet of three dozen pink tulips in his hand.

"Just a misunderstanding," the doctor said.

"Why are you upset?" Nicholas asked. "Hold on!" he said, pivoting toward the doctor when he noticed him slinking away. "You're not going anywhere until I know what upset her."

Trevor shot furious daggers at Mia. He was silently threatening her. Mia shrank back in fear until she realized it was Trevor who was menaced. He was as frightened as an insect aware he was about to be squashed.

Mia's resolve strengthened, and she straightened. "That's Trevor." She pointed to the doctor. The name didn't seem to register with Nicholas, and Mia couldn't remember if she ever mentioned his name. "The one who tried to rape me."

Nicholas' face contorted in fury. He shot Trevor a murderous glare.

"Nothing happened." Trevor threw his hands up in defense.

"You son of a bitch." Nicholas furiously flung the bouquet to the ground, the petals scattering around the floor. Nicholas lunged for Trevor, grabbing him by the throat. "Get the fuck out of this room," Nicholas ordered.

"Let go of me or I'll call security."

"Nicholas!" Mia called.

Nicholas' laugh resonated with an evil rumble Mia had never heard from him before. Before he let go of Trevor, Nicholas slammed the doctor unmercifully into the wall. "Go ahead. Give that a try and see how it works out for you. I'll tell you what. I'll call the hospital administrator myself. He might be interested to learn what one of his doctors is capable of."

"You can't prove a thing," Trevor said, regaining some courage.

"Oh, but I can." Nicholas poked Trevor in the chest. "A little less arrogance would serve you well. Now go find another doctor to discuss the scan results with us. Now! And don't even think about coming within twenty feet of Mia."

Trevor left the room, his face fuming with vehemence, his posture surrendering defeat.

Nicholas pulled up a chair by Mia's bed. "You're shaking." He ran his hands tenderly up and down her arms.

"What else will I have to face today?" Mia quivered.

"Nothing, if I have anything to say about it." Nicholas pressed the back of his hand to her forehead. "You're warm. I'll get the nurse."

Mia shook her head. "I'm not due for my meds yet. I just need sleep," she said, her eyes growing heavy.

Chapter 42

Nicholas

Nicholas remained in the chair by Mia's bedside while she slept. She'd fallen into a slumber, yet it was far from a peaceful one. Maybe it was her fever or the unexpected encounter with her would-be attacker; Nicholas wasn't sure. But her mournful cries and indecipherable gibberish rang of anxiety. Nicholas held the hand unencumbered by IV tubes, pressing a kiss to her palm.

Nicholas tapped out a text to Penelope, updating her on the little he knew. Grappling with whether or not to call Mia's family, he decided to wait until he had some definitive answers.

A rap on the door drew Nicholas from his thoughts.

"Mr. Aristides?" A rotund, balding, middle-aged man stepped into the room. "I'm Dr. Abboud. I understand you requested Dr. Ward be taken off Ms. Andarakis' case."

Nicholas stood. Walking over to him, Nicholas extended a hand to the doctor. "They have a history that's not pleasant," Nicholas affirmed. "If pressed, I could share the details. Alarming details that I expect would make you re-evaluate his position at this hospital."

Dr. Abboud took on a look of concern. "Dr. Ward is one of our younger residents but he is an excellent doctor with a clean record. Even the suggestion of an accusation is disconcerting, to say the least."

"It would be up to Ms. Andarakis to decide what to do. So far, it was a matter she's kept to herself for years."

Nicholas was aware of how incriminating his words were, and by Dr. Abboud's expression, Nicholas' implications were clear.

"Can we get to the results," Nicholas said curtly.

"You're not her husband or her next-of-kin—" the doctor started before he was cut off.

"I am fully aware of the HIPAA laws," Nicholas said impatiently. "If you'll look at your paperwork, she signed to share medical information with me."

Dr. Abboud scrolled through his iPad. "My apologies." Meeting Nicholas' fierce glare, he hurriedly continued, "The CT scan shows a severe inflammation in the colon and small intestine, which indicates bacterial gastroenteritis. The type of bacteria will be determined with the stool culture."

"How long until we know?" Nicholas asked.

"The average culture takes seventy-two hours. The treatments for most bacterial strains are the same," Dr. Abboud explained. "Once we determine if the cause was from contaminated food or undercooked meat, particularly poultry, we could refine the treatment."

"She'll fully recover though?" Nicholas looked for reassurance. That old, familiar panic was resurfacing.

"In severe cases, certain bacteria can cause damage to the central nervous system or bring out undetected autoimmune diseases," the doctor said with little empathy.

Nicholas thought the doctor's bedside manner could use some work.

"We're doing everything possible to make sure she makes a full recovery," Dr. Abboud routinely reassured Nicholas. With a nod, he exited the room.

Nicholas returned to Mia's side, plopping down in the chair, deep in thought. Deep in worry. Soul-deep with inner-terror. His mind drifted to a very dark place, dominated by death, where abandonment wreaked havoc on his heart.

Mia stirred when Nicholas grazed his fingers along her cheek. "Nicholas, Nicholas," she murmured softly in her sleep. Rocking her head from side to side, she confessed, "I love you, Nicholas."

It was a subconscious declaration but one he realized must be true. Mia was kind to him in ways no one else was. Nicholas believed she cared for him but never before had he allowed himself to believe Mia loved him.

Suddenly, Nicholas felt as if the wind had been knocked from him. The constriction in his chest crushed the air from his lungs. The possibility of loving and losing once again paralyzed him. As it was, the metaphorical shreds of sinew hanging on his heart by a thread were fragile. What was he thinking? It was so much simpler to live as he had—uninvested, free of entanglements. Detached—not having heartache inflicted upon him or allowing it to eat away at what was left of him.

Nicholas stood, his breathing labored, sweat pebbling at his brow. Anxiety clawed his insides. Pacing like an animal trapped in a snare, Nicholas raked his hand through his dampening hair. In a split-second decision, he fled Mia's room and left the hospital.

* * *

In his office, Nicholas, with his elbows propped on his desk, head in his hands, ignored the incoming text message notifications on his phone. After seven in the evening, the only activity on the floor was a janitor humming to the music filtering through his earbuds.

Nicholas attempted to catch up on work but his mind had no capacity for concentration. He groaned when yet another text message from his sister popped up on his screen, followed by a call. Finally, he relented.

"What is it, Pia?" Nicholas asked, annoyed.

"What is it?" Penelope threw back at him. "Where are you? I came to the hospital after work, and you were nowhere to be found."

"I stayed as long as I was needed. There was nothing more to be done," Nicholas answered, his tone detached.

"What's the matter with you?" The question was an accusation. "Where are you?"

"At the office. I'm trying to catch up on lost time." After a moment of silence, he asked, "Are you still with her?"

"Of course!" Penelope said. "I wasn't about to leave her alone. I don't understand why you did. Mia said you were with her until she fell asleep. When she awoke, you were gone."

"So she's fine?" Nicholas sounded hopeful.

"No, she's not fine. Mia's temperature spiked, and she began to convulse."

Nicholas closed his eyes, his breaths growing shallow and rapid. Beads of sweat began to form on his forehead. He tried to get up for a glass of water but he was too lightheaded. The earmarks of an anxiety attack were underway, and it was too late to rein it in.

"Nicholas, stay with me. Calm down. Breathe slowly," Penelope urged. "Stay put and try not to panic. I'll be right over."

Twenty minutes later, Penelope entered Nicholas' office. He was staring off into nothingness and didn't even acknowledge his sister's presence.

Penelope came up beside him, bending to meet him eye to eye. "Nicky." She stroked his face in the same way one would comfort a child.

"Please talk to me," Penelope pleaded, her eyes full of concern. "Tell me what's on your mind."

Nicholas shook his head slowly. His voice came out as a whisper. "I can't do it. I can't."

"Can't do what?" Penelope asked.

He didn't answer. Penelope knelt by his side, waiting for him to open up to her. When he didn't, she gently forced the issue.

"Mia was . . . distressed to find you gone."

Penelope waited for a beat, looking to her brother for a reaction. On a sigh, she continued, "I don't understand why you left her side."

Nicholas' eyes flew up to meet Penelope's. "I had to leave sometime."

"Don't be a bastard," she reprimanded. "I saw how frantic you were. There was no way you were leaving her for even a minute. What changed?"

"She said she loved me," Nicholas confessed.

"And you left her? No wonder she was so upset."

"She wasn't aware. She mumbled it in her sleep but she said it all the same."

"Regardless, that's beautiful. You should be happy."

Nicholas fisted his hands so tightly, his knuckles whitened. "She can't love me. I don't want her to. I'll admit I care for her, but I don't and won't love her. I can't."

"Yet the thought of her growing more ill threw you into an anxiety attack. What does that tell you?" Penelope sighed deeply. "Love isn't a choice. It just is. You can deny it but no good can from it. It's time to free yourself of old wounds. Tragically, people die. Lovers break up, sometimes shattering our hearts. But when the right person comes along, they not only glue those shards back together, they also penetrate your soul in a way no one else can."

Nicholas dismissively rolled his eyes. Not accepting his repudiation, Penelope took his face in her hands, forcing him to look at her. "I've watched the two of you. If you miss this chance at happiness, at true love, you'll regret it for the rest of your life."

Nicholas sat stoically in his chair. Much of what his sister said made sense, but his protective walls stood firm.

"Mia loves you. She'd never do what Devalina did to you," Penelope assured him.

"I know that," Nicholas said, his tone harsh. He slammed his fist on the desk. "But she could die!"

"Not from this," Penelope said. "She'll be fine."

"But from something else." Desperation coated his words. "An accident, cancer, who knows."

"We are all going to die someday. My dear brother, you need to move beyond the broken twelve-year-old boy you once were. Life holds no guarantees."

"I know, I know," Nicholas said, exhausted. "I just need some space right now."

Penelope stood. "Okay. I'll leave you. Please call me if you need to talk."

Bending, she kissed him on the cheek and left him to his thoughts.

Chapter 43

Mia

Mia propped herself up against the hospital bed headboard, her laptop elevated by a pillow. She'd asked Penelope to bring it to her so she could get some work done while waiting for the culture results. Whatever they were pumping into her IV was helping, yet Mia still felt weak. But her lack of concentration was more due to the absence of one very unpredictably moody man, namely Nicholas.

It had been a full twenty-four hours since Mia had seen him, and she was beginning to fear he had no plans to visit her at all. She refused to ask Penelope about him but, without prompting, she had made excuses for her brother, stating that he was inundated since Mia was out of the office. But Mia read right through her apologetic tone.

"It's fine, Penelope," Mia said. "When you see Nicholas, tell him I appreciate all he did to get me the best medical care."

"You'll be in the office soon enough, and you can tell him yourself." Penelope smiled but the expression on her face was weary.

"Thank you for bringing this," Mia said, referring to her laptop.

That had been hours ago, and there was still no word from Nicholas. Mia had once confessed to Nicholas that she had never loved anyone enough to have her heart broken. That no longer rang true. Mia could now relate to the pain and angst chronicled in sad love stories. Mia felt as though part of her soul had died. Anguish dominated every cell in her body and each thought running through her mind. Still, there was an emptiness inside her, numbing her spirit.

Reluctantly, Mia typed a letter of resignation to Nicholas and Penelope. Lesson learned, she scolded herself. Never get involved with the boss or else the dream job goes up in flames.

Mia buzzed the nurse, asking for a new HIPAA form before she sent Jenny a text.

Two hours later, Jenny entered Mia's room. "How are you feeling?" she asked.

"My body is healing. My heart is another story," Mia said, her eyes fogging with unshed tears.

"Are you sure I can't call your family?"

"No, please," Mia begged. "I'm fine. Had my condition worsened then maybe. Right now, I just can't deal with everyone hovering over me asking a lot of questions."

"When can you come home?"

"Tomorrow. Will you be able to pick me up?" Mia asked.

"Of course." Jenny sat at the foot of her bed. "Did you send it yet?"

"The resignation? No. I'm waiting until I get home," Mia said. "I hope Penelope isn't too angry with me."

"Are you certain you can't keep your work life and personal life separate?"

Mia nodded. It was time she made a decision. "I'm certain."

The next afternoon, Jenny took Mia back to their apartment. Mia was still lightheaded, most likely from sitting in bed for three days. She didn't have her full strength back but she had recovered from what the doctors called campylobacter, most likely caused by eating under-cooked chicken.

Once Mia was situated comfortably on the sofa, she pressed the send button on her letter of resignation.

"It's done," Mia said to Jenny. The desolation in her voice was accentuated by a sob. "I feel even worse about doing this to Penelope. She's been so good to me. I wrote her a separate email thanking her and saying that I'd be happy to complete my unfinished projects from home." Mia hugged her knees to her chest. "I feel like I've lost everything."

"You'll get through this." Jenny set down the bowl of soup she'd prepared for Mia and hugged her. "Why don't we watch a comedy?"

"Sure, whatever you want, as long as it's not a romantic comedy."

For two hours, Mia blankly stared at the television screen. Jenny tried to engage her but to no avail. "Jen, it's okay. It's not up to you to entertain me," Mia said. "I love you for it but I just need a little time."

But that was not to be. The doorbell rang, and when Jenny opened the door, Nicholas was standing on the other side of it.

Chapter 44

Nicholas

Nicholas was a mess. For years, he'd prided himself on being in full control of his life and emotions. He worked hard, never engaged in any behavior that would cause his family embarrassment, and sought out uncomplicated companionships with women on his own terms.

Now, in just a few short months, all of it had gone to hell. All because of a petite, sable-haired beauty who managed to infiltrate his every thought. Nicholas never missed a day of work. Yet after leaving—correction—fleeing the hospital, and later, dodging his sister's wrath, he went to his apartment, drank himself into oblivion, and passed out.

The next morning, it didn't take long for Penelope to figure out that Nicholas wasn't coming in. After reading her string of texts, he was grateful she gave him some slack, understanding he needed to sort through some things.

His sister's words from the night before played over in his mind. Logically, he knew she was right. But the fear that clawed away at his spirit prevented Nicholas from declaring his love for Mia. Instead, he tortured himself, scrolling through photos of the girl who haunted his every thought. Pictures as she worked on-location. Ones he had taken on the sly. Another he'd captured as she peacefully slept beside him. Nicholas was tempted to delete them all but the message his brain transmitted failed to deliver as far-reaching as the muscles in his fingers.

When Nicholas, once again, neglected to make an appearance at the office the following day, Penelope sent him a fiery text. *Get your shit together. We have a magazine to run.*

Though his sister made a valid point, Nicholas ignored it. He wouldn't be productive anyway. He went to his home office and sent an email to the graphic designer who works under Mia. Outlining explicit instructions and tasks for her to complete, Nicholas figured this would keep himself somewhat on track. At least he was doing something.

Picking up his phone, he contemplated what to do. Like picking off petals on a daisy, 'She loves me, she loves me not,' Nicholas pondered, 'Do I call or do I not?'

There was never really a choice. "Hello, this is Nicholas Aristedis. Can you give me an update on Efthymia Andarakis' condition, please?"

After being told to hold, the floor nurse came to the phone. "I'm sorry, Mr. Aristedis, but Ms. Andarakis took you off the HIPAA approved list."

"There must be a mistake," Nicholas argued, confused.

"No, there's no mistake. She signed new papers this morning."

Nicholas let the phone drop from his hands. A new realization began to set in. The anxiety he felt from his grief-laden past was minuscule compared to what he was experiencing at this moment. A life without her smile, her comforting words, and her generous heart was no life for him at all. Mia, in her own effort of self-preservation, trusted few. She had once taken him into her confidence. Now Nicholas feared he had broken that fragile trust.

"I'll come in tomorrow," Nicholas barked into the phone before Penelope could say anything. He had finally answered her after the third call.

"Have you opened your emails in the past hour?" Penelope asked.

"No. Is there something crucial I need to look at?"

"I'd say so," she said. "Mia sent us her letter of resignation."

"What?" Every muscle in his body tensed.

"You heard me." His sister was beyond angry. "I can call an agency to send us a freelancer, I suppose. But the rest . . ."

"I'll fix this," Nicholas vowed before ending the call.

He went to his bedroom and threw on a pair of jeans and a black Henley, not bothering to look in a mirror. His hair was uncombed and two days of stubble covered his face.

When Darren pulled up in front of the hospital, Nicholas jumped from the car and headed right to the visitors' reception.

"I'm sorry, there's no patient here by that name," the elderly woman said.

"Check again. I brought her in myself. She's in room 914," Nicholas said impatiently.

"Oh, dear," the woman said. "Yes, she was here but she was released a little while ago."

Nicholas huffed out his frustration. "Thank you," he said, racing to the exit. He called Darren to bring the car around.

"Take me to Mia's apartment."

Fifteen different possible ways to plead forgiveness ran through Nicholas' mind. Which one would work, if any, he had no idea. By the time he ran from the car and up her fourth-floor walk-up, Nicholas was spent. Jenny opened the door, looking at him with disdain.

"I need to speak to Mia." His tone was not demanding or intimidating. Instead, Nicholas was contrite. For the first time in his life, he had no idea what he was doing. Jenny forced a smile as she waved him in.

Chapter 45

Mia

'We were on a break!' Ross shouted to Rachel Green. How timely, Mia thought. She kept her eyes trained on the television screen, pretending she hadn't noticed Nicholas enter the room. In reality, Mia always sensed him before he approached. It was as though there was a magnetic force electrifying her skin, making her heart leap whenever he was within twenty feet of her. More and more, she had begun to understand her grandmother's unconditional faith in her missing husband. The old woman felt his life still breathed inside her soul. But she and Nicholas had not been gifted with the deep and rare love her grandparents shared. Mia didn't want to simply be cared for or desired. Mia wanted to be loved.

Jenny quietly slipped away to her bedroom. Nicholas came up beside Mia, humbly clasping his hands in front of him.

"Mia, I'd like to speak with you," Nicholas said when she made no acknowledgment of him.

Mia picked up the remote, increasing the volume.

Nicholas hung his head in, what? Frustration? Disappointment? Mia simply didn't care.

"You can deafen me with the sound. You can get up and lock yourself in your room. But I'll wait," Nicholas said calmly. "I'm not leaving until you and I talk."

"Go home, Nicholas," Mia said flatly. "We have nothing to discuss."

"The hell we don't." Nicholas paced. Running his fingers through his hair, he admitted, "I screwed up." He exhaled heavily. "I need to make it right with you—to do right by you. And damn it, resigning would not be in your best interest."

For the first time since Nicholas stepped into her apartment, she looked at him, her eyes dark with fury. Mia stared at him with such vehemence, he flinched.

"That's why you're really here," Mia spat bitterly. "The magazine." She shook her head slowly, willing only to let Nicholas see her anger and not the deep, emotional wound he'd inflicted on her heart. "No need to worry. No one is indispensable. I'm quite replaceable."

"If you'll listen to me, it's not about the magazine. This is about you." Nicholas dared to step closer. "It's about us," he whispered.

"No, it's clearly about you," Mia accused. "What works for you at this moment. You go all protective and alpha, barking orders and demanding the best for me, never leaving my side . . . until you did. And then for two days I don't see or hear from you. Not even a text. You discarded me like yesterday's newspaper."

"I know. I was wrong," Nicholas confessed. "I wasn't thinking clearly. Give me a chance to explain."

"No. It won't do any good." Mia turned her head away. Looking into his eyes would only weaken her resolve. "I was doing just fine without a man in my life," Mia said through gritted teeth. "Especially one as complicated as you." Snapping her head around, she poked a finger in his direction. "I don't need someone who hasn't a clue what he wants, or someone who finds it easier to run away the second a woman gets too close."

"Well, maybe that's better than never letting anyone in at all," he jabbed back at her.

Nicholas may as well have pierced her heart with a serrated blade, twisting it around just to ensure every drop of blood had drained out of her. Mia's throat burned from the tears she tried to hold back.

"I told you things I've never shared with another soul," she whimpered, challenging him. "I tried to remain professional in our workplace for all our sakes." Mia stood, holding onto the arm of the sofa to steady herself. "In private, I gave you every part of myself. But I was a fool to think I could elicit a true emotion from you." Slowly, she walked to her bedroom, slamming the door behind her.

Mia flopped onto her bed, burying her face in her pillow. At first, she took her rage out on the upholstered headrest, banging it with her fist. Soon, her fury gave way to quiet sobs. Mia heard footsteps approach her door. There was silence on the other end but for one quick knock. Even with the door between them, Mia's body responded to Nicholas' pull. If she were to lay her hand over his heart, she was sure it beat in rhythm with hers. But where Mia's pounded in longing, Nicholas' throbbed only with guilt. She had love to offer while Nicholas offered nothing. After some time had passed, Mia heard the door to the apartment shut. Nicholas was gone.

There is no fear in love, but perfect love casts out fear, because fear involves torment. But he who fears has not been made perfect in love.
— 1 John 4:18

Chapter 46

Nicholas

Nicholas had been a fool. In an attempt to shield himself from future anguish, he'd sheltered his heart. His plan had worked flawlessly until he looked into the eyes of Mia Andarakis. Instinctively, he knew everything was about to change, yet Nicholas did everything in his power to deny what couldn't be controlled.

The result of all this inner chaos was only more chaos. The torment Nicholas tried to avoid lived in his present and it was far worse than what he anticipated or what he'd experienced in his past.

Nicholas feared he was doomed for an existence like that of his grandfather, greeting the morning sun with only work on the horizon, at night comforted by memories alone.

Nicholas found himself in the lobby of his grandfather's apartment building.

"I'm sorry I didn't call ahead," he apologized when his grandfather answered the door.

"I'm always happy to see you, *agori mou.*" Pavlos eyed him with concern. "You don't look well."

"I'm not."

"Sit down, and tell me what's weighing on your heart." Pavlos poured amber liquid from a crystal decanter into a pair of tumblers, handing one to Nicholas.

A melancholy silence hung in the air, each man lost in his own thoughts. Nicholas swirled the libation around in his glass, occasionally stopping to gulp down a sip.

Pavlos remained quiet, waiting for his grandson to unload the burden plaguing him.

"I don't know how you do it," Nicholas started. "Get through day after day when the only person you ever loved is gone."

"Did something happen to Mia?" Pavlos asked, alarmed. "Penelope said she was recovering nicely."

"She is." Nicholas knocked back the remainder of the contents in his glass. "Mia left the magazine . . . and me. I can't say I blame her." On a sigh, Nicholas leaned his back into the sofa cushion, scrubbing his hands over his face. "One way or another, everyone I love eventually leaves."

Pavlos, seated stately in a wingback chair across from Nicholas, listened with concern.

Nicholas looked at his grandfather, heartache etched on his face. "Only this time, it was me who ruined everything. I pushed her too far. All because of some deep-seated, irrational phobia I can't shake."

Finally, Pavlos spoke. "I'm afraid much of the fault lies on me."

Frowning, Nicholas was confused by his grandfather's statement.

"Penelope called me, worried about your state of mind."

Nicholas was trying to get a read on his grandfather. He'd raised him to be strong, to fight through the knife thrusts life threw his way. It took losing Mia for Nicholas to see that he hadn't fought or overcome anything. He'd only succeeded in suppressing the turmoil of emotions running through him by shutting doors.

"This has nothing to do with you, *Pappou*."

"But it does." The distress his grandfather felt was etched in the deep lines on his face. "When your parents were killed, your grandmother and I were grief-stricken. If it wasn't for you and Penelope—" Emotion caught in Pavlos' throat. Tears brimmed the edges of his lower lids. "Before your father was born, my Ioanna suffered three miscarriages."

With his hand covering his face at the mention of his parents, Nicholas, hunched over, looked to his grandfather through spread fingers.

"Your father was an answer to many prayers. Our miracle." Pavlos pulled a handkerchief from his trouser pocket. Dabbing the corners of his eyes, he continued, "The death of a child is life's cruelest agony." The sigh that followed bellowed of enduring heartache. "I don't know how we would have gone on if not for you and your sister. Penelope was older, resilient. She wore her grief like a rite of passage, journaling her way through every emotion."

Pavlos stared ahead, trance-like, losing himself in the memory as if it only happened days ago.

"You were different," he said, turning his focus back to Nicholas. "Quiet, isolated, anxious." Anger bubbled to the surface of his expression; self-blame etched on his features. "And what did I do? I pushed you to rejoin the world like nothing was different than before."

"You taught me to be strong. To be a man," Nicholas spoke up. "I owe everything I am today to you."

"And everything you're not," he spat with self-deprecation. "Your grandmother pleaded with me to have you see a therapist. You needed help we couldn't provide. But I said no."

"I'm not sure at twelve years old I would have been receptive," Nicholas said. "You did your best."

"I didn't equip you to deal with life's blows. Not your grandmother's death and not the betrayal of your trusted friends." Pavlos leaned forward, patting Nicholas on the knee affectionately. "Strength is not putting on a brave face and pretending nothing affects you. It's knowing when to be vulnerable. Knowing when to take risks. *I alithiní agápi chreiázetai dýnami kai thárros.*"

"Is that a quote from Socrates?" Nicholas joked.

"No. I just made it up," Pavlos smiled.

"True love takes strength and courage," Nicholas repeated under his breath. "I'll try to remember that."

"Do you love her?" Pavlos asked with great seriousness.

Nicholas swallowed, his throat thick with emotion. "So much it hurts," he answered in a whisper.

"Then figure out how to win her back, and let nothing get in your way."

Chapter 47

Mia

"And that's that." Mia slumped.

After moping around her apartment for days, Jenny ordered Mia to either get out and do something productive or find solace in her family. Since mustering any form of motivation was not in her immediate future, Mia went home.

"That's that?" Melina threw up her hands. "You land in the hospital, and no one calls to let me, your own mother, know?"

"She's fine," Egypt waved Melina off. "Let's focus on the problem." Turning, she scowled at Mia. "But if you ever keep us in the dark ever again, I'll kick your ass from here to Jupiter."

Mia examined the faces of the women seated around her mother's kitchen table like they were an assembly of deliberating jurors. The trouble was, they all had a different idea on who to condemn.

"The man came to speak to you, Mia. Didn't you at least owe it to him to hear him out?" Kally asked.

Before Mia could reply, Krystina chimed in. "He left her alone in the hospital, like a stranger he happened to stumble upon in the street."

"But wait! Hasn't the guy shown how much he cares for you so many other times?" Loukas added his two cents. "He screwed up. Give him a break."

"Who asked you?" Krystina lambasted Loukas. "Why are you here anyway?"

"I was already here before everyone else," Loukas said, unperturbed by Krystina's hostility.

"Just in case you didn't notice, this meeting—" Krystina circled her hand around the table, "—is just for women."

"Yet here I sit," Loukas beat his chest with his thumbs.

"That's enough, you two!" Kally reprimanded. Turning her attention to Mia, she asked, "You haven't heard from him since he came by your place?"

"No but Penelope has been texting me."

"What did she say?" Egypt asked.

"Only that she needs to speak to me."

"Maybe it's work-related," Melina suggested.

"I resigned, remember?"

Egypt gave Mia's shoulder a shove. "Answer the woman's texts. You've never been rude!"

All eyes went to Mia's phone as it suddenly rang. "It's her again," Mia said nervously. Holding her cellphone in the palm of her hand, she waited for a beat, contemplating what to do. Finally, she tapped the green button on her screen. "Hello?" Mia said, rising to find some privacy.

"Mia, thank God!" Penelope said. "You and I need to have a conversation."

"Penelope," Mia started, climbing the stairs to her old bedroom. "I have the utmost respect for you, and I'm so sorry I left without notice. If there was another way . . ."

"My brother's happiness means everything to me but I also know what it's like to be hurt, so I won't push you," Penelope promised. "But I'm just as passionate about my magazine as I am about my brother, and I need your particular talents on a special project."

"I don't know," Mia said reluctantly. "Is it something I can do from home?"

"No, not for this, I'm afraid. I've rented Dance With Me ballroom dance studio for a photo shoot on Tuesday evening," Penelope said. "I'm a little out of my depth, and I could use your help."

"I'm confused. Shouldn't Nicholas handle that?" Mia wondered.

"Normally, but for personal reasons, he can't direct this one."

"Okay, of course. I'll be there," Mia agreed on a sigh. "I owe at least that much to you." Aside from her guilt at abandoning Penelope, the project sounded too tempting to turn down.

Mia crept slowly down the stairs, mulling over Penelope's words. Where was Nicholas? Concern seeped through her senses, filling Mia with an uneasy dread.

"Tell us everything," Melina demanded when Mia rounded down the steps.

"Nothing exciting." Mia brushed it off, finding her seat. "Just one last project Penelope needs help with." Mia's eyes dimmed even more so. Gone was their usual brightness.

Up to that point, *Yiayiá* had remained silent. But nothing escaped the wise, old woman. Mia recognized that look on her grandmother's face—the darkening, narrowed, assessing look in her eyes; the creases in her brow, deepening with worry. "*Efthymia mou*, I know love when I see it. That boy loves you."

Mia opened her mouth to argue but *Yiayiá* shot her hand up in protest.

"*Scáse!* That first day *Nikólaos* came here to bring you back to Newy Yorky," she said in her funny way she always referred to the city, "it was there. The way he looked at you. He might not have known it himself, but I did."

"It doesn't matter anymore." Mia's tone resonated with deep sorrow.

Yiayiá slapped her hand on the table. "It matters." She stood, shaking a wrinkled finger vigorously in Mia's direction. "What? You think this happens every day? It doesn't. Don't throw it away." She sank down into her chair and drew out a Kleenex from inside her sleeve. Defeated, she whimpered, "Time isn't always on our side."

Melina rose from her seat and embraced her mother. "Shhh, it's not good for you to upset yourself," she cooed.

Mia hid her face in her hands. The last thing she wanted was to make her grandmother cry. "I'm sorry, *Yiayiá*. I promise, if Nicholas gets in touch with me, I will listen to what he has to say."

Guilt had driven her empty promise. After all, it didn't matter what she agreed to. Nicholas had no reason to contact Mia anymore.

Chapter 48

Mia

On Tuesday evening, Mia took an Uber to the SoHo address Penelope had listed in a text along with her instructions. She'd explained that since it was a special project, behind-the-scenes photos would be uploaded on several social media platforms. Mia was to wear clothing that would blend in with the Big Band Era theme.

Despite having her heart stepped on and pulverized, a thrill coursed through Mia over the chance to art direct such a shoot. Mia had emailed Penelope a well-crafted outline of suggested shots, poses, and a set design. She could picture it all in her mind—still photographs reminiscent of swing dance movies like *Hellzapoppin'* and *Swing Fever*.

A familiar song immediately put a smile on Mia's face as she pushed through the dance studio's lobby door. She removed her coat, hanging it over a chair, and smoothed out her crimson dress. The flattering bodice had caught her attention with its sweetheart neckline cinched at the waist, but it was the full skirt that had swung her final decision. Yes, Mia was commissioned to work, yet with a glimmer of hope, she might be lucky enough to find herself in the mix of just one swing number with a dance professional.

Cheerfully, she hummed along to 'Chattanooga Choo Choo' as she followed the music. When Mia opened the door to the main ballroom, she expelled an appreciative gasp. The space on its own was impressive. A dozen chandeliers hung from an open industrial ceiling. Mirrors ran the length of one wall and, on the opposite, floor-to-ceiling windows offered passersby an unobstructed view.

Penelope had orchestrated the set design just as she imagined. She'd even gone as far as hiring a live jazz band. Model extras seated at tables set for two were situated around the dance floor, and professional dancers were giving instructions on blocking. If Mia hadn't known better, she'd have sworn she had stepped back in time to a 1940's movie set.

"What do you think?" Penelope asked as she came up behind Mia.

"I'm speechless," Mia said in wonderment. "My only question is, why did you need me? You have every detail covered."

Penelope chuckled. "Come." She looped her arm around Mia's as they walked into the thick of the activity. "I definitely need you." Penelope signaled to the bandleader, and he began the next song. The dancers took their place on the floor, and, after the photographer took a series of photos in various poses, he instructed them to dance. Mia was mesmerized.

"Have a seat at that table." Penelope pointed to the only unoccupied one. "I want to get a copy of what I've mocked up to show you."

"Okay," Mia said, taking a seat.

Moments later, Penelope came back with a copy of *Opul* in her hand. "I need you to look through this for approval. Particularly the letter from the special issue editor," she suggested, setting the publication down in front of Mia.

Puzzled, Mia scrunched her face in confusion. Turning, she wanted to ask Penelope what this was all about, but she was already halfway across the room, heading to one of the dancers. Glancing down at the magazine, Mia gasped in surprise. The cover of the magazine featured a picture of her. One she didn't recognize.

"What on Earth?" she muttered to herself. As she flipped through the pages, a rush of adrenaline coursed through Mia's body, causing her heart to pound forcefully in her chest. Every page was another photo of herself. Remembering what Penelope had suggested, Mia opened to the second page to read the editor's note:

Dear Reader,

In this very special edition of Opul, a most beautiful, talented, and indescribably incredible woman is featured. Page after page explores her kindness, compassion, and drive. She has captivated my soul and consumed my every thought. Yet, I failed to tell her how deeply and unconditionally I love her. Yes, I love her with all my heart. My only excuse was fear. But building walls didn't spare me any possible anguish I had hoped to avoid. Instead, it ultimately intensified. Like an inferno burning brush through a forest; it seared my spirit. But a very wise man once told me that to love takes strength and courage. I'm drawing on those qualities now, and humbly asking her for forgiveness.

I could declare that this enchanting woman has stolen my heart. But that would be a lie. The truth is, she didn't steal a thing. Every part of me belonged to her all along—my heart, my spirit, my soul.

So many years ago, I met an unforgettable young girl, barely a teenager, on a garden bridge. Fate brought us together, and fate generously brought her back to me. My sister once asked if I believed in destiny. The answer was no until this compassionate woman stepped into my orbit. She's my life source, the air I breathe, the reason I wake up each morning to greet a new day with a smile. If moments with her were to be measured by the grains of sand in an hourglass, I'd choose to savor every single one, no matter how many or few I'm favored. She is the only woman I want and need, and I will love and adore her for eternity.

With unending honesty and sincerity,

Nicholas Aristedis

Special Issue Editor

Mia stared down at the words written on the page, unable to catch her breath. Her mind was muddled with a myriad of emotions. Suddenly, everything seemed to fade away. The vibrant sounds of forties' jazz softened to mellow, background strains. The lights dimmed, or was it her tears clouding her vision that created the illusion? In her periphery, bodies quietly floated away, leaving her alone in the expansive space until a tall figure in a dark, double-breasted suit appeared before her.

Turning, she gazed up to see Nicholas, his hand extended in an invitation. His expression a hopeful plea, carried an underlying look of trepidation that Mia recognized. She could now read what was truly in his soul. It only took one look into those eyes of hazel, his emotions etched into the various hues as they changed color like a mood stone. As she took Nicholas' hand, Mia stood, smiling up at him, his eyes exuding all the warmth of comforting hot chocolate after a cold spell.

Tears streamed down her cheeks, and as Nicholas wiped them away with the pads of his thumbs, Mia melted from the tenderness of his touch.

"Don't cry. *Agápi mou, tesoro mio.*" Nicholas uttered endearments in both Greek and Italian. "I love you so very much. And I pray you feel the same."

"I've loved you from the very beginning," Mia croaked, barely able to get the words out through the tears tightening her throat. "From the second I laid eyes on you; I just knew."

Nicholas exhaled deeply, as though he'd been holding his breath for an age. Taking Mia's face gently in his hands, he kissed her passionately, devouring her very being, making up for the time he'd wasted. It was blissfully consuming for Mia, an intoxicating moment she never wanted to end. The world spun on its axis at a rate twice its speed. She was dizzied as much by his physical affection as she was by his declaration of love.

"Dance with me," Nicholas asked, guiding her to the dancefloor.

"I can't believe you staged all of this," Mia said as Nicholas took her into his arms. "And this song? You planned this too?" she asked, touched by the lengths he had gone to. As they swayed to 'Someone to Watch Over Me,' Mia sank contentedly into his chest.

"You mentioned it was one of your favorites." He smiled down at her, kissing the tip of her nose. "I'll always watch over you, if you'll let me, Mia. But I'm not sure who the lost one was here. I think it might be you who needs to watch over me."

"Always," Mia promised, stroking the side of his face affectionately. "Always."

"Perhaps it is our imperfections that make us so perfect for one another."
— *Jane Austen*

Epilogue

Mia

Christmas Eve 2019

Christmas at the Andarakis home had always been a loud, high-spirited feast of a holiday with more food than the exuberant gathering of family and friends could possibly consume. This year, the number of guests had grown even more, with Mia inviting Nicholas and his family to join them. There would be no more impersonal holiday restaurant meals for the Aristedis family, not while Mia was in their lives.

Athena, Kally's future step-daughter, wasted no time in ripping open her gifts. As a storm of glittering wrapping paper littered the space around the child, Kally's dog, Emma, yapped, scampering around her and nipping at the discarded paper.

Nicholas hugged Mia from behind. "Do you want one of those?"

"What?" Mia laughed. "Elsa's ice palace or a dog?"

"Actually," he said, pressing a kiss to the side of her face, "I was referring to the little girl."

"Oh!" Mia wasn't expecting that question. "Yes, of course. I'd like a baby. Boy or girl, or . . . one of each, if I'm so fortunate."

"Me too," Nicholas whispered in her ear.

"You've got to see this!" Penelope strode over to Nicholas and Mia.

"You weren't kidding when you said your Yiayiá had a lot of fire in her. She's got my grandfather balancing a shot of ouzo on his head while dancing!"

"Is that why all that laughter and noise is coming from the living room?" Mia asked with a laugh.

Nicholas eyed Penelope with suspicion. "Our Pappou? The starchy conservative man we've known all our lives?"

Penelope shrugged her shoulders. "You can take the man out of Greece but you can't shake the Greek out of the man, I guess."

Mia and Nicholas followed the clapping and the opas! There he was, Pavlos, in the thick of it, a napkin between himself and Mia's grandmother as they danced the slower steps of the Sirtaki. Indeed, Pavlos had a glass planted atop his head. A string of men followed his lead— Max and his brothers, and their grandfather, Milton. Mia's father and her Uncle Markos, had also joined in on the festivities. Even Loukas' father, who had managed to pull himself from his usually depressed and often drunken state, ended the line.

Furniture had been pushed aside. This was, by far, the most jubilant Christmas Mia could recollect. Maybe she was just happier than she'd ever remembered before.

"It figures. She's the only woman up there." Mia grinned, shaking her head. "I'm sure she instigated the whole thing."

"I hope you have her energy at that age," Nicholas chuckled. "Come with me." He pulled her from the crowded room. "This is an ideal time to slip away. No one will notice we're gone."

"You naughty boy," Mia teased as they climbed the stairs. "Are you going to try to sex me up in my parents' home?"

"That's a splendid idea," he growled, cupping her bottom as they reached the top step. He pulled her into her old bedroom. "As much as I'd like to, I have other motives."

"Okay." Puzzled, she turned to close her door.

When Mia turned back around, Nicholas was bent down on one knee, a ring dangling from his forefinger.

Mia sucked in a deep intake of breath. Their eyes locked and tears sprung to hers with immediate understanding. She rushed to him, forgetting to even glance at the gem he was holding.

"If I had it my way, I would have done this weeks ago when I asked for you to love me. To forgive me. But I wanted you to be sure. So, I'm asking you now to be my wife. To spend your life with me. To be sure that you are as in love with me as I am with you."

"I am sure. So very sure," Mia whispered. "I want to marry you. Have your babies. Grow old with you and embarrassingly dance balancing crystal glasses on our heads, if that's what it takes."

Nicholas took the three-carat, radiant-cut diamond ring and tenderly placed it on Mia's finger. The brilliant stone was accented by a delicate, diamond-rimmed, platinum band. "Do you like it?" Nicholas asked nervously.

"I love it. I've never seen anything so beautiful," Mia said softly as she admired it on her finger. "But I love you more. I can't wait to start our life together."

"It's already begun, *Cara mio.*"

The End

Krystina's Story

December 2019

"I'll get you another one, sir," Krystina said as politely as she could stomach to the rudest customer to walk into her sister's café. Upon hearing the agitated man's litany of complaints, Loukas hovered by, wiping down a table, ready to lend support if required.

"Are you okay, Minnie?" he asked as Krystina muttered inaudible curses under her breath.

"I've been better," she rounded on Loukas. "And your nickname for me isn't helping my mood."

Krystina stomped her way behind the front counter to remake the vanilla soy latte with two tablespoons of stevia, precisely to the man's liking. Way to kill a cup of coffee, she thought. Two more hours and she was out of here. Not that she didn't like helping out her sister, but this place was Kally's dream, not hers.

At seventeen years old, Krystina had aspirations. With a little over fifteen thousand followers, she was already on her way to becoming an Instagram influencer. Not to mention the list of subscribers to her blog, Island-trotting with Krystina. Someday, she hoped to change the title to Globetrotting with Krystina.

Today, she was heading west of her Port Jefferson town to the

Bayville Winter Wonderland. Now if she only heard back from Chynna, her best friend and 'Instagram boyfriend.'

"Here you go, sir," Krystina chirped, setting down the replacement beverage. Pivoting, she walked away quickly. She wasn't about to wait for another complaint to come out of the jerk's mouth.

Pulling her phone from her back pocket, she checked for a text. Nothing. She tapped one out to her friend and waited. Ten minutes later, Chynna responded.

Chynna: *So sorry. Was sleeping. I'm sick*

Krystina: *:(What's wrong?*

Chynna: *Sore throat. Fever*

Krystina: *Can I bring u anything?*

Chynna: *No xoxo*

Krystina: *Call u tomorrow xoxo*

"Why the glum face," Kally asked Krystina. "If it's that customer, don't give him another thought."

"No," Krystina said, disappointed. "It's Chynna. She's sick, which I feel terrible about. But she was also my ride and photographer today."

"I can help you out with that," Loukas offered, draping his arm around Krystina's shoulder.

Kally could barely hide the amusement on her face. Krystina flashed daggers at her before turning and aiming her anger at Loukas.

"Hands off," she snapped, slipping from his hold.

"Listen, Minnie, I've got the wheels and a pair of able hands to snap the pics. It'll be fun." He flipped away the silky, black hair falling over his topaz-blue eyes. "What do you say?"

Krystina let out a long, contemplative breath. No matter what she did, he always seemed to be around—at school, church, the café. She couldn't even escape him at home. What was the point in trying?

"Okay, but here's the deal—no telling me what to do, how to pose, or what shots to take. No touching me like you just did. And absolutely no calling me Minnie," Krystina insisted.

"So many rules. What do I get out of this?" Loukas groaned.

"I'll pay for your admission."

"I'd rather pay my own admission and forget all the restrictions."

"Take it or leave it," she deadpanned.

"I'll be ready to leave when you are," he relented.

When Krystina's and Loukas' shifts ended, he drove her home to change. Noticing a disturbing commotion two houses down, Krystina diverted Loukas' attention. "Let's hurry up before it gets dark," she said. Jumping from the car, she shuffled over to the driver's side. Grabbing Loukas' hand, Krystina urged him out and hurried them into her home.

"I thought you said no touching," he smirked.

"Extenuating circumstances," she answered quickly.

Loukas spent more time at the Andarakis home than he did at his house down the block. That house hadn't been much of a home since his mother passed away four years prior. Before that, his family life was very much like the one he found comfort escaping to. The day she passed, all that had changed. Grief-stricken, Manny Mitsakis had gradually drunk his pain away until there was nothing recognizable of the man he'd once been.

"Give me ten minutes, Loukas," Krystina said. "Go up to Theo's room, and amuse yourself with a video game until I'm ready."

"You're full of orders today," he joked.

But as Krystina knew he would, Loukas complied. Her nemesis spent a good amount of time in her brother's room while he was away studying in London, often crashing at their home when Loukas feared his father's wrath.

Once Loukas disappeared up the stairs, Krystina questioned in a whisper, "Mom, what's going on over there?"

"Manny got in his car, apparently drunk. Thankfully, he didn't get too far. He crashed into his mailbox, swerved, and landed in the middle of his lawn," Melina explained. "Loukas didn't see?"

"No. I got him into the house in a hurry," Krystina said.

"Hmmm." Melina cocked her head. "It's nice to see you being kind to him for a change."

"I'm not a monster," Krystina defended. "I know how bad it must be for him."

"I called Max directly instead of the police station," her mother explained. "He and Leo are over there now."

Krystina stepped out onto her front porch. Her soon-to-be brother-in-law, Max, and his partner, Leo, were on Loukas' front lawn. Max moved the car back into the driveway while Leo, a large muscular man polished in the martial arts, had a stronghold on Loukas' father, forcing him into the house.

Krystina hoped that by the time she changed and they left the house, nothing would look too much out of place to draw Loukas' attention down the street.

The weather was unseasonably warm for December. Pictures were more aesthetically appealing when she wasn't donning a heavy coat. So Krystina slipped on a pair of warm, chocolate velvet leggings, most of which wouldn't show under her above-the-knee suede boots and oversize sweater.

She touched up her makeup with a bit of lip gloss and cheek bronzer. Krystina's hair was lighter than that of both her sisters. Mousy brown, if you asked her. It was her one complaint about her looks. Hair should either be dark brown and lush with a rich hue or light with luminosity. Hers was neither, so she gave Mother Nature a helping hand by adding sweeping highlights to her hair in a technique called balayage. As a bonus, she'd been paid to promote the hair salon on her Instagram account.

Krystina walked into Theo's room to find Loukas already invested in some version of Assassin's Creed. "I'm ready if you are," she said with a kinder voice than her usual tone when it concerned him.

"Sure," he said slowly, as if he was trying to figure out her angle.

Krystina stepped further into the room to coax him out of the game chair. In a swift move, Loukas grabbed her by the wrist, pulling her down onto his lap.

Yelping, Krystina reprimanded him. "I said no touching."

They were practically nose-to-nose. She could feel the warmth of Loukas' breath graze over her skin.

"You didn't rule out kissing," he whispered.

She blocked his mouth with her fingertips.

Loukas grinned. "One day, my little Minnie Mouse, you're going to realize that I'm exactly who you need."

"In your dreams."

"Yes, it is," Loukas admitted. "One day it will be yours, too."

Other books by Effie Kammenou

The Meraki Series:
Love is What You Bake of It

The Gift Saga Trilogy:
Evanthia's Gift
Waiting For Aegina
Chasing Petalouthes

Love by Design
The *Meraki* Series

If you enjoyed *Love by Design* please consider leaving a review on
Amazon and Goodreads.

Feel free to connect with Effie Kammenou on social media

Twitter – @EffieKammenou
Facebook – facebook.com/EffieKammenou/
Instagram – instagram.com/effiekammenou_author/
Goodreads – goodreads.com/author/show/14204724.Effie_Kammenou
Bookbub – bookbub.com/authors/effie-kammenou

Sign up for Effie's newsletter to learn about promotions and events
subscribepage.com/effiekammenoubooks

For additional recipes follow Effie's food blog
cheffieskitchen.wordpress.com

Printed in Great Britain
by Amazon